JULIA

Books by Sandra Newman

The Country of Ice Cream Star

The Only Good Thing Anyone Has Ever Done

How Not to Write a Novel (with Howard Mittelmark)

The Men

The Heavens

Julia

JULIA

A Novel

Sandra Newman

MARINER BOOKS

New York   Boston

JULIA. Copyright © 2023 by Sandra Newman. All rights
reserved. Printed in the United States of America. No part of
this book may be used or reproduced in any manner whatsoever
without written permission except in the case of brief quotations
embodied in critical articles and reviews. For information, address
HarperCollins Publishers, 195 Broadway, New York, NY 10007.

HarperCollins books may be purchased for educational, business,
or sales promotional use. For information, please email the
Special Markets Department at SPsales@harpercollins.com.

First published in Great Britain by Granta Books in 2023.

FIRST MARINER BOOKS HARDCOVER EDITION PUBLISHED 2023.

Library of Congress Cataloging-in-Publication Data has been applied for.

ISBN 978-0-06-326533-2

23 24 25 26 27 LBC 6 5 4 3 2

To Jeff

PART ONE

1

IT WAS THE MAN FROM RECORDS WHO BEGAN IT, HIM all unknowing in his prim, grim way, his above-it-all, oldthink way. He was the one Syme called "Old Misery."

He wasn't truly new to Julia. Fiction, Records, and Research all took second meal at thirteen hundred, so you got to know everyone's face. But up to then, he'd really just been Old Misery, the one who looked like he'd swallowed a fly, who coughed more than he spoke. Comrade Smith was his right name, though "Comrade" never suited him somehow. Of course, if you felt foolish calling someone "Comrade," far better not to speak to them at all.

He was slight and very fair. Good-looking—or might have been, if he hadn't always looked so sour. You never saw him smile, unless it was the false smirk of Party piety. Julia made the error of smiling at *him* once, and got back a look that would sour milk. People said he excelled at his job but couldn't advance because his parents had been unpersons. One supposed that made him bitter.

Nonetheless, it was a shame how Syme tormented him. At the Ministry of Truth, Syme worked in Research, devising Newspeak words. These were meant to purify everyone's mind but were mainly a pain in the arse to learn. Most folk muddled along, but Old Misery Smith couldn't even say *ungood* without looking as if it scalded his mouth. Syme saw in this a reason to follow him around and act like his best friend, the better to pepper him with Newspeak terms and watch the fellow squirm. Smith also hadn't the stomach for public executions, so Syme would talk about the hangings he'd witnessed, making the noises of the strangling men and saying how he enjoyed it when their tongues lolled out. Smith turned positively green. That was the sort of fun Syme liked.

Julia had spoken to the man just once, when they got stuck together at a table in the canteen. She'd still harbored hopes for him then. There were so few attractive men at Truth and she'd thought she could nurse a crush on Smith to while away a tedious day. So she'd chattered with more warmth than was warranted about the new Three-Year Plan, and how Fiction had luckily got new workers, all praise to Big Brother, and how was Records bearing up?

Instead of answering, he'd said, not meeting her eye, "So you work on one of the Fiction machines?"

She'd laughed. "I fix whatever breaks, comrade. It's not just one machine. That would be a fine machine, one you had to fix all day!"

"I always see you with a spanner." His eyes went to the red Junior Anti-Sex League sash at her waist, then darted away hastily, as if he'd had an electric shock. She'd seen the silly blighter was afraid of her. He thought she was about to report him for sexcrime—as if she could see whatever filthiness he had cooking in his head!

Well, there wasn't much point after that. They had finished their meal in silence.

The day it changed was the morning O'Brien was in Fiction, a low April morning of evil winds, when all London rattled and moaned and seemed about to blow down around its own ankles. With O'Brien in, Fiction was a madhouse—everyone showing off how hard they could work—but Julia's side dried up. She spent the whole morning up on the walkway, watching in vain for the yellow flags that meant someone needed a repair. Normally, they sprouted like weeds, and Julia was dashing about all day to a refrain of: "Comrade, it's making a rattle . . . Oh, it's not doing it now. Could you just check?" Most service requests were just an excuse to sneak out for a chat and a gin, and Julia always played her part, shutting down the machine and pretending to hunt for the source of the phantom problem.

Today, not a rattle in the house. Everyone was too afraid of being taken for a saboteur by O'Brien. Julia spent the morning pacing the walkway, gasping for a fag but knowing all it wanted was a cigarette for her to look criminally idle.

Fiction was a vast and windowless factory floor that took up the first two basement stories of the Ministry of Truth. The space was dominated by the plot machinery, eight mammoth machines that looked like simple boxes of shining metal. When you opened them up, their guts were a bewildering array of sensors and gears. Only Julia and her colleague Essie knew how to crawl around inside without doing damage. The central mechanism was the kaleidoscope. It had sixteen sets of claws that selected and transported plot elements; hundreds of metal sorts that were grabbed and discarded until a group was found that fit together. This successful pattern was assembled—again by machinery—on a magnetized plate. The plate was dipped into a tray of ink, then swiveled out and was stamped onto a roll of paper. The printed length of paper was cut away. A production manager lifted it free.

The result was a gridded print, jocularly called a "bingo card," that coded the elements of a story: genre, main characters, major scenes. A Rewrite man had once attempted to explain to Julia how these were interpreted, but to no avail. Even after five years on the floor, to her they might as well have been Eastasian picture-writing.

Now she watched as a production manager snatched a new print off the roll and waved it about to dry the ink. When he was satisfied, he rolled it, inserted it into a green cylinder, and shoved the cylinder into a pneumatic tube. From her vantage point, Julia could watch the cylinder's flight through a tangle of translucent plastic hoses on the ceiling to plop into a bin at the southern end of the room. That was Rewrite, where men and women sat in long rows, muttering into speakwrites, turning bingo cards into novels and stories. But by that stage, no machines were involved and Julia's interest was at an end.

She was perpetually fascinated by the plot machinery, how it worked and the ways it could go wrong. She knew how the inks were formulated, and loved to explain why the blue gave trouble. She knew how the paper was held steady, and what could make it bunch up or crease. She was excruciatingly aware of when a part would soon need replacing, and knew how to submit the order so it wouldn't get knocked back by the Capital Goods Committee. But about the books that were the end result, she knew little and cared less.

Once a Rewrite chap told her he was the same, having formerly been a voracious reader. "People say if you love sausage, you should never see it being made. It disgusts you after that. That's me and books." For Julia, this dictum wasn't true of sausage. She'd made and eaten sausage without a second thought. She'd even eaten sausage raw once to win a bet. But it was true of *Revolution's Victory: All for Big Brother* or *War Nurse VII: Larissa*.

As she thought this, she realized she'd idly fallen into watching O'Brien. He was working his way around the floor, making impromptu speeches, asking questions, smiling genially at everyone. In the regions far from him, the workers kept their heads down and their faces blank. They were doing their best machine imitation, which in many cases was impressively good. Close to O'Brien, however, all faces turned to him, alive with timid hope, like flowers turning to the sun. Several people had been coaxed from their posts and were gathered by him, listening raptly to whatever he was saying. Of course, an Inner Party member's chitchat always took precedence over your job.

From Julia's vantage point on the walkway, what was most striking was the physical contrast between O'Brien and his listeners. O'Brien wore jet-black Inner Party overalls of thick American cotton that fit so well they must have been tailored. Everyone else was Outer Party and wore blue rayon overalls, either too tight or comically voluminous. After one wearing, the rayon bagged at the knees; after twenty, the knees grew thick with darning. The dye came out in the wash, so every pair was a slightly different blue, and blotchy where the color had faded unevenly. O'Brien was tall and powerfully built, while the Fiction people were either painfully scrawny or potbellied. They hunched in the permanent cringe of the meek, while O'Brien was a straight-backed, bull-like man. One kept fancying his big hands scarred across the knuckles and his snub nose broken, though in fact he had not a blemish. Then there was his charm: he treated every man like his particular friend, and made every girl feel as if she'd caught his eye. All sham, of course, yet you couldn't help liking him.

He reminded Julia of a moving picture she'd seen where an Inner Party man got stranded in Second Agricultural Region and ended up saving the harvest. Only he could see that the trouble with the corn was a tiny insect devouring it from the inside. This thanks to his superior intellect, symbolized by the neat eyeglasses he wore on the end of his nose. When it came time to help with the reaping, though, he folded those eyeglasses, put them in his pocket, and his brute strength was the wonder of the peasants. Girls sighed over him, and the laborers roared with laughter at his down-to-earth jokes. O'Brien was just like that, down to the gold-rimmed specs and sighing girls. Even now, Margaret from Julia's hostel had materialized beside him at Machine 4, laughing at whatever O'Brien had said, her cheeks pink, one hand in her sandy hair. Margaret didn't even work in Fiction, and had no earthly cause to be here. And behind her were Syme and Ampleforth, both of whom worked with her on the tenth floor. All three must have been alerted to O'Brien's presence and come running.

Julia looked away in irritation, for she herself should be chatting up O'Brien—not for love of his blue eyes, but to see if he wanted any home repairs. Most did: the Housing people took forever, and never had parts when they finally came. Julia did home repairs for the challenge—so she said—but almost everyone was kind enough to slip her fifty dollars. And with Inner Party members, it was well worth it, even if they paid nothing. Indeed, it could be better if they paid nothing. That was treating you as a friend. Julia had heard of people getting jobs or flats thanks to friends of just this type.

O'Brien would make the ideal "friend." Yet Julia remained on the walkway, her face a mask of dutiful alertness. The thought of approaching the man made her flesh crawl. O'Brien was from Love.

At that moment, all power was cut to the machines. They whirred and slowed with a groan like a great beast sighing ponderously and easing its huge bulk down to the ground. In the silence that followed—a funny-bone silence, a silence like the deafness after a bomb—the whistle blew for the Two Minutes Hate.

Fiction, along with a dozen other departments, had its Hate in Records. Records had the space; half the office had been cleared out in the Small Adjustment of '79. It also made a nice break for Fiction, because they worked in the lightless depths, while Records was on Floor Ten, with banks of windows on all four walls. The catch was that they weren't to use lifts—healthy exercise, comrades! To add insult to injury, there were three "ghost" floors, which had once contained bustling offices but now stood empty, so Floor Ten was really Floor Thirteen. This meant not only three extra flights but that you had to pass those floors-of-the-dead.

Every landing on the stairs was dominated by a telescreen. Syme and Ampleforth, who struggled with the climb, kept pausing to comment in apparent fascination on whatever the telescreen was saying, while panting and mopping the sweat from their brows. Julia had a habit of smiling at each telescreen as she passed, imagining some bored man in surveillance being cheered by her appearance. Stairs held no terrors for her. At twenty-six, she'd never been stronger, and certainly never so well fed. Today she was especially lively after the long, dull hours of idleness, and trotted up, chattering with everyone she met, pressing hands and laughing at jokes. Syme's name for her was "Love-Me," which sometimes gave her pause, but could have been far worse. Only at the end did she slow abruptly, when she saw she might overtake O'Brien. As a result, she was right on his heels when the group came pouring into Records.

The first thing she saw was Smith—Old Misery. He was moving chairs into rows and, absorbed in this chore, looked surprisingly likable. A lean man of roughly forty, very fair and gray-eyed, he resembled the man from the poster HONOR OUR INTELLECTUAL LABORERS, though of course without the tele-scope. He appeared to be dreaming of something cold but fine. Perhaps he was thinking of music. He moved with obvious pleasure, despite his slight limp; you could see he liked to have physical purpose.

But then he noticed Julia, and his mouth thinned with re-vulsion. It was startling how it changed him: hawk to reptile. Julia thought: *Nothing wrong with you a good shag wouldn't fix!* This almost made her laugh, for of course it was true. His real trouble wasn't that his parents had been unpersons, or that he couldn't keep up with Party doctrine, or even his nasty cough. Old Misery had a bad case of Sex Gone Sour. And naturally the woman was to blame. Who else?

Without giving it much thought, when Smith sat down, Julia went to sit directly behind him. She justified it to herself because it was the seat right by the windows. But when he stiff-ened, uncomfortable with her presence, she was meanly pleased. Beside her was a low bookshelf with only one book: an old Newspeak dictionary from 1981, now lightly rimed with dust. She imagined running her finger through the dust and writing on his nape with the dirt—perhaps a *J* for Julia—though of course she never would.

The only trouble was, from here she could smell him. By all rights, he ought to smell like mildew, but he smelled like good male sweat. Then she noticed his hair, which was thick and fine and might be quite nice to touch. So unfair that the Party warped the good-looking ones. Let them take the Ampleforths and Symes, and leave the Smiths to her.

Then, wouldn't you know, Margaret came to sit next to Smith, and O'Brien followed after and sat on Margaret's other side. Margaret and Smith ignored each other. All the Records people were like that. It was a treacherous job, reading oldthink all day, and Records workers kept each other at arm's length. But what troubled Julia now was the question of why O'Brien was tagging after Margaret. Surely he couldn't *enjoy* plain Margaret simpering and sighing at him?

Julia looked away—always the safest option when anyone was doing something peculiar—and gazed out of the bank of windows. At that moment, a scrap of newspaper sailed past, hectically spinning in the air, before it abruptly spread itself and dived to the rooftops far below. From this height, you couldn't tell prole neighborhoods from Party neighborhoods; that was always queer. It also took a moment to pick out the gaps where bombs had fallen; on the street, they were all around you, and London sometimes seemed more crater than city. There was a private-use fuel ban for daylight hours, and you could make out the rare wisps of smoke where the A1 dining centers were. Electricity cuts were in force as well, and the grubby, unlit windows of office buildings had the gloomy radiance of the sea.

A little chunk of the view was obstructed by the massive telescreen on the nearby Transport building, whose moving pictures created the illusion that the daylight kept flickering and subtly changing. The images repeated on a simple loop. First one saw a group of pink-cheeked children innocently playing in a playground. On the horizon, a shadowy group of perverts and Eurasians and capitalists grew, reaching toward the children with brutish hands. Then a cut-out of Big Brother rose and blotted the villains out, and a slogan appeared in the sky: THANK YOU, BIG BROTHER, FOR OUR SAFE CHILDHOOD! After this, the same children reappeared, now in the uniform of the children's organization, the Spies: gray shorts, blue shirt, and red kerchief. The jolly Spies marched past with an Ingsoc flag, and the slogan in the sky became: JOIN THE SPIES! Then all faded, and the first image returned.

Weaving busily above this scene were helicopters. First you noticed the large ones, whose passage was audible even behind thick windows. These were manned by a pilot and two gunners, and you sometimes saw a gunner sitting casually in the open door of a copter with his black rifle resting against his knee. Once you thought of copters, you started noticing the flocks of microcopters below; then the big ones looked like the little ones' parents. The micros weren't manned but operated by remote control. They were only for surveillance, and in Outer Party districts, you'd often glance up from a task to find a micro hovering by your window like a nosy bird.

But by far the most striking thing in the view was the Ministry of Love. It rose from the jumble of ruins and low houses like a white fin breaching turbid brown water. On its gleaming surface, you could make out the tiny figures of workmen, attached to a slender tracery of cables, scrubbing its eerily snow-white flank. Apart from the tiny detail of those workmen, the building was so white it gave the impression of being an absence: a portal to nothingness cut through the shabby city and the cloudy sky. Love had no windows at all, giving its austere beauty a suffocating effect. Julia had heard a story that the mice there had no eyes; with no light, they had no need. That was bollocks, of course. Even when there was a power cut, the four big Ministries always had electric light. Still, those mythic blind mice troubled her. They stood for the real terrors behind those walls, terrors one couldn't see and must imagine in ignorance.

Beyond Love to the southwest was the more modest glass tower of the Ministry of Plenty, aglitter with light. Farther to the south, the Ministry of Peace was visible only as a glow in the mist. Beyond even that, Julia could see a faint green haze, which might be the fields at the very edge of London. She always thought of that haze as Kent—or Semi-Autonomous Zone 5, as it was properly called—where she'd grown up.

Most other Truth workers were born in the city, and passed the windows without a glance, but Julia could never get enough of London. She even loved how blasted and tumbledown it was, how wild, if you strayed from the Party neighborhoods. It was the greatest city of Airstrip One, the most populous city in all of Oceania, from the Shetland Semi-Autonomous Zone to the Argentine Economic Region. Julia never stopped feeling lucky to be here, born as she was in a SAZ, amid the cows and the camps.

While she was gazing out the window, the room had filled, and the Smith man's scent had vanished in a general fug of dirty laundry, sour breath, and cheap soap. Some people's faces were already indignant in preparation for the Hate. It was always queer to see them snarling and glaring rigidly at a blank telescreen. Julia was feeling her usual anxiety that this time it wouldn't come off, that they would try to rage and give up in embarrassment or simply burst out laughing. Whenever she imagined this, she saw herself standing up and righteously scolding the mockers. In reality she would be the first to laugh.

Then it was starting. One felt it before one heard it: a vibration like thunder that resolved into a too-loud, grating voice. It seemed to buzz in the metal chairs themselves and make the lighting seethe with migraine. All cried out in anger as the telescreen filled with the familiar, loathsome face of Emmanuel Goldstein.

It was a lean, intellectual face with a kindliness that soon came to seem conniving and false. Behind the spectacles, the eyes were childish and lewd at once. The thick lips were always moist. They made you want to cross your legs. The bloom of woolly white hair around his head was sheeplike, as were his bulbous features. Even his voice had a bleating querulousness. As the clip began, he was making a speech that at first seemed much like any Party speech. In fact, for long stretches, it was Newspeak: *sickthink overtaked plusgood of truefighters.* You had to listen closely to hear it was a string of attacks on Oceania, the Party, and their way of life.

Emmanuel Goldstein had once been a hero of the revolution, who had fought at Big Brother's side. Then he turned against the Party, and now devoted his considerable cunning and energy to the destruction of Oceania and its people. No one was safe from his malice. If he couldn't turn citizens against the Party, he would poison the water supply. If he couldn't pervert little children, he would bomb their schools. He detested anything chaste or brave, because he lacked these qualities, and, for this reason, he hated Big Brother with all his warped, parasitical heart. Though his speeches were always full of obvious lies and meaningless jargon like "free speech" and "human rights," he still managed to gull some people. His acolytes were responsible for everything that went wrong in Oceania, from the sabotage that meant no one had enough food to the undermining of soldiers' morale that kept Oceania from winning the war.

Of course, one knew this couldn't all be true. There were so many stories of Goldstein's crimes, they would have taken him a thousand years to commit. London was meant to be crawling with his terrorists, but no one had ever seen one in the flesh. The tales of Goldstein's escapes from justice were particularly far-fetched, always involving thrilling feats of courage by our Boys in Black, and a humiliating episode in which Goldstein fell on his backside or sniveled, begging for his life, only to be rescued at the last minute by some villain—usually a Party higher-up who'd fallen out of favor the day before.

Today, Goldstein was talking against the war, in the most puerile and offensive way, as if the war were all Oceania's fault. He cared nothing for the people killed by bombs that morning. Just in case you were in danger of being won over, behind his head the screen showed ranks of marching Eurasian soldiers— an endless flood of massive, hard-faced men. The Hate was in full swing now, the whole room heaving and yelling. Margaret was prettily flushed, her mouth straining wide in sensual rage, and O'Brien had manfully risen to his feet as if to confront a hated enemy. Even Smith was roaring with surprising venom and kicking spasmodically against the rung of his chair. For a hazardous moment, Julia became detached, wondering clinically if Smith was shamming. Then a jolt of panic went through her. She'd forgotten to keep yelling. Now she felt a yawn coming on.

On impulse, she grabbed the old Newspeak dictionary from the shelf beside her. Taking a deep breath, she screamed, "Swine! Swine! Swine!" and hurled the heavy book over everyone's heads. It flew end over end to slam into the screen with a resounding clang. All started, and, in that instant, Julia was struck by second thoughts. Her act could be seen as an attack on the screen. Telescreens were remarkably sturdy, and a book couldn't really do one harm—but was O'Brien aware of that? Might he think her action was sabotage?

But O'Brien bellowed on, oblivious, and other people were now peppering the screen with whatever came to hand. One man threw a packet of cigarettes at it, another his own shoe. Julia was perspiring with fear, but it had come off. The treacherous yawn was gone.

Now the image on the screen began to change. Goldstein's face turned into that of an actual sheep, while his voice became a long shrill *baa*. Just as people began to laugh and jeer, the sheep was replaced by a burly Eurasian soldier, leaping toward the viewer with a submachine gun. Some people in the front flinched back.

But this image immediately melted into the comforting face of Big Brother—the Party leader—a man of about forty-five with thick black hair and a black moustache. This Big Brother was both like and unlike the young, bare-armed Big Brother on army recruiting posters, or the child Big Brother who appeared on Spies badges. The mature leader was handsome and supremely masculine in a clean, reassuring way. He was a man who had fought for his people for decades, and survived to see his vision made real. Along the way, he'd been betrayed by countless men he'd thought of as true comrades, and had almost been murdered by the capitalists scores of times, but he still stood firm against the Flood. He understood the ordinary man and entered into all his problems. He was great but also good. You didn't have to be a fool to love Big Brother; whatever else, there was always that.

As Big Brother spoke, everybody shifted toward the screen, as if basking in its light. He said, "We stand as one. Ours is truth…" More grand, plain words followed that faded from Julia's mind as they were spoken. Margaret stretched forward over the back of the empty chair in front of her, murmuring, "My Savior!" and buried her face in her hands. Smith, too, strained forward, his fair head raised.

In the final seconds, Big Brother's face faded and was replaced by the three core Party slogans, written in thick black letters on red: WAR IS PEACE. FREEDOM IS SLAVERY. IGNORANCE IS STRENGTH. Then the telescreen blanked out and left the watchers facing their own dim reflections. They began the chant: "B-B! B-B! B-B!" It started out uncoordinated and messy, but soon settled into a slow, sure beat. Those who were still sitting rose to their feet; some stamped along or drummed on the backs of chairs. This part of the ritual was always a release. Everyone relaxed and beamed. Another thought had been correctly thought, another feeling rightly felt. One saw how little the Party asked, after all. You needn't know all the latest Newspeak words or struggle to believe contradictory things. If you hated the enemy, you could be loved. People smiled dopily at each other, and some eyes welled with tears. They had had a good Hate.

Now all that remained was the petty problem of knowing when to stop chanting. You wouldn't want to be the first to quit, but being last was no good, either. Julia decided to take O'Brien as her cue—but as she thought it, he turned his head, and she was startled to see he'd already stopped. His face was also queer, expressing not joy but a humorous interest. At first glance, Julia saw this as sexual, and thought with surprise that homely Margaret had somehow really attracted him.

But O'Brien wasn't looking at Margaret. Impossibly, he'd locked eyes with Smith. And Smith's face was open, quiescent, bright with some enigmatic softness. He was like a meadow glowing in a bath of sunlight.

Instinctively Julia turned away, and in that moment, the chant had ended. She shut her mouth on a last superfluous "B!" and, when she glanced back, O'Brien and Smith were both facing forward again with somber faces. You'd never know they'd given each other a thought.

Immediately she was unsure of what she'd seen. People looked at each other. How was that significant? Smith's loving expression hadn't been that distinct from anyone else's during the chant. And how was it surprising if O'Brien looked at Old Misery with detached amusement? It was no more than Syme did every day.

People now began to rise from their chairs. Ampleforth

wandered up and began to talk obsequiously to O'Brien about the new poetry quotas. Nodding and making interested faces, O'Brien again radiated sincerity. When Smith starting gathering chairs again, he was pinched and sour, quite restored to himself.

No, nothing had happened after all. Julia put it from her mind and rose to start the long trip back to Fiction.

2

AFTER HATE, JULIA SIGNED HERSELF OUT FOR TWO hours on a Sickness: Menstrual. In actual fact, she was going to her hostel to deal with a stubbornly blocked toilet. It was a repair she should perhaps have postponed, with O'Brien nosing about, but the hostel only had two toilets, and, in Julia's experience, it was inevitable that the other would be blocked by sundown. Anyhow, Sickness: Menstrual was a privilege all the girls used and abused. Any pretense that it corresponded to sickness, or even to any particular time of month, was a thing of memory. At the guardroom, no one even blinked at the fact that Julia also signed out a plumber's auger. Of course, the guards were all blokes; perhaps they thought it was a necessary tool of menstruation.

At this hour, the bicycle bay was deserted. The only person there was a monitor drowsing on a chair, with a bottle of Victory gin between her feet. Hundreds of battered tomato-red bikes slouched on their kickstands beneath a line of BIG BROTHER IS WATCHING YOU posters and a banner with the slogan BICYCLE FOR HEALTH! Most of the machines were unusable, of course, their chains chapped with rust, their spokes bowed. That morning, Julia had hidden a reliable Atlantic between two warped old machines, but someone must have spotted it and filched it nonetheless. She scanned the racks for ribbons and strings—

markers people used to indicate a working bike. Not a hope. It took her ten minutes to find a sturdy old International she trusted to last the trip home.

As she left, the Ministry's external telescreens were showing the second-meal musical program, with an image of crashing surf over which "Maid of Oceania" played. The walls of the other nearby buildings had ranks of B.B. posters: BIG BROTHER IS WATCHING YOU, BIG BROTHER IS WATCHING YOU, BIG BROTHER IS WATCHING YOU. It was only those words and his grave, caring face, which filled the poster so it seemed to expand beyond its bounds and rush toward you. When Julia came to a crossroads, to left and right the posters covered every available space. She'd once seen a man do a card trick where all the cards turned into the king of spades. Then he riffled the deck so the faces all rushed by, uncannily the same. The posters were mesmerizing in just that way. All down the road, they passed her like marching soldiers, while the maudlin refrain of "Maid of Oceania" came from every open window, from bus stop telescreens, from the speakers mounted in trees in Martyrs of December Park. It was moving even to Julia, who liked to think of herself as a hardened cynic. Riding with the wind in her hair, the music swelling, and B.B. gazing from every direction made her feel like the lovely factory worker in the movie *Airstrip One the Free*, who renounced her true love to devote herself to the fight against Ingsoc's enemies. The song and the fantasy only faded when she turned into the old legal district, where prole London began.

This was a world of bashed and crumbling houses shored up with higgledy-piggledy bits of wood. Some walls had been buttressed with sections of tree trunk trimmed to size with an axe. Not a window was whole; all were boarded up or re-placed with government-issued blackout material, rimed with dirt. There was no electricity here. In the daytime, everyone in the district, and their furniture, was out in the street. People sat there drinking tea, playing cards, mending clothes under makeshift shelters cobbled together from blackout material, cardboard, and the ruins of bombed-out homes. Julia had to keep an eye out for errant children, drunks, wet armchairs, discarded bottles. It was nerve-racking, too, how the proles' voices all died down as her bicycle approached, but no one looked up to watch her pass. Her Party overalls might as well have been a cloak of invisibility.

Cutting through this bustling area were two dusty ravines where rocket bombs had flattened everything. In both, the road surface was gone, and Julia had to dismount and lift her bike over chunks of wreckage. The first bomb site was relatively new. Plaster dust still swirled in the air, and a family of ragpickers dug through the wreckage. Their prettiest daughter—a black-eyed waif of nine or ten in a velveteen frock twice her size—was stationed on a blanket at the side of the road to sell their meager finds to passersby: battered shoes, old nails and screws, a pair of scuffed eyeglasses.

The second site was of far longer standing, and had already filled with squatters' huts. All about them, willow herb grew on the rubble. Some squatters were the people who'd lived in the shattered buildings, but there were also nomads who traveled from site to site, mostly demobbed soldiers who hadn't been issued with a London residence permit. Sites like this were held to be dangerous, and girls would gravely warn each other against them. But here again a gaunt man, glancing up from his cookfire at the sound of Julia's passing, spotted her blue overalls and gazed right through her as if she were empty air.

When she got to the Party streets of Highbury, and the ranks of B.B. posters resumed, her tension eased enough for her to realize how jittery she'd become. She saluted the patrolman at the boundary, and his stance brightened in a way that let her intuit the grin behind his mask. All was quiet then until she passed the high wall of the football stadium, with its mural showing Butler's famous goal against Eastasia. The Eastasian uniform had recently been painted over with white, a hint that the alliance with Eastasia was on its last legs. On Julia's street, a line of chestnut trees was in bloom, looking especially festive with the fat red ribbons around their trunks that showed they were marked for deletion. A band of children played in the road, and as Julia jumped off her bike and wheeled it to the hostel wall, they all began to chant, gathered around one girl who was hopping over a chalk pattern and bouncing a rubber ball around her feet. Julia recognized the game: it was Hang 'Em. The chalk pattern represented a gibbet, and you hopped over it to the rhythm of a chant. If you hit a chalk line with foot or rubber ball, you became the "enemy" and were "hanged."

Hang 'Em had been devised by the legendary Mamie Faye from the Children's Department at Truth—she who'd written the songs "The Little Spy's Promise" and "Piggy Cannot Hide." It was made to commemorate the hanging of the three most famous Enemies of the People, the turncoats Rutherford, Aaronson, and Jones. The signature Mamie Faye touch was adding an imaginary uncle to the list of enemies—in children's stories, an uncle was always being unmasked as a spy by a sharp-witted niece or nephew.

The chant went:

> Rutherford, Aaronson,
> Your uncle, and Jones
> Supper for the gallow-birds
> Eyes and bones

They kick and they kick
They blubber and moan
But we don't care
We know what they've done!

Hang 'em up naked
In the rain and the snow
Rutherford, Aaronson,
Your uncle, and Jones

At the end, the player threw the ball high in the air and tagged another player, who had to catch the ball before it hit the ground, or else become the enemy and be "hanged." That meant performing some penalty—lapping up puddle water or letting all the other players pinch your arm.

Ordinarily Julia thought the game's nastiness was a laugh. The horrid things children liked! Today, though, her mind went back to O'Brien, and Smith gazing at him with adoration. Out of nowhere, she remembered Smith's first name: Winston. A lot of chaps that age were named Winston, no doubt for some hero of the revolution who'd later turned traitor and got himself vaporized. That Winston would have gone through the Ministry of Love—or whatever it was called back then. Julia's mum used to say, "He went through Love when it was only Fond Regard."

The children had noticed Julia now, and a weasel-faced boy in the uniform of the Spies was squinting at her suspiciously. Julia smiled amiably at him and turned to the door of Women's 21 with pointed casualness, making a note to herself to keep her chocolate ration for the kids this week. If they knew you were good for the occasional treat, they wouldn't be so keen to make up stories about you. Anyway, only a child could really stomach that Party chocolate.

The other girls had left her a slab of bread and cheese at the monitor's desk in the foyer. The cheese was the ration stuff they all called "shoe," but Julia was ravenous after her ride, and she was going to miss second meal altogether. She wolfed it, standing by the desk while the monitor, Atkins, chattered.

Atkins was a Nationality, and her face was a very deep brown, which had fascinated Julia at first. She'd even wondered if the color came from eating African food, though she now knew that was silly. In every other way, Atkins was the typical London Party stalwart in late middle age. She smiled through everything, showing all five of her remaining teeth, and could express almost any idea in the form of Party enthusiasm, like a dog communicating all its needs by barking and wagging its tail. Her overalls were ostentatiously patched, as was fashionable when she was young, and on her collar she wore the bronze badge of the Hero Mother, awarded for the feat of raising ten children to conscription age.

On the wall beside her desk were photographs of seven of those children. Six were transport portraits, taken at the Wall of Martyrs before they were sent to the front, and each was embellished with the Red Lion stamp that meant its subject had fallen in the war. One daughter, still living, was represented by photos at every age from infancy to forty. She was a dogsbody at the Transport Department and had grown into the image of Atkins. Comrade Atkins never mentioned the three children not represented, so one knew without asking they'd become unpersons. Queer to think they'd left nothing behind but their three-tenths share in that bronze badge.

Many monitors were Nationalities. It was a way to get Party membership and be safe from the camps, so for them the long hours might seem a small price to pay. Malicious mouths said Nationalities were more willing to inform on their white charges, and merciless at squeezing bribes from them. The same sorts of things were said about people from Semi-Autonomous Zones, though, so Julia always took it with a large pinch of salt. And, in fact, Monitor Atkins was nothing like that. She took little gifts with grace, but never ill-treated girls who had nothing to give. She worshipped the Party, exclaiming over every new item of dogma with naive excitement, but showed no interest in reporting others for getting the dogma wrong. Second only to the Party, she doted on her charges, and had never been known to initiate a Conduct/Yellow or a Conduct/Red, much less a Conduct/Black. In Julia's time at Women's 21, they'd only lost three girls. With a more draconian monitor, it easily could have been thirteen.

If Atkins had a weakness, it was her love of talk. Now she kept Julia standing by her desk while she gossiped about the latest triumphs of Ingsoc, nodding in happy agreement with herself. At first Julia focused on her bread-and-shoe, scarcely listening to what Atkins was saying about the resolutions in support of the troops at last night's North London Monitors' Union meeting. Behind her, the telescreen comfortably droned about rice production in America's agricultural regions, and the combination was gently soporific. Even when Atkins's talk turned to the most recent squabbles in the hostel, Julia only made commiserating faces while tidying up the crumbs she'd left. She was abruptly jolted back to attention when she heard the name "Vicky."

Atkins was saying, ". . . so exhausted. I went up to do the beds this morning, and what do I find but little Vicky, curled in her bunk with the blanket pulled over her head. Who knows when she'd have woken without me. Fancy being late to work at Central Committee!"

"It's the job that does it," Julia put in hastily. "Vicky's only tired."

"Don't I know it!" Atkins nodded. "Central Committee! It's too much for mortal man, or girl. I only think it's a shame if she suffers for it, after all her plusgood work for Deputy Chairman Whitehead."

At the mention of Whitehead, they both paused, deliberately not looking at the telescreen. One could feel the snoops leaning forward at the name.

Julia said with practiced enthusiasm, "Oh, Comrade Whitehead is doubleplus clever. We all admire him ever so much!"

"Oh, yes," said Atkins. "He's a marvel. He doesn't half go through the girls, though. Wears them right out, for all he gets them so young. What's Vicky, eighteen?"

"Seventeen. Just turned."

"I know it's such important work, Central Committee, but it's a shame to see her so poorly," said Atkins. "She can hardly keep food down. That's nerves, I suppose."

Atkins frowned down at her hands. Julia waited, feeling the cheese in her stomach like lead. On the telescreen, a woman was cheerily reading a list of agricultural products that had been produced in greater abundance than was projected in the Three-Year Plan. "Avocados—fifty metric tons over plan! Bananas—seventy metric tons over plan!" These glowing agricultural reports always seemed to feature goods one never saw in the shops. Julia wouldn't have known some of them existed if newsreaders weren't always enthusing about how plentiful they were. You could have hit her on the head with an avocado and she would be none the wiser.

Atkins went on in a low, confidential tone, "Do you know what I think Vicky should do?"

Now Julia saw where this was heading and wanted to groan. But she made herself say brightly, "What?"

"Artsem!" Atkins said. "That's what. She ought to go in for the artsem treatment."

Artsem was artificial insemination. This was now the Party's preferred method for its members to have babies. Sex outside marriage had always been criminal, but now even marriage was regarded suspiciously as a source of divided loyalties. The only good comrade was one who devoted every ounce of energy to the Party. Yet these comrades could not be conjured out of thin air. So they were to be produced by artificial insemination, then separated from their producers and raised in infant development centers by dispassionate workers. Artsem was at the center of the Party's "new direction on the family," and every allowance was made for girls who signed up.

It was also how unmarried girls covered up for sexcrime when they got pregnant.

Atkins was saying: "Whitehead's bound to understand if Vicky takes time off for artsem. Of course you girls should all be thinking about it, but in a case like Vicky's, you only ask yourself why she hasn't done it already. It's just the thing when you're feeling tired. She could be getting extra rations now, and looking forward to time in medsec, with her feet up and tea being brought by nurses. Oh, it's jolly work, having a baby. And artsem's so clean and scientific. I'd do it myself if I hadn't already had mine the oldthink way. And she'd still be a virgin! Think of that."

Julia studiously kept her face blank. Of course Atkins knew Vicky was no more a virgin than she was an avocado. What Atkins *didn't* know was that the girls had already spent weeks enthusing about artsem to Vicky, telling her what a jolly time it was—a sovereign remedy for "disorders of the womb." Of course they had. Vicky was their baby, the pet of the hostel, who still cried when one of the cats caught a mouse. Julia had tried especially hard, talking up her own two failed artsem courses, and the sweets she was given, and the badge she'd received, as if these were her fondest memories. She had even, ever so carefully, hinted that the reason she'd had these courses wasn't solely patriotic. Julia was Vicky's great crush, the one Vicky followed around like a gosling at the heels of a mother goose; it should have worked.

But Vicky was also a moody teenage girl who didn't want to think about her problems and turned sullen and stupid when reminded. In the SAZ, you could have taken a girl like that by the scruff of the neck and talked sense into her. You could have said plainly, "Don't be a damned fool. You're pregnant, and if you don't make it look right, you'll have the baby in the camps." In London, you had to speak in riddles, and with Vicky, half the time you were talking to yourself.

Atkins said, "I know there's no use my bringing it up. Who listens to a daft old thing like me? But she looks up to you. I know she does."

Julia said with deliberate blandness: "Perhaps Comrade Whitehead might have a word."

Atkins winced. "Oh, he'd be far too busy. Such a great man! A selfless worker for the Party!"

"A great man. Gives his all."

"Well, if she only thought about it." Atkins shook her head. "She mopes. That's not the way."

Her eyes went to Julia's face beseechingly, and Julia felt helplessly furious. It was the nicest people who made things difficult. Atkins ought to know you couldn't help everyone, not when they wouldn't help themselves.

But she found herself saying: "I'll speak to her. I can't promise she'll listen, but I'll see what's what."

Atkins brightened as if the day was saved. "I knew I could count on you, comrade! And now, don't let me keep you. Time and toilets wait for no man."

At Women's 21, the dormitory, monitor's station, and community room were at ground level, and everything with plumbing was on the floor above. This arrangement was maddening to Julia. It ensured the water pressure was weak, so of course you'd get clogs like nobody's business, and any leaks went straight through the floor onto the beds. People said it was designed to give a layer of protection if a rocket bomb hit while the residents were sleeping. That was a fine theory, but Julia had a different one. She thought the Party did it to get on her nerves.

The kitchen no longer functioned, and was used only for drying laundry, so people went up mainly for the ownlife room. *Ownlife* was a Newspeak word for time spent alone: going for long walks, staying up with a book, watching sunsets. It was always pejorative, used to remind comrades that time not spent on the good of the collective was wasted. On a hostel door, though, OWNLIFE just meant toilet. When Edie, who was from the back of beyond, first arrived at Women's 21, she'd frowned at the OWNLIFE sign and said, "Are they trying to say our lives are poo?" Margaret had looked nervously at the telescreen, and Edie took the hint and added loudly: "*I* don't think my life is poo! I think my life's spectacular!" Julia had heard the name was a relic of the time when hostels still had baths, so of course workers must be discouraged from lazing in them. Now you used the Party bathhouse, and washed under the eagle eye of a political officer who blew a whistle if you loitered.

The last room on the upper floor was the locker room. That was where Julia went now, slightly tense, as she always was when she had to change clothes. The locker rooms had telescreens on all four walls, angled down from the tops of the lockers, and it was impossible to change out of sight of them. It was also against the rules to put up anything that might obscure the view. Supposedly this was in order to make it harder to stash black-market goods. But it was generally believed it was really because the snoops liked to peep at naked girls. The official line was that the infosec crews who watched such screens were all female cadres, but rumor said otherwise. Anyway, if Julia had learned anything from her years of Junior Anti-Sex League, it was that there was no shortage of women who admired the female form.

As she opened her locker, her mind was on this, and she almost didn't notice the chit of paper that had been thrust into the vent. When she did see it, she took it absently, assuming it was a note about the toilet situation. Seeing what was written there, she froze, then immediately closed the chit in her hand. By then, her heart was racing. She forced herself to breathe evenly and turned back to rummaging in her locker as if nothing untoward had occurred. She felt a heat all over her body, a heat that would soon be sweat.

Too late, she realized a good Party member would have made a scandalized fuss for the telescreens, then run down and lodged a Conduct/Red with Atkins. If she did it now, any fool would see her shock was false. The idea of Love's eyeless mice gnawing at her in the dark passed through her mind. The sweat had come out now and she was chilly in the drafty room.

The note had said: I LOVE YOU.

In her first panic she irrationally imagined it was from Winston Smith. Of course it couldn't be. Even if he'd thought to write such a note, he'd never have got inside Women's 21. The more likely candidates were the housing inspector, who often lingered in the dormitory smirking at the underthings hung up to dry, or the post boy who brought parcels in and was always mooning over someone or other. The bloke Julia had been sneaking around with should have been the prime suspect, but wasn't. He was an inventory worker from Plenty who was easy on the eye but did his business in a minute and was talking about Party duty again while Julia was still finding her shoes.

The note itself gave no clues. The letters were clumsily formed; it was clearly written by someone unaccustomed to using a pen. But that could be anyone under thirty. Since the advent of speakwrites, most people seldom held a pen or pencil in their hands. The ink was watery and bluish, and the latter half of the *U* was just an unpigmented groove in the paper, but, again, that could be almost any pen in London. Good black ink would have told her more.

She was almost certain the snoops would have noticed nothing odd: just a note, such as often passed between girls, about chores or shared rations. They might not have seen the note at all. She'd had her back to the screen and the locker door was in the way. At worst they would have seen her glance at it, then go back to what she was doing. And now that she'd had half a minute to reflect, she was chilled at the thought that she might have made a fuss. Fancy sending the little post boy to Love, or that poor sap from Plenty. Anyway, no denunciation was without risk, especially where sexcrime was concerned. If a man was fingered for anything like that, he often took the girl down with him for "encouragement." No, she'd landed on her feet. Her SAZ instincts had pulled her through.

Keeping the note tucked in her hand, she pulled out the "nasties" she used for dirty jobs. These were overalls so worn that the knees had a lichen-like appearance from darning. The seat was almost transparent. Tiny holes in the front showed where burning crumbs of tobacco had fallen from cigarettes over the years.

She turned to the telescreen with a pleasant smile and said, "I'll just change from my good clothes, not to get them soiled. If there's a male comrade on duty, I'd ask you to avert your eyes." Julia often made announcements of this kind to entertain the other girls. The assumption was that it would bring every male comrade within earshot running. Julia didn't care who saw her naked arse, which was a fine arse, and nothing to blush at. Sometimes she even felt a thrill from imagining the snoops getting hot and bothered.

Now, of course, she was counting on her backside to distract attention from her hands. With a flourish, she unzipped her overalls. As she stepped out of them, raising one leg, then the other, her hand quite naturally went to the top shelf of the locker to keep her balance. There she left the note, shoved between her dress boots. While she hung up the good overalls and hastily pulled her nasties on, she replayed the incident in her mind. It was all right, she was almost certain. By the time she was dressed and had the locker shut up, she was almost calm.

By then, the hostel's two cats, Tiger and Commissar, had materialized behind her and were fighting over a discarded sock. With the instinct of cats for giving trouble, they had chosen to do this directly in front of the ownlife door. Julia laughed and said, "Go catch our rats, you lazy capitalists." When she hefted the auger and came toward them, they stopped midattack, and Tiger jumped to his feet. Commissar remained stretched out, the sock wrapped over his orange haunch, one paw still curled aggressively in the air. He leaned back his head and yawned. Julia wormed her foot underneath him until he sprang away in annoyance. When she opened the door, both cats darted officiously into the ownlife ahead of her. She laughed again and said, "I've got my eye on you, you wrongthinkers. Pair of bleeding Frenchmen, you are."

The stall of Toilet 1 had no door, and looked directly onto the telescreen, so the shyer girls wouldn't use it, and Toilet 2 was perennially overworked. Even when it was clogged, there were some who used it and left the growing mess for someone else. Still, when Julia had left that morning, the toilet hadn't yet overflowed. She'd even plunged it (unsuccessfully) without getting any dirty water on the floor.

Now a puddle spread from the toilet stall almost to the opposite wall. There was enough water in the mix that the image from the telescreen was dimly reflected there, but there were also some brown splotches and a fair bit of Sickness: Menstrual. A folded piece of paper lay in the mess, soaked through. I LOVE YOU flashed through Julia's mind before she remembered what the page must be. That morning, Edie had written a note to remind people not to use that toilet: PLEASE DON'T ADD TO THIS UNGOOD SITUATION, COMRADES! They'd laughed over it, and Julia had folded the paper and hung it over the stall door.

Some girl must have flung the door open, in such a hurry to add to the ungood situation that she never saw the note and sent it right into the soup. How that girl failed to see the ungood situation itself, and why she'd not only used the toilet but flushed it afterward—by the looks of things, several times— well, if it hadn't been so predictable, one might have scarcely credited it.

For a moment Julia felt close to crying. It was O'Brien and Vicky and the I LOVE YOU note and now this mess. There were hardly any cleaning rags left. It was the middle of the day, so no hot water either. Not a hope of getting through it without getting filthy, which meant a trip to the baths. Another bath coupon gone, another hour lost, and if O'Brien was still in Fiction, being that late could even be dangerous. All for some girl too good to let snoops see her take a shit. Not too good to let others mop it up, though!

In the meantime, the cats had scented the blood, and Commissar was standing gingerly at the boundary of the water, sniffing at the nearest clot, while his brother looked over his shoulder more fastidiously. Setting down the auger, Julia swooped down and grabbed one cat in each hand. They still strained their heads back toward the interesting mess as she lifted them away. In the air, they twisted, and Commissar got his claws hooked into Julia's sleeve, but when she opened the door, they allowed themselves to be tossed into the locker room. She shut the door in their faces and turned back, muttering to herself: "The Party is strong, our problems are unstrong." Then she stepped toward the stall, not giving herself time to feel anything about it, and opened the door to assess the damage.

Her first response was relief. Someone had already had a go at mopping up, so the puddle wasn't as large as it appeared from outside. Whoever it was had used the scraps of newspaper provided to wipe yourself with and, for reasons best known to themselves, hadn't taken them to the bin but left them in the corner of the stall in a sodden heap. But at least they hadn't dumped them in the toilet, where Julia would have had to dig them all out. That was when she noticed the thing in the toilet bowl. At first she thought her eyes were playing tricks, but when she squinted and leaned closer, it was still there.

It was no bigger than a mouse, and most of that bulk was a bulbous, misshapen head. The head had blanks where eyes should be. Its skin was translucent purple, mottled red and streaked with bright blood. It had wizened limbs, coated in some places in a substance like black aspic, but one arm was clean and startlingly fully formed with a neatly articulated elbow. A foot had five distinct toes and was tucked up to the belly as if in satisfied sleep. Its nudity was its most human quality. She instinctively wanted to wrap it in a blanket. It lay in reeking brown water and dilute blood. A turd nestled against its forehead.

Vicky's baby.

3

ONCE JULIA HAD MADE THE REPORT, THE PATROLS AP-
peared with horrible swiftness. All was terrifying then for a
spell. Two men took Atkins to the dormitory, dragging her so
she lost her footing, then cursing at her clumsiness. Julia was
left at Atkins's desk, with three men shouting accusations in
her face. More patrols arrived, looking flushed, invigorated, and
agreeably nervous, like people gathering to watch an execution.
These new arrivals trotted upstairs, and Julia was icily conscious
of the note still there on the top shelf of her locker.

Through the fright, there was the steadying feeling of knowing one's part and performing it well. As a child of the SAZ,
Julia had been raised with the lore of police interrogations. She
knew you didn't name names if you could help it. It was as fatal
to accuse those with protection as it was to defend those who
had none. You must also never let the patrols draw you onto
other subjects. If they asked about anything but the incident,
you talked about the incident, playing the part of a simpleton
who couldn't keep up. Above all, you kept your story simple and
repeated it word for word, so they couldn't find inconsistencies.
Never mind if you sounded daft. Daft was good. Daft lived
while clever died.

So it went:

"Who gave you the poison to abort the infant?"

"But the unbirth wasn't mine, comrade. I only saw it in the toilet, so I came directly to report it. I work at the Ministry of Truth and I know my duty to the Party."

"When you lie, you only make things worse for yourself. Tell us when you committed the sexcrime. Who was your accomplice in the crime?"

"But the unbirth wasn't mine, comrade. I only saw it in the toilet, so I came directly to report it."

"So you admit you colluded at abortion with another girl? What's her name?"

"I would never do anything like that, comrade. I work at the Ministry of Truth and know my duty to the Party. I only saw the unbirth in the toilet and came directly to report it."

At last the door came open a final time to admit a smiling, black-overalled man with the undefinable stink of Thought Police. It was something about his shape-shifting face, how all he said contained a subtle wink. He might kill you any time he liked, and enjoy it—but for now you were his friend, and wasn't that a pleasant thing to be?

His first act was to wave around a telescreen report and announce that a culprit had been found—a culprit who wasn't Julia. It was comical then how the patrols changed face. They seemed a full foot shorter as the thinkpol scolded them for "badgering a patriotic woman who'd only done her duty." Atkins was ushered back in, and graciously accepted a cup of tea from the same louts who'd been manhandling her before. In a minute, all were gone but the thinkpol, who was sitting chummily with Atkins and easing his way toward the important topic of his bribe.

When Julia went back up the stairs to change, there was no one in the locker room. All the lockers had been broken open and their doors were warped and ajar. Odds and ends were strewn about on the floor—nightclothes, chess pieces, a shattered hand mirror. But when she went to her locker, her dress boots were still on the shelf. In pulling out her work gloves, she let her hand traverse the shelf and felt a chill of relief when her fingers encountered the slip of paper: the I LOVE YOU note was still in place. She considered disposing of it now, but decided to leave it for a few days. The snoops would be watching the hostel now, and the gesture of slipping something into a pocket might well attract their notice. And this room had just been thoroughly searched. It was as safe as a place could be.

She found the auger and did the job she'd originally come to do. The patrols had taken the thing—the baby. With it gone, it took seconds to clear the clog. She spent far more time cleaning the floor, taking care not to soil her clothing, then washed the auger in the sink, using the caustic all-purpose soap that turned your skin crimson and left you itching all day. Today the harshness was a relief. Julia washed her hands with it twice.

The rest of the day passed in a spell of strange peace. Julia cycled back to Truth to make up her hours, and when she returned the auger, the guardroom boys thanked her for its cleanliness and gave her a square of chocolate as a reward. In Fiction, O'Brien was gone. She was able to lose herself in fixing the mechanical gripes that had arisen in her absence. It was lovely how no one here knew what had happened. All was wonderfully the same as every other day. At some moments, the thinkpol's voice came back to her, and she was tempted to dwell on Vicky—Vicky, who so recently was only a lovable pest, a child who laughed too much at Julia's jokes and copied her way of cutting her hair, who had the great plum of being at Central Committee and made so frustratingly little of it. And Julia had taken Vicky under her wing. When she herself was a young goose, fresh from the

SAZ, other women had done it for her. When she was a child—but Julia put it from her mind. She had to fix these machines. That was all she had to do.

She worked late, catching up, and was pleasantly ravenous by the time she signed out. The canteen was already closed, so she decided to pamper herself by going to an A1 dining room. It would let her put off going home. In any case, she still had two 1983 meal coupons, which had to be used before the first of May, when the revolutionary calendar was reset.

Here, too, she was lucky. The meal was shepherd's pie, and though the carrots were rubbery, it had a good amount of tripe and the potatoes were browned just right. She relaxed among the lower-echelon office workers who populated such places, those who hadn't made the four big Ministries but had eked out a London residence permit and were clinging to the bottom rungs of the hierarchy. There was a sweetness to this company, their voices so quiet and their manners so obliging. They made room for each other at the long tables and brightened when they spotted a familiar face. An older woman smiled at Julia and said, "A plusgood bit of tripe in this."

"Oh, yes," said Julia. "They feed you well here."

"They feed you *goodwise*," a gray-faced man corrected her with a friendly wink. "Mind your Newspeak."

"Oh, I can't ever get Newspeak right," Julia said. "I'm not a bit intellectual."

"It's really only the kids who do it rightwise," the man said, then added gallantly, "Not that you're much more than a kid yourself."

"Now, 'feed,'" said the woman. "Is that a proper Newspeak word? Can you still say 'feed'?"

All at the table chimed in, debating whether *feed* was oldful. Julia relaxed, laughing at the mild jokes and nodding solemnly at the assertions. The dining room was chilly and had a sad odor of bleach and cabbage, yet Julia felt a struggling love in her chest. The windows had fogged up, so the rain outside was visible only as a dim unsteadiness, and the place had the cozy feeling of nightfall, of the coming curfew's benign enclosure, of dark outside and safety within. When the waitress came round to warn them it was ten minutes to the electricity cutoff, Julia bid her new friends farewell with real regret.

It was too dark to think of riding a bike, so Julia caught the bus home. That trip remained in her mind long after as a last taste of peace. Stop by stop, the bus emptied. People lit cigarettes. Buses had no internal lights—even headlights were dimmed for blackout—and in the darkest stretches, they swam through a nothing like the chaos before the world was made. Where they came into a bomb site, the moon appeared, showing the crazy shapes of ruins, and one felt giddy at seeing the ground not quite where one had supposed it to be. The last passengers of the evening flagged the bus down by brandishing white rags. Julia leaned her forehead against the chilly window, drowsing and feeling immortal. She'd survived another trial and here was night. Nothing more would be asked. She had won another day.

She was the only one to get off at the football stadium. The hostel door had been left unlocked for her. Inside, the monitor's desk was empty. Atkins would be in her little basement room, drinking gin and watching the evening program. The telescreen was turned down to a mutter—Atkins could never be convinced it didn't save on electricity—but its light still played across the desk and dully flashed on the glass of Atkins's children's photographs. Tonight's evening program was one Julia had seen before, about "Our Friend, the Potato." A tinny male voice informed her that the potato was first discovered by an

Airstrip One boy called Walt Raleigh, who'd been beheaded by the capitalists for his pains. Julia found a stub of pencil and made an *X* by her name in the register, then held the page up to the telescreen through a count of ten. The program's drone was briefly interrupted by a crisp woman's voice saying, "Worthing, Julia, registered at Women's 21"—a bit of magic that never failed to amaze Julia. Then the program went on droning about the cultivation of the potato by plantation owners; instantly it was hard to credit that the woman's voice had really been.

She thought of going upstairs to change, but couldn't face the locker room—or, worse, the ownlife room. She decided to sleep in her overalls, as she often did after an especially long day, and went down the hall to the dormitory. Already she was uneasily aware of its abnormal silence.

The door was half open. As Julia paused outside, she was chilled by the stillness, the flat gray dark. Not a candle showed. No clusters of gossipers gathered by the popular girls' bunks. At twenty-two hundred, all were already in bed. The usual chatter of bedtime had been replaced by a creeping whisper, barely audible above the telescreens. Steeling herself, she stepped in.

The dormitory had rows of bunk beds against the east and west walls. As the girls here were all Ministry, they had all the conveniences of modern life. This meant each bunk had its very own telescreen overlooking the pillow, from which now came a ubiquitous babble about our friend the potato. Beside each telescreen hung a gas mask, which must be there by regulation, though they gave the new girls nightmares. Between bunks were strung propaganda banners: SLEEP IS VIGILANCE, SIX HOURS FOR HEALTH, BIG BROTHER WATCHES OVER OUR PEACEFUL REST.

Julia's was a lower bunk by the door, the second-most desirable spot. You had the privacy of the corner, and were near the door, so you were first out in the mornings and never had to queue up for the sinks. Edie slept in the bunk above Julia, and their neighbors were the artsem girls, Bess and Oceania. Bess was artsem/one and getting extra sweet coupons to help with nausea. Oceania was artsem/due, which meant she now spent her days at the Chestnut Tree Café with her artsem sash prominently displayed, having teas bought for her by patriotic men.

The volume on the telescreens here was nearly as high as it was in the day. Some girls were disturbed by the noise, but most couldn't sleep without it. Julia was the latter sort. If she woke from a nightmare, she needed to be lulled by the old Big Brother speeches that were broadcast after midnight. His deep, calm voice was the sound of sleep, just as the scent of sleep was stale cigarette smoke, the reek of chamber pots that grew more insistent as the night wore on, and the rude musk note of unwashed girl. All Julia asked was to be left to sleep in rooms like this for the rest of her life.

At the far end of the room, framed between the rows of bunks, was one single bed, sitting snug against the room's one radiator. On the few winter nights when the heating came on, to sleep in that bed was bliss. It was also beneath the window, and thus had no telescreen of its own, so no barking rebukes if its occupant thrust a hand between her legs in sleep. The curtains could be left open, telescreens not being accounted a violation of blackout rules. It was possible to smoke and look out at the moon if one were of a romantic disposition. That bed was always given to the girl who was nearest the top of the Party hierarchy. For the past six months, it had been Vicky's.

She sat there now, half-wrapped in her bedclothes, facing not the window but the door. The hostel's two cats were curled beside her, Commissar grooming himself, while Tiger watched him intently as if waiting for him to make a mistake. Vicky was blond, with hair so pale it could look white in certain lights. Atkins had once called her a "seafoam child." She was plump, as no other girl here was, from a thousand Central Committee canteen meals—so plump that, in anyone else, it might have given an impression of greed or luxury. In Vicky, it seemed an enhanced innocence. At first glance, she looked not seventeen but twelve; then one noticed her generous breasts. Still, she was beautiful as a child is beautiful: pure-skinned, tender, new. She now sat forward and beckoned to Julia.

The whispers stopped. Without them, the telescreens sounded louder, almost painfully clear: *The potato in nature is a rich source of vitamin C. Thanks to advances in scientific socialism, potatoes now also provide protein, vitamin B, iron . . .* The silence underneath was alive with malice. Julia understood: they'd been enduring Vicky for hours. That was why the whole hostel was in bed so early, to rest from the work of ostracism. Julia had seen it many times before. The doomed girl would come home preoccupied, jittery, expecting the last blow at any moment. What she didn't expect—somehow never expected—was her dorm-mates flinching from her and turning their backs, the hostile eyes, the spiteful whispers. Some unfortunates grasped it immediately, revised their expectations of life, and shrank to the space allowed. Others—and Vicky surely would be one— bumbled about in confusion, approaching one old friend after another, each of whom would feign deafness or snap, "What the hell do you want? Can't you see I'm busy?" Vicky would have wept. That was the worst; it made one helplessly loathe the blubberer while also bitterly despising oneself. How one loved the few who got through it without crying! *Them* one would have liked to comfort—but of course one couldn't. Guilt was a catching sickness.

All her life, Julia had obeyed the unwritten rules that kept her far from guilt. She had known who was safe, and felt an unfeigned disgust for unsafe people. Instinctively she'd loved the lucky and clever. If she ever took a risk, it wasn't for fools. It wasn't for the dead or those half dead. It was actually cruel to give them hope.

Julia thought this now, but walked to Vicky—impossibly walked, as if crossing a path of moonlight across an expanse of black water. The whispers still weren't there. They were the blackness beneath her feet. Vicky's eyes dwelled on Julia, shining; they filled and overfilled with trust. The telescreens droned: *Potato was a rare delicacy in the capitalist era, obtainable only by the owning classes. Hard for us to imagine now, when the potato takes pride of place on every table! Thanks to our potato diet, our children grow two inches taller . . .*

As Julia sat down on the end of the bed, the two cats flinched away from her, and Commissar lashed his tail. Vicky whispered, "Oh, I knew you would come!"

For just a moment, Julia was filled with rage. Then she said in a determinedly cheerful voice: "It's early for bed. I couldn't ever sleep yet."

"Nor I. Not after . . . well, I simply couldn't."

"Would you like a cigarette? I've just got my ration."

"Thanks ever so much, but I don't smoke."

"Not ever?"

"I did, but Comrade Whitehead doesn't like it."

"Is that it? Well, then."

"He says the smell of it on a woman turns his stomach."

Again that fury rose in Julia. She said hoarsely, "Can't have that."

"I feel all right now myself. The nausea's gone."

"Yes, you've been ill. Atkins said."

"Oh, I've been so ill. I was afraid."

Julia was nonplussed. Might the girl truly not know what had happened? She imagined Vicky producing *that* in the toilet and not seeing it for what it was, perhaps not looking in the toilet at all. Going back to her bunk in mysterious pain, then being rousted out by Atkins. Staggering to CentCom Tower in that condition, never knowing she'd been pregnant.

But then Vicky haltingly, faintly whispered: "Do you think . . . do you suppose one might be forgiven for a crime, if they saw it truly wasn't one's fault? If they saw that one was led by a powerful person, that one couldn't say no? They *might* see, mightn't they? If one simply made a clean breast of it, I mean?"

Both cats were looking at Vicky now. The whispering had risen again in the room, a vicious sound. The telescreens brightened, showing a potato field under blue skies. By their light, Vicky's face was white and luminous, with a sheen of sweat on her cheeks. Then the screens darkened again, and Julia heard Vicky's sob. It wasn't sweat: of course it wasn't. Vicky was weeping.

Julia said, without thinking, "Oh, why ever did you do it?"

Vicky shook her head and whispered, "But I didn't! That is, I never meant to. I never even thought I could be pregnant. He made sure it couldn't happen, but it did, you see. And when I saw that was how things were, he gave me a preparation to make it go away. I supposed the birth would be digested inside, that it would dissolve or . . . anything but what it was. Atkins said you found it?"

"Yes."

"But I was bound to believe him, wasn't I? To do as he said? I never knew it was a baby already. When I saw the—what you found—I thought it was my mind playing tricks. Is it truly gone? It's not still there?"

"It's gone."

"Of course it would be." Vicky nodded, looking fearfully at the door. "Could they have saved it, do you think? Could it live?"

"Of course not," Julia whispered savagely. "Remember where you left it. How can you?"

Vicky nodded faster, pressing the sheet to her cheek. "I know it couldn't really. I know."

"It's murder. You do see that, don't you?"

Vicky stared at her in fright, tears welling silently from her eyes, her mouth a distorted slash. Belatedly, Julia felt her own cruelty. But it was how she must be—for the telescreens, for the other girls listening in the dark. Vicky must realize that herself. Nothing said to her now meant anything. They were just the words that one must use.

Julia said stiffly, "I'd best get off to bed now. It's no good. I'm sorry."

"Oh, yes, you'd better go. I do see."

"Perhaps it will be all right. I must go, but it may yet be all right."

"I do adore you," Vicky whispered. "Oh, I do. You'd think it wasn't much that you spoke with me, but it's the world. I shall remember it always."

When Julia rose from the bed, the whispers altered in timbre. Then, as she passed the bunks, they died before her and rose again in her wake, like a wind passing through a wheatfield. When she came to her own corner, Oceania's eyes were shut, her face tense, her hands clasped tightly under her chin. Edie lay above, unseen and silent. Julia tried to act as if nothing was wrong, but couldn't help moving furtively, cringing as she crept into bed. Tonight Edie wouldn't lean down to gossip with her and share a last cigarette. The artsem girls wouldn't complain of their pains or speculate about their babies' futures. All the bunks nearby were silent. Beyond, the whispers surged and hissed. More than anything,

Julia wanted to pull the covers over her head and curl up as she had in childhood. But she lay as she always did, on her back with her arms splayed around her head. She mustn't seem different this night. She must show no sign of guilt or fear.

She didn't expect to sleep, but the dread exhausted her and weighed her down, and she fell at once into fitful dreams. Through them came the cozy voice of Big Brother, telling Julia she was loved, that her failings would be overlooked, but first she must save Vicky's baby. She was laboring at that toilet to find it, turning over sodden, bloody paper with the plumber's auger. Behind her, she heard patrols searching lockers, their clamor getting closer and closer. If one of them reached her, she would die. Then the scene changed, and she and Big Brother were fleeing through a prole street that was ablaze. Proles watched them pass from windows, unconcerned by the flames that raged around their heads—and, with no transition, Julia was back in her bunk, awake and bitterly cold.

Heavy footsteps were approaching. There was an indefinable change in the air and an absolutely leaden silence. When she opened her eyes, the telescreens were off. The realization struck her like a physical blow. The only light was a flashlight whose beam flitted restlessly around the room. She heard the footsteps again and realized what was happening—but oh, why must they have the screens off? What could they do that couldn't be seen, even by snoops? Julia flinched as the light from the flashlight flicked over her bed. Behind came a complex, heaving flow of dark: ten men at least. Among their heavy footfalls one heard Atkins's familiar squeaking shoes. Even after they'd passed, Julia couldn't stop clenching up from fear. Her shoulders already hurt. If they turned back toward her, she'd never bear it. They couldn't. She would die, she would die.

As she thought this, the footsteps stopped, too close. A

cheeping sound came out of the dark: a girl crying out in surprise. In that first moment, Julia knew there was something wrong about it. It was in the wrong place. It was wrong altogether. But only when the girl said, "Oh, what is it?" did she know it wasn't Vicky.

A man's voice spoke, the words indistinct.

Then Atkins said, "It's no good being like that, dear. You just go along with these comrades. They'll see to you."

"But there's been some mistake," said the girl. "I haven't done—"

Atkins cut in anxiously: "You won't want to talk about that, not here, where decent Party girls can hear you."

"But I've done nothing! I'm trying to tell you—"

A man said coldly, "Enough. Get up or we'll help you get up, and you won't like that."

Julia turned her head and saw Oceania twisted strangely in the dark, her hands clasped on the hill of her belly.

"But could you speak to my superior?" the girl said more softly. "Please, I work at Truth. I'm in Records."

A man guffawed. "It would be Records."

"There are those who will vouch for me, that's all I mean," the girl said. "I'm—"

There was a scuffle, then a thud. A half breath, a half shriek. Julia realized her fingernails had sunk into her palms and automatically loosened them. Oceania was pressing both fists to her mouth as the footsteps came back toward their bunks. The group of men washed past them in a formless shadow. Julia instinctively cowered. Unseen inside the mass, one could hear the girl gasp. Then there was a skip, a scrambling that became a wild din of boots on floorboards and cursing men. The dark shape heaved. A slight, struggling figure appeared atop it and was borne forward lurchingly, the flashlight's light skating crazily over the ceiling. The mass caught momentarily at the door, then narrowed, grunting, and forced its way through. Behind, a shrill, wild voice trailed: "But I could never—please listen! It's Vicky Fitzhugh who was pregnant! It couldn't be me! I've never even wanted sex! Please, comrades, listen! There's been some mistake! I'm Margaret! Margaret Fellowes!"

4

JULIA'S PARENTS WERE OLD REVOLUTIONARIES, MEMBERS of the Party before Big Brother. Her mother, Clara, was a child of the former aristocracy. She'd grown up reading Tennyson and riding ponies on a Wiltshire estate, and was presented to the King at Queen Charlotte's Ball. Clara's first great adventure was insisting on going up to Oxford to read Classics. There she met Julia's father. They were young Party cadres together; they asked their branch secretary for permission to marry. The revolution came and took her lands and her Greek, but Clara loved it no less, and carried sheaves of red carnations in early victory demonstrations. She defended all the Party's early crimes—the burning of Parliament, the massacre at Sandhurst, the murders of the two princesses. Even when the Party condemned her husband, it was him she blamed.

This episode she described very sourly and slightingly. Poor health made Michael peevish, she said, so he quarreled with everyone, high and low. "He fancied himself a man of principle, the last honest man. Well, no one likes that." They were exiled to Kent for his intransigence, but he continued to write peppery letters to the newspapers about the Party's wrong direction, for which folly he was finally hanged in the street in front of Maidstone Police Station, with his wife and child in compulsory attendance. Baby Julia screamed and fought to reach her father long after he was dead. "Oh, well," Clara said, "I suppose it felt good to get it off his chest."

In Julia's first memories, they lived in Maidstone, then a town of political exiles. Among Clara's friends, reasons for exile included possessing a German dictionary, not wearing red to a May Day demonstration, winning a footrace against the son of a Party higher-up, painting a landscape a critic recognized as being in Eurasia, and making a typing error that changed "Big Brother" to "Big Bother." All exiles wore a white armband, which in theory bore a symbol indicating the wearer's crime. In practice, the only armbands available had the sabotage boot, so all wore those. For this, the exiles were called "boots" by the local population. Most were socialists of some stripe, and privately saw the crimes of their neighbors as slips no true Party member could have made, while regarding their own troubles as a foolish misunderstanding.

The boots were always meeting to talk, for them an activity in itself. They talked about the conduct of the war and the direction of the Party. They talked about decadent materialism, the false dialectic, and petty-bourgeois infantilism. They talked about the menial jobs they were reduced to, which they agreed were jolly educational and gave one a marvelous understanding of the workers' troubles, but were such a dreadful waste of one's abilities. They talked as they wrote appeals for reinstatement, they talked as they queued at the police station every week to register their continued presence, they talked as they accompanied an unlucky friend to the train station for his "secondary exile." They talked as if talk were the real work of life, and the world's problems would soon be resolved if it were only rightly done.

At weekends they threw parties, at which they talked but also danced to a gramophone or sang to an acoustic guitar.

These parties featured food of a splendor that later struck Julia as simply incredible. Was it possible Clara once soaked three chickens in cream and herbs, then roasted them with figs? That a neighbor liked to offer five kinds of fruit, and one was always African pineapple? That the Italian wife of an anarchist once made a pasta dish with fresh tomatoes and real prawns, which—most wonderful of all—little Julia had refused to eat? Just as strange, however, was the noise—the sound of fifty people arguing, laughing, dancing, while jazz music played and a baby shrieked. It was a wild, gay din Julia never heard again, not at any community-center dance, not even at balls for departing soldiers.

Then came the days when the talk of the exiles was all of schemes for hiding books. These books Julia remembered as utterly different from those she later knew at Fiction. They were lovely, heavy things, clad in cloth or leather, from which adults read bewitching tales of queens and chimeras and glass slippers, books redolent with a kindly scent that now existed nowhere on earth. Then there was the night the exiles obediently brought those books to be burned. Julia remembered the ponderous wheelbarrows creeping up to a hill of fire, the reflections of flames on the river's surface, and the cheers, in which the exiles joined. Nonetheless they were shoved and kicked in the crowd, their white "boot" armbands giving them away. But far worse was the memory of the Party "uncle" who visited Julia's mother at night and was arranging something for them. Then Julia must be taken out of bed and left on the chilly stairs outside until the uncle was gone. One night it was not one uncle but three, and Clara clung to Julia afterward and sobbed and spoke in a strange, hoarse voice.

But after all, what childhood was not fearsome? Was it not

ever the lot of a child to be terrified among the giant adults and their sudden blows and their unfathomable pain?

What that Party man had been arranging was a favorable place of secondary exile. This was a dairy farm in a village with a sprawl of prison camps on one side and an air force base on the other. Such out-of-the-way postings were at a premium, as the atom bombs had now struck London, and the Second Security Period had given way to the First Patriotic Purge. Hundreds were shot every day in public justice demonstrations, and thousands more beaten to death in police cells. In Maidstone, it was no longer safe to wear a white armband on the street.

The village, Hesham, was where Julia first came to understand her life as unhappy. She loathed the farm director, Mrs. Marcy, who scanted Julia's and Clara's food and was always threatening to report them for parasitism. She never overcame her fear of cows, even after she was doing the work of a dairymaid and had learned to also love them. She dreaded school, where she shivered in an unheated room while reciting the Twenty-Seven Principles of Ingsoc and the Hundred Maxims of Big Brother Thought, and was regularly caned for saying them wrong. Then there was the stench from the camps, which waxed and waned in changing winds, and made any pleasant thing seem false. At first Julia believed it came from unwashed criminals, thinking it only natural their smells were worse than other people's. Then one day Mrs. Marcy wrinkled her nose and said, "They could bury them a little bit deeper," and the scales fell from her eyes.

There were two consolations in this new life. One was the socialist Youth Leagues, where there was always a warm coal fire and thick rugs and music and the smell of baking tarts. The first club was Spies, for children up to ten; then the girls graduated to Mayflowers and the boys to Socialist Youth. Activities altered little with age. In fine weather, they marched about with toy rifles and staged mock battles. When it rained, they drew educational posters and sang patriotic songs around the piano. The Mayflowers were also taught cookery, and real food was provided for this purpose, though some ingredients always had to be represented by drawings.

The main lesson taught in Youth Leagues was suspicion of one's elders. Adults had been raised in capitalist times and were all prone to wrongthink. It was a solemn duty to report their missteps, and certain children acquired a horrible glamour for their feats in that direction. They got medals designating them "Eagle Eyes" and "Guardians," which came with extra rations. The best medal, "Hero of the Socialist Family," guaranteed Party membership and a place at a London polytechnic when one turned eighteen. This, however, was only awarded for turning in a parent, and most children in Hesham village were evacuees and orphans, cruelly deprived of any parental misdeeds to report. As one of the few with a mother in situ, Julia enjoyed a certain prestige. She was envied by the other children, who saw her as in possession of a gold mine, and was tacitly admired by the adults for never mining that dark gold.

The other light of Julia's life was the airmen. Enlisted men were housed in barracks, but the People's Air Force officers were billeted on villagers, and the dairy farm always housed two or three. Even the stingy Mrs. Marcy accepted this imposition with good humor. All knew the young pilots were soon to die, and so you couldn't begrudge them. They were also tall young men with patrician accents and swashbuckling manners, in a place where all other able-bodied men had been sent off to war. One of Julia's first tasks was answering the door to tell lovelorn neighbors the officers weren't at home, often while they could be heard playing cards and cursing each other in the next room.

Part of the airmen's charisma was their thrilling scorn for government. At that time, they still had no fear of denunciation. As they said, they would soon enough be blasted from the air above some Eurasian town. So they casually damned all Yanks and Londoners and sneered at the rot that came out of the radio. They couldn't be made to take Newspeak seriously, and loved to invent profane versions of its words: *twatspeak, arsethink, doublepluscunt.* They despised the Eagle Eyes and Guardians, calling them "beastly little sneaks" and saying they ought to be roasted with apples in their mouths. Once two airmen got hold of Julia's *Spies' Handbook* and roared with laughter at the list of telltale signs of wrongthink, which included "Unusual beard" and "Farting during our Leader's speeches." When prisoners from the local camps were hired on farms as labor, only the airmen would speak to them. One officer struck up a friendship with a German prisoner of war, and had long conversations with the man in his own language, a crime for which the airman was denounced—but time passed and nothing was done about it, and finally he died an airman's death when his engine failed in a storm.

Julia had started falling in love with them when she was still a child. She made them posies of wildflowers to carry in the cockpit for luck, and gathered hawthorn to brew them strengthening tea. Some made a mascot of her, and took her with them on errands in their jeeps, Julia hanging ecstatically from a window, making faces at any other children she saw. When an airman died, she hid in the hayloft and wept awful tears for hours. But another would come, and she would happily mend his shirts and ask him breathless questions. All her youth, she was in love. The pilots belonged to the sky, and to the clean, black realm outside of life. When she first imagined sex, it was mixed in her head with planes and noble death, with flying at night in a wilderness of stars, aloft and lost forever. Later she could sometimes feel bitter that planes had been produced in such abundance while farm machinery rusted away, and horses were eaten in hungry years, and starving men pulled the plows themselves. But at that age, she would have starved the world to make another soaring plane and the gallant crew who manned it. What else would a world be for?

Only once she got to go up in a plane. The pilot was Hubert, a burly, enthusiastic man of twenty, and she never knew why he took her. He surely could have had no amorous motive, as Julia was then a scrawny twelve, and one couldn't wish for a man more decently dull. His one passion was listening to the cricket on the radio. Of course she had loved him desperately at that age. Of course he was soon to die.

Of the flight, she remembered every detail as if it were her only life. There was the engine's great noise that came to her ears through her whole body, and the moment the plane lost touch with the ground and changed from machine to animal. It dangled and caught as if fighting a leash, then bore down and turned with a fearful drop like hunger. They rose and rose, and Julia couldn't stop imagining how it would feel to slip and crash. She was terrified, yet the fear was dazzling. It made her laugh and straighten out her legs. It felt as if they must fly forever.

On that flight, she saw the bright of the sea from above, and the wavering line where it met land. She'd never seen ocean before, and it looked nothing like it did in pictures. The water was utterly flat, black-gray, and metallic light swarmed over its surface. It looked the same in all directions, and she couldn't tell how low they were flying until Hubert pointed out a little sailing boat. At first she thought this was a spy boat and was suitably thrilled, but Hubert shouted into her ear, his hot breath sending chills to her toes: "Smugglers! From France! They're bringing us chocolate!"

But her most cherished memory from that trip was her sighting of the Crystal Palace. This was the vast glass castle where Big Brother lived when he was in Airstrip One. It was built on the ruins of a capitalist palace that had burned in the wars that were then common; the socialist version was, of course, far grander and more scientifically made. A drawing of the Crystal Palace was the frontispiece of Julia's scientific atheism textbook, and an etching of it hung on the schoolroom wall. Transparent from all sides, it represented the fact that Big Brother had nothing to hide. In class, they were taught that, when communism was achieved, all people would live in such fabulous buildings. Outside class, the children speculated about whether the toilets had glass walls too, and what the glass would do to a person if the palace were hit by a bomb. All her life, Julia had taken the Crystal Palace for granted, while somehow never imagining it was a real place she might see.

Hubert hadn't warned her they might fly past it, nor did he point it out. Julia spotted it herself the moment it appeared on the crest of a hill. Miniature with distance and unsettlingly perfect, it was lovelier than she could have ever imagined. Its glass reflected the rosy clouds of sunset. It seemed composed of silver jewelry and light. Neat lines of trees were planted around it, their boughs flowing visibly in the wind, and that tiny, watery movement made the scene arrestingly real. A chill went over Julia. Big Brother could be there. She might see him now.

Then the plane tipped a wing and nimbly turned. The celestial vision fell away.

5

IT WAS A WEEK LATER THAT JULIA NEXT SAW WINSTON Smith. It was then it all properly began.

The intervening days had been eerily quiet. There were no more arrests, no patrols at the hostel. Every night, Julia looked for Vicky to be gone, but she was always there. The other girls had accepted Vicky again, and sat with her on her bed doing mending and trading cigarettes. Julia, too, pretended to forget. She even feigned delight when Vicky joined the Junior Anti-Sex League and started to appear at every meeting, avidly soaking up the cant about purethink and repeating it with seeming conviction. Of course Whitehead must have protected her—whether from tender feeling or because he didn't like the axe to fall so near his own head. What was chilling, though, was how quickly Vicky lost her wan and wretched look. One couldn't help feeling she should have the good taste to look sick, for the baby's sake, if not Margaret's. But seventeen was seventeen. Julia remembered very well what it was like to be startled by one's rosy face in the mirror when one felt near death from heartbreak.

The day it happened was the first day Julia dared to visit her black-market woman again. She made up her trade parcel in the hostel kitchen, which was home to everyone's cache; it had many cabinets and cupboards, and the telescreen's view was obstructed by drying laundry. The bulk of the parcel was the usual stuff: several bottles of third-class gin, a nearly new pair of men's slippers, and a comprehensively broken umbrella, whose fabric was used by proles for raincoats. But the real treasure was ten nail clippers, the sort of rare item one might seek in vain for years. Julia had luckily stumbled on a queue for them at Household Goods 16. Each customer was only allowed one pair, but Julia said she was buying for the hostel and slipped the salesgirl five dollars, so an exception was easily made.

Julia loaded all this in her tool bag, piled a layer of Anti-Sex leaflets on top, and slipped a ten-dollar bill into the top leaflet, for the benefit of any patrol who stopped her and asked to inspect her bag. Then she cycled to the northern prole border and left her bike just inside the line. Crossing the unmarked boundary on foot, within a block she was in a slum where all was grimy, shabby, broken, befouled. The smell was indescribable, since the quarter's privies and overflowing rubbish tips were regularly blasted sky-high by bombs, and there were also the rotting corpses of men and beasts, pulverized or lost under rubble. Added to this was a pall of malodorous smoke; anything that caught fire was burned for warmth here. Above, the awful naked sky had not a single barrage balloon or net, an open invitation to more bombs. One did wonder why the Eurasians would bother to bomb such mean places, but bother they did. Meanwhile the Party districts had skies full of wires and rooftops thick with antiaircraft guns, and were left untouched: worth remembering on those days when the careless life of a prole appealed, with its freedom from cameras and constant meetings and "voluntary" Party work.

The Meltons' was a low two-story terraced house with a battered doorway giving straight onto the pavement. A dead rat lay gaping at the curb, and one had to sidestep it and hop over a puddle of filthy water to gain entry. But there was glass in all the windows, taped up tidily against future bombs. The chimney showed a flag of smoke; this house was well supplied with coal. Inside was running water and electric rigged up through a "bleeder" that stole it from neighboring Party lines. Julia had been honored once with a tour of all the Meltons' electronic conveniences, which included a handsome cream-colored refrigerator and a "Phoenix" water heater that could dispense enough hot water for a shallow bath. Mrs. Melton was visibly pleased when Julia said they didn't have these things at the hostel. Ever after, she always offered to let Julia wash her hands and face in hot water and would say, with a satisfied smile: "So you haven't got that at home, then?"

Mrs. Melton answered at the first knock. She was a heavyset woman with a plump, softening face that retained its prettiness, despite her coarsened skin and the crimson veins that had appeared on her nose. As always, she wore trousers, the mark of a prole woman who considered herself a respectable socialist, and a scarf on her head to hide her thinning hair. Today's was a souvenir from the "Airstrip One Can Build It!" exhibition. The slogan had been twisted into a knot and the cartoon of the smiling wrench was displayed across her crown.

Seeing Julia, she frowned and balked, and Julia felt a preliminary disappointment. Black-goods merchants always had many schemes afoot. Not all were fit for strangers' eyes, and she could be turned away. But after a momentary calculation, Mrs. Melton unhooked the chain, saying, "As you're here, you'd best come in. You haven't half picked a rotten time for it, though. Mrs. Bale was telling us—well, you'll see."

Julia followed her into the sitting room, a cramped den whose only furniture was three dingy armchairs. Both the Meltons' lodgers were now seated here, hemmed in on all sides by miscellaneous junk: heaps of cardboard, army blankets, bricks, gin bottles full and empty. The first of the lodgers Julia had met before, though she'd never heard her speak—a wrinkled, helpless-looking creature in a cheap blond wig that sat uncomfortably on her head. Today her eyelids were swollen from weeping, and she clutched a soiled handkerchief in one hand.

The other woman was a hard-faced character of the true proletarian type. She wore three layers of clothes, all threadbare and aggressively laundered. A perpetual frown of grievance was etched between her coal-black brows. She bristled at Julia's entrance, saying, "Now, that ain't right. Having one of *them* here this day. 'Taint decent!"

"You know my work," said Mrs. Melton shortly. "And you'll know I don't hold with blaming them, neither. We're all English."

"All English!" The hard-faced woman scoffed. "There ain't no English now. It's Airstrip bloody One, thanks to your precious comrades."

Mrs. Melton said, "I thought you was telling a story, Mrs. Bale. If it's all like this, I'd as soon get on and see to this lady's business."

The hard-faced woman—Mrs. Bale—glared a moment, then turned from Julia pointedly. "Well, I'll tell you, as I've begun it. Might be a useful lesson for some."

Mrs. Melton winked at Julia, but any reassurance Julia might have felt was undercut by Mrs. Melton's instantly going to occupy the one remaining armchair. Of course Julia never did take a seat here. One had to be so careful of bugs in prole homes. Still, not to be invited was jarring. To make things worse, the wigged woman was staring balefully at Julia with her reddened eyes. Julia found herself wishing Mrs. Melton had turned her away at the door. It was so tiresome to be disliked.

Mrs. Bale went on, "So as I was saying, before we was so rudely—as I was saying. It weren't an hour ago when it happened. I was out by the house where the Irish live, that building that was the Dog and Trumpet before the landlord got hisself purged. T'weren't no one in the street but myself and Mrs. Brattle and her little one, Rosie. The bomb was the sort you don't hear till it strikes. I'm a Cockney, though, so I feels 'em in me nerves. All the air grows hard. That's the sign. I feels that, and I'm flat on me belly before I've the time to wonder why.

"The bomb come down on that new block of flats, where they put the people what was bombed out of Kilburn. I got knocked about somewhat meself—bits of brick, bits of masonry. I don't complain of that. But as I wipes the dust from me eyes, there before me I sees the Brattles' Rosie. I've had that child on my knee. Only three years old and already talking up a storm. If you live in these streets, you've heard her voice." She nodded grimly at Julia. "I don't suppose *this* one has, or wouldn't care if she had. I speak of them that lives here."

"Enough of that," said Mrs. Melton.

"Oh, as it's your house, you choose your guests. I know. But Nan, 'twas a baby! A three-year-old baby!"

At this, the wigged woman began to sob, pressing her soiled handkerchief to her nose, her gaze still fixed on Julia. Her eyes were a startling pale green.

Mrs. Bale went on, "Well, little Rosie was still alive then, but in a dreadful state. Moving her head so queer, as when you've trodden on a beetle, but it ain't yet dead. And, what I hadn't seen at first, her little hand wasn't there. It was away on the pavement, a good five meters from where she was lain. The bomb had torn it clean away. All the street round was red with her blood, and the dust falling into it. Her poor mother somewhere screaming. I shall never forget it.

"And I'm still thinking if there's any help to give, when a man appears round the corner, right out of the clouds of dust, and he goes strolling past, just as cheerful as you like. And as he goes, he raises his foot, like that, and *kicks* the baby's hand into the gutter. Kicks it out of his path like rubbish!" She turned to Julia and added venomously, "One of yours, he was. A comrade."

All three women looked at Julia then. The woman in the wig still wept, her eyes pale green and empty. Mrs. Melton's face was blank.

"Oh . . . how beastly," Julia said.

"Beastly," Mrs. Bale repeated scornfully. "Well, he *was* a beast, whether you say it or not. And I know who *you* are. You're that one what's in Fiction. So why don't you write about *that* in one of your books? You won't, will you? No, we all know you bloody won't!"

Julia wanted to say she wrote no books and most certainly didn't choose what was written—no one did; that was done by machines—but of course she wouldn't be believed. She thought of asking after the child's mother and offering money for her if it was being collected. But that risked sounding glib. Anything she thought of saying felt offensive, like the gesture of kicking a baby's hand from one's path.

At that moment, they were mercifully interrupted by a clattering on the stairs, followed by the noisy entrance of Mrs. Melton's daughter, Harriet. This was a willowy, red-haired girl of seventeen, the acknowledged beauty of the neighborhood. Her Party marriage prospects, and the "refined" education required to cement them, were the great work of her mother's life. One couldn't escape the Meltons' house without a demonstration of Harriet's handwriting or a recital of her singing. Her speech was an ongoing project. For years the Meltons had housed a seedy old codger who pilfered from them and lived on gin, but whose accent was pure Inner Party. Every Party client of Mrs. Melton's was also pressed into service, and Julia had often been roped into helping Harriet subdue an intransigent vowel.

Today Harriet was dressed in a deep-green satin dress that ended at her shapely calf, and she sang out cheerfully as she came in, "Hullo! I heard Comrade Worthing here, and wanted her opinion on this frock. Julia, am I too screamingly prole in this?"

Her mother said sharply, "Ain't you ashamed? A little child's just been killed. Mrs. Bale saw it happen."

Harriet made a hasty sympathetic face. "Oh, I *am* sorry, Mrs. Bale. How dreadful. But *you* won't mind if I ask this question? It's only, my chap's calling here at seven."

Mrs. Bale said suspiciously, "What chap?"

"Oh, you *do* understand," said Harriet. "It's only Freddie, my fellow from Peace, so you won't worry about him. You know I bend them to my will." Harriet turned back to Julia. "Now, Julia, can I wear this to a Party lecture? I do think he's serious, so I want to look right."

Julia looked at Mrs. Melton, but she seemed mollified. In fact, all the women were now inspecting Harriet's dress with feminine surmise, glancing at Julia for her verdict.

"Well," Julia said judiciously, "it's very lovely, but . . . perhaps a bit showy."

"I was afraid of that!" Harriet said despairingly. "But what *can* I wear? I couldn't wear overalls. It's so unclassful when prole girls do that. More vulgar than the vulgar, *I* think."

"It's only, you'd best not show any leg. That risks being embarrassing for him. If you still have those gray trousers..."

"Oh, the dreaded mouse trousers! Blast! Might it make a difference what sort of lecture it is?"

"Truthfully—no."

"Well, if that's how it's to be . . . but if I married him, might I still wear this at home?"

Julia made a little face and slightly shook her head. "Telescreens."

"Oof! You lot *do* have your own troubles, don't you? Never mind, I'd wear potato sacks all my days if it got us out of these ruddy trenches. Oh, as I'm thinking of it, Julia, do you want to borrow a frock? Not this—I'd not part with this. But you could have my violet wool."

Julia often borrowed Harriet's clothes to visit the nearby market as, in prole garb, she got better prices. But now she said, "Not today, thanks. I've got no time before curfew."

Mrs. Melton took the hint and stood up, saying, "That's right, you'll want to be getting on. Well, let's see what you've got."

They did their business in the kitchen, a room that was a curious combination of spotlessness and squalor. Not a speck of dirt was tolerated, and yet the cracked walls and ancient stains made an overwhelmingly dirty impression. The vermin of the district were also represented; Mrs. Melton stamped her foot as she entered to scare away beetles and mice, but nothing could discourage the marauding flies.

As always, when Julia unpacked her wares, Mrs. Melton put on a show of disappointment, tutting and muttering that all were suffering now, and none as rich as they used to be. "I see it in what they bring. I feel sorry for 'em, but I can't cheat myself. I've got my girl to think of."

Julia said, as if she hadn't heard, "Those clippers are worth three hundred, I should think."

That shocked Mrs. Melton out of her funk. "Three hundred! You're having a laugh! I'd give forty."

"Yes, you don't see clippers like that very often. Even Inner Party would love to have these."

"And I'd meet Inner Party when? No, for me it's the in-between folk, and right thieves they are. I can't pay more than I get."

"Of course if you could pay in goods ..."

Now the struggle began in earnest. Harriet was sent upstairs and returned with a carton of French cigarettes, which Julia must sniff disparagingly while Mrs. Melton sang their praises. A packet was opened. They all lit cigarettes and talked about the hard times. Harriet took off a shoe to clip her toenails, Mrs. Melton watching and complaining that the clippers looked blunt. Mrs. Melton measured the umbrella, then did a circuit of the room in the men's slippers and pronounced them "thin." Still, Harriet was dispatched upstairs to fetch Julia a bag of coffee and another carton of cigarettes; these joined the first carton on the table.

It was now Julia's turn to be regretful. "It's only that I risk such a lot ... I should hate so dreadfully to have to go elsewhere ... when someone doesn't know the value of my goods ..."

Mrs. Melton said, "It's always sad to lose a customer, but I won't be robbed in my own home."

At last Julia signaled an end to hostilities by suggesting the shortfall be made up by twenty dollars to her account. Mrs. Melton smiled—that rare, personal smile that meant Julia was one of the "good ones"—and agreed to ten.

The safe was unlocked, and Harriet fetched out the "Friends of Harringay Widows" ledger. It was opened ceremoniously, and the lodgers gathered round to watch Harriet perform her trick. She shook the pen grandly, found Julia's page, and, knitting her brows in pretty concentration, wrote in a flowing, elegant cursive no Party member would ever use: *10 Oceanian dollars, received with gratitude this Tuesday, 10 April 1984, from anonymous donor 129.* Mrs. Melton watched over her daughter's shoulder, not understanding the letters but smiling and sneaking looks at Julia to see the impression they made. The other women sighed in admiration, and Julia caused general delight by saying she'd never seen a finer hand.

Five minutes later she was back on the street with her coffee, her cigarettes, and a lipstick Harriet had slipped in as a parting gift. She paused to sniff her bag to make sure the coffee was adequately wrapped, then headed back by the market street.

When she'd first come to the district, this market had been so rich it stunned her: joints and chickens roasting on portable stoves, seas of walnuts and fresh berries, gleaming ranks of fresh-caught fish. Now even the eggs were sold out by morning, and the walnut stands were replaced by emaciated women selling the "protein" biscuits that notoriously contained ground beetle. Some government stalls were empty altogether, and the injured veterans who minded them were dozing in their chairs. Half the space was taken by make-do-and-mend girls, their variously colored spools of thread set out on tables in front of them. Then there was the legless veteran in a wagon who played a French horn for coppers while his bored wife smoked behind him, and the cheerfully shabby man with a Siamese cat on his shoulder and a sign on his chest: INNER PARTY STILE KITTENS AT RESONABLE PRISE: GOOD RATTERS, GOOD FRENDS.

Today the poverty of the scene was rivaled by its hostility, and Julia was painfully conscious of her blue overalls. People affected not to see her as she passed, but if she looked back, she found them glaring. Even the kitten man lost his smile at her approach. She turned off the market street with a mournful feeling, remembering the anger of Mrs. Bale. Could that man have truly kicked a child's hand from his path? Why should he, when he might as easily step over it? One would think a simple care for his shoes would prevent such an enormity. Of course people easily believed the most preposterous stories about other classes. She'd like to see Mrs. Bale's face if she heard what Party members said of proles!

At that moment, as if conjured by her thoughts, down a side street she saw a flash of blue: a man in Party garb. The chap had stopped on the pavement, peering into what might be a pub window or a shopfront. Proles passed in both directions, giving him a wide berth without looking directly at him. It crossed Julia's mind that here was the brute who had kicked the baby's hand. But surely it couldn't be him. Even if such a monster existed, he would be long gone.

This was a fellow of about middle height, very slight, with striking, pale hair like a child's. His head was bowed, one hand held protectively to his cheek as if he were conscious of crime. There was something appealing in the stance—perhaps the combination of vulnerability and the manly set of his shoulders. Julia prided herself on her ability to tell a great deal about people at a glance, and she decided this man had a secret, a secret that ennobled him and made him lonely.

Then the figure raised its head and was Old Misery Smith.

6

BEFORE SHE COULD REACT, SMITH OPENED A DOOR AND vanished inside. Julia almost continued on her way, but, at that moment, she was caught in a flood of passing youth, all noisy and boisterous and oblivious to her attempts to get through. The boys were bare-chested and stained purple to the chin; from their chatter, she grasped they'd been bathing in the canal and had got caught in the effluent from the dye works. The tallest boy was complaining it itched, while the others laughed and called him an old woman. A girl said teasingly, "That ain't the half of it. It's eating away at your flesh, and by night you'll be a skeleton. Goodbye, you!" The boy said, "I don't mind the being a skeleton. Bones is no trouble. What I minds is the itch."

Then they were past, and a decision had somehow been made. Julia turned down the road whence Smith had vanished.

She didn't intend to speak to him, only to casually spy out where he'd gone. Of course she'd never inform on him. Still, she couldn't help wanting to know if he was meeting a tart or slipping into a prole card game. And it never hurt to have a little damning information on people, in case of need. It was one of the ways one avoided being turned in to the police oneself.

As she came up, she slowed her step as if in idle curiosity. The door he'd entered belonged to a shop whose window was full of all manner of bric-a-brac: bent picture frames; tarnished watches showing different times; a stuffed badger with a bulky head. The space behind was heaped with more such dubious treasures, and the walls were hung with smeary paintings. In the depths of the room, she saw Smith with his slim blue back to her, in conversation with a prole man in late middle age. The man was the first thing that jogged Julia's memory. He wore a shapeless velvet jacket in an indeterminate purple-brown color, and his silver hair was tousled and overlong. He had a plausible face, a face too affably simple—a face she'd seen somewhere before. He turned. Smith followed him to the rear of the shop, where they both disappeared up a narrow flight of stairs. Then, for the first time, Julia noticed the name stenciled on the shop-window: WEEKS. A chill went through her.

With that, she was past. There was a bright new sweat down her back. She felt as if she were striding on unsteady air. The next door was a mean-looking pub, and she could decently quicken her step to get past it. At the corner she turned, went halfway down the street, and stopped in front of a hoarding. She fished out a cigarette and stood there smoking, staring blankly at the passing proles.

She'd first heard of Weeks from Harriet Melton. It was back when Harriet still had a prole boyfriend, and the two of them were always perched, bantering and laughing, on a rolled-up rug in the Meltons' sitting room. That day Harriet had mentioned a friend of theirs "hanging about at Weeks." The boyfriend shoved her and said, "What you want to say that for? You trying to get us all nicked?" Both were laughing, but Mrs. Melton wasn't. She snapped, "Speak of that again, miss, and I'll warm your arse for you."

When Julia asked Mrs. Melton later, the woman said darkly, "Nobody knows what *that* place is, or they better not. All's I can say, Mr. Flanagan went in once—one time! And now he's not been heard from for weeks, and the jumble man's selling all his clothes."

Another day, Harriet was seeing Julia out, and in the doorway she suddenly grabbed Julia's arm and motioned to her to keep still. A shabby gentleman was going by. In passing, he smiled at Harriet in courtly appreciation and touched his hat. The hat was what struck Julia most: it wasn't a prole cloth cap, but a felt hat with a brim and checkered band, a kind one only saw in films. When he was safely past, Harriet whispered, "That's the Weeks fellow. He gives me the shivers. Brrrr—his face isn't right!"

"But whatever *is* Weeks?" said Julia.

"That's the question! Some say it's just a worse sort of brothel. Or an opium den, if you can believe that. Then there's people who say it's a hive of the Goldstein Brotherhood, but don't tell Mum I said so. I think that's all rot, anyhow. I don't believe there is a real Brotherhood, do you? Well, if there is, you've just seen a Brother in the flesh!"

That was the man Julia had seen in the shop in lively conversation with Smith—Smith, who had seemed the very image of dullness; Old Misery Smith, who'd been the butt of all jokes. Who was now revealed as—what? An opium smoker? A Goldsteinite terrorist?

Slowly, her nerves eased. She took a last draw on her cigarette and, still disoriented, turned and glanced at the hoarding behind her. It bore a huge poster showing Big Brother leading ranks of marching blond soldiers, under the slogan VICTORY IS FREEDOM. She laughed to herself, hardly knowing why, and set off back toward Weeks.

As she went, she was already having second thoughts. Surely she wouldn't dare go *into* Weeks? Even if she did, how would she go about asking? You couldn't very well say, "Here, are you Goldsteinites?" What if it was some horrid kind of brothel?

As she turned the corner, she'd decided to walk straight past without looking in. She kept her gaze on the houses opposite, and was halfway down the street when she realized Smith was in Weeks's doorway, standing almost in her path.

He was faintly humming a tune, but stopped abruptly when he saw her. He looked gaunt and strained, as always, and had the dust of a bombing in his fair hair and on his forehead. On the narrow pavement, she had to pass closely, and all the way, his eyes were on her with their peculiar gray severity. Her face went stiff. She kept her steps measured, while her heart beat wildly. He was scarcely taller than she was, just a spare, blond man in the usual shapeless overalls, who should have meant nothing.

His eyes went down her body and his whole manner changed. He glared with lust and rage.

Then she was past him. She felt his gaze on her back, but walked on at the same pace, deliberately keeping her body natural. For a moment, she felt she must look back—but there, she'd turned the corner. Done. But how the man had reacted! It couldn't have been clearer that she'd caught him at some unspeakable crime. And yet he hadn't quailed—he'd glared right at her. He'd even let her see he wanted her. There was a man, if you liked! And not a soul at Truth suspected what he was. Of course, ordinarily he looked such a mouse—made sure to look that way, no doubt. A Goldsteinite! Or a debauchee! She couldn't think which she liked more. She remembered his look of complicity with O'Brien. Might O'Brien be another? Might the whole world be different from how it seemed?

She was smiling foolishly, flushed and sweaty, although the evening had grown chilly, when she realized she'd missed her turn. She was alone in a stretch of burned-out buildings and boarded-up houses. It was almost dark, the declining sun obscured by smog. A light rain had begun to fall, and the few undamaged stretches of tarmac sparkled weirdly as the fine drops struck. Belatedly, it occurred to Julia that, if Smith were a Goldsteinite, he might not take kindly to being seen at Weeks. He might feel the need to silence her—to pursue her to a lonely place, such as this, where he could strangle her and leave her body in a ruin. It was just the sort of thing Goldsteinites did. He might not give her time to explain—and if he did, what could she say?

She was relieved to see a couple up ahead, even though the woman appeared to be a tart; her face was brightly painted and she wore a soiled yellow dress that drooped off one shoulder. The man had a dramatically scarred face and was yawning while the woman complained. No doubt he was her pimp. Both fell silent when they noticed Julia. She slowed uncertainly and glanced back into the shadows—and from them came a man.

She was too shocked to cry out when he swooped upon her. They grappled, his hands all over her horribly, and now she was shrieking as loud as she could, afraid he would soon stop her mouth. In the first moment, she was certain it was Smith, but soon his smell and size got through to her. It wasn't like Smith at all—it was a burly prole, who stank unspeakably of beer and unwashed flesh. The next second she felt her tool bag being yanked from her shoulder in a horrid slipping movement. She instinctively grabbed at it. Then something happened—a thudding blow to her shin—and she was falling through empty space.

She landed on one hand and tumbled jarringly on her face, knees, shoulder. Her hand turned beneath her, and the pain in her wrist was a flash of sickening heat. Above, the man shouted with rage. Her fall had yanked the bag from his grasp.

At the same time, footsteps came running, and the tart was suddenly looming above, shrieking, "Are you fucking mad? Can't you see she's a blue! You bleeding imbecile!"

"Fuck off!" the robber said. "Get off, you thick bitch!"

"We can't have none of that here! She's a comrade, look! Are you mad?"

Now the scarred man appeared too, saying, "What's all this, now? What's he done?"

"He's only gone and tried his antics on a blue!" said the tart.

"What?" The scarred man peered at Julia, then reared back and swatted at the robber. "You twat! Bleeding twat! You trying to bring all the coppers of London down on us?"

"I ain't done nothing!" the robber said, dodging his hands. "If she'd stayed in her own place—"

"Oh, it's *her* fault?" The tart laughed. "Charming."

As they squabbled, Julia was conscious of an awful pain that at first seemed to have no source. No, it was her wrist—she had twisted it in falling. It was only lightly skinned, and the bleeding didn't look that bad. But when she prodded it exper-imentally, the agony was so great her vision went black. When her sight cleared, she was crying helpless tears of pain, tears that rose of themselves like sweat.

The scarred man was bending down to her. "You all right, love? There, you're all right. No harm done, is there?"

"No," she said. "No harm."

"Right, then. Up you get." He extended a hand to Julia. She shrank from it instinctively, and all three proles laughed.

"Blimey," the tart said. "That's put the wind up her!"

"No," Julia said. "I—I was only startled."

"Never you mind." The scarred man winked at the tart and put both hands behind his back.

Julia rose unsteadily to her feet, pulling the tool bag onto her shoulder. She made herself smile, feeling somehow culpable, but none of the proles smiled back. The robber was staring at her sullenly, like an unjustly chastized child.

The scarred man nodded down the street behind her. "Off you go, then. This one won't pester you no more. We'll see to that."

Julia nodded and turned away, the smile still fading on her lips. She wanted—she didn't know what. To be made a fuss of. To be told she was brave. They could at least have offered to punish the robber—but what nonsense to expect rightful behavior from a pack of criminals! As she walked off, she was miserably conscious of the pain that throbbed in her wrist with every step, the injury none of them had cared to notice. And if the wrist were broken? She daren't go to hospital. Most doctors there worked for the Thought Police, and were known to regard any injury of a young woman as a probable sexcrime. A broken bone could turn into a long convalescence in a hard-labor camp. She'd better go to Anti-Sex, where she might find Dr. Louis— but she would also find Agnes and Thomas and a dozen other keen-eyed informers. Waves of frustration and helplessness went through her. Those cannibals! To knock a girl down in the street, then laugh at her terror! All the evil said of proles was true.

It took her twenty minutes to find her bike, then another twenty to ride to Anti-Sex House, going slow so she needn't use her hand to brake. In that time, the rain intensified. When she turned into Cleanlife Square and added her bike to the dozens in the racks there, Julia was soaked to the skin.

7

ANTI-SEX HOUSE WAS A VAST HIGH COLONIALIST BEHE-
moth that occupied one whole side of Cleanlife Square. It was
grand and quaint and imposing and fussy; all ornamental clocks
and narrow arched windows. Its roof bristled with so many
spires and gables, new ones seemed to grow with every rain.
The upper floors housed a hundred-odd bedrooms for visiting
delegations of Junior Anti-Sexers. These provincials' time in the
city was taken up by cleanthink rallies, tours of syphilis wards,
and trips to the Museum of Venereal Diseases. They had their
own entrance, and were forbidden the use of the ground-floor
club rooms, which were reserved for London Branch, and while
the upstairs was spare and functional, the club rooms were a
welter of pre-socialist frivolity: floral rugs, painted ceilings, velvet armchairs, gilt wallpaper, stained-glass lamps. All this was
worn and shabby, and yet these rooms had a wonderfully sooth-
ing quality. They seemed to dote upon their occupants with all
their failing might.

In reception, Julia found a lecture in progress, with a throng
of Anti-Sexers listening raptly in folding chairs. The speaker was
the usual Inner Party lordling, emitting a flood of Newspeak
even he surely didn't understand. Julia searched the faces as casually as she could for Dr. Louis's distinctive, elegant face, but he
was nowhere to be seen. Instead her eye snagged on Vicky, who

had turned her pretty, inquisitive face to stare. Julia rushed on hastily and passed through the rear door into the corridor. Here the portraits of illustrious Airstrip One virgins—Isaac Newton, Elizabeth Tudor, Alan Turing—stared from the walls, alternating with telescreens. The latter now showed the Oceanian stars and stripes flying over the tower of the Ministry of Truth: the opening image of the twenty-two-hundred newscast.

At the end of the corridor, the door to the tea room was open. Julia felt its emptiness long before she drew up to the door. Indeed, the room was utterly deserted: no gossiping knots of London Branchers, no aproned girls bearing teapots from table to table, no throng of invalids and valetudinarians paying court to Dr. Louis. From all four walls, large golden-framed telescreens showed the African front, a scene of bursting explosions and floating dust. The newscast had begun. To Julia, this only served as a reminder that she'd arrived too late; anyone with an excuse to miss the lecture would have already had their tea and gone, and Dr. Louis must be among them. Now she would have to hide her injury until she got to the Truth infirmary next morning.

She entered the tea room nonetheless, from the disappointed person's need for privacy, and sat at a table to stare despondently at a telescreen. The sound was turned down as low as it would go—it couldn't be turned quite off—and she could only make out occasional words: *unfearwise*, *23rd battalion*, *uncomrades*. She let herself be distracted by the quietly bursting bombs and the little dark figures fleeing through cascading dust—those would be the uncomrades, running fearwise. As she watched, one by one, they were snagged by gunfire. Their helplessness, combined with the pain radiating up her arm, made her want to cry. But of course she kept her face in the excited half smile that was appropriate to victory news.

Then she heard the door to reception come open, letting out a dim flood of Newspeak that ebbed again as it swung shut. For a moment, Julia feverishly thought that here was Dr. Louis after all. But the footsteps coming down the corridor were a girl's. She realized who it had to be just as Vicky appeared at the tea room door.

"Oh!" said Julia. "Hello."

"Hello! I saw . . . well, are you all right?"

"I was caught in the rain. I thought I might have a tea before I went to the lecture."

They both regarded each other while Vicky chose not to indicate, by word or glance, that she noticed Julia had no tea.

Then Julia said thinly, "Lecture not to your liking?"

Vicky looked startled. "No, it's doubleplus good."

"Which is it? Chastity as Weapon of War?"

"Socialist Chastity and Capitalist Chastity. There are five differences, five main differences. Those break down into thirty minor ones. One can remember them by—well, I can't. But there's a chart."

"Plus interesting. Perhaps you'd like to get back and hear the end?"

"I shall. But I couldn't help noticing . . ." Vicky's eyes went to Julia's hand.

"Oh, this? I've come off my bike, that's all. It looks far worse than it is. But I was hoping to find Dr. Louis. Has he gone?"

Vicky looked uncomfortable. "No, I believe he's still about. He's had this lecture before, you see, so he went to do inventory with young George. They went a little while ago, so I shouldn't wonder if they're still in the storeroom. That is, I know they're there, as I would have seen them leave. They're there." By the end of this seemingly innocuous speech, Vicky's face had turned bright red.

The storeroom was one of those rare spaces with no tele-screen at all. Its view would only be blocked by shelves, so there was no point. Access was therefore restricted, and the rules for its use were posted on the door. Crucially, no one was ever to enter with a member of the opposite sex. Certain people of the same sex, however, regularly went there in pairs, locked the door behind them, and came out some time later looking tousled and at peace with the world.

Dr. Louis was a storeroom regular, and young George his latest partner in crime. Both belonged to a common Anti-Sex type called "Reggies." These took their name from Reggie Perkins, an old revolutionary stalwart who'd been arrested in the First Patriotic Purge for indecent relations with another girl. She was ultimately acquitted, the judge having ruled that, while male homosexuality was all too possible, sex between women could not occur. "The corrupt mind dreams perversions to which human anatomy is not equal." Her acquittal did poor Reggie Perkins no good; once arrested, no one ever really escaped, and she died that week of "unknown causes." But her name had been immortalized by the corrupt minds of Airstrip One, and was whispered wherever perversions, both possible and impossible, were performed.

Vicky said, "I could just run and knock. I don't like to disturb them, if they're still doing inventory. They get quite absorbed. But they might be finished."

"Well, that would be fine. Or I could go and ask myself, if you don't like to do it."

"No, I don't mind. But ..." Vicky looked up shyly at Julia. "If Dr. Louis can't come, might I have a look at it? I don't know if you knew, but I studied nursing. That's what I was doing when Deputy Chairman Whitehead found me, when he asked me to be his secretary. I was his nurse."

"Oh, were you?"

"I didn't finish training. But I can treat scrapes and sprains. I often play nurse for the girls at CentCom. I miss it so dreadfully, you see."

Julia hesitated, but could find no excuse. She could hardly say she didn't want Vicky's help because the girl had no discretion. Vicky had already noticed the injury anyway, and the telescreen had heard all about it, so that ship had sailed. And her wish to help seemed utterly sincere. One could easily imagine the eager student nurse she must have been at fifteen, when the obscene Whitehead crossed her path.

Julia said, "Well, if Dr. Louis can't come . . . yes, thanks."

Vicky clasped her hands together in triumph, and, without another word, ran out. Julia laughed in her wake, then looked apologetically at the nearest telescreen. It occurred to her belatedly that the snoops would have wondered at it if she'd turned Vicky down. Thank goodness she'd said yes. Anyway, she had nothing to hide. She'd fallen from her bike, and a comrade had offered to patch her up. That was all it was.

Keeping that thought foremost—she'd fallen from her bike—Julia went to the sinks along the wall. There teacups were heaped, waiting to be washed, but there was ample room beneath to wash her wrist. The soap here was Inner Party quality, cake soap that made a fine white lather. Luckily there was hot water today. Though the flow aroused the pain again, it felt good to rinse away the blood and grime. That done, she could see the cuts really weren't bad. The wrist was swollen, but she'd had any number of injuries that were worse. She'd only fallen from her bike. It was an everyday occurrence. It would all be forgotten in a week.

Julia startled when the door opened again, and Vicky came in, pink with pleasure. "I called to Dr. Louis, and he *will* come, only he can't just yet. But the plusgood news—I've found bandages! I was rather worried, as there's always a shortage. But good old Anti-Sex came through." She held up the first-aid kit—a battered tin with a red cross painted sloppily on its lid. On the other arm she carried a tattered pair of overalls people had been cannibalizing for patches.

Julia nodded to the overalls. "I hope those aren't the bandages you mean."

Vicky laughed breathlessly. "Silly! No, that's for a sling. You will need one, even for a sprain."

"I'm not certain it even is sprained, though."

"We'll see. Or Dr. Louis will see. Oh, you've washed it yourself! That's clever. Ordinary soap works wonders, you know. How I wish we had ice!"

"You're not at CentCom now."

"Yes, well," Vicky said self-consciously. "Now, if you like, Dr. Louis said it would be all right if I helped with the bandaging. If it's not a break. Or not a bad break." Vicky looked hopefully into Julia's eyes.

"Well," Julia said dubiously, "I suppose he'll do it over if it's not right."

"That's just what I think!" Vicky smiled. "It's doubleplus good of you to let me, though. I know it's silly, but I do miss nursing. I would ask to be transferred, but that would look so queer, to ask to leave Central Committee. I mean, wouldn't it look queer?"

"It certainly would. Where shall I sit?"

"Oh! Anywhere. Thank you. I shall just . . . yes."

Vicky now became brisk and efficient, washing her hands with professional thoroughness, then coming back and positioning Julia's arm carefully on the white tablecloth. She raised a pair of tweezers thoughtfully over the cuts, nodding them along the skin as if letting the tweezers themselves see what was what. A tiny speck of grit was plucked out neatly and the tweezers got set aside. It was then the turn of the iodine, which Vicky swabbed on with such delicacy that there was only the bright sting familiar from childhood skinned knees. Julia began to feel embarrassed at having made a fuss over nothing. But when Vicky probed the wrist with her fingers, Julia had to distract herself by biting her tongue.

Vicky said musingly, "I shouldn't think the bone there's broken. If it is, it's nothing gruesome. But to really be sure, you'd need an X-ray, and you'd only get that at hospital."

"Oh, I shouldn't think it needs that," Julia said hastily. "If I went to hospital every time I fall off my bike!"

Vicky looked as if she would like to argue more, but only said, "Well, we shall see what Dr. Louis says." Then she took out a neat white roll of bandages and went to work. Again she was wonderfully deft, but the tugging and changing pressure were agony. Julia was conscious of her wet overalls again, the horrid chill of the material over new sweat. She tried to do Big Brother breathing—drawing in a breath to a count of seven, then letting it out on a count of twelve—but whenever Vicky pulled the bandage tight, she gasped and lost her count.

As Vicky secured the bandage at last, her hands paused on Julia's wrist. There was the suspense of the job perhaps not done, of more pain still to come.

Then Vicky said softly, "I was wondering . . ."

"Yes?"

"I left you a note some days ago. I was wondering if you ever had it."

Julia understood immediately—so immediately she wondered if she might have already suspected. In the same instant, she was filled with anger. She almost snapped at Vicky to get on with what she was doing and not talk rubbish. But showing emotion at such a moment could only make things worse.

Of course it was no news that Vicky had a crush on Julia. That sort of thing was rife in hostels. In fact, it would be a poor sort of girl who didn't fall in love with a pretty bunkmate from time to time. Julia had Reggies on her mind just now, but such crushes weren't really *that*. Even when a sexcrime happened between two girls in a hostel, it was almost never *that*. In the girls' home where Julia had been sent from the SAZ, she herself had had a few impossible encounters with a handsome older girl called Edna, and it had been very heady and lovely at the time, but of course it wasn't that. It was just part of feminine nature to love and be loved at the drop of a hat, to make a romance of sharing a pair of slippers and putting them on warm from another's feet. If it ended in a sneaking embrace in a closet, well, that was feminine nature too. One needn't call it *that*.

But beneath this was the awareness that Vicky had left that note when she was facing death, when she knew her crimes could no longer be hidden and she might have only hours to live. "I love you"—a final confession before the patrols took her off to prison. And, just as had happened that night, Julia found herself treacherously moved. She was thinking furiously that Vicky's behavior was rash, impossible, dangerous, but part of her wanted to seize the girl's hand and say, *I got it, and I love you too*.

Meanwhile she made an appropriately vague face. "A note? I'm not sure. When was it?"

"It was...you'll remember, that night they had the telescreen program about our friend the potato. You came and sat on my bed. I left the note that afternoon."

"Oh, yes," said Julia. "I did find a note. I remember it now."

Despite herself, Julia looked at Vicky and found the girl's eyes on her with a frantic brightness. Her heart dropped. Given half a chance, Vicky would start whispering. A lot of arrests began that way, when someone desperately wanted to speak and decided to believe the snoops wouldn't hear.

Before this could occur, Julia said, very calmly and clearly, "You might have saved yourself the trouble, however. I saw straightaway that the toilet had overflowed. No need to warn me at all."

Vicky nodded, her eyes now treacherously soft. "No need."

"Funny how one writes notes like that, when nothing can come of them. But it has no meaning now, has it? Let's forget it."

Vicky tightened her jaw and looked back at Julia's arm. "Of course it means nothing. Yes, I see."

After this, the making of the sling took place in an agony of consciousness. Julia had once imagined a language of touch one could use to defeat the telescreens. There was something like that between them as she held still for Vicky to wrap the overalls about her to measure the length, then watched her cut the fabric, then again held still as Vicky tied the material in place. They didn't speak, but moved in concert. A sublime discomfort bloomed over Julia's skin. Vicky's scent was real tea—Central Committee—and behind it a hint of youthful sweat. At one moment Vicky's breast touched Julia's shoulder and that scent overwhelmed her.

Then down the corridor, the door to reception again opened, releasing its blast of droning Newspeak. Footsteps approached, and Vicky and Julia drew sharply away from each other as the door opened.

Dr. Louis stuck his head in. "Hello there. Are we still alive?"

"Oh, hello!" Julia called out. "Only just!"

"May I?"

"Please do!" said Vicky, standing up hastily to cede her place.

Dr. Louis was one of those rare, magical beings who seemed invulnerable to denunciation. Although his Reggie activities must have been known to a couple of hundred people, and he was involved in a dozen questionable enterprises, no harm ever came to him. Some of this was understandable. As a doctor, he was valued at Anti-Sex for his ability to write authoritatively on the health hazards of the sexual act and, less officially, for his willingness to treat those hazards discreetly when they occurred. He also prescribed and dispensed "anti-sex" drugs. These took several forms, but all were known to make a person feel exceptionally nice. If you were high enough up in the Party, he took no payment for these services. If you were not, his sister would coincidentally meet you in the street and request a donation to the "North London Inter-Party Medical Fund."

He also possessed the indefinable quality called rightlook. Now he came into the tea room radiating his signature cleanliness and calm. His hair was damp and he brought a pleasant air of Socialist Purity soap; he had clearly taken time for a bath in one of the upstairs rooms. He was carrying his usual three medical bags, all stout with useful goods. His appearance had the usual effect; both Vicky and Julia relaxed and their faces fell into grateful smiles.

"I came off my bike," Julia said, as Dr. Louis divested himself of his bags. "And then I must have turned my wrist where I hit the pavement. I can't think it's much."

"A hurt wrist." Dr. Louis shook his head with an expression of mock gravity. "More people die that way. I shouldn't think you have much of a chance."

"Oh, don't joke," Julia said. "Must I undo the bandage?"

"Not yet. Your nurse has done such a fine job. Let's see if we can preserve her work."

Vicky stood by anxiously while Dr. Louis sat to examine Julia. This mainly consisted of palpating her wrist and asking Julia if it hurt, to which the answer was generally yes. Still, there was something sedative in his manner. Even when the pain brought tears to Julia's eyes, it was somehow manageable and not dreadful.

Finally, Dr. Louis said, "I'm quite certain it's only a sprain. That's luck."

Julia said, "Does that mean it's not very serious?"

"No, you won't be very happy for a while. And it needs rest. No working with that. But a break gets reported two levels up. No end of bother with a break. Sprain's nothing."

"Oh . . . well, thank you."

"Don't look downcast. Let's see . . ." He used his foot to coax one of his bags within reach. In it, he found a tiny bag of waxed paper, fat with pills. "These little fellows will help with the pain. Only don't take more than two at a time. And never with gin. A girl your size can put an end to herself with twenty of these."

"Perhaps Julia shouldn't have them," Vicky put in. "If they're not safe."

"Oh, stuff," Julia said. "I shan't want more than two."

"Indeed," said Dr. Louis. "The girl I'm thinking of did it on purpose. For a chap. We Anti-Sexers are safe from all that foolishness, I hope."

"Oh, yes," said Vicky, recovering herself. "I am so glad I'm Anti-Sex, aren't you? Sex makes people do such horrid things."

"Plus true," said Dr. Louis.

"Yes," Julia said. "I do promise I won't put an end to myself."

"No, you won't," said Dr. Louis. "I've only given you ten."

kept one eye on Smith. In this light, he was a shabby, color-less figure—until his face gathered suddenly in thought. Then a depth appeared and vanished in his eyes, like a great fish pass-ing beneath dull waters. And if he were a Goldsteinite, mightn't his drabness be a clever disguise? When he rose to carry his tray to the racks, she surreptitiously watched and was pleased by his slim frame, by the broad shoulder blades showing beneath the thin rayon. After he left, the motion he'd made in rising from the grimy table repeated in her mind.

In case she didn't know what all this was about, that night she found herself in her bunk, lying on her belly with a hand inside her overalls, slipping a finger under the threadbare crotch of her knickers. She rubbed slightly, with a tiny, invisible mo-tion, thinking of Winston Smith. He rose from his seat in the canteen, took out a cigarette, and tapped it on the table to firm up the tobacco, but his eyes were locked on hers. He wanted her and *would have her*. It was in his eyes. There was nothing she could do about it. He would *have his way*.

That was all the fantasy was, but it did its work. She played it through several times, and achieved her satisfaction.

The next day she lingered on the tenth floor when the Two Minutes Hate was over, wandering as if in search of a lava-tory, offering to fix a drafty window, chatting to her old flame Tom Parsons. From the corner of her eye, she observed Smith's movements. Once he struck her a disliking glance, a sharp deep glance that was gone as she looked. It lit her up. When she sat down again, she felt it: a keen point of pleasure in her cunt, a softness where she was richly wet. She crossed her legs tightly as if to keep it from escaping.

In Julia's affairs, the chap had always made the first move, or at least met her halfway. Her most recent lover, for instance, had come to sit beside her in a cinema. She hadn't been sure of his intentions, so she let her knee drift to touch his and left it there a moment too long. Taking it away, she gave him a sidelong glance. Sure enough, he was looking at her. A minute later, he let his knee drift to hers, and again it lasted just a fraction too long. This was repeated until their knees rested together and they yearned in the wonderful dark. Amid the bustle of the audience leaving, she'd whispered a time and place to him.

From there, the affair created itself. Every step was preordained and part of the routine of such affairs, like a story stamped out by a Fiction machine. The man even reproduced some of the muttered endearments of her previous lovers. Of course, that was no great wonder: certain words and phrases had become watchwords that showed one was of the fucking class. The words *dear* and *darling* were staples. There was also a transgressiveness at trysts that seemed part and parcel of sexual play. A casual profanity was almost expected. Many people liked to curse the Inner Party and call them swine and bastards. Julia had had one fellow who'd got aroused from saying, "Emmanuel Goldstein isn't all wrong"—always those same five words, then he leapt upon her in urgent passion. Another liked to fart after sex, long and loud, with a smirk of joyful impudence, and say, "*That* to the Inner Party."

What Julia loved was nudity, especially out of doors. She loved to fuck in the grass, the whole sky seeing her, then to sprawl with legs akimbo, feeling the breeze on her cunt and scratching at her armpit like a sleepy monkey. She liked rough dirt beneath her arse while she was fucked. She would dig her bare toes into the earth, and the man atop her would use the coarsest language, then call her "dear," or "mother"—just as he pleased. Afterward, they shared their black-market finds and said the worst things they could think of, laughing until they cried, all naked. She felt exceptional then, as daring as a pilot flying in the teeth of a storm. She was fucking though it killed her, so it was only natural to moan, "I love you," in the ear of a man she would never see again. She loved him because she was forbidden to do it. She loved him to be fearless.

It couldn't have been more obvious that Winston Smith was not of this profane, irresponsible company and could never be.

She might never have approached him, then, if it weren't for Dr. Louis's pills. She had never taken anti-sex pills before, and was unprepared for how they turned ordinary things into romance. Everyone seemed dear and admirable; all the old dangers felt like gay adventure. The factory floor with its raucous noise and bustle was a festival. She had little to do and could dream on the walkway, smoking, so happy she felt a keen nostalgia for these hours even as they happened. Her mind went off to unusual places, yearning, embroidering, remembering. There it found Vicky's note—I LOVE YOU—and jumbled it together with Winston Smith in the door of Weeks's mysterious shop, glaring at her with lonely rage. In a moment, this turned into a plan that made her smirk behind her hand. She'd thought she was being careless by not tossing that note in a canal long ago. Now it revealed itself as the solution to a puzzle. Had anything ever been so clever? The next morning she was changing in the locker room and found the note still untouched on the shelf between her dress boots. She slipped it casually into the pocket of her overalls, chattering all the while with Edie about the latest musical flick.

Having come this far, she was lost. She was dreaming of Weeks and brothels and opium dens where the Brotherhood met, and her body soared with pleasure. The Beastly Brothers! What were they after? *Freedom*—that was what Emmanuel Goldstein said. She imagined freedom as exuberance, a clumsy romping; it made her imagine two dogs leaping on top of each other in meeting. In her mind, it was tied to her childhood days, the hours the exiles had spent complaining, fighting, singing at kitchen tables, while Julia played soldiers with hairpins at their feet. The rich food the exiles had eaten was freedom, and the music called jazz, with its horns and wails like wonderful sickness. Her mother had told her those songs were made in another universe. That universe, then, was freedom. People smoked opium there, and every house was a worse sort of brothel: bliss. One song had talked of a time when saints came marching in and the sun refused to shine and . . . what was the rest? Julia couldn't remember. She remembered her child self peering out from under a nest of coats, the gramophone skipping with the stamping of the dancers, and the anarchist man who had danced with his Italian wife so slowly; both closed their eyes as their faces touched. Freedom was in that touch, its bald sexuality in the hot crowd. And it was in that later time when she climbed into the plane with Hubert and took flight above the dark-bright ocean, her whole body singing with noise and fear. It was in the smugglers' boat they had glimpsed, drawing out its slender tail of foam, a boat full of chocolate from another universe, one with different trees, under which people smoked French cigarettes and drank wine and were "free." They said, "I love you."

Such were Julia's thoughts in the days before she did the thing that killed them.

She was on the tenth floor with a legitimate excuse, popping by Research to fetch a Newspeak update for the Rewrite crew. On her way out, she slowed as she entered the long, bright corridor leading to the stairs. Of course she was thinking of Smith, so when he appeared in the flesh it felt both ridiculous and inevitable. In her surprise, she almost let the opportunity pass. It felt too soon, too sudden. The pills made her feel not herself, and one could so easily make a mistake.

The lighting was harsh and bright, medicinal in its intensity, and his slight figure and stooped shoulders gave him the look of an invalid. His limp was more pronounced than before, and the effort of walking down the hallway seemed almost more than he could bear. His face was deeply lined. His very fair hair seemed almost white. There was a mix of the geriatric and the boyish in his struggling form.

This lasted until he saw her. Then his eyes turned cold with lust and contempt. His shoulders squared, and his face altered completely. He seemed five inches taller. Now, as he advanced, the limp seemed the relic of some war exploit in which he'd had no mercy—none!—on enemy women. Julia felt it deliciously all through her flesh. Growing closer, he looked beyond her, adopting a face of careful blindness, but his body was still expressive of intimate rage. Oh, it was that she wanted! And if he were truly a Goldsteinite?

In a moment, the choice was made. She let a foot slip from under her and fell headlong.

To make such a fall convincing, one must truly lose one's balance and flail and hit the floor with one's full shocking weight. Julia managed to land on her good side. Still she cried out in real agony as her sprained wrist was violently jarred and her other elbow struck the floor and was crushed beneath her body. A second later, she was sitting up, feeling horribly cold. Pain throbbed up both arms. She frowned downward and made a quick adjustment to her sling. The note was in her hand.

Smith had come forward, his manner altered. He was manly in a different mode, his lean face serious with response. When he said, "You're hurt?" his voice was hoarse. Again, she felt that point of pleasure.

"It's nothing," she said in an offhand way. "My arm. It'll be all right in a second."

"You haven't broken anything?"

"No, I'm all right. It hurt for a moment, that's all."

With a sudden natural gesture, she held out her good hand to him. Just as naturally, he came to help her up. She turned her face away as she took his hand, frowning as if braced for pain.

She had passed many notes before, and the mechanics were always satisfying: how the paper was pinched between thumb and palm, then swiftly, decisively, pressed into the other's hand. As she'd feared, he stiffened in surprise. To cloak it, she put too much weight on his hand. He staggered just a little, then caught his balance. Regaining her feet with a grimace, she said, "It's nothing. I only gave my wrist a bit of a bang. Thanks, comrade!"

She let go of his hand and turned away with only a cursory glance at his face. She was braced for him to raise the note triumphantly to the telescreen, or stupidly let it flutter to the floor. But he was smiling noncommittally, holding the note just as he should, out of sight in a loosely closed hand.

She walked on as if nothing had occurred. Behind, she heard him walk away as if nothing had occurred. Nothing had. She had fallen, and a colleague helped her to her feet. She let that thought be foremost—nothing had happened, just a foolish fall—until she reached the door to the stairs. There, with her back to the telescreens, she drew a sharp breath and a thrill of delight swept over her. He'd taken it! Oh, he was hers! Belatedly she felt the warm pressure of his hand, its masculine strength. Those bleak and pitiless eyes! He would have her! On the stairs, she started singing a patriotic hymn that meant love only to

Julia. It was one the airmen used to like, about the halcyon days
to come when the war was won. It went:

> I'll never forget the people I met
> Braving those angry skies
> I remember well as the shadows fell
> The light of hope in their eyes
>
> And though I'm far away
> I sometimes hear them say
> Thumbs up!
> For when the dawn comes up
>
> There'll be red flags over
> The white cliffs of Dover
> Tomorrow
> Just you wait and see!
>
> There'll be love and laughter
> And peace ever after
> Tomorrow
> When the world is free!

By the time she reached the fourth floor, she was singing it
so lustily a Textbooks fellow, coming up past her, made a little
comedy of cowering and covering his ears. She laughed, but left
off as she took the last few flights to Fiction. Part of her mind
was still marveling at her folly. To pass a note at Truth—not on
a hike, not at a crowded march, but in a corridor at Truth! And
to Old Misery, a man who'd never smiled at anything but a Two
Minutes Hate, who, above all things, detested women!

But the note wasn't hers, it was Vicky's—that was the brilliance of the plan. Oh, if he'd reacted the moment she'd handed it to him, he could have pinned it on her. But now? Julia's handwriting was well known. As a mechanic, she was always writing orders for equipment and leaving notes on temperamental machines. Two dozen people would know at a glance that note could not be hers. And if it came to Julia's word over Smith's, he would never be believed. She was a well-liked, attractive girl, and one who could compromise twenty well-placed men if she were ever interrogated. Smith was a friendless prig who worked in the disreputable Records Department. At a pinch, she could mention seeing him at Weeks.

But, thank B.B., it wouldn't come to that. Smith had taken the note like a lamb. With any luck, he and Julia would be fucking in a month. And he must have experience, after all. He might even be a real Goldsteinite. The summer was saved from boredom.

Back in Fiction, agreeably breathless, she checked the factory floor for flags—all clear—then headed up to the walkway. But on the stairs, her way was blocked by Essie.

Essie was a barrel-shaped woman of forty, dreadfully scarred by the combination of Fiction machines and gin. One cheek was twisted and seamed, her left hand only had three fingers, and there were other scars on her legs and flanks that she liked to show off on Fiction's annual seaside excursion. She was plainspoken to an alarming degree—her parents had been proles—but no one was more doggedly loyal to the Party. Her greasy fingerprints were perpetually visible on the receiver of the white "discretion" phone that went directly to Love. Luckily Julia had always got on with her. It had been settled in her first week that Essie, as the senior mechanic, got all the perks of the job, while Julia did the donkey work. It didn't hurt their relations, either, that Essie was proudly married, and saw Julia's Anti-Sex sash as a tacit admission that she couldn't get a man.

Now Essie cried out, "There you are! We've been hunting high and low. Did Comrade O'Brien find you?"

Julia stopped dead, the excitement curdling in her chest. "Comrade O'Brien?"

"Yes, he's just been here."

"That is—Inner Party O'Brien?"

"Well, I'd not call him that!" Essie laughed. "Inner Party O'Brien! But, yes, that's the one. He wants you for a private repair at his flat."

"His flat?"

"I can't say I wasn't surprised myself. I did try to offer my services, but he ran right off. Didn't even stop to listen!"

Julia saw the dawning jealousy in Essie's eyes and said hastily, "He probably didn't know you were in repairs."

"All right. But why he asked for you—that's the puzzle."

"Oh, I'm sure he hasn't a clue who I am. He will have picked a name from a list, that's all." Julia said this, and wanted to say it again, as if that would make it true.

"But why come for one of ours at all?" Essie said. "Unless they haven't got mechanics of their own. No machines to repair over there, perhaps. Here, look. He's left you an address."

Essie held out a note and Julia took it automatically. It was the square sort of paper used for intra-office communications, shockingly identical in size and appearance to the note she'd just given Smith. For a moment she expected to see I LOVE YOU written there, and subtly shuddered. Of course it wasn't that. It was an address in the Inner Party neighborhood between the Westminster compound and Martyrs of December Park.

"I do wish he'd asked me, though," Essie said. "I could do with an Inner Party friend just now. You don't see a lot of them down this way."

Julia was feeling faint, staring at the paper, when she registered Essie's words. She said, as naturally as she could, "Well, why shouldn't you go? I'm sure Comrade O'Brien will see no difference."

"Couldn't. Wasn't asked."

"But it's only a repair, and you're the better mechanic. You *should* go. I'm sure it's what he'd want if he knew."

Now Julia extended the paper casually. Essie didn't take it, but her fingers twitched.

"Well, he did say it was just a repair," said Essie. "A *simple* repair, he said that twice."

"If he wanted it done tonight, I couldn't go anyway. Not easily. I've got a volunteer shift and I oughtn't to beg off at such short notice."

Again Julia held out the slip of paper. This time Essie accepted it, and both smiled in relief. Essie said, "I wish I could be sure he won't mind."

"Why should he? A mechanic's a mechanic."

Essie looked faintly dubious at this, but then looked back at the address—the enticing Inner Party address—and allowed herself to be convinced. "I'll go, then. Though I do seem to be doing a lot of your work this week."

This gambit was so shameless Julia almost showed her amusement. But she kept her face earnest as she said, "Yes, and I'm ever so grateful. When my hand's better, I shall do all the heavy work for ages to pay you back."

That night Julia dreamed of Love—or of the things Love made.

When a person was taken by Love, he sometimes vanished utterly. Other times, however, a version of him was released—a broken, skeletal creature that shambled, muttered to itself, and groaned in pain. The skin of these wretches was blotched with overlapping bruises and sores that never healed. Their bodies had lumps in the oddest places; their heads were often dented in a way that turned one's stomach to see. Fingers might be missing, or the fingers were there but the fingernails gone. They often came to the Chestnut Tree Café, the only café that was halfway luxurious—or it was when none of Love's creatures was there. When one was, everybody's eyes were drawn inexorably to the spectacle of them trying to eat. Some couldn't use a knife and fork. They must eat by putting their faces in their plates and lap their gin from bowls. She'd seen one that had to crawl on hands and knees to leave, and, as he went, nodded obsequiously at everyone he passed, a line of drool on his chin, head trembling. The diners stared through him, continuing their conversations as best they could—it wasn't safe to show you noticed these unfortunates, never mind to speak to them. They went about the city in a zone of solitude, exhibiting their sickening damage for weeks or months, then one day vanished.

Julia's dream began with a telescreen program about such creatures, which she'd been asked to narrate. This task presented a terrifying difficulty, since one couldn't very well describe them without speaking ill of the Party. Julia started to babble nonsense syllables, thinking this would be safe. But this too was unacceptable, and she now found herself inside the program. She was one of the creatures, struggling down a crowded pavement while people shrank in dread. The damage to her body kept changing. First both arms ended in grotesque stumps from which the naked bones projected. Then she decided she would need one arm to work, and her right hand reappeared. To make up for this, she now found her jaw and throat were mutilated so badly she could not form words. She thought, *No, then I couldn't eat.* At this, the horror moved again, and she found her skull had been sawed open, and her damaged brain was exposed to the air so flies could land and feed. Again she refused to accept this, and was trying to find a mirror so that she could see it wasn't true. But when she put her hand to her head, she always found that awful gap, that wetness, and the flies still came.

From this, she woke in the dimness of the dormitory. She half sat up, almost crying out, then automatically arranged her face into the somnolent smile considered appropriate to that hour. On the telescreen at her head, Big Brother was speaking, silhouetted darkly against the Oceanian stars and stripes, saying something soothingly meaningless about the flowers of toil. Through the bunks, she could see the moonlight streaming through the one un-blacked-out window. Beneath it, Vicky lay in bed. Both cats were curled up with her; she was stroking one while the other licked her hand. Her eyes were wide open. She stared at Julia.

That was all; then Julia slept again. Perhaps she'd never really woken. Whether she had or she hadn't, next morning she rose well-rested and untroubled, remembering the nightmare only as a distant misery. She queued for the sink and did her Rhythmic Jerks without consciously seeing Vicky; the Vicky of morning somehow had no connection to the ominous Vicky of the night. On the ride to the Ministry, Julia even dozed off. Only when she arrived at Truth and was descending the stairs to Fiction did she suddenly remember O'Brien. He had asked for her: that was real. The terror from the dream returned in a flash. All was damaged! Too damaged to ever be whole!

But as she thought it, a hearty cry came behind her, then the sound of boots running down the stairs. It was Essie, grinning so broadly her scarred cheek bunched up, half closing her left eye. She called to Julia, "Comrade! What a man that O'Brien is! And were you right? I'll say you were. Not a word from him about who the worker was or wasn't. And what do you suppose wanted fixing? A machine that washes clothes! Well, we've all heard of them, but to see how it works was quite another thing! I fixed it all right, too, for all that I'd never seen one before. A machine's a machine. I suppose you might have done it as well." Essie gave Julia a condescending smile that said she supposed just the opposite. "He spoke highly of my work, as well he might, and said he'll have me back again for any other little jobs. There's a friend to have! Oh, yes! I'd say you've done me a service there."

They walked together down the last flight of stairs to Fiction and shared a cigarette before going to begin the starting sequence. All that time, Essie chattered about O'Brien and his wondrous machines and his decency, and Julia hung on every word. When they parted to their various duties, Julia was annoyed to find her heart still pounding and her palms damp. But surely it had all passed safely. Essie had a good instinct for trouble; if she hadn't, she would have been dead long ago. An informer's life was precarious: the careless ones got denounced in turn, as their work bred so much hatred. No, it had all come off. Julia must only do her part and put all thought of Winston Smith from her head. With O'Brien sniffing round, anything of that nature could be fatal. In fact, it might be time for her to give up sexcrime altogether. Better to live out her life in chastity, sweetening the time with fags and chocolate and a little self-pleasuring in the dark, than to have another tryst or two, then an agonizing death in the bowels of Love.

Julia maintained this sensible resolve for a day and a night, then another few days. She changed her schedule to avoid the canteen when Records took their meal. When an old boyfriend sidled up to her at a rally, she kept her arms crossed and her face turned away. She sang louder during patriotic hymns and was quicker to volunteer her services at the piano. At her Mechanical Workers' Union branch meeting, she avidly joined in the criticism of Local 21, which had allowed the taint of Goldsteinism to creep into the notices on their bulletin board. She marched with the Maidens for Patriotic Love at a demonstration in support of the platform of the Party's 42nd Congress. By then, her arm had recovered enough for her to carry a placard depicting a baby dismembered by Eurasian bombs, and she screamed "Love is hate!" with such abandon her voice was hoarse for the next two days.

This impeccable conduct persisted until one day she let herself take second meal at her old hour. It had become too great a bother to avoid Smith; changing her routines meant Essie's routines were upset, and Essie had begun to dangerously grumble. Anyway, such precautions seemed silly, when Smith had done nothing about the note for days.

This first trial passed without incident. She sat with a group of other girls, and though Smith gave her a peculiar stare, he made no attempt to approach. Julia returned the following day, and once again he left her in peace. By the third day, she thought it perfectly safe to sit at a table alone. Taking second meal at one hour or another made no difference at all. One could scarcely call it incautious—so Julia was thinking, when Smith set his tray down across from her, sat down, and baldly asked, "What time do you leave work?"

She was mostly concerned in that first moment to show no visible shock. To buy time, she took a spoonful of her soup, a bean-based swill with a pronounced odor of dog. As she did, she realized with relief that Smith's voice had been low and indistinct, and he, too, was gazing at his bowl as if she were a matter of total unconcern. Farthermore, there were no tele-screens nearby, and no one close enough to hear.

Nonetheless, she was about to rebuff Smith, when she glanced up and saw his face. Even as he dabbled in the soup with his spoon, his eyes showed the feral need they'd shown when he glared from the doorway of Weeks. She looked away hastily, but in her mind's eye still saw the fair hair, the spare, worn face. He would have her. There was nothing she could do about it.

Bending over her bowl, she said, "Eighteen-thirty."

9

ON THE MORNING OF HER FIRST TRYST WITH WINSTON Smith, Julia did two hours of street cleaning. It was her favorite volunteer shift. You got to wander the predawn streets of curfew, when your only company was owls, rats, foxes, and night patrols who were bored with their lonely duty and glad to offer a cigarette to a fresh-faced girl. Occasionally a long car passed, bearing some Inner Party member home from a banquet or war conclave. Then Julia stood at attention, hiding her dustpan and broom behind her for decency. The patrols stood straighter too, as perhaps did the owls and the startled rats, but never the foxes, whom nothing daunted.

Street cleaning earned her a chit for the warm-water baths at Goodspeak Circle. If you timed it right—Julia always did—you could stretch the bath to fifteen minutes. As she soaked, she gave herself over to qualms. It was true that Smith had handled the first stages well. He'd met her in Victory Square as instructed, and knew without being told that this first meeting was for arrangements only. He'd held off approaching her until there was a crowd, then spoke without meeting her eye, his voice almost inaudible. As the mob pressed them together, he'd let her take his hand and had fondled it in his, which certainly showed the right spirit.

On the other hand, the plans had all been Julia's. He'd made that approach in the canteen, but then had simply waited for her instructions. He'd shown no sign of prior experience. He hadn't whispered "dear" or touched her arse—none of the quirks or shibboleths that would have marked him as part of the merry conspiracy. There was a timidity about him, too, that made it seem unlikely he was a terrorist. He seemed rather to be venturing beyond the bounds of Party propriety for the first time, and to be breathless at his own daring. It felt increasingly probable—dreadful thought—he had only entered Weeks to look at the merchandise. But she'd come this far, and no other man would be arriving to fuck her that afternoon. One made do with what one found.

From the baths, she went to the Meltons' and used two dollars of her Harringay Widows money to buy a slab of chocolate. It came in silver foil and pretty red paper with Eurasian writing and a sketch of mountains, but Mrs. Melton removed this neatly and rewrapped it in a page from a prole newspaper. The elegant wrapping could only get Julia in trouble, while proles would buy it separately as decoration for their rooms. For her countryside trysts, Julia carried chocolate partly as a welcoming gift, but more as an alibi. If she were searched, it would tell patrols she was going to a farm to trade for butter or meat. They would take the chocolate for themselves, of course, but do her no worse damage.

All her buses were miraculously running, and she was on the train to the meeting place by thirteen hundred. The trip took a little under an hour, and went through countryside that was unsettlingly reminiscent of the SAZ. On the journey, she entertained herself by folding paper horses for a little prole boy who stared at them in wonder and repeated after her, "Orse." His mother glared all the while, and only grudgingly accepted the delicate things as a gift, shoving them so carelessly into her bag that they would surely be ruined. This dampened Julia's spirits somewhat. Why must proles be so uncomradeful? But when she disembarked, she was cheered to find she was the only passenger alighting. It would have been awkward to encounter Smith here, or—still worse—a group of hikers eager to engage her in conversation, or even to propose she join their picnic. On fine days, such pests were everywhere, ready to latch onto a girl alone and rescue her from the threat of ownlife. Many a tryst had been spoiled by a band of convivial strangers with a bag of protein-paste sandwiches.

She left the little platform and took an ill-kept road leading past some tumbledown farm buildings to a patchy wood. Here she found to her delight that the bluebells were out. The path she'd chosen was carpeted in the lovely things, and the scent was otherworldly. Doves cooed in the thickets. The stronger breezes fetched a faint scent of manure, but the fragrance of the flowers mostly cloaked it. The whole way was shady and alive.

Beneath all this ran the heady feeling of being away from telescreens. This close to a railway station, there might be microphones in the trees, but one could be sure one wasn't *seen*. As long as one made no suspicious sound, one might be naked, one might even be fucking, and the snoops would never know the difference. Julia took off her boots and socks and went along barefoot for a way until the pain of treading on broken sticks defeated her. As she laced the boots back up, she made gruesome faces and mouthed: "*That* to the Inner Party!"

She came across Winston on the path, crouched down to pick bluebells and gather them in a sloppy bunch. The sight of him struck her forcibly. He was really here. It was going to happen.

Though she made a great racket coming up, he didn't turn to look. Perhaps he was frightened she was someone else; still, he ought to have offered the comradeful smile of a hiker glad of a potential companion. When she laid her hand on his shoulder, he didn't flinch. The muscle was hard beneath her hand. The masculine body! It was always a surprise. He turned to look, and his face changed at the sight of her. He looked older in sunlight, but far more handsome. His face was grave and sensitive. Any doubt she still had fell away.

She shook her head to warn him not to speak, then passed to lead him forward. She felt his eyes on her as he followed, and kept her gait self-consciously feminine, always difficult in Party boots. She was aware again that she didn't know him. What if he was here to kill her, to silence her? There were no protective telescreens. It might take weeks for her body to be found. Of course she didn't believe that—if she had, she would have run from him. Still, the notion added a keenness to everything. The clouds of bluebells were deliciously ominous, the sunlight wild like one's last sunlight. For romance, for erotic delight, she was courting death.

At last, Julia leapt nimbly over a fallen tree and paused by the wall of dense-grown foliage that marked their destination. With her still-stiff hand, it was more difficult than usual to force a passage through the branches. But at last she fought her way into a clearing surrounded by tall bushes and saplings that hid it on all sides. She waited in suspense until she heard Smith coming after her. Then she ran to the center of the clearing and whirled to face him as he emerged. She said, "Here we are!"

He stopped a few paces away, holding his bunch of bluebells to his chest. The freshness of the flowers contrasted with the worn blue of his overalls and with his worn, masculine face.

She went on, "I didn't want to say anything in the lane in case there's a mike hidden there. I don't suppose there is, but there could be. There's always the chance of one of those swine recognizing your voice. We're all right here."

For a terrible moment he looked as if he was about to turn and flee. Then he repeated faintly, "We're all right here?"

She smiled. "Yes. Look at the trees. There's nothing big enough to hide a mike in. Besides, I've been here before."

He came forward then, dropping the bluebells at his feet. To Julia's disappointment, he only took her hand, but the intensity in his face was just as it had been in her fantasies.

He said, "Would you believe that until this moment I didn't know what color your eyes were?" Before she could answer, he added, "Now that you've seen what I'm really like, can you still bear to look at me?"

She felt the joy of being set a simple task, and said, "Yes, easily."

"I'm thirty-nine years old. I've got a wife that I can't get rid of. I've got varicose veins. I've got five false teeth."

"I couldn't care less."

That did the trick. She was in his arms, and it was just as she'd hoped, a savage embrace. He would have her! Too late to change her mind! He'd waited so long, and now he would brook no resistance.

But in the next breath, something went wrong. His mouth became awkward on hers, and he was only going through the motions of kissing her. He grappled with her body rather than feeling it. He pulled her to the ground, as if determined to fight his way through the problem, but there he fared no better. Everything clashed, as if the man were made of elbows. First his weight bore down painfully on her hip bone; then he shifted, and sprawled half on, half off her, in the most peculiar pose. He seemed not to know his place was between her thighs, and when she tried to pull him there, he resisted. Then she felt what the trouble was. His prick was so limp it felt entirely absent. She kissed him more avidly and squirmed against him, trying to bring him back to life, but nothing doing. He ebbed; he dribbled away.

At last she let him go, and he instantly drew into himself as if offended. She said, as lightly as she could, "Never mind, dear. There's no hurry. We've got the whole afternoon."

He sat up, adopting a careless air. That was good—far better than defensiveness. There was hope, if she managed him wisely.

She went on in the same easy tone, "Isn't this a splendid hideout? I found it when I got lost once on a community hike. If anyone was coming, you could hear them a hundred meters away."

"What is your name?"

"Julia. I know yours. It's Winston—Winston Smith."

"How did you find that out?"

"I expect I'm better at finding things out than you are, dear." She said this in a bantering tone, but he accepted it meekly. That wouldn't do. The sexual charge was dying, and she was halfway to the role of mother. Julia tried, "Tell me, what did you think of me before that day I gave you the note?"

This was a far greater success than she could have anticipated. He said, "I hated the sight of you. I wanted to rape you and then murder you afterward. Two weeks ago I thought seriously of smashing your head in with a cobblestone. If you really want to know, I imagined that you had something to do with the Thought Police."

She laughed out loud. "Not the Thought Police! You didn't honestly think that?"

To her dismay, this took the wind out of his sails. "Well," he said, "perhaps not exactly that. But from your general appearance—merely because you're young and fresh and healthy, you understand—I thought that probably..."

From here, it went by fits and starts. She laughed off the

thought of being a thinkpol, gushing about her hatred of the Party to dispel any fears he had on that score. She made a great deal of not being intellectual; some men thought Fiction girls were all readers, and felt inadequate because they were not. This didn't seem to be his trouble, but he looked pleased to hear it nevertheless. She also played the brash young tart, in case he was unmanned by the idea of her purity, and even made a show of tearing away her Anti-Sex sash. She'd half intended to follow it with her clothes, but when she touched her zip, he looked panicked, so she reached in her pocket and offered him chocolate instead.

This backfired. He asked in wonder, "Where did you get this?" and was naively enthralled by the taste. Of course, she couldn't have guessed that the man would have never tasted black-market chocolate! He looked on her now as a powerful magician. This quite undid all her good work, and she had the dispiriting chore of building him up again from nothing. She took the gamble of asking why he'd been at Weeks. If he were a Goldsteinite, the memory of his daring would surely puff him up, and if he'd just been visiting a shop, there would be nothing lost.

It was the latter, but luckily, he grew puffed up at the memory of visiting a junk shop—a thing Winston clearly felt few other men would dare to do. Immediately he began to lecture her that the shop wasn't "Weeks," not properly. "The shopkeeper is named Charrington. I talked to him, you know; we spoke for quite some time. He has been meaning to change the name, but he seemed rather downcast. Not many people appreciate his sort of merchandise, or dare to show it if they do."

Winston Smith, of course, was the rare exception to this rule. He'd bought a notebook there before, and on this visit had purchased a paperweight. This turned into a rhapsodic description of the paperweight, which, from what she could glean, was just a glass dome with a bit of rock in it. He promised to show it to her if he got a chance, and she said gravely that she would like that very much.

He also boasted of having been upstairs at the shop. Julia was wistfully hoping he might at least have spotted an opium pipe, but he said there was only a shabby bedroom that looked to be infested with bedbugs. To Winston, though, this had a peculiar charm. "It was like stepping into a room of fifty years ago, even a hundred. It had no telescreen. Only think!"

"Oh!" she said. "One might meet there."

"Yes. I was even thinking of renting it for myself. Just to sit alone and know one wasn't seen."

She had been feeling variously disappointed. The notorious Weeks was just a junk shop whose owner had an unfortunate manner; Winston Smith, far from being a terrorist, was someone who saw buying a paperweight as the height of manly valor. But as he spoke dreamily of being alone and knowing one wasn't seen, she felt a dawning sympathy.

"Yes," she said. "I know just what you mean. Being here—I could come here just to look about myself all day. Just to know *they* aren't here."

"Yes." He smiled into her eyes. "One can properly think."

"And feel. Even be. One is quite different at those times."

He took her hand again. "Yes, I might really do that. You have given me the courage."

Here he rose and proposed a walk. She agreed, feeling warmly toward him and sensing that this might be the way back in. Indeed, he walked with his arm around her waist, and when they had to separate in a narrow path between bushes, he touched her cheek and whispered gravely, "You are so lovely and fresh. I do like you." His body was delightfully hard against hers, his hand conscious on her hip. Everything was as it should be. The treacherous mother-feeling was gone.

At the edge of the wood, he stopped in surprise at the beauty of the scene before them. She paused, pleased, and let herself feel it with him. They stood nestled into each other, shielded from view by a patchy screen of leaves. Before them was an over-grazed, threadbare pasture, eroded from the recent rains, and showing some scars of brown-gray earth. A faint footpath led across it, almost sparkling in the May sunlight. It was the path Julia had come along on the hike when she first found this place. Beyond the pasture was the edge of another forest whose boughs stirred in the breeze. The light in the massed leaves prettily flowed like the changes of light on water. It was a plain scene, but inexpressibly charming if one but looked at it. It was all alive.

Winston said in a near whisper: "Isn't there a stream some-where near here?"

"That's right," she said dreamily. "There is a stream. It's at the edge of the next field, actually. There are fish in it, great big ones. You can watch them lying in the pools under the willow trees, waving their tails."

"It's the Golden Country—almost," he murmured.

"The Golden Country?"

"It's nothing, really. A landscape I've seen sometimes in a dream."

She was taken by this. A dream! Of course he'd probably seen it on a hike, and only half remembered it. Still, it was lovely that he turned it into a dream and gave it a fanciful name. As they leaned against each other, a bird alighted on a bough a few meters away. It got a grip with its feet, tucked in its wings, and became quite prim and tidy on its branch. Julia didn't know what sort it was: a pale brown bird with a cheerfully spotted breast. At that moment it seemed extraordinary to her. How would one go about making a bird like that? It couldn't be done. No one could do it.

"Look!" she whispered. Winston's arm tightened about her with his pleasure. As they watched, the bird ducked its head as if reflecting, spread its wings, tucked them again, and began to sing.

At first it was the sheer volume that was startling, then the sweetness and variety of the music. They were near enough to see the trembling of the feathery throat and how the bird's tail jerked with the effort of the louder notes. It would fall silent and cock its head as if considering, then casually sing a new variation. Twice it turned itself entirely around on the branch as if excited by its own tune. Julia and Winston clung to each other, hypnotized. He seemed to be holding his breath, his face a study in manly rapture. At last, he turned her to him and kissed her lips.

She felt the difference immediately. Their mouths changed together, went deeper, softer, found the way to sex. Here was her man at last! He touched her breasts, her buttocks, and all was natural, desire that grew and invented itself and tried new variations like the wild bird's song. She became languid in his arms. He crushed her urgently against him. When their mouths moved apart at last, both sighed.

From here, all went very simply. She led him back to the hideout and hastily kicked off her boots, then shed her overalls with one sweeping gesture. Smith knelt before her as if to a goddess. There was one more tricky moment when he balked and suddenly had to know about her previous lovers. How many had there been? Were they Party members? Did she enjoy sex for itself?

In the SAZ, they'd had a cow that gave more milk than

any other, but liked to kick the bucket over just as it was full. Smith was like that frustrating cow. But she knew him now, and got ahead of him. She admitted to many lovers but none more highly placed than he; she adored sex and had it whenever she could. At last the catechism was done. Then, when he embraced her, she felt him hard against her belly. All the milk was saved.

They fell to the earth together, sprawling wantonly among the bluebells from his discarded bouquet. He kissed her throat, her breast, her thighs. There were no difficulties now. He even managed to remove his own overalls without it being comical. As he thrust into her for the first time, there was the usual amazement: a man's prick had really gone inside her! Could such a sublimely obscene thing happen? Then the pleasure of it hit her, again, again, striking deep and retreating, threatening to leave, then striking again. Oh, wicked, deep pleasure unlike anything else! She let herself cry out, a little wail as natural as the bird's song. There was the magic of broad male shoulders, the rasp of his stubble against her neck. He knew just how to fuck, hard enough that it jarred her whole body and resonated through her. He rang her like a bell.

But far too soon, he groaned and tensed. She wanted to cry out, *Not yet*, but his body trembled and went weak. A moment later, he rolled off her, and there was that cheated feeling of a prick sliding out. She lay taunted by her receding pleasure, like a story that would never now come to its point. He'd left one hand proprietarily on her breast, where it now irritated her. Belatedly she realized she might get pregnant. Winston, meanwhile, looked blissful, like the cat that got the cream.

At length the near-climax dissipated, and she was able to see things more philosophically. No man was at his best on his first outing. He mustn't have done it in ages. And even at half-weight, he had a little gift. He was already better than poor Tom Parsons, the last man she had brought to this spot, who'd lasted a minute and sweated so much that, when he rolled off Julia, her whole belly glistened. Parsons once told her, as a salacious titbit, that he'd heard French girls could climax seven times a night. Julia had replied a bit tartly that, given the chance, she too had that remarkable ability. He'd stared at her in shock, then asked, "Do you think you might be part French?"

Her mind then drifted naturally to the first time she'd ever come to this place. She and a girl named Lou had left the main hike to scour the woods for mushrooms and lost their way. They had stumbled on this clearing and marveled at its privacy. Lou opined that some criminal must have made it. She hunted on the ground for evidence of crime, while Julia lingered warily on the periphery, wondering what she would do if Lou tried to kiss her. Lou was rumored to be a raging Reggie, though of course people said this of any girl who was unusually tall. No traces of crime were found, and at last Lou agreed to leave. Only then did they realize they didn't know their way back to the trail. It was Julia who heard the stream and remembered streams were meant to lead to civilization, though she couldn't recall which way one followed them. They were debating this, going up, then down, and becoming increasingly hot and cross, when Lou suddenly said, "Oh, to Love with all this. I'm going in for a swim." In a minute, she'd stripped off her overalls and knickers, waded splashingly into the water, and was swimming, crying out with pleasure and shouting to Julia to come in.

Julia was then very young—seventeen—and she'd dithered on the bank a long time, uncertain if this was a Reggie snare. Lou kept laughing at her cowardice and exclaiming how lovely the water was. At last, Julia stripped and ventured in with extreme self-consciousness. When the water reached the tops of her thighs, she shivered and ducked down, feeling much better once the water covered her up to her shoulders.

But Lou was now looking away. She said, "Do you hear that? Listen!" When Julia stopped splashing, she heard, very dimly but distinctly, the voices of the other Anti-Sexers, tunelessly singing "The Ballad of Goldstein's Blood." They couldn't have been more than five hundred meters off.

"Oh, the misery of it!" Lou said in comic despair. "We're found!"

"Are you disappointed? Truly?"

"Horribly. You?"

"A little. I'm not sure."

Lou grinned wickedly and plunged beneath the water. There was a pause where all above was quiet. Julia looked at the tree-tops and tensed, anticipating the other girl's hands on her. But Lou surfaced five meters off, bright water streaming from her dark hair. Julia caught her breath, surprised and stung. Then she plunged her own head down.

10

ESSIE HAD VANISHED. ONE MORNING SHE WAS MISSING from work, without warning or explanation. In the first hours, some thoughtless people commented on her absence. By second shift, no one mentioned her at all. Julia went to the Fiction noticeboard to check the lists of the Gardening Club, whose treasurer Essie had been, time out of mind. The treasurer was now a Joan Wollenska. Essie's name was also gone from the coat pegs, and her washing-up gloves had disappeared from the sink. The most artful erasure was on the chalkboard where people signed up for cleaning shifts, and the names overlapped in a messy tangle. By some legerdemain, Essie's name had been spirited out from the middle, and the gap neatly closed.

Julia's first, unworthy feeling was that of having escaped a trap. O'Brien had claimed a victim, but it hadn't been her. Then a chill passed over her as she remembered her antics with Winston Smith. Could O'Brien's invitation have been related to her sexcrimes? If it were, Love would be after her still. But that couldn't be right; if she were wanted for sexcrime, there would be no dubious invitations to Inner Party members' flats. She would be bundled into a van and vaporized without further ado. But what, then, could it have meant? And why do away with poor Essie if the trap was meant for Julia?

At length she concluded it must have really been a repair and nothing more. Perhaps Essie's arrest was unrelated, or perhaps she'd offended O'Brien—easily done, given what she was like. Anyhow, Julia might feel dreadful for sending her, but she had no more to fear.

Still, these reflections cast a shadow over her meetings with Winston Smith. For the rest of May, these consisted mainly of furtive conversations in public streets. They couldn't simply walk down the street together; any such intimacy could be noticed by a telescreen. There were even times when they reached their rendezvous to find a flock of microcopters buzzing about, or patrols checking everyone's papers, and had to pass each other without a sign. Sometimes, in a prole district, they walked at a careful distance from each other, speaking when no one else was near, in an almost normal fashion. But mostly they used a procedure known as "speaking by installments." Julia would walk some way ahead, then pause, pretending to inspect a war-bonds poster or a shop that mended shoes. He would then stroll by and mutter something in the moment of passing. Two minutes later, it would be his turn to pause, hers to mutter as she passed. Both tried to speak without moving their lips, though Winston was singularly bad at this, and ended up making demented faces.

Laborious though these machinations were, there was a thrill in conversing with one's secret lover. Smith was also rather interesting, even if he wasn't the sort of company Julia ordinarily liked. He had a peculiar obsession with truth. Half of his conversation consisted of asserting what was true and what was a lie. He could spend a whole meeting proving to his own satisfaction when airplanes had been invented or what the chocolate ration had been last year—always different from whatever the

Party said it was. Once she asked if it made him feel better to know more than other people. He said tartly, "My feelings don't matter in the least. What matters is what's true."

Allied to this truth fixation was a taste for negativity—what Julia called to herself "bloodythink." He abominated the Party, but was sure its reign would last for generations. Only in the distant, unimaginable future might a free child at last be born. Once she'd asked him what point there was, then, in keeping track of the Party's lies. At that moment, they'd had to separate. Two minutes later, Winston swept past and said with dark satisfaction, "No point at all."

Another time he'd lingered beside her to say: "Party members can't think independently. They have lost the capacity to dream of something different. If there is any hope—I don't say that there is—it must lie in the proles." A patrol appeared then, and they had to go their separate ways. Walking home, Julia felt unspeakably annoyed. *She* couldn't think? *She* couldn't dream? Who did he think had devised their affair? Was that not dreaming of something different? But, no, Winston Smith was the only one in London who could think! He and proles! To be sure, any prole was worth twenty of Julia when it came to thinking!

But as she walked in the pleasant evening, her temper cooled and she began to see the funny side. Bloodythinker or no, Smith wasn't entirely wrong. Every Party member did repeat the same old rubbish. Smith's difference was what made him piquant, for all his gloom and self-importance. And proles did have more freedom. It only made sense that any rebellion must originate there.

The next time they met, she accordingly told him he was quite right about proles. They were far more quick-witted, anyway, than the Party would have you believe. But Old Misery wasn't having that! Oh, no, that smacked too much of optimism! He instantly dashed cold water on it, saying that proles had no political awareness. They thought only of their lottery numbers and where to find an egg for supper. He then told a story about how he'd once quizzed an old prole in a pub, hoping to learn about capitalist times, and was bitterly disillusioned when the man rambled on drunkenly about top hats and told him nothing of value. The man couldn't even grasp what Winston wanted. Fancy hoping for an uprising there!

Julia said, "So you've spoken to a great many proles?"

"How could I?" Winston said, affronted. "I risked a great deal by speaking to that one old man."

At this, Julia dropped back and stooped to fiddle at her bootlaces so he wouldn't see her laughing. Poor Winston! He'd talked to a single prole, and felt he knew all there was to know about them! She didn't have the heart to tell him how many proles she'd dealt with over the years.

Still, the one afternoon they managed to make love, Smith played his part admirably. They met in the belfry of a ruinous church, in a region of deserted countryside that had been hit by an atom bomb many years before. One had to walk five kilometers from the station, and for the last stretch one could see the whole abandoned village on the crest of a hill. To the east, the buildings were shattered and blackened and now, in places, tufted with green, while the western side was intact but for the effects of abandonment and weather. All doors and ground-floor windows had been boarded up and embellished with red warning tape, which fluttered hectically in the breeze and had the festive look of bunting.

The belfry was a little square chamber, stiflingly hot and smelling overwhelmingly of pigeon. When the wind blew, though, it was quite tolerable. It also gave a good view of the land all around, so one could watch to see one hadn't been followed, though it was unclear what one would do if one had. As Julia arrived, a storm was gathering overhead, and it seemed they must submit to being soaked, the church having no roof worthy of the name. But the clouds speedily passed, and the sky was again blue, which Julia called a jolly good omen. Winston surprised her by agreeing and kissing her on the cheek.

That day they talked at length, really chattered, like two hostel girls at bedtime. And just as she would with a hostel girl, Julia trimmed and embellished as she went along. The SAZ could not be mentioned, nor, of course, could her criminal parents. She did mention being branch secretary in the Youth League—no matter how much a fellow despised the Party, this reliably impressed him—but not how she'd acquired that position, nor what, in the SAZ, it really meant. She said nothing of Vicky or Essie; that would hardly put a man in the mood for sex. In fact, she made out she had no friends. If you mentioned girlfriends, some chaps got the wind up, thinking you would gossip to them about your affairs.

As many men did, Winston asked how Julia was "initiated" into sex. She said she'd lost her virginity to a sixty-year-old Party member when she was sixteen. This was nearly true: fourteen was much the same as sixteen, it just didn't sound as well, and Julia had wearied of people's exclamations on this point. Gerber, meanwhile, had been nearer forty than sixty, but Winston's eyes brightened at the number, as she'd intended; it made him feel comparatively young. She added that the man had ended up shooting himself to avoid arrest, since Winston doted on such dark tales. "And a good job, too," she said. "Otherwise they would have had my name out of him when he confessed." Of course this wasn't half of what had happened, but she judged the full story to be beyond the scope of even the grimmest tastes.

On a lighter note, she was able to tell him about her first job at Truth, producing pornographic novels for proles. The Pornosec factory was housed in a warehouse in the bombed-out regions to the south of Plenty, and its workers were told to say they worked in "agricultural statistics." Those workers were all unmarried and female, the Party thinking virginal girls too pure to be corrupted by the material. When Winston asked what the books were like, she said they were boring—ghastly rubbish. True enough, though it didn't account for the dazed, hot state in which the girls went about all day, and the hidey-holes everyone knew where one could safely masturbate. In her experience, men didn't like that part—some even grew angry and insisted it couldn't be true—and so she left it out.

She did end up describing quite a lot of the ghastly rubbish. She especially dwelled on her favorite book, *Inner Party Sinners: "My Telescreen Is Broken, Comrade!"* This featured a female mechanic like Julia, called to a private flat for a repair and obscenely mishandled by an Inner Party man. The reader knew that the telescreen was secretly working all the time, and the snoops were mightily aroused by the scene and driven to their own criminal orgy. In the light of what had happened to Essie, this story now had macabre connotations (though surely that was not what had happened to Essie). Winston was more interested in *Spanking Stories*, of which she remembered only that there was spanking, some of which was done with a shoe.

Like many Party members, Winston, too, was cagey about his life. He claimed to remember nothing of his childhood. His family were all conveniently dead. He had never lived anywhere but London, and seemed to have only the frailest concept that any other place existed. No military service: he suffered with his lungs. He had once had a wife, from whom he was separated, and about whom he was willing to talk as long as Julia would listen. This wife conformed to the rule of all ex-wives: she was handsome, but a mental and moral nullity. A joyless virago, whose only conversation was Party bromides, she was devoid of sexuality but nonetheless insisted on regular sex in the hope of producing a baby. Winston did a fine imitation of the wife's long-suffering posture as she submitted to his embraces, and was touchingly pleased when Julia laughed. Well, perhaps his story wasn't exactly true—the wife wasn't here to give her side—but one would make a poor companion if one refused to laugh at a fellow's ex-wife.

Julia also gamely played along when Winston began to reminisce about a time he and his wife were walking alone beside a steep cliff, with no one to see or hear what happened. The wife leaned out, and Winston thought...

Julia said, "Why didn't you give her a good shove? I would have."

"Yes, dear, you would have," he said complacently. "I would have, if I'd been the same person then as I am now. Or perhaps I would—I'm not certain."

Julia felt rather put out by this. Of course she wouldn't really shove someone off a cliff! It had clearly been a joke. But Winston seemed to be pondering the question in absolute seriousness.

She said rather cautiously, "Are you sorry you didn't?"

"Yes. On the whole, I'm sorry I didn't."

They were sitting side by side on the dirty floor, and he now drew her close. She wanted to pull away, but let her head rest on his shoulder. He said musingly, "Actually, it would have made no difference."

"Then why are you sorry you didn't?"

"Only because I prefer a positive to a negative. In this game that we're playing, we can't win. Some kinds of failure are better than other kinds, that's all."

Now her distaste got the better of her, and she squirmed, trying to get free from his arm. He let her go with a mournful smile, saying, "Dear, have I told you about my diary?"

This diary turned out to be a notebook Winston had bought at Weeks—or Charrington's, as he persisted in calling it—in which he wrote down all his forbidden thoughts and deeds: his hatred of the Party, his visit to a tart, his idea of killing his wife. One day he'd even found himself writing, DOWN WITH BIG BROTHER, over and over, without being fully aware he was doing it.

This struck her as simple madness—what fool made a note of such things, which were of interest only to police? But Winston would not admit it made any difference. "From the moment of declaring war on the Party," he said, "it's better to think of yourself as a corpse."

"You're welcome to that!" said Julia. "And who's declaring war on the Party? What rot!"

He shook his head condescendingly. "Think what we've just done. Don't you see they would regard that as declaring war?"

"They won't regard it at all, if you don't play the fool. I'll tell you what, you must destroy that diary. Have you written about us? Swear you won't."

"No. At any rate, I wouldn't put down your name."

"My name! If you write what we're doing, they won't need that. Listen, dear, I've been at this game for years. Think of all the men I've been with—and each of them has had other lovers too. I shouldn't think there are ten men in the London Party who haven't had a mistress. All corpses, I suppose!"

He said, with a trace of waspishness, "You think it's possible to construct a secret world in which you can live as you choose, that all you need is luck and cunning and boldness, and then you're safe. But the individual is always defeated. You must realize yourself you're doomed—yes, in your heart, I expect you know it well enough." By this point, he'd recovered his aplomb and added in a tone of triumphant melancholy, "We are the dead."

"We're not dead yet. For goodness' sake!"

"Not physically. Six months, a year—five years, conceivably. I am afraid of death. You are young, so presumably you're more afraid of it than I am. Obviously we shall put it off as long as we can. But it makes very little difference. So long as human beings stay human, death and life are the same thing."

"Oh, rubbish!" she said with real anger. "Which would you rather sleep with, me or a skeleton? Don't you enjoy being alive? Don't you like feeling: This is me, this is my hand, this is my leg, I'm real, I'm solid, I'm alive! Don't you like *this*?"

She turned to press her breasts against him, and fished mischievously between his legs. His dick grew stiff again like a dear. He stammered, "Yes . . . I like that."

Then all was well again, or well enough. Because the point, of course, was the sex. They did it three times that afternoon, and in this one matter he was willing to be taught. He even took happily to licking her, although he was clumsy at first and did it too soft or too hard, so it took a long time to achieve the desired result. But he kept at it nobly until he did, then reacted as if it were a miracle—as if he'd kissed the ground and a flowering tree sprang up before his eyes. He earnestly assured her that this was not only a sexual feat but a revolutionary act. Well, let it be what he liked. Let him call her "the dead," and spin unwholesome fantasies about woman-murder. She was here for his long hard thighs, his tight arse, his fair hair falling into his eyes as he bent over her, his spent prick lying curled against his hairy thigh, seeming utterly exhausted—but when she touched his leg, it stirred intelligently, quickening again. Oh, bliss! What did it matter if the man was an oddity? He climbed on her and fucked her a third time. He cradled her buttocks in his hands and licked her cunt. He moaned in pleasure and called her marvelous, beloved, best of women. When he whispered, "I do love you," she answered easily, "And I love you!" She would deal with the diary another day. She would surely be able to convince him to destroy it. What need for such morbid toys when he had a real woman to share his secrets?

The day following that afternoon at the church, Julia came to work to find Essie had a replacement. This was a very willing but ignorant girl with the preposterous name of Typity. It was one of the new ultra-Party names; its letters stood for "Three-Year Plan In Two Years." The fate of such names was to be resented by their bearers, and, with each new person Typity met, the first words from her mouth were a hasty "Everybody calls me Tippi." Julia was tasked with training Tippi, of course; the only other mechanic left in Fiction was a man with a highly placed brother, who knew nothing of the work but couldn't be sacked. This, among other things, must be explained to Tippi, who seemed to feel something should be done about the man, and even asked about the process for reporting a grievance, so she seemed well prepared to fill Essie's shoes as an informer, if nothing else.

The next weeks were a blur of work and more work, punctuated by increasingly frustrating meetings with Winston Smith. He was in the best of moods after his exploits at the church, and talked cheerfully about a prole uprising, while turning a deaf ear to her suggestions that he destroy his diary. He did swear that nothing of his meetings with Julia would appear in it, which she found she believed. If he were writing about her, he wouldn't lie. He would make it a point of pride to defy her. Still, it wasn't very comforting to know such a thing existed. It haunted her while she did extra shifts, fixed Tippi's mistakes, and covered for her ignorance. She felt as if she was carrying a fool on either shoulder.

The day everything changed should have been Julia's full day off for June. Instead, she only dared take the morning off, and was meeting Tippi at second meal to shadow her through the afternoon. At ten hundred, she went to meet Winston in the prole district nearest the ministry. She was feeling especially out of temper with him and thinking of ways of tactfully ending the affair. But, once rejected, he was sure to write about her in his blasted diary.

She was trailing Winston down the pavement, feeling depressed by her predicament and the day ahead of her—the months, the life ahead of her!—when the earth pitched underfoot. There was a deafening roar, and she was flying in sudden darkness, peppered by a thousand tiny projectiles. She hit the ground with her shoulder, then was flat on her back with the wind knocked out of her. It was a rocket bomb. She'd never had one so close. She lay stunned and electrically alive, feeling frightened perhaps, or was it thrilled? Winston's face, just an arm's length away, was white from the billowing mist of plaster dust. He was blinking and she was distantly relieved. The next instant he'd seen her, and a terrible spasm of agony crossed his features. He scrambled for her, kissing her face. When she kissed him back, he startled violently and whispered, "You're alive! Are you hurt? My dear!" He was weeping then, clutching her against him.

But now a prole woman ran past, screaming for her children. The dust was settling. Soon they would be seen. Julia pulled free from Winston sharply and said, "Oh, do let go! I'm not hurt a bit! We'd better get away." He nodded, a dazed smile still on his whitened face, and turned from her reluctantly.

Only after they'd separated did Julia feel the force of what had happened. When the bomb hit, all Winston's thoughts were for her, while she hadn't even asked if he was all right. She had no human sympathy. Then again, she'd been shocked by the blast. If he'd left her to herself for a second, she would have had time to become concerned. She might even have shed some tears of feeling. Now she would never know.

At the same time, she only had an hour to get to the Truth canteen and meet Tippi, and here she was, begrimed from head to foot. She found her way to the Meltons', suffered being scolded by Mrs. Melton for being "more lucky than you deserve," and was charged three dollars for the use of a basin of warm water and a flannel. Julia stripped to her underwear in the cockroach-infested kitchen and, while she scrubbed herself as well as she could, Mrs. Melton used a carpet beater to get the worst of the dust out of her overalls. Winston, of course, could go back to his private flat to wash in comfort—a flat large enough to have a corner out of sight of the telescreen, where he could write in his diary. Why was the damned man always complaining? He was as well off as one could be without being Inner Party. And all his talk of abolishing the Party was the purest vanity. "If there is any hope, it must lie in the proles"—all that meant was that Winston wanted the proles to do his fighting for him. People like the Meltons were expected to risk their skins, so that Winston Smith might be free to say that the Party hadn't invented the airplane. Meanwhile, proles would fare no better under the rule of Smith. He would even take away their lottery tickets, just so he might be spared the sight of them enjoying something he thought low.

At the same time, Julia was guiltily conscious that her vexation was due to the fact that Winston loved her better than she loved him. She was haunted by the wild joy on his face when he'd seen she wasn't hurt. And she hadn't thought of him at all! She'd shoved him away and rushed off, thinking only of how her dirty clothes would look to Tippi. Why was she so hard on the man? She'd never been so critical of Tom Parsons, who was twice the fool and half the lover.

When she put her overalls back on, they were still smudged with plaster dust. Still, she was clean enough to make it past the guards at Truth. That would have to be good enough. Racing back on her bike, she was glad to feel her sprained wrist had not been harmed. Her shoulder and hip were bruised from her fall, but, thank B.B., she had no worse injury. She would make a point of asking if Winston had been hurt when she next saw him. As she rode through London, she imagined this and her face went through a series of commiserating frowns.

At Truth, she dashed to the canteen and arrived with two whole minutes to spare. This was lucky, as she found the canteen doorway blocked by Alfred Syme.

Once Julia and Syme had been friends of a sort. But then he'd started to talk about the loneliness of the widower, and to wonder aloud if Julia had ever felt the appeal of matrimony. She'd put him off with talk of Anti-Sex and the comradeful life of the women's hostel, but he'd never forgiven the slight. Every time she encountered him now, she must endure some unpleasantness.

He was standing with Ampleforth from Records, a colorless, shapeless sort of chap whose job was "scrubbing" old poetry to make it appropriate for modern readers. Ampleforth sometimes used a cane, and more often visibly wanted one. In every posture, he drooped. His attitude toward all things was apologetic weakness. When Julia and Syme were still on good terms, he'd once told her that Ampleforth had had polio in childhood, and his great terror was becoming ill enough to be sent to an invalid camp. Julia quite understood it; there had been such a camp in SAZ-5, which regularly had its rations stolen by the criminals from the adjoining camp. In the hungry year of '72, every one of the invalids died.

To Julia's annoyance, Syme had spotted her. She forced a smile and came forward saying, "Comrades! Hello!"

"Just the woman we were looking for," Syme said. "Tell us— did Comrade O'Brien find you?"

She stopped and blinked, then ventured a smile. "No, that was weeks ago. That's long sorted out. He didn't want me at all."

"No, O'Brien was just here," said Syme. "He was asking for you particularly. Wasn't he, Stan?"

Ampleforth nodded and mumbled something, smiling at Julia with unfocused good nature.

The shock of the rocket bomb came flooding back. She felt sick, but said with determined carelessness, "Well, that's queer. I wonder what he could want?"

"He said he needed a repair."

"But that was done. His clothes washer."

"Not that. He said his telescreen's not workful."

"His telescreen? Not—workful?"

"'Workful' is Newspeak, comrade. Not working. Broken."

"Well, I know what the word means."

"What, then?"

She wanted to say broken telescreen repairs were a plot for a Pornosec novel. No man would really invite a female mechanic to see to a repair like that. Why, just a week before, she'd been laughing with Winston Smith at the very idea. The memory gave her another thrill of terror. Surely that couldn't have been overheard?

"I can't see what there is to be so surprised at," said Syme. "The man's telescreen isn't workful, and he doesn't like to wait until Housing can get to it. Dab hand like you, it won't take twenty minutes. He said you have his address."

"Oh, I did, but I gave it to—well, it's gone."

"Gone?" Syme's eyes shone with mean curiosity. "What a thing to misplace! Well, never mind. He's still about somewhere. I'm sure he'll hunt you down."

Julia suppressed another shudder while nodding with feigned relief. Then, to her horror, Syme's eyes slipped downward to her soiled overalls. His eyebrows subtly changed. A chill went through her as she imagined O'Brien finding her in this state. Of course anyone could be cycling through a prole area and get caught by a rocket bomb. They could—but they didn't. They weren't so careless. And a man like O'Brien might see at a glance where she'd been, and be able to guess why she'd been there. Oh, why could they not all just stop *seeing*?

She smiled brightly at Syme and said, "That *is* exciting! I'll look out for him."

Then she had to get a tray, fetch a plate of stew, and look for Tippi, who helpfully stood up at her table and waved both arms. Julia's body enacted the cheerful stride to join her without any conscious thought. She even produced some rote Party chatter, while wolfing her food and monitoring the doorway for O'Brien. He didn't appear, though she learned she was capable of mistaking anyone, of whatever size or shape, for O'Brien when she was sufficiently nervous. At last she apologized to Tippi for her dusty state, saying she'd taken a tumble in a bomb site. "I'll run home and change, in fact, but I'll be back as soon as I can. You won't mind?" Thank Big Brother, Tippi didn't. She was an avid cyclist herself, she said. Her eyes sparkled with the wish to be pleasing. Everybody liked Julia—if only that were enough!

She escaped from Truth without incident, and the ride through the streets was a wild release. Here at last no one was watching her, and she could make any desperate face she pleased. At the hostel, she darted past Atkins, calling out a cheery, "I took another nose dive, look!" and went straight up to the locker room. She stripped without a thought for the telescreens—now the least of her concern—then scrubbed herself again at the ownlife sinks. She noticed her period had started, and wiped away the first trace of blood, then came back and opened her locker briskly. In that moment, she was only grateful to find she had clean menstrual rags, and almost didn't notice the chit of paper thrust into the vent of the door. When she did notice, her mind at first refused to believe in it. It couldn't be real: it was just nerves. As it persisted in being there, Julia was filled with irritable fury. Had Vicky learned nothing? Was everyone in the world determined to kill Julia?

The locker door had come fully open, and the screens would have already seen the note: too risky now to hide it. She managed to take it out casually, but seeing what was written there, she froze.

For a full minute she stared and could not find a safe reaction. When she finally thrust it in her pocket and continued the routine of dressing, her posture had shrunk to a defensive crouch. Her throat hurt with the rise of tears.

The note was the same one Essie had given her, with the address of O'Brien's flat. A new message had now been added in a different hand, unlike any Julia had ever seen before. The writing was elegant, thickly black, and so perfect it seemed incredible a human hand had made it. The letters were exquisitely, curiously formed and joined together by slim curving lines. It was an artifact of a higher culture. It made one aware of penmanship as drawing, and of fine penmanship as art.

It said: *I shall expect you on Monday evening at 18:30. W. O'Brien.*

11

JULIA HAD VISITED AN INNER PARTY DISTRICT ONLY
once before. She was in a party of orphans, brought there to
present appreciation wreaths to Party officials. One of the recip-
ients was Vicky's future boss, Deputy Chairman Whitehead—
though he was then Agricultural Secretary Whitehead. He'd
invited two orphan girls to stay behind for a celebratory dinner, and Julia had been cruelly disappointed not to be among
the chosen. That disappointment waned and grew complicated,
however, as days passed and the two girls never returned. One
morning their names had vanished from the registers. When
Julia's bunkmate incautiously asked what had become of them,
she was savagely caned.

At that age, Julia had imagined all Inner Party members
inhabited smaller versions of the Crystal Palace, and she was
keenly disillusioned to see they lived in houses and flats like
everyone else. Now she was more able to discern the telltale
signs of luxury. In Outer Party districts, trees were rare, their
upkeep being considered a frivolous luxury in time of war. Here
the streets were lined with them. Many of the houses were embellished with ornamental iron railings; in the rest of the city,
all the iron had gone in scrap drives long ago. Even though the
sun was about to set, lights gleamed in all the windows. Not
a one had been blacked out. Nor was any facade disfigured by

bombs; the terraces stood in unbroken ranks, their faces clean and white.

Julia didn't know her way—there were no maps that showed the streets of Inner Party districts—and she turned into a park, looking for some kindly person who might help. In the park's center was a fountain with a statue of Big Brother where the water flowed from his outstretched hands. To either side, beds of flowers spilled over each other in cascades of purple and white. Strangely, there was no telescreen overlooking the park. No music played, and no voice informed the visitors of recent Party proclamations. In this unnatural quiet, black-overalled women pushed prams down shady paths. There were also servants, the men in white jackets and the women in black dresses with white pinafores and neat white hats. Several of the servants were Eastasian, enough that it hinted at some Inner Party fad. Many people were walking dogs, odd creatures of every size and shape with peculiar physical embellishments: flowing manes, curled tails, truncated legs, comically wrinkled faces. The only dogs Julia ever saw were guard dogs, snarling at the ends of chains, and she was wary of approaching these. On the other hand, the thought of accosting an Inner Party woman was still more unnerving. To make matters worse, she was attracting hostile stares. She heard one woman saying to a servant, "I call that brazen! At this hour of day!" He muttered something conciliatory, but the woman still glowered at Julia, her hand tightening on her tufted dog's leash.

At last Julia timidly approached a servant boy walking a long-faced spaniel. The boy amiably bent over the address, but when he read what was written there, his face changed. "Well! Yes, I should say I know the place. I couldn't take you right to it, but I'll walk you to where you can see it, if you like."

"Oh, do you know Comrade O'Brien?"

This question caused him some difficulties. "I know the building. That is, only as everyone does. I say, don't go mentioning me, will you?"

"I wouldn't know whom to mention."

"No, you wouldn't, would you? That's all right."

The boy then set off at great speed, so not only Julia but the spaniel had to struggle to keep up, the spaniel occasionally twisting its head to look back at her with what seemed like commiseration. The boy didn't look back at all. His posture implied he regretted his generosity, and Julia even wondered if he might deliberately lead her astray. At last he stopped at a corner and pointed. "You see? It's the modern building, the tall one there with the flags at the corners. And see you don't mention me!"

"Why would I?" Julia said.

But the boy had already taken off at a trot, with the spaniel galloping at his heels.

It was a short walk then to the building, which was rectangular and mostly composed of glass—a sort of urban Crystal Palace indeed. The entrance was flanked by two red-coated guards. It took all her courage to approach one of them with her now-rumpled paper and its brusque message. But the guard smiled as he read it, becoming cordial, even courtly, as no guard was. The other guard opened the door and ushered her in with a white-toothed smile. Inside was a vast hall, three stories tall, its walls papered in an intricate pattern of flowers and leaves that intertwined cunningly. She tried to imagine the paper hangers standing on ladders three stories high, pasting down that paper without bulges or creases—did the length matter? How would it be done? Everywhere she looked, she found some similar feat. The skirting boards were all perfectly flush with the wall, and the paint laid on without a single brushmark. The floor was carpeted from wall to wall in rich green wool that was unsettlingly flat and perfect, as if the carpet had been poured. The smell was no smell at all. It was, she supposed, the smell of air. It struck Julia that luxury was as much the absence of things as their abundance. Most of all, she noticed the absence of dirt, an absence that would make no sense in any other part of London, where the air was a tenth part dirt and one blackened the handkerchief when one sneezed.

The guard led her to the lifts. There were six, all with unblemished silver doors. Not one wore a SCHEDULED FOR SPEEDY REPAIR sign. The guard pressed an up button for her, and instantly a faint thrumming came in the wall, then the settling of the lift into place. The doors opened almost silently. The compartment inside was carpeted in the same rich green, its walls paneled in gleaming oak. There was a servant already standing there, and Julia stood aside to let him out. He didn't stir. Instead he said in a deferential tone, "Which floor, comrade?"

The guard answered for her: "O'Brien."

At that, all expression vanished from the lift man's face. When Julia entered gingerly, he made himself smaller. Her own terror, which had dissipated in the chase down Inner Party streets, came back in full force. The doors closed, and all sound vanished. Even when the chamber moved, the machinery's working was scarcely audible; it was more like a silent vibration. Or perhaps the lift *wasn't* moving. She strained her ears, and found herself imagining eternity spent in this odorless, soundless chamber with only the white-jacketed man for company. His hair had been oiled flat, and the comb had left stiff pathways in it. Could that man ever have fucked?

When the lift doors opened, at first she didn't understand what she saw. There was no lift bay, no corridor with doors on either side. Instead she was looking at a high-ceilinged room with four armchairs and a low glass table: the lift opened into the flat itself! An Eastasian servant in a snow-white jacket waited there, silhouetted in gentle light. This man had the upright posture of a soldier, and his eyes were alive with intelligence, but his face had a queer immobility. As a child, she'd seen a man who'd had plastic surgery after a plane crash, and although that man was left disfigured and this one had very regular features, the effect was similar. It was as if the face had melted into a new shape and stiffened as it cooled.

The man turned wordlessly, and she followed him into a larger room whose size and elegance gave her a fresh thrill of fear. It had cream-papered walls and white wainscoting, every inch of it as spotless as the servant's coat. From the ceiling hung a chandelier. It was unlit, but its tiers of crystals glittered in the last sunlight. The air was scented with fresh-cut flowers, set out in vases everywhere, and from another room came the song of a canary, doodling around ineffectually. Most of one wall was taken up by an enormous window, in which the towers and ruins of Outer Party London showed in a hazy gray-red sunset. One could even see a shining stretch of the Thames with its complement of little prole boats. All was alien, impossible, the only familiar note the tinny burble of the telescreen. But as she thought this, the servant casually went to the telescreen and turned it off. Not down—off! She thought feebly that here was the malfunction. One oughtn't to be able to turn it off. At the same time, she knew there was no broken telescreen. There would be no pretense at a broken telescreen. All such games were done.

O'Brien was sitting comfortably on a settee of black leather, his long legs stretched before him. He was larger than Julia remembered, or perhaps being alone with him made her more conscious of his size. His posture was alert, with the ease of an athlete who might at any moment spring into action. He wasn't wearing his spectacles. His face was nakedly ugly. Still, in him, the snub nose and knuckle-like brow bones seemed the only proper features for a man.

The servant went to sit somewhere behind her. She wanted to see where he went, but couldn't take her eyes from O'Brien. She thought of asking to use the lavatory, although she didn't need it—anything to be away from O'Brien. She thought of creeping out of the lavatory window, and whether there might be a way to climb down. She thought of asking that the tele-screen be switched back on. The silence was suffocating. It was particularly dreadful, somehow, that no one would see what became of her.

O'Brien's eyes rested on her. He still hadn't spoken. He hadn't stirred.

At last she cleared her throat and said, "I received a note that said I must come at this time. And Comrade Syme said you wanted a repair. That is, I was asked once before, but I sent a comrade in my place, as we thought she was better at the work. I do hope that wasn't wrong. If I oughtn't to be here, of course . . . I'd never want to disturb you."

At this, the servant made a sound that might have been a scoff or a laugh. She glanced back at him but found him gazing at O'Brien with no expression at all. Then, with a jolt of panic, she realized she'd taken her eyes off O'Brien. She looked back and found him smiling.

"You are afraid," O'Brien said. "You are thinking I know every secret you have sought to hide, every disloyal thought, every treasonous speech. You are thinking I know you are a sex criminal, that you trade in black-market goods, that you collude at the treason of others. You are thinking you must be killed for these crimes."

Julia stared at him, in a fear beyond fear. All the strength had gone from her legs. His ugly face seemed to float quite apart from the harmless things of the room, to be the secret meaning of the world. When he smiled again, she felt it in her throat.

He went on, "You are right. I know you more intimately than you can imagine. I have watched over you for seven years. I have been your companion in every moment of doubt, every crime, every treasonous speech." He let the smile ease from his face and said gravely, "You are quite wrong, though, to be afraid. If what I wanted was to destroy you, I might have done it at any time. And now—you are less in danger now than you have ever been in your life."

This speech left her more petrified than before. When such a man told you not to be afraid, you must die. She couldn't hold his gaze and looked away at a painting beside her of a great brown horse, very thick-bodied on its delicate legs. She'd never seen a horse that shape; in the SAZ, all horses were skin and bones. She had loved them and wept when they were killed for meat. She would die without seeing another.

"You are not to be harmed," said a new voice, one so harsh it seemed to come from no living thing. She shuddered and looked at the servant. Yes, it was he. In the strange, immobile face, his eyes were amused and kind.

"Martin does not speak lightly," said O'Brien. "So you may take this as a fact. You are not to be harmed. You will believe this, I hope, before you leave this room. You are one of our people and no one can harm you again. This I can promise. Now, sit." He gestured toward an armchair. "We have a great deal to discuss."

The armchair was upholstered in pale yellow fabric, and was quite the cleanest piece of furniture Julia had ever seen. She perched on it with a painful self-consciousness. Instinctively she looked at the servant, and found him gazing at O'Brien with a look of candid affection. O'Brien met his eye, and some thought passed between them that made both smile. It was this that first eased Julia's nerves—that O'Brien could inspire that wordless friendliness. Then the quiet of the flat and its spring-like air, the inconsequential voice of the canary, asserted themselves. Of course no violence was done in this room. While she was here, at least, she was safe.

O'Brien said, "You may ask whatever questions you have."

She said tentatively, "May I ask..."

"Whatever you like. The telescreen has been turned off. We are quite among ourselves."

She hesitated another moment, then said, "How can I be one of your people? You said yourself that I'm a criminal."

"I think you must trust me to know who I am dealing with. And of course you have worked with us before. That counts for a very great deal with us."

It took a moment for Julia to understand. Then she was unable to prevent her face from becoming a mask of tragedy.

He said, "You don't wear the badge. The Hero of the Socialist Family."

She shrugged. "One can't."

"Yes, it isn't understood by the average person. You would be feared. You would be hated."

"Yes."

"Julia, what do you think of those who would hate you for what you did? Please, you must say exactly what you think. I shall know if you don't."

She said plainly, "They don't know what it's like. It's very easy to judge what you don't understand. They think themselves superior, but they don't know."

"They have never been faced with a choice so difficult."

"Yes. They don't know how they would act. They have parents living, many of them. They can visit their parents. They have never felt the need to—you know."

"To denounce a mother."

"Yes."

He nodded. "They are like children still."

"Yes. They're like children. In that way, anyway."

"I see you think it cruel. To make a child condemn its own parent—yes, many people think it cruel."

She said stiffly, "I know it is cruel."

"Perhaps you are right. But perhaps it is meant to be so. All great things are painful. We say that a child who makes that choice will never grow crooked. You chose the Party above all else at an age when such decisions are true signs. You betrayed a parent and killed her, knowing she would never understand, and all who knew you would condemn you. Few can do it. Fewer can do it and survive. You, Julia—you have thrived."

She was almost fatally distracted by the realization that here was something O'Brien didn't know. He knew all Julia had done in London, but what had happened with her mother, in the SAZ, with Gerber—that he didn't know. There had been no telescreens there, and all who remembered it were dead.

O'Brien went on, "You want to ask what was done to your mother. I will tell you. She died as such people die. It is long. It is all the worst things you can imagine. It is worse—there are things only we can conceive. But of course you knew this already. That knowledge has been with you all your life. It was with you when you made the choice. So I must ask: Would you choose differently now?"

Her mind was swarming. For a moment, she didn't dare speak. Then she thought of the question narrowly and was able to say without falsehood, "No, I would do the very same. I could do nothing else."

He nodded. "That is right. You would do the same. And why do we prize that choice so highly?"

"Loyalty," she said stiffly. "It proves loyalty to the Party."

"No."

She looked at him in surprise. "But why—"

"Why else would we ask a thing so monstrous?"

She frowned, then nodded. "I can't see why."

"If we ask such things of children, it is not because we are in any doubt about someone's loyalty. We can tell loyalty from treason as easily as we tell day from night. Nor is it that the criminals can't be unmasked without such help. In every case, we have seen the parent for a criminal long before the child makes his report. Yet we wait for that report, even if it means the criminal lives in freedom for a very long time.

"Why do we do this? It is for what you have become. You were a person like others around you, a fatuous creature that called its weakness virtue. But by this choice, you were transformed. Through the years that followed, the years of hiding what your fellows called a crime but you knew to be courage, you were transformed. It is how a lump of coal is changed to a diamond, by pressures that deform and crush it. No diamond can be made without this violence. It is what a diamond is.

"You do not yet know your strength, not yet. But you are more than a woman; more indeed than a man. You are *Homo oceanicus*, the race yet to come. In our work, every one of us has made such a choice. It is the choice that we call Love."

As he said it, she felt it could be true. She *was* stronger than others. After all, she'd escaped the SAZ when no others could. She had become a member of the Party, though her parents were both criminals. She had found work at one of the big four Ministries. She sat now in front of O'Brien of Love and hadn't begged or cried, hadn't said a wrong thing. Yes, she was a diamond. She would live.

O'Brien said, "Do you know the fifth goodstory of Big Brother Thought?"

"Of course," she said. "We recited the goodstories every morning at school."

"Can you say it for me now?"

At first, she was afraid her boast would be proved hollow. Then the schoolroom flooded back to her: the fear of caning, the cold and the stink of latrines, the desperate need to get every word right, and then she was able to recite: "This is the fifth goodstory of Big Brother Thought. Here begins our learning; here ends our resistance. A prole was arrested for raising rebellion among the workers of a district. He was brought before the District Party Chairman by the union leaders.

"The Chairman said, 'What charges are you bringing against this man?'

"The union leaders answered, 'If he were not a criminal, we would not have handed him over to you.'

"The Chairman said, 'So take him yourselves and judge him by your own rules.'

"The union leaders objected, 'No, he must be executed, and we have no right to execute anyone.'

"The Chairman then went into the Palace of the People and had the accused prole brought to him. He asked him, 'Are you the king of the proles?'

"'Is that your own idea,' said the prole, 'or did others talk to you about me?'

"'Am I a prole?' the Chairman replied. 'Your own people handed you over to me. What is it you have done?'

"The prole said, 'You say that I am a king. In fact, the reason I was born and came into the world is to testify to the truth. Everyone on the side of truth listens to me.'

"The Chairman said, 'What is Truth?'"

Here O'Brien, who had been listening intently, leaned forward to ask, "And how did the prole answer?"

"He had no answer," said Julia. "Anyway, none is given in the story."

"And did the Chairman spare him? Since the prole wished only to speak the truth?"

"No, the prole was given to the executioners. He was flogged and made to wear a crown of thorns and nailed to a gibbet, where he died. And the Chairman washed his hands and forgot."

"So why did the Chairman punish the prole so harshly?"

"It was wrongthink and dissemination of wrongthink. It was speakcrime in a public setting."

"Yes, but why is wrongthink deserving of such a cruel penalty? Answer for yourself, Julia. Why do we punish these crimes with such a death?"

"Well, I really couldn't say. I'm not a bit intellectual."

At this, O'Brien and Martin both burst out laughing. Julia flinched, saying, "No, it's true! I never thought!"

"But you did think," O'Brien said. "You were thinking just now. You thought the man needn't be killed."

"Well, perhaps. But it's just a story. It's easy to be sorry for a criminal in a story, as he can't harm you. It's not real life."

"That's true. I should call that a very wise observation. Yes, I think we may find that you are rather more 'intellectual' than you say. But let us test your hypothesis. Let us suppose our prole king is a real person. For instance, Winston Smith."

Now Julia saw where this had been heading, and felt a sick

weight in her stomach. Of course it couldn't pass without a victim. O'Brien was death. These were the rites of death.

O'Brien said, "You must answer honestly, Julia. I shall know it if you do not."

She said cautiously, "Well, Smith isn't king of anyone. Has Smith any power, I mean?"

"None."

"So he might be exiled. Or taught to know better. That is—I don't know. I'm only a mechanic."

"Shall I tell you why he must be killed?"

Again she felt the sick weight. But she said, "Yes, please."

"You have been taught that the prole king in the goodstory stands for Emmanuel Goldstein. In fact, there have been countless Goldsteins and countless states that faced these Goldsteins. Goldstein has had a million names and worn a million faces, but always he believes he fights for truth.

"Truth! How the terrorists love that word! First they dream of giving their lives for it—that is how the sickness begins. Of course, at this point, it remains a fantasy. Our fledgling terrorist does not think to really sacrifice himself. In fact, he goes to his job as before, does his work, and appears like everyone else.

"But soon truth demands the blood of others. It is at this stage that dreams turn into action. The terrorist is driven to find others like himself. Once they have gathered in a cell, the truth-lovers will not rest until they have their blood. They will commit acts of sabotage that cause the deaths of hundreds of innocents. They will betray their country to enemy powers, bring hostile armies to their own cities to blight and kill and rape. They will commit every low crime, too—cheat, forge documents, blackmail, corrupt the minds of children, distribute habit-forming drugs, encourage prostitution, spread venereal diseases—anything to harm those people they see as obstacles to truth. If it might somehow serve the cause of truth to throw acid into the face of a child, the truth-lover will happily do it.

"They hate doublethink—so they say. But they will readily lie for truth. In fact, a truth-lover will assume a false identity and live in it all his life, even marrying and fathering children to whom he never speaks a truthful word—all in the hope of someday killing them for truth.

"All this may seem incredible to you, but a Goldstein Brother will boast openly of these intentions. What is truth? It is acid in the face of a child. It is a father who schemes to murder his family. It is every atrocity of the Eurasian horde, brought to our doorsteps."

He paused and asked, "Does this seem unbelievable to you?"

"I suppose," she said cautiously. "I can't see why anyone would want such things."

He nodded, approving her candor. "In time, you will hear a devotee of truth confirm this from his own mouth. Then you may judge for yourself what moves him. For now, let us say it is insanity. We have made a study of this sickness and can now spot it in the early stages. We know the least flaw of this type leads to homicidal madness."

"You don't think—I haven't got this sickness?"

Again both men laughed warmly.

O'Brien said, "No. You are immune. That is why you are so valuable to us. You are proof against all lunacy. You can safely commit the crimes of pleasure—in you, they are even healthy. That is the mark of *Homo oceanicus*. In time, all people will be so. Already, all those of the Inner Party can boast of this immunity. But of course you too will be of the Inner Party in time."

As he said it, his eyes subtly moved to acknowledge their surroundings. She sat up straighter, trying not to show how this arrow had found its mark. Again she was conscious of the elegance of the flat, its sweeping view, its finer air. Could she belong in such a place? Now she felt she could. Already it was inconceivable that she must return to the hostel, with its noise and rats and stink of chamber pots. She could sit at a window like that, alone, and smoke an Inner Party cigarette as night fell. She could have a spaniel that napped at her feet. She could wear black cotton overalls, fitted to her body, and wash them in a clothes washing machine. She tried to imagine what sort of bed the flat had—but this turned into a vision of Julia spread-eagled on a bed while O'Brien approached her, unzipping his overalls, a merciless expression in his eyes. Yes, he was ugly, he was dreadful to her. But if—

"You lack only one thing to be a fit mother of the race. Shall I tell you what it is?"

She was brought back to reality with a jolt. "Oh—yes, please. Do tell me." Her voice came out hoarse, as if she were freshly woken from sleep.

O'Brien met her eyes with a hardness that was new. He said, "You do not hate."

Julia's first impulse was to brush this aside. She'd performed the rites of hate acceptably since she was a child. She had stabbed and burned dummies. She had burned books. She had screamed and chanted and sung Hate Songs. She had even once denounced a schoolmate and joined in the ritual pummeling that ensued. She'd taken part in pummelings when others denounced schoolmates or fellows in the Youth Leagues. Perhaps she had done it half-heartedly, but was she so much more half-hearted than anyone else?

"You do not hate," O'Brien repeated. "You are the healthiest mind I have ever encountered. You have none of the mental perversion of the truth-seeker; none of the ersatz virtue of the weak. But you must learn to hate, or all this is for naught. It will burn away like tinder." He smiled again. "But it is always the work that is the best teacher. We will put you to work, and you will learn.

"Now, you have made a very good start with Smith, so you may continue there. We are interested in that psychology, and he is very safe, very compliant. He shall be your training subject. We will give you time to get used to the work, and you will have a space to use."

Here he paused and seemed to think, gazing into the air. Julia put in timidly, "Yes, I don't mind Smith. I am quite used to him. But what—"

"Yes." O'Brien nodded with a faint impatience, only half listening. "And you shall bring other men in, just as you can. Thomas Parsons, there's one. You have had him before. Then Alfred Syme you could easily get. Any man from Records would be useful. And of course you will not be alone in the work. I will put you in the hands of a very good man. He is the one whom you call Weeks."

Julia frowned. "The man at the junk shop?"

"Yes. He is already known to Smith. That is helpful. You yourself know the place and can find it on your own. Go tomorrow; he will expect you. And don't worry, we wish you only to do what you already do. There will be nothing difficult, nothing strange. But you must do it for the Party, not against it."

"You mean I am to work—well, not as a mechanic."

"As a whore."

This he said factually, as if it were of only practical consequence. Then he nodded to Martin and the man rose to his feet and went from the room without a backward glance. Julia knew immediately what must come next. She was electrically aware of O'Brien's strong frame, of the big hands resting on his knees. There was relief in it. It was what she understood. Perhaps they would do it on the floor, right here. There might be some refinement of cruelty or humiliation—some first teaching in hate. She could bear that easily. He would beckon her wordlessly from her seat. Then she must stand and obediently take her zip down. Or he would say it: "I am going to fuck you now, Julia." She was a whore, she was only a whore, after all. What else could Julia give?

But O'Brien didn't move from his place. He said, without the least change in manner, "Our time is almost done. After this, we may not meet again. It is of the utmost importance that no one realizes your connection to us. So if you have any other question, you must ask it now."

At first, all Julia understood was that he didn't want her. The humiliation struck her belatedly, as if he'd only now called her a whore. She was to be sent back into the street. The dream was over. She would walk to the bus stop, scorned by Inner Party women and their servants. At the hostel, she would drink ersatz tea, then sleep in the stink of chamber pots. She would wake in the morning and go to the Ministry—for of course, she wouldn't be excused from her old duties. Work would be piled on work.

And she would be a thing of Love, of murder—never again would she be anything else.

But as she thought it, she remembered Martin. What must that man have done for O'Brien in his years of service? And yet Julia hadn't disliked him. For all his strangeness, she had trusted him. Was he worse than Winston? No, she didn't feel that. So one could do this work, perhaps, without being quite bad. And *he* was Inner Party; or lived in these spaces as if he was. So that part might be true. At the same time, she felt it was a thing she couldn't do—to make love to a man as a means of killing him. But if she admitted this now, she would die, and that too seemed impossible. No, she must go forward and see what came of it. There was always the chance that something would change—Love would have second thoughts about hiring her, or possibly Julia would die in an accident. Perhaps O'Brien would die.

Then she remembered that O'Brien was waiting for her question. She wanted to ask how many men she must "bring in." She wanted to ask if they all must die, or if some might redeem themselves. She wanted foolishly to ask if she could still say no, if she could go back to her machines and her hostel, give up being Inner Party forever, and still be let to live.

But these were not the questions O'Brien wanted. She was not that fool.

She said, "Can you tell me—what is hate?"

He smiled. "Very good: you have begun."

12

JULIA KILLED HER MOTHER IN '73, A YEAR WHEN, IN London, there was no hunger. From Hesham village, to Julia's knowledge, she was the only one who survived.

It began, as great horrors always begin, with a change to the Party platform. Agriculture was to be put on a rational basis. Party cadres were dispatched to the countryside by the Ministry of Plenty to oversee this change. These cadres were called Plentymen by the locals, and at fourteen, like most village girls, Julia looked forward to their arrival. They were imagined to be like the Party youth sent to the SAZ on voluntary work details. The "vols" pitched tents in the fields, and SAZ girls haunted them day and night, fascinated by the boys with their lordly stature and the girls with their stylish short haircuts and scent of Socialist Purity soap.

When a SAZ girl had a vol boyfriend, she called him her Romeo, after the hero of a popular play in which an Inner Party boy eloped with a prole girl. In the play, this led to a general slaughter. The last scene showed the local Party chairman standing in a litter of corpses, bewailing the corrosive effect of sex and the carnage it brought in its wake. For the girls of the SAZ, though, all that mattered was the scene where the lovers had secretly married and corrosively romped in bed together. This was treated as historical fact, while the ending of the play was doubted. All knew such stories got rewritten by the Party eggheads. The real Romeo and Juliet might have moved to London and had ten children. One did hear of Party men marrying proles, or even classless girls like themselves. A popular legend told of a SAZ girl who'd had her wedding in the Crystal Palace itself; at the peak of the festivities, Big Brother himself had given her her Party card. None of the girls believed such tales, not exactly, but all were happy to repeat them. They were only careful never to do it when a vol might overhear.

All expected Plentymen to be stricter about Party dogma than vols, but this did not dismay the girls. Rather, in preparation, they were seized with revolutionary fervor. A new youth study group was formed, at which the meaning of Big Brother's Maxims was discussed. On Sunday nights, the girls terrorized the village with their patriotic caroling, going from door to door singing "Rule, Oceania!" and "The People's Flag," and expecting to be rewarded with cups of Victory tea. Like other children of "boots," Julia must now submit to group criticism, in which the other girls filed past her and snarled accusations in her face. An hour later, however, this was forgotten, and all sat chattering happily together while embroidering handkerchiefs with Party slogans.

Julia had always privately considered the vol boys disappointing stuff—slender-armed and flimsy, with accents like a limp handshake. They also made her feel dirty and coarse as the airmen never did. She was once admiring a vol girl's white, manicured hands, when the girl insisted on seeing Julia's, saying she was sure they were lovely, only to fall silent with a stricken face on seeing Julia's chilblains and broken nails. Still, Julia went to the tents with the others. She allowed a vol girl to cut her hair and the boys to instruct her in socialist dance. She was infected, too, with the general enthusiasm at the Plentymen's arrival. The day Comrade Gerber was to arrive on the farm, she washed herself all over and wore her only presentable frock.

Gerber was to be billeted on Mrs. Marcy and to preside over four adjacent farms. When his train was heard, all those soon to be under his rule assembled in Mrs. Marcy's yard. Since, for SAZ boys, military conscription now began at fifteen, almost all were women, mostly of the kind who traveled to the countryside when the picking seasons started, then in winter were reabsorbed into the slums of various towns and cities. Julia's mother, Clara, said of such women that you could safely hit them in the face with a brick if you didn't mind what happened to the brick. There were also the four farm directors in their shiny-elbowed committee suits, a few young milkmaids and elderly farmhands, and Mrs. Marcy's two resident airmen. These already regarded the newcomer with suspicion, predicting he would cause "no end of bother," and saying that, if he turned out to be a Yank, they would carry him to the pond and drown him.

At last the man himself was spotted, striding up the path with a railway worker behind him carrying his two suitcases. Comrade Gerber turned out to be a heavyset, middle-aged man with a hearty look and scarred, used hands. The blue overalls of Outer Party workers were still made of thick cotton then, and his had been tailored to flatter his robust figure. He carried himself with a certain rigid importance, as if he were part stone.

His first act was to summon all the workers to a speech in the disused parlor. This was a place of various ruin. It had once been the lair of Mrs. Marcy's brother-in-law, who'd come back "not quite right" from the war. Marcy never washed, and often drank himself into unconsciousness and pissed himself, so the room had an indelible gamey smell. He also liked to vent his feelings by striking about himself with a hoe, so the floorboards were torn and splintered, the walls gashed. Several panes of the windows had been broken, then mended with tape that was now brown with age and curling at the edges. On one of his difficult nights, Marcy had taken a sledgehammer to the mantelpiece and left it half destroyed. The larger marble chunks had been left lying about through a negligence that seemed somehow native to the room. Marcy had finally reenlisted and died—heroically, it was assumed—in Africa, and the room was now the province of seasonal workers, who slept on bedrolls on its floor in the company of various farm equipment. The parlor was regarded as belonging to the out-of-doors, and no one would have thought of cleaning it, any more than they would have thought to wash the pastures or scrub down the trees.

Comrade Gerber's suitcases were the new revolutionary type, made of bright blue polymer. He kicked the larger of the two on its side and stood atop it to address the workers. He began by lamenting the degraded state of the room in which they were standing, calling it "the very symbol" of the state of farming in SAZ-5. He spoke of decadence, corrosion, treason; of proletarians and soldiers who starved because of the crimes of bourgeois-capitalist elements in the Semi-Autonomous Zones. These attacks on the revolution, he said, had been tolerated far too long. As he spoke, his eye dwelled unpleasantly on Mrs. Marcy, who stared back, refusing to be cowed. The temporary workers smirked, and Julia, who'd been chagrined to find Comrade Gerber so old, now decided he could be liked. This good impression was strengthened when his pale eye paused on her and his face changed subtly in appreciation.

That week, all were set to putting the offending room in order. Even the floorboards had to be replaced and the walls replastered. The next days saw new tasks, invented by Gerber to remedy the wrongful habits of Mrs. Marcy and her ilk. All routine was overturned and a holiday atmosphere prevailed.

Gerber's ability to obtain goods like timber and plaster elevated him in the workers' eyes, though his ignorance of farming soon became manifest, and some orders had to be tactfully ignored so as not to kill the blameless livestock. Even this ended happily, however, as Gerber never noticed. Only Mrs. Marcy and Clara looked bleak, and the cows, who were always sensitive to upset and change, milked poorly.

Gerber moved into Mrs. Marcy's bedroom and set up the restored parlor as his office. All the best pieces of furniture migrated to these rooms, and Clara and Julia were set to sewing curtains for his windows. Mrs. Marcy now slept in the attic with the airmen (Julia had volunteered to undergo this hardship, but was ignored). The temporary workers made their beds where they could—in the yard, in the barn, beneath the dining table. The airmen no longer presided over dinnertimes with their jokes and scurrilous stories; they'd persisted at first, but Gerber kept interrupting to point out their errors of thought. Now everyone spent mealtimes listening to him hold forth about socialist husbandry. This annoyed Julia less than she would have expected, as he peppered this talk with descriptions of London's skyscrapers and commissars, and addressed many of his comments directly to her. She also never tired of his exotic accent. He was a Scouser, Gerber had explained at his first meal, then thrillingly winked at Julia and said he might be trusted nonetheless.

The greatest fascination of Gerber, however, was the marvelous things in his rooms. There were shiny magazines with pictures, satin sashes Julia was allowed to rub against her cheek, a chess set with pieces made of real ivory. There was a framed photograph of Gerber with the Minister of Plenty, and another in which he stood in an array of dapper Plentymen in front of the Crystal Palace. When the village began to be hungry, there was always tinned meat and biscuits with real sugar, which Gerber served to her daintily on Mrs. Marcy's willow-pattern china. Most wonderful of all were the fruit cakes sent by his sister each month in bright-red tins. A fire was always lit in the cold of the night, and Gerber always seemed to be awake, working at his desk on his marvelous typewriter—the first machine Julia ever learned to repair. She adopted the habit of visiting him in the unreal hour before the cows were milked, and he would tell her stories of London until she felt he'd promised to take her there. He showed her photographs of Westminster compound, and told tales of the ingenuity and kindness of the high officials. She closed her eyes and thought of airmen while he touched her under her clothes. He would say at these times, "Let's see ... let's see..." Afterward he always gave her food, and it was he who secured her the post of secretary of the Youth League, with the extra rations that entailed. If she thought of hope or comfort, she thought of Gerber. The sexual pleasure, too, was a revelation; he might as well have taught her to levitate. It didn't matter that she had to close her eyes and pretend he was an airman. It didn't matter that she sometimes couldn't bear his hands on her and trembled with the need to stop him. All that was only psychology, Gerber explained, which was healthy in a girl but must be restrained. In later years, she would have no memory of Gerber taking her virginity, only of going to the cowshed after, and how she put her hand between her legs and was disappointed to find no blood. She had milked her cows and told Big Brother a version in which she horribly bled.

In the day, there were times when the sight of Gerber disgusted and unnerved her. She couldn't then believe all that had happened: that she'd seen that body naked, that she'd let him touch her between her legs. It was a thing outside of life. But again in the predawn hour, she would wake in excitement and go to his door. She would knock with fingernails only. He would call her in and she was ready, the look on her face so plain he sometimes laughed. He said, "What am I to do with you?" and then, "Let's see ... let's see ..."

There were mornings, too, when he talked to Julia as if she were a friend. He confided in her about his quarrels with his sister, asking her to give "the woman's viewpoint." He spoke of his loneliness in Hesham, and the unjust prejudice he faced. When he was allocating quotas to his four farms, he asked Julia for advice, as one familiar with the place, and she went along with it importantly, pretending more knowledge than she had. All this she found enthralling; she would remember the wise remarks she had made to Gerber and feel power.

When it later turned out the quotas were too high for any-one to fulfill, and the villagers began to suffer hunger, it didn't occur to her that it was strange to let agricultural quotas be set by a child. She only lived in terror that her neighbors would learn she was responsible. The guilt clung to her long after she'd understood that, whatever she'd said, the result would be that all the grain was taken, that every ounce of milk was taken, that every chicken was counted and expected to lay its daily egg, which would be packed in Party cartons and removed by Party vans; that even vegetable gardens and single fruit trees would be inventoried, and their produce removed as it was picked, and any worker who took a bite from a pear arrested for sabotage.

Of course, it was promised that the locals' needs would be met by the Party. To this end, a new commissary was opened, and ration coupons were issued for one hundred and fifteen classes of goods. But most days the building stood empty. The only items that ever reliably appeared were bread and a hard, unusable kind of soap, and the bread ran out within hours. Schoolchildren were now excused from class when the delivery trucks arrived, as parents couldn't be excused from work, and otherwise the family would lose their rations. All raced pell-mell to be first to the doors, and vicious fights broke out for precedence.

There was also food that was for children alone; this became of greater and greater importance as the year progressed. Some days the students were sent into the woods to gather rose hips, which could be boiled to make a nourishing syrup, or acorns, which could be soaked, then ground into a kind of flour. The Youth Leagues dispensed supplementary foods—anything from powdered eggs to dried currants to a nutritional paste called chicken essence, which all knew was made of worms. One week, there was real meat, with a cat's face on the tin and writing in some Eurasian tongue. A girl suggested it was made of cats, but the opinion of those who believed the cat was only a mascot prevailed, and the children ate it without a qualm. All the food—the acorns as well as the catmeat—could only be consumed on the premises by the children themselves. The mistress felt underneath their armpits and down their legs before they left to ensure no one had secreted food about their person. To take these "state resources" home to a starving parent was theft.

There had been a time when the local prison camps were a world apart. Stories were whispered of the horrors within, and of the beastly crimes that merited such treatment. Children crept to the fence sometimes to listen to the amplified announcements or to poke sticks through the wire at the raging dogs. The tall fence itself, festooned with barbed wire, was an object of fascination, and boys vied to explain to each other how they would easily escape. Sometimes prisoners could be seen at a distance, engaged in incomprehensible business, or a column of new inmates was seen being marched in from the station. When one could get close enough to make out their features, they looked satisfyingly disreputable—their skin reddened and visibly dirty, their hair crudely shaven, their faces gaunt and dull. Some had a dragging, rocking gait and a stupid look, and the children told each other authoritatively that these ones would soon die; this was the condition called "last legs." Such prisoners weren't the monsters of propaganda. Still, one wouldn't call them men.

But in the drive to meet the new quotas, more and more prisoners were sent out to work on the farms. They were always on the roads, being marched to and fro, looking comical in their striped pajamas. The villagers learned to tell politicals from ordinary criminals, and criminals from POWs. POWs were favored as workers, as politicals were too weak to do a day's work, and criminals had often paid off their guards and acted with impunity. Indeed, POWs were generally petted, as they reminded locals of their own sons and husbands lost to war. Some criminals, too, were popular: they were terrible rascals, everyone knew, but they'd had hard lives and were good for a laugh. Even some politicals were invited for cups of tea in the kitchen and pronounced good lads. Opinions began to be shared in the village about which men were rightly imprisoned and which (the majority) should be set free. Several local houses came to be decorated with the drawings of one young POW, showing views of his native Lisbon. When two criminals were shot for pilfering chicken feed, the villagers grumbled at the cruelty, where they once might have approved. By this time, some villagers themselves had reddened, scaly skin and showed the dragging gait of "last legs."

As winter closed in, the first villagers began to die—the old, the infirm, infants whose mothers' milk had dried up. When a baby went missing from a field—the prey of stray dogs, said his mother—many suspected he had really been devoured by his own family. Now the Youth Leagues stopped receiving shipments of tinned meat and chicken essence, and, when children foraged in the forest, the definition of food was expanded to include every crawling thing. Julia herself was ravenous all the time. There were days when a slice of Gerber's fruit cake was all she had to eat.

About this time, a group of village boys who were approaching conscription age disappeared into the woods. A few crims escaped to join their ranks, and now the village grew dangerous after dark. One night a window at Marcy's farm was broken; the burglars crept inside, stole the little food they found in the cupboards, smashed a table in the parlor, and pissed on Gerber's armchair. The airmen thought it a joke and called the invaders "wild young devils," but Gerber and Mrs. Marcy were united for once in being shaken and darkly saying it would end in violence. Indeed the bandits grew bolder and more cruel. Soon, when people were robbed on the roads, even their clothes and shoes were taken, and those who resisted were savagely beaten. Once a girl staggered home having endured worse. People said then it was a funny sort of rebellion, to rob the weak and dishonor women. Still, when the bandits were rounded up at last and three of their leaders publicly hanged, the crowds at the execution were ominously silent.

The other bandits weren't shot but sent to camps. Some turned up working in the fields again in the familiar striped pajamas. The camp had once been a hell beyond imagining. Now it was the neighboring settlement where some of Julia's school friends lived.

There was a time when one could regard these events as a crisis that must end—and then there was a time when one could not. For Julia, this was marked by the hangings at the airfield.

She remembered only one such scene; she knew there had been others. The audience was all women and children. Some women wept openly; one knew these were the condemned men's sweethearts. The gallows could only accommodate three, but seven were to be hanged that day, and everyone had to wait while one set of bodies was taken down to make room for the next. When the condemned men were made to help with this work, a woman in the crowd cried out, "Shame!" Then the guards turned their guns on the crowd. It seemed especially cruel that the last airman must still help, and then be hanged alone. What Julia remembered particularly was how the bodies spun gently at the ends of the ropes, and the wind ruffled their hair as if they were alive.

Another memory from this time was of the night Julia first hallucinated from hunger. Gerber was on her, pressing and groping, a thing that could still give her pleasure, but now the pleasure was malign. He put his hand over her throat as he sometimes did, and the choking weight of his thick hand and the tiring misery of fear overwhelmed her. She found herself floating on the ceiling, looking down at the wriggling, obscene figures. She thought, *That girl is starving*, and found it funnier than anything in the world. When she thought: *But the man will die before her*, the little figure of the naked girl below began to gaspingly laugh. The man's hand closed on her throat, and Julia was back in her body, having an intense orgasm.

This memory was worse than the memory of the hangings. She always carefully thought of it as something that might have really happened to someone else.

By this time, the daily Two Minutes Hate had been introduced in the SAZ. They had no telescreens, so this consisted of someone standing in a field reading the day's hate column from the *Times* while the workers shrieked in rage. One could hear the screams and the concluding chant of "B-B!" from one farm to another, never quite in synchrony. The more distant ones sounded thin and unconvincing. That spurred one on to greater vehemence.

Julia's friends had invented a related game of spinning around with eyes shut while chanting "B-B!" She who lasted longest would become a Party member and go to London, fabled as a place of ease and abundance. The first part of the game consisted of each girl deciding what her first meal would be on arrival in the city. One day Julia was spinning, feeling weightless, indefatigable, and went on long after the others stopped chanting. When she opened her eyes to the blank white sky, a detail tickled the edge of her vision. She focused in sudden fright on a line of prisoners staring from the top of a hill. They were the scarecrow figures of those last days, their clothes hanging empty as if there were no bodies inside at all. Their faces were yellow and weirdly bloated. One man's tongue lolled from a toothless mouth, bright red where his gums were bleeding. He was making repetitive bowing movements, both hands lodged in his crotch. But it wasn't a man. It was a woman. The figures were skeletal, shaven, toothless women. At that moment, one of the other girls screamed. Then Julia breathlessly screamed and all the girls ran off in terror. They were pursued by an unearthly sound, the lovely, ringing laugh of a quite young girl. Julia looked about wildly but couldn't find its source. Only later in the evening did she realize it must have come from one of the prisoners.

This memory was tied to another in which one of those emaciated women emerged from the cowshed with a pitchfork over her shoulder, bent and weaving from exhaustion. She was breathing heavily through her mouth, which hung open, so her missing front teeth and bleeding gums were visible. This woman didn't have a shaven head, but her hair was falling out, showing broad strips of chapped scalp. This wasn't a prisoner. It was Julia's mother. The sight filled Julia with agony and shame and a treacherous resolve to escape such things—to go somewhere where she never need see them. At the same time, she thought that she must get food to her mother somehow—from Gerber, from the woods—from the meager resources she still had. But when she inspected these ideas more closely, each of them crumbled into futility. She was visited by the desperate thought of offering to feed her mother on her own flesh.

There was also a damp spring night, very near to the end, when Julia and Clara were out in the fields, alone, and Julia's mother spoke about Big Brother. "He can't be as young as they show him, but that's his real face. I should know it. It was always the same hundred people at those protests, before it got properly going. He wasn't anybody at the time, not yet, but he was older than we were, so he was noticed. Once, on a hot day, I offered him a bottle of pear juice, but I can't remember if he drank from it."

"You've never spoken of it before," Julia said.

"No. If I'd wanted to say he shone like the sun and all went in awe of him, I might have. But it wasn't about Big Brother then, or any other particular man. That was rather the point, I thought. But once they had power—well, then it was a throne, and all fought for the throne. Michael, too." She looked at Julia and added unnecessarily, "Your father."

"Surely *he* couldn't have won, though. He couldn't be Big Brother."

"Oh, I don't know about that. We think Big Brother so unique, but it might have been Michael, and made little difference. It might have been any of them. Well, not me." She laughed shortly. "It couldn't be me."

"It couldn't be a woman," Julia guessed.

"I don't say that. There was a woman then, Diana Winters. It could have been her. I can't think she's still alive."

"Was she very clever?"

"Clever, yes. Formidable. Icy Winters, we called her. She had very strange green eyes, like a cat's. Her tutor at Oxford, Kenilworth, said to me once, 'Doesn't one have the feeling Miss Winters would eat one down to the bone?' I thought it very funny such an old man would say a thing like that. We all feared Icy Winters dreadfully, but she did me a good turn once."

"What sort of good turn?"

"I had my period and I'd bled through my skirt. She told me and gave me her cardigan to tie about my waist. It doesn't sound much, but not many would have done it. Too embarrassed. Winters just said, 'Look here, you've bled on yourself. Take this.'"

Julia tried to imagine the scene—what sort of cardigan it would have been, what Oxford looked like. Big Brother had walked the streets in those times. He'd seen Clara. He'd taken a bottle of pear juice from her hand, or said to her, "No, thank you." Clara hadn't seen his greatness. It was funny to think a person could miss a thing as obvious as that.

Then Clara said in a different voice, "That Gerber. I wish you'd keep away from him. You're on a hiding to nothing there."

Julia tensed and turned away, filled with a sense of violation. Her mother hadn't the right to know. It was foul. That sort of creeping into all one's affairs—it was the capitalist generation all over.

She said bitingly, "Oh, you only hate him because he's a Party member."

Clara scoffed. "I like him better than you do. But I understand him and you don't."

"You don't know him at all. You think because he didn't go to Oxford he can't be clever."

"I know some girls are attracted to an old man like that. But if they don't marry you, you're the butt of the joke."

"I know he won't marry me. I'm not stupid."

"What's it about, then?"

"It's not about anything. You're just full of oldthink and anti-Party attitudes. All this rot about marriage and Oxford. If people heard how you talk. If I told them what—" Then Julia just stood trembling.

Clara touched Julia on the head—it wasn't quite a caress—and turned back to the house. She walked now with a lagging gait, and her feet were too swollen and covered in ulcers for shoes. She wrapped them in rags and plastic. They left weird, overlarge prints in the mud. Julia saw this without seeing it, and wanted to call her mother back. What Julia had said shouldn't count. It was Clara's fault if she'd been cruel. She didn't call. She only stood alone in the night for as long as she could bear it. Then she went back, instinctively stepping in Clara's footprints, trying to efface them with the crisp marks of her boots.

The starving winter passed. The time of sowing came, but no seed grain had been left, and the Party seed that had been promised never came. The fields were mud and weeds. New bandits appeared in the woods; these were rumored to kill people for their meat. The commissary was officially closed, and heavy chains were put on its doors. People decorated these with notes saying, *We are dying*, and *Have you no shame?* Livestock began to disappear; if one woke to the smell of meat, one hastily put on shoes and pursued the smell in the hope that the carcass would be shared. Correspondingly, the pace of arrests accelerated, and Hesham and the surrounding villages were designated an Area of Endemic Criminality. Every road out of the SAZ was closed, with makeshift roadblocks and trucks full of soldiers parked alongside. There were days, too, when swarms of Party activists and police descended on the village in jeeps, and went from house to house, dragging people out while the other villagers stared. Even Plentymen were being arrested; their ranks were said to have been infiltrated by bourgeois-capitalist conspirators. Without the depredations of these enemies, socialist husbandry would have doubled yields.

Striding among the gray, diminished villagers, the police and activists looked supernaturally thick-bodied, healthy and upright—godlike. One couldn't help admiring them. Sometimes the people they were coming to arrest would cheer them as they came. Other villagers abused the arrestees, cursing them as wreckers and parasites, and laughing sycophantically when one was beaten. This was not a matter of belief. It was because, if enough enthusiasm was shown, the Party activists gave out bread.

The night it ended, Julia was acting in the Youth League play. In a normal year, this play was one of the great events of spring. The airmen were given leave to attend, and the audience would also be swelled by vols, who would be in their first week of work. There was a stage in the Youth League clubroom, and by borrowing chairs from all over the village, they could create seating for eighty people. Arriving at an age to be given a part was a rite of passage for the local youth. This was Julia's first time.

The play was *The Sin of Big Brother*, in which an adolescent Big Brother comes to learn that pity is actually the greatest cruelty. Julia was playing Woman with Contagious Disease, a part that had thirty lines, and was thus a great coup for the daughter of a boot. For theatrical performances, girls were allowed to wear makeup, and Julia's costume was a cotton nightgown that was no more immodest than her usual clothes, but was white and had lace at the collar. In it, she thought herself beautiful.

The first disappointment of the evening was that there were no airmen in the audience. To add insult to injury, the opening lines were drowned out by a roar of planes taking off, and some in the audience rushed out to see. A little later, gunshots were heard, in the spaced, slow pattern all now recognized as executions. No one went out, but everyone became distracted, trying to pinpoint whether the sounds came from the airfield or Hesham village. Every change of wind carried awful smells. Even in a normal year this was a problem; a poignant line might be undercut by a sudden rude stink of manure. The smell now was of shallow graves. Often Julia breathed through her mouth, though the smell was so potent it then became a taste. A few parents were the only audience; they coughed pathetically and smelled of illness. Gerber wasn't there. Clara wasn't.

Julia said to the twelve-year-old playing Big Brother: "But I am weak and in pain. Can you not spare a bed? Oh, please, have pity!" He replied, "No, I cannot, for you will infect the workers. You bring death and poverty to the people. You are to be hated. That is love."

After the play, Julia walked home alone in her absurd nightgown. It was raining, and she looked up into the drizzle, imagining the makeup would run and she would look as if she'd been crying. She was thinking of food. This was now so involuntary and constant, it didn't really count as thinking; it was a process more like the falling of the rain. Gerber hadn't been at the play. That might mean he would give her no food. He'd been short with her lately and had even once slammed his door in her face.

The house was silent when she went in. Clara was at the kitchen table. This in itself was unnatural; Clara never sat indoors. She had Gerber's cake tin in front of her, her bony hand resting atop it. A fire was lit, a thing only Gerber was allowed, but Gerber would never light a fire in April. The kitchen was uncomfortably hot. There was a smell in the house that was new.

Clara told her daughter to sit down, then told her Gerber was dead. "He knew they were coming for him, so he's gone and shot himself. He's there in the attic. Don't go up." The police had come and gone, Clara said, and she noted with a smile of contempt that they'd offered no help in disposing of the corpse. "You thought me a prude for disapproving of your affair, but if they'd got him alive, that man would have given them your name in twenty seconds. He would have had them hang you without a second thought. Well, the man's done one thing well."

Then she said, very clearly and passionlessly, that everyone here would die. It was a camp now, or worse than a camp. All the people in the village were dead already. They were corpses that didn't know enough to lie down. Then she took both Julia's hands and explained to her what must be done. Clara said her old connections made her a high-value coin, a coin that Julia now must spend. She reminded Julia of her maiden name, a name she shared with a colonel who'd fought on the wrong side in the revolution. She now told Julia for the first time that this colonel was Clara's brother. She told Julia the crimes for which he could be blamed, and how Clara could be made to seem complicit. She listed the old revolutionaries she'd known who had since been shot as traitors. "It is they who gave me my orders. They planned this famine, and I helped execute it. You must remember that." She told Julia how to behave, the emotions she must feign, and Julia was too stunned to argue. Surely she would have argued, if she hadn't been stunned. But Clara gave her no time. When she wanted to object, Clara shook her head and opened the cake tin. She made Julia eat the last thick slab of fruit cake and dab up all the crumbs in the tin with her finger. Clara said, "The dead don't eat," and laughed. Then she put Gerber's thick wool coat on Julia—the dead did not wear coats—and walked her to the police station. At the edge of the station's lawn, Clara stopped and nodded Julia forward.

Julia walked over the grass in the chill, damp night, her stomach hurting with the unaccustomed meal. Only after she'd arrived at the station steps did she notice there was a footpath she should have taken. She looked back to check if her boots had marked the lawn and saw her mother shivering, unsteady on her feet. Clara was looking up at the few stars in the cloudy sky and hugging herself against the cold. Behind her, the low buildings of the village center were indistinct in mist. Clara saw her daughter looking and made an impatient gesture: *go on, go on.* Julia turned hastily and went into the station. She never saw any of it again.

PART TWO

13

ON A SULTRY JULY AFTERNOON, JULIA STOOD BY THE
window of the room over Weeks's shop. Behind her was an
enormous bed, made up only with fraying wool blankets and
a stained and coverless bolster. She'd asked for sheets, but was
told by Weeks it wouldn't be authentic. In the bricked-up fire-
place was a little oil stove with a saucepan and two dented tin
cups. On the mantelpiece sat an old wooden clock with hands
and a twelve-hour face. The armchair beside the window had a
crooked leg; it listed to one side and had the indefinably sordid
look of a piece of furniture teeming with bedbugs. The bed, the
curtains, and the seams of the bookshelf were similarly infested.
Julia scattered pepper to drive them off, but the effect was sadly
short-lived. A little table held Winston's beloved paperweight,
a glass dome with a piece of coral inside. The coral was the only
thing in the room that was ever really clean.

Across from the bed hung an engraving of a capitalist-era
church in a wooden frame. The picture was spotted and yellowed, and couldn't have looked more of a piece of oldthink
junk. In fact, it was an ingenious sort of spying device, supplied
with microcameras, microphones, sensors—everything a snoop
could wish for. No doubt it could tell your weight and take your
temperature, if required. The day Julia first came, Weeks had
spoken to the picture to ask if it was working. It answered in

O'Brien's voice: "We can see and hear you perfectly, comrades." Since then, it had been silent. Julia had been warned not to speak to it or look at it, never to pay particular attention to it, even if she were alone. "Good habits," Weeks had said. "Everything in our work is founded on good habits."

Julia spent little time alone here, but even that short time felt long. She fought the bugs and filed her nails and felt the absence of the telescreen's companionable voice, a loneliness like the deep hole of toothache. One day in her boredom she was driven to the extremity of seeing if she could fit the paperweight in her mouth. She succeeded, only to remember belatedly that the snoops must be watching in mystification.

The room's one window looked out on a little cobbled yard with a sea of shabby roofs beyond. A stout, red-faced prole woman was often down there, pegging nappies up to dry—so often, in fact, that it must have been her trade. The woman sang as she worked, and always the one song, a cloying ballad that had been playing on the radio everywhere that summer. The song went:

> It was only an 'opeless fancy
> It passed like an April day
> But a look and a word and the dreams they stirred
> They have stolen my 'eart away

Its tune was hauntingly simple and fraught with mournful sentiment, even though, like all new songs, it had been written by machine. The song-writing device, known as a versificator, was the pride and joy of Truth's Music Department; whenever one ran into the Music people, they would boast of how the new models could beat any human composer at his game. Indeed, this tune was uncannily potent.

One began to imagine the versificator to be possessed of a wistful, yearning soul.

By this day in July, Winston Smith had visited Julia in the room a dozen times. She'd first suggested it during their usual sort of rendezvous in a prole street. They were meant to be arranging a second trip to the forest—the Golden Country, as he called it. When she put him off with the excuse of her period, he'd looked not just aggrieved but murderous. He wasn't to get his treat, and so she became his hated enemy. She felt no scruples, then, about suggesting things would be very different if they had a place to meet indoors—really any old place with a sink and a bed. And hadn't he spoken of such a place? That shop in the prole district—what was its name? Just then a microcopter appeared above, and they had to separate. But when they met the next day, he told her he was going to speak to Weeks—or Charrington, as Winston called him. By then, of course, he had convinced himself it was his idea.

She'd always wondered at the fortitude of married couples with telescreens in their bedrooms, who must copulate in stony silence with bored expressions on their faces, for fear that the snoops would judge it sexcrime. But of course that wasn't Julia's part. She could moan and spread her legs to the camera and finger her own cunt. She could go on hands and knees and let Winston fuck her like a dog and spank her. The first few times, in fact, she found the presence of the camera stimulating. She imagined a line of snoops at their screens, men of various ages and builds, mesmerized by lust and painfully erect—a scene taken directly from the pages of *Inner Party Sinners: "My Telescreen Is Broken, Comrade!"*

As time passed, though, her awareness of the watchers faded. The same thing had happened when she came to London and first lived with the presence of telescreens. She'd started out feeling self-conscious and important, panicked by every care-less word and proud of every Partyful comment. At night, she would review her day in her mind, imagining how the snoops had reacted to everything she'd done. But in a matter of weeks, all that was gone. What was left was a set of habits, a personal-ity that was a compendium of behaviors the watchers wanted to see.

In this room, that meant a Julia with a boundless appetite for crime, who loved to incite men to every obscenity, who found any slander of the Party just. She was also a girl in love; that was certainly part of what was wanted. Julia knew it with the instinct of someone who had hidden such feelings all her life.

The romantic part was real enough, at least with Winston Smith. Weeks had provided oil lamps, and, in that dim light, Winston looked dashing, piratical, the terrorist of her dreams. She would be painted and perfumed for him, in a thin prole dress given to her by Weeks, whose flared skirt made her nether parts accessible in a way that inflamed them both. When Win-ston opened the door, she hurried to press herself against him, breathless. They often spent an hour in bed before they thought of anything else. Afterward, she wove fantasies with him of how they might someday be married, how they would hide them-selves as proles, get jobs in a factory, live in connubial poverty. Sometimes she clung to him with real despairing passion, not properly remembering who she was and how they'd come to be here.

Then, lounging by the light of the lamps, she led Winston to share his most criminal ideas and to think things still more criminal. This he liked better than anything; it was remark-able how his interests and Love's interests were alike. He held forth happily about his murderous resentment of the Party and every individual Party member. With her encouragement, he talked about joining the Brotherhood and taking part in arson, bombings, assassinations. Amusingly, it turned out he believed he knew one member of the Goldstein Brotherhood already—Comrade O'Brien. This was based on a look in O'Brien's eyes, an understanding he thought existed between them. "I sometimes feel an impulse," he said, "to simply walk into O'Brien's presence, announce I am an enemy of the Party, and demand his help."

Julia would have dearly loved to know what O'Brien made of this, but he hadn't spoken to her since that day at his flat. She had a souvenir from that visit: a brochure O'Brien had given her in answer to her final question, entitled *Why We Hate*. Its cover was filled with warnings that it wasn't to be circulated outside the Inner Party, and that if it fell into the hands of an unauthorized person, it must be destroyed unread. Inside were four pages of small print, headed by four slogans: "Truth Is Hate. Plenty Is Hate. Peace Is Hate. Love Is Hate." The text then explained that the names of the four big Ministries were decoys for the ignorant. Truth was not truth, love was not love—the Party had never embraced such weak delusions. It was not even true, as the Outer Party was led to believe, that these concepts lived in a dialectical, doublethink relationship to their opposites. Oh, it was certainly the case that peace was war, as anyone could see from history—the point was so well understood by Party members as to need no explanation. But this was still to valorize "peace," to justify war by saying it amounted to "peace." The Party then was still holding up peace—that feeble idol of feeble races—as a principle.

All true Inner Party members understood, long before they were taught, that this could not be right. No, these names had another, occult significance, revealed to the Inner Party alone. Each was a face of hate. "In the place of the voluptuousness of plenty, the cowardice of peace, the dependency of love, the empty sanctimony of truth, we place hate. Hate is the highest capacity of mankind. Every other sentiment we share with the animal kingdom—anger, greed, mother love, fear, curiosity. Only hate is human. No lower animal can access its mysteries. A beast can feel transient rage, but never hate. That is why he is morally null; there can be no goodness without hate. One hates when the good within one identifies evil. Hate is goodness in operation. And without operation, without action, goodness is the mere corpse of goodness.

"Only hate is good. That is the great revelation of Big Brother Thought. Perhaps future human beings will evolve some still higher faculty, purer and more ruthless. For now, this is the greatest of what is human: to hate and to be led by hate."

Julia found this terribly impressive and had read it countless times with pleasure. And yet when she tried to practice hate—to feel hatred for a person—the best she could summon was annoyance or resentment. Trying too hard could set off bursts of fondness—for Winston, for O'Brien, for the prole washerwoman singing naggingly as she hung her eternal laundry. Most of all, Julia was troubled by surges of misplaced affection for the thinkpol Weeks.

Weeks was her companion in all her work, her confidant and scourge. If she felt perplexed at the meaning of hate, or needed advice on what was expected of Winston, or just wanted Inner Party goods, she went to him. Of course properly there was no "Weeks," though he didn't object to Julia using that name. In fact, he had no name, no self. He was a creature composed entirely of pseudonyms, disguises, lies, and wigs. The Weeks persona the Meltons had known had died some months before and been buried (or a coffin full of earth had been buried) with a dozen uneasy proles in attendance. Weeks was replaced by old man Charrington, the persona Winston met—a mild little fellow, perpetually adjusting a pair of bent spectacles on his nose and letting his jaw hang open to show discolored teeth. Charrington was a personification of nostalgia. He sang old arias to himself as he fussed over his old junk; he chatted to his customers about past events and talked about old books. Despite his prole accent, he had an air of decayed gentility, and wore a velvet jacket that was still surprisingly fine despite its age. Charrington was never seen abroad and didn't approach the shop's windows, as the artificial aging of his face wouldn't hold up to direct sunlight. Under oil lamps, it did very well.

Julia soon realized all the Meltons' imaginings about the shop were true. In the room upstairs, a group of would-be Goldsteinites was allowed to hold meetings, whose numbers were always dwindling as arrests were made, then being supplemented by new recruits. There were also days Julia arrived to find a faint sweet odor that Weeks explained was opium, Mr. Charrington's secret stock in trade. "In itself, that won't make a fellow talkative, but we can add what will." As for the shop being "the worst sort of brothel," that was clearly Julia's part. What worse brothel than one whose bed was overlooked by Thought Police?

Weeks liked to talk to Julia about their work, for which he had various high-sounding names: "the sum of all the arts," "the greater life," "the lie that is truth," "the mercy of the condemned." He explained this last—*the mercy of the condemned*— to Julia one day while desultorily dusting shelves. "This shop is a haven for spiders. You'll see them lazing about in their webs, and they seem such idle, harmless fellows. But only let a beetle lay a foot on that web, and Comrade Beetle is doomed. Our spider cares for his victim, however. He swaddles him in silk and even administers a drug to ease his passing. There are some who think the beetle is only paralyzed and feels what happens to him as he is consumed. I think differently. I think the drug that paralyzes him also gives him lovely dreams. You'll see that here. The criminal has never been so happy in his life; he has come to the golden land of his hopes. That brief interlude in the web—those are the criminal's sweetest hours."

"He won't be so happy once he's arrested," said Julia.

Weeks waved this notion away with his duster. "Not our department, comrade. What does a spider know of hell?"

This speech was typical of Weeks, who loved comparing people to vermin: not only beetles and spiders but flies, bedbugs, rats, pigeons, germs, and the mold that ate at walls. It often sounded whimsical or even affectionate; still, Julia came to know it for the art of hate. Indeed, Weeks had learned to hate so completely that all his moods were hatred. He hated Julia even as he sincerely liked her; he showed his liking in tormenting. He hated his own face in the clouded mirror and delighted in blotting it out. He hated all who came through his door, with an attentiveness that foresaw all their needs. He hated more unselfishly and devotedly than most can love.

He especially liked to hate Winston Smith. He quickly discovered all Smith's infirmities, and asked solicitously if the fellow's wet cough didn't turn Julia's stomach, or if she'd noticed the ulcer on the leg. Didn't she agree old men ought to stick to old women? "To see that loose, discolored flesh alongside fresh skin—one feels it a violation." He badgered her to bring other men to the room, saying anyone must be a great improvement. "And really we will need the cameras for other things than Comrade Smith's bony arse." Julia came to bitterly regret confiding in Weeks about Winston's talk of killing women. Weeks loved to dwell on this, asking if she was quite sure the wife was still alive, speculating about the dismembered bodies Winston had left all over London and wondering what indignities he'd visited on them before they breathed their last. "You may be certain he's not told you the worst of it. No, they always keep a good deal back."

He was also pleased to inform her that Winston was the monster from Mrs. Bale's story of the bomb, the man who had strolled past the dying baby and kicked her severed hand from his path. "Oh, yes! I know everything that happens in my district. Your Smith is the Beast of the Bomb. My neighbors could talk of nothing else for a week." Julia wanted to think this was a slander, but when she asked Winston, it turned out to be true. He couldn't remember why he'd done it, and seemed to believe it was of little consequence. "All these horrors!" he said very tragically. "They finally come to seem quite normal." He added that, under the Party, people couldn't really love their children anyway, as they were only spies in the nest.

At their next meeting, Weeks asked if Winston had admitted his guilt. Julia said defensively, "Oh, what difference does it make, after all? It's not as if the hand could feel."

To this, Weeks laughed with pleasure. "Oh, it's the baby's hand that can't feel? Not the man? Are we so very sure that's right?"

Weeks had a theory that a man would always resemble whatever he feared most, and he was delighted to learn that Winston had a morbid fear of rats. "Oh, yes! A fine rat! One sees it in the eyes. Not a wild rat, but the fair-haired species, bred for use in experiments." Another time, Weeks spoke of the fatal appeal of his shop to men with mental sickness, boasting that every wrongthinker was irresistibly drawn there. Some fought the urge for months, instinctively knowing the shop would doom them. But they were drawn back again and again, until at last they must choose between the shop and madness.

"Now he enters at last. He looks all around. And he goes directly to this table." Weeks went to a small table in the corner, heaped with a slightly better class of junk: lacquered snuffboxes, agate brooches, a china horse with a broken leg. He let his hand rest among the dubious treasures and looked at Julia, smiling. "Oh, yes, their noses lead them here. It's a feast I've laid on especially for them, and they smell it and can't help themselves. They must eat, though they know it's poisoned. A rat will do that, you know. It will take a poisoned bait, though it quakes in terror. Its intellect knows the meat will kill it, yet brute instinct makes it eat." He lifted an agate brooch to his mouth and made his face into that of a nibbling rat. She could see the pointed nose and bright small eyes, the appetite and the terror. Then he let it all fall away and said, "I speak, of course, of Smith."

One of Weeks's finer cruelties was that he never let Winston learn of the meetings of Goldsteinites at the shop. Winston was never to be welcomed into any revolutionary circle, never to have like-minded friends or hope, be it ever so fleeting. No, for him, old Charrington was an impotent creature who lived and breathed old stories. Winston loved to repeat Charrington's reminiscences of London in the forties—a time when the real Weeks was not yet born. Winston also often stood in front of the picture of the church that hung in the bedroom—unaware, of course, that he was gazing into the faces of a row of Thought Police—and repeated a rhyme old Charrington had taught him:

> Oranges and lemons, say the bells of St. Clement's;
> You owe me three farthings, say the bells of St. Martin's.
> Here comes a candle to light you to bed,
> Here comes a chopper to chop off your head!

The song was supposedly of great antiquity, and there was a game that went with it, in which children joined hands and raised their arms in the air while one of their number wove beneath, until the arms came down and "chopped off" the victim's head. It so happened that Julia knew the song, and was able to contribute one more line: *When will you pay me, say the bells of Old Bailey.* This interested Winston more than anything else she'd ever done. He demanded to know where she'd learned it, but she put him off by inventing a wise old grandfather, long ago vaporized. The last thing she wished to do with Winston was reminisce about school days in the SAZ.

Julia suspected the nasty rhyme was of no greater antiquity than the Two Minutes Hate. In fact, she imagined it to be the work of Mamie Faye at Truth. She suggested this to Winston, mentioning the similarity to the classic Mamie Faye rhyme "Hang 'Em," with its gloating over the executions of "Rutherford, Aaronson, your uncle, and Jones." But not only did Winston dismiss this theory; it sent him into a gloomy reminiscence about having seen the real Rutherford, Aaronson, and Jones at the Chestnut Tree Café. They'd just been released from Love, though they would soon be rearrested and hanged. Winston talked at length about the pitiful demeanor of the men as they drank their clove-flavored gin, shuddering as he said that Rutherford and Aaronson had both had broken noses. He was also very struck by the fact that the telescreen had played a jeering tune at them, and Rutherford then began to weep. The song went: *Under the spreading chestnut tree, I sold you and you sold me*—rather tame, Julia thought, by comparison to Charrington's rhyme, but Winston repeated it again and again, as if it were the pinnacle of horror.

When Winston spoke of such things, Julia was subject to

a strange exhaustion that came upon her in a flood. It was a flattening boredom or desolation, a teeming sort of impotence. Sometimes, from one moment to the next, she simply fell asleep. Because she knew what came of all this. Winston would be taken to Love and tortured, turned into a ruined, sobbing thing that crept on the ground, that exhibited its broken bones and dribbled pink froth from a toothless mouth, then at last was taken out and shot. The images came to her, and the room detached from life and became unreal. She slept and only woke to him dressing to leave. When she rose to kiss him, she was weak in all her limbs, and her face felt strangely numb. She often got a twitch in her eye at such times, though luckily he was the most unobservant of men and never noticed. Washing afterward in the shop's dark kitchen, she felt immortal, lonely, strange, so pitiful it was like being in love. As she dried her face with a foul-smelling cloth, she believed all things in turn: that she was evil; that she was a victim; that O'Brien was right and she was a "diamond"; that people were animals and what they did meant no more than the buzzing of flies. Once she hunted through the drawers for a rope or sharp blade, with the thought of ending her life, and cried when she found none. She could see no way back to herself.

But when she returned to the bright, false noise of the hostel, how she missed that darkness! She had never been so real.

And so she had come through June, still alive in the stuffy, odd-smelling room, still finding bug bites on her arse, still waiting for the washerwoman's song to end. She couldn't find Syme—Research was doing twenty-four-hour shifts, putting the finishing touches to the tenth edition of the Newspeak dictionary—but she got a note to Parsons, who visited the room and fucked her very anxiously, peering at the walls as if a telescreen might grow behind his back, but still was done in thirty seconds. Afterward he sat on the bed and upbraided himself for betraying his wife, his Party, and "all that was finest in old Tom Parsons." He swore he could never come back. She *was* a sweet tumble—that was how he'd always put it—but he'd never get away with it, not now that his kiddies were old enough to sniff him out. "They get a very good training in the Spies that way. They're sharp-eyed kids. Keen as mustard! Yes, they keep us on our toes, all right." Then he talked for an hour about the hapless people his children had denounced, seeming terrified and proud by turns. She tried to get him to speak ill of this practice, but there was nothing to him but prick and Party; "a sweet tumble" and "a very good training in the Spies." And the song went on outside, and he left and Winston came and left, and another day came. There was Fiction, there was coming home to the hostel, and one night Vicky staring at Julia in the mirror while Julia washed her face. Julia loved Vicky flashingly, then turned away with a grimace: *Let me be. Can't you see I'm no good?* There was Fiction, there was riding to Weeks on the bus, napping fitfully in her seat while the proles all around complained of the shortages: beans were absolutely not to be found. There was Vicky in the back of her mind, there was Winston saying, "We are the dead," and Julia falling into deep sleep, fleeing. Parsons came and left, and she went down to the kitchen to wash and cry. She leaned against a wall and went into a reverie, in which she imagined a greater purpose that made what she was doing right. She remembered, as if it were a fact long known, that Big Brother loved her—only he. It was what she had been taught at school, and it was true in a way. It might be true. She raised her face to the little slot of window, just as the clocks in the Party districts struck nineteen, faraway and dull, portentous, as if the distant ocean tolled. In a minute, she would understand. The feeling was coming in the damp-smelling room. In a moment she would see the Party's teachings as perfect. O'Brien, who was so much cleverer than she, understood them and believed them. The airmen had had their jokes, but they had died for Oceania and Big Brother. They had killed for Oceania and Big Brother, without any quibbles or fatuous questions. The feeling was there, and perhaps it didn't matter if the Party's teachings were true. "What is Truth?" It was nothing, or nothing of use. A plane was strong, not true.

And it came to this day in July. She stood by the window sweating in the heat. Behind her on the bed now was Stanley Ampleforth, a long, tall man with dark blond hair, not shapeless now, not drooping as he'd been. He was thriving in the web.

She had first invited Ampleforth three weeks before, when, despairing of ever running Syme to ground, she had given Syme's note to him. It specified only a place and time, but Ampleforth from Poetry received it with the face of a man who was witnessing a long-awaited miracle. He came to the appointment and was easily coaxed into Weeks's shop, making instantly for the fatal table and being convinced by old man Charrington to buy a little carved pipe. Julia led him up to the room. He was bright-faced with anticipation, but when she stroked his face, he stumbled away. He cowered by the door and stammered miserably that he hadn't meant that. "Oh, I was afraid you might think that. And you have every right to expect—you are so lovely, and if I weren't such a poor thing . . . I shouldn't like to die without being in love. But can I love? Well, you see what I am."

She said, as gently as she could, "But why have you come? Are you a Goldsteinite?"

At this he looked still more horrified. "A Goldsteinite? Of course not!"

"But I can't make it out. What on earth have you come for, if it isn't that?"

What he thought they were there for, it turned out, was poetry: the old, lost poetry he and his colleagues rewrote to cleanse it of wrongthink. Ampleforth had been committing the original verses to memory for years, jotting lines on scraps of paper he secreted in his shoes and read over to himself when he was sure he wasn't seen. He'd always hoped someone might guess his secret, so he could share those lost old poems. "The rewrites we do, I don't say it isn't necessary. Such things are certainly dangerous. They send the mind down very unhealthful pathways. I may feel something for them—I do—but I see why they must be suppressed. Why, my favorite poem of all has degenerate images, glorification of capitalist hoarding, and a positive depiction of an Abyssinian maid, who is of course Eurasian. Only think if a child were to see it! Yes, such a poem is a deadly poison for the mind, expressly designed to warp and corrupt, and its author is a criminal. It can't be safe!"

Then he blinked at Julia and said shyly, "Might you like to hear it?"

Soon Ampleforth was perched on the bug-infested bed, intoning some gibberish about Kubla Khan and a pleasure dome and caves of ice, and "Weave a circle round him thrice and close your eyes with holy dread!" To Julia, it might as well have been meowing. Still, she clapped her hands and made rapt faces, and Ampleforth straightened and became very bold. He now suggested such poems might be saved, to be distributed only among the politically mature, of course—but mightn't they really be saved? "I believe in my work at the Ministry, but when

187

we're finished—it's the butterfly without the wings. It must be done, but—the butterfly without the wings!"

He came back again and again. At every visit, he looked less defeated and less shapeless. One would have said he had grown a skeleton. His shoulders were still stooped and his blue eyes guarded, but his face was clear and bright. He was the butterfly with the wings. Old Charrington sold him two notebooks, and he would lie on his belly on the bed, transcribing verses from his compendious memory, while Julia brought him tea and slabs of Inner Party chocolate. His feet, shod in a pair of velvet slippers she'd found, kicked in the air to the rhythm of the verse. There were times, too, when he sprawled and recited, luxuriously closing his eyes. Then he would let her hold his hand. He called the room his Xanadu, his Arden, and her his Abyssinian maid. It was as Weeks said of the beetle in the web: this was his sweetest life.

Now he frowned up from his notebook, the pencil pressed anxiously to his chin. "I've been meaning to say, but I kept losing my nerve. You had asked if I still saw Syme."

"Oh?" she said, turning sleepily from the window.

"Yes, I couldn't find the courage to say before. But the funny thing is, Syme's gone."

Julia frowned. "Gone?"

"I mean to say, he didn't just go. He said he was going, that's the queer thing. I did think to tell you, but I was afraid."

"So Syme's been vaporized?"

"Not vaporized."

"Gone but not vaporized—what's that?"

"Oh, he might have been vaporized. One can't truly know. But he said he would go, and next day he'd gone. They've taken his name off all the schedules."

"I can't see what you mean. Taking his name off the schedules—that's just what they do when someone is vaporized."

"But they'd do it just the same if he left."

In an instant, Julia saw what he meant, and felt an almost ungovernable urge to hush him. She wanted to cover the picture, to drag him from the room. This was a thing Love couldn't know.

But she only said stupidly, "Left? How, left?"

"Left the city. Gone where the Party can't find him. Escaped."

"Where the Party can't find him? Where's that?"

"Well, a man could escape to Eurasia, or—"

"Eurasia!"

"I don't say it's that. There might be quite wild places in Airstrip One itself."

This struck Julia forcibly. She wanted to object that in the SAZ there had been wild places where one could hide for a time, but people who did this could only survive by robbery, and sooner or later they were hunted down. But then she thought of Eurasia and remembered the boat she'd seen from Hubert's plane. Smugglers! Smugglers must go back and forth to Eurasia all the time. If one could pay them ...

"When he told me," Ampleforth went on, "we were in that mews behind the community center, having a smoke before the bus, and he muttered it in my ear quite suddenly: 'I'm leaving the city'—just like that. Then another fellow came out and joined us, and I hadn't a chance to ask more. Well, I told myself it meant nothing, that I must have misunderstood, but then he was gone. His name on all the schedules—gone."

"But that it should be Syme!"

"Oh, I don't wonder at that. He was quite the hero when he did his military service, you know. A scout."

"I didn't know."

"For a time I was sure he would denounce me. Isn't that funny to think of now? He was always such a devil for Newspeak and hangings. The week he left, he was going around saying that soon the very idea of freedom would be abolished, and people wouldn't even be able to think of it—wouldn't be able to think of anything, as there would *be* no thought. And he made it sound as if he liked such a prospect!"

"I wouldn't mind not being able to think."

"You don't mean that," Ampleforth said absently. "You know, if I thought my damned legs would carry me, I'd have half a mind to follow him. Then some of this"—he lifted the notebook—"might be saved."

"I really don't want to think," Julia said. "I don't."

"I have said I believe in my work at the Ministry. Well, that's a lie—I don't. Not a bit! They're rotten vandals—that's the truth. Even when there's nothing wrong in a poem, they change words here and there, and then more—just to make the beautiful ugly, to make it fall like a mallet on the brain, to refashion the butterfly into a cockroach. No, if I could save but one of these poems, I wouldn't care if I must die for it!"

Now the black exhaustion descended on Julia. She saw Ampleforth broken and toothless, crawling across the floor of the Chestnut Tree Café. She saw him shot in the back of the neck, dragged out by his feet.

She looked at the clock and made a grimace, saying, "Oh! What a nuisance! I've just seen the time. And I had so hoped I could hear another poem."

That night she dreamed of Eurasia. She and Vicky were in a smugglers' boat, crouched together in its damp hull. Julia had promised to recite some of Ampleforth's poetry as payment for the oarsmen, but couldn't remember a single line. Instead she was reciting the fifth goodstory of Big Brother Thought, but she knew they would soon spot the imposture. To make things worse, she was mixing up the words, and Vicky was disgusted by her stupidity.

Then O'Brien was in the boat somehow, oars in his hands, bare-chested, muscles working. He gazed down masterfully at Julia. The moonlight picked out his manly features. Now the other oarsmen were gone. Vicky was gone; she was safely on the Eurasian shore, where she couldn't see what Julia and O'Brien did in the boat. No one could, no one anywhere. They tossed on the sea, and only moonlight shone on their naked bodies.

14

AS JULY WORE ON, THE CITY WAS SEIZED BY STIFLING heat. The prole streets filled with mattresses at dusk as people escaped the heat and bugs indoors, and every day a dozen prole men were roughed up by patrols for going shirtless. People from all classes gathered around fountains to splash their arms and faces. Public baths had such long queues that anyone as busy as Julia couldn't think of going, and the stack of bathing coupons Weeks had given her were all for naught. She must scrub herself at the sink with a flannel like any hostel girl.

Like everyone, she was caught up in the frenzy of preparations for Hate Week. Fiction had paused production of novels to work round the clock producing reports of Eurasian atrocities. After work, there were endless committees to organize the necessary demonstrations, military parades, rallies, lectures, puppet shows, waxwork displays, and even a mock sea battle on the Thames. As a mechanic, Julia was much in demand for the making of clockwork Eurasian soldiers, which could aim a gun all about them from the eminence of a parade float. This year, too, Fiction had won the honor of producing the effigy of Goldstein for the Ministry of Truth's official Hate Fete, and endless compulsory meetings were devoted to perfecting the details of this likeness.

Women's 21 had a harder task; for their neighborhood Hate

Fete, they must produce an acceptable dummy of the turncoat Attlee. While Attlee was always mentioned in the lists of traitors, his likeness was only shown during Hate Week, when he was burned in effigy. The girls' memories of previous Attlees conflicted even in such points as whether the dummy wore a beard and whether it was stout or thin. All were squabbling into the night, then going to bed late and in an ill temper, and the day was only saved when Edie ran in crowing one day with a copy of the *Mail*; it had printed specifications for all the traditional Hate Week dummies on its front page.

The streets grew chaotic before Hate, and this year, it had started early. Three weeks out, every other housefront was already daubed with slogans wishing death to various people, from Goldstein to "false botanists." The year's Hate poster, of a menacing Eurasian soldier, was posted everywhere, and everywhere it was loyally defaced: the soldier's head was torn away, or given black eyes and blacked-out teeth, or a speech bubble was added saying, *I'm a filthy coward.* In prole districts, all such posters ended up with patches missing at the crotch, as youths drew tiny penises on them, and more mature citizens tore them away.

Hate Week was traditionally timed to coincide with the regular summer blitz, but this too had begun a few weeks early. Bombs fell more often, killing more people, and the newsflashes were all bodies and wreckage. In Stepney a cinema was destroyed in the middle of the evening program, and hundreds of people burned to death. This prompted a massive, trailing funeral that became a protest march. Julia ran into it on her bike and felt it wiser to flee when prole boys in the rear began to hurl dirt at her. The next day, another bomb fell on a piece of waste ground used as a playground, and several dozen children were blown to pieces. That afternoon, from the upper floors of Truth, one could hear the sound of the protests, an unearthly howl like the screams from an open arena. In these days, too, there were enormous explosions in the distance, roaring gales of demolition that went on for long minutes. One of these came early in the morning, and was followed by a haze that dimmed the city and made the sunrise a lowering red. Some said the era of atom bombs had returned, but the telescreens were silent on this subject.

Day and night, major streets were filled with marches, both spontaneous and planned. On her way from place to place, Julia joined in protests—against, well, she didn't always trouble to learn what it was—in which she lustily shouted slogans and waved whatever banner was thrust into her hand. When a shop had been singled out for destruction by the marshals, she happily threw bricks through its windows. If a book was handed to her, she gladly tossed it into the waiting fire. Who didn't like the sweet, hysterical sound of breaking glass? Who didn't like the brave smell of gasoline and the brightness of the conflagration? Gin bottles were also handed to her everywhere she went—the gin ration had been trebled temporarily—so she, like everyone else, was drunk or tipsy all day long. Like everyone, she sang the new Hate Song as she went about the streets. It had been simplified from previous years, so now it scarcely had a tune or lyrics. It went:

> Death to the wrongthinker, death death death!
> Death to the ownthinker, death death death!
> Death to Eurasia! Death! Death! Death!

Hate itself still eluded her. In the mob, what she felt was the thrill of the crowd, the physical pleasure of yelling and waving fists that was like the fun of dancing. Most others seemed to feel the same. They destroyed and sang with beatific smiles, threw arms around each other's shoulders, laughed loudly at the slightest jokes. They might believe Goldsteinites should be hanged, and happily go to watch an execution, cheering when the others cheered, but then they went home, looking forward to their supper without feeling personally concerned.

A few times, though, Julia found the real article, a man or woman who screeched hate slogans with a face distorted by real fury. These people were dissatisfied with the scale of the violence, and muttered about the real reckoning to come. It was intolerable to them to think that an enemy existed who was not suffering. They instinctively worked to hate the enemy more, and to convince other people to hate them more. If a Party member was too casual in his hatred, they saw it as a monstrous moral crime. The very thought of such things could make them lose control and sputter with incoherent rage. Their hands trembled and tears came to their eyes as violent scenes played in their minds, in which the atrocities of the enemy mingled with the gruesome punishments coming to him. Once Julia was listening inattentively to one of these people and startled him by sleepily replying, "So you think we should burn the Goldsteinites' children alive?" He snapped, "No! *They* want to burn *our* children! The whole point is we're not like that! But, if you're asking me, their children aren't so innocent, either. If their spawn were to be disposed of—I don't say burned, but to rid us of the enemy, if that's what's needed, then burning it will be. Yes, burn them, if that's what's needed. Burn their children! Burn them alive!"

In the midst of this tumult, Julia went to get the artsem treatment. Her period had come in lighter than it should be and her breasts felt sore and full. She'd even begun to experience bouts of nausea whenever she took the bus. There was reason to hope it was a false alarm. She'd had such symptoms twice before. On both occasions, she'd done artsem, but those courses had both failed, and she was sent away at the end with vitamin supplements, brochures on healthy habits, and slighting remarks about her "uncomradeful" womb. However, she could take no chances. When she'd asked Weeks what she should do if she were pregnant, he'd said cold-bloodedly it made no difference.

"But how am I to explain it?" Julia said. "That's the thing."

"Explain it just as you like."

"So you can't—that is to say, there isn't a preventative?"

He tutted and shook his head. "Oh, no, we don't traffic in that. What a question! No, I hope we are not so degenerate as that."

At the clinic's entrance, all was just a little seedier than before: the WELCOME, PURE MOTHERS OF OCEANIA banner more grimy and faded, the pavement more littered with fag-ends, the children posted outside to hand paper flowers to the patients more dejected and thin. Inside, however, it was quite another world. The waiting room was air-conditioned, like a Ministry. There were comfortable chairs, and the windows gave onto the tended lawns of Socialist Prudence Park. On one wall, a mural showed Big Brother dandling one blond child on his knee while another stood grinning at his side with a toy horse in its hand. A carousel of leaflets advertised the Artsem Fathers Selection Program, the health benefits of virgin birth, and the happy lives the artsem children led in government homes. Since Julia had last been here, a new leaflet had been added to the display. On its cover Big Brother stood beside a demure, beaming woman in late pregnancy, his hand resting paternally on her shoulder. The slogan beneath read: BIG FUTURE—A NEW RACE FOR A BETTER TOMORROW.

There were two dozen girls in the waiting room, looking variously uncommunicative: some furious, some forlorn, most gazing dully into space. A few looked far too young to be here, and a few were already visibly pregnant. Julia always wondered if these big-bellied patients were permitted to go through with the charade, or if they were sent away to suffer the penalty for their unchastity. All the patients were Outer Party. Inner Party women weren't eligible for artsem: they all married and raised their own children at home, their positive influence on the young being seen as more valuable than purity. Prole women, it went without saying, weren't welcome here. They could not be pure.

Julia gave her Party card, union membership, London residency permit, and passport to the nurse, who turned to a speakwrite in the wall, read all the relevant numbers into it, then handed back the papers and told Julia she must wait for the results of her classification.

"Classification? Is that new?"

"Yes, just this week. Have you been with us before?"

"Third time. Never took, I'm afraid."

"Oh, that's a shame. They don't like to waste the good stuff on a tricky womb. But three's not so bad. We get girls coming in with ten unsuccessful courses, and they still want to try for Big Future."

"Big Future?" Julia glanced back at the leaflets with the misgiving Party initiatives always aroused.

"That's the new program," said the nurse. "The doctor will fill you in. But don't fret if you don't qualify. All the fathers are excellent here. Every one is an Inner Party member in first-class health, with all his teeth."

"Doubleplus good," said Julia absently. "That's very reassuring."

The speakwrite buzzed. The nurse put the receiver to her ear. At the faint squawk of the voice on the other end, her eyes turned to Julia with new respect. She hung up, saying, "Well, here's a thing! You've been approved for BF already. I've never known it to happen so fast." She smiled almost flirtatiously. "Well! You can come right in, then. Follow me."

Julia followed the nurse through a pair of swinging doors with a prickly feeling of self-consciousness. She felt as if everyone waiting could tell she worked for the Thought Police. What other reason could there be for Julia to be so favored? At the same time, she felt an increasing trepidation. What was Big Future? Would it be possible to decline? *A New Race for a Better Tomorrow*—what was that? Could the Party be engendering scientific monsters?

With these unhappy thoughts, she was ushered into a tiny room with the familiar stirruped table and shelves arrayed with frightening implements. The nurse gave her a paper gown and left her alone with the telescreen, here fixed to the ceiling and quite blank; the conception-boosting image would only be switched on when the procedure began. Julia had changed and was perching on the table, trying to position the meager gown so it wasn't obscene, when the doctor came in without knocking. This was a stout woman with a tired, pale face, who immediately launched into what was clearly a memorized speech of congratulations: "With Big Future, you are to be a true bride of Ingsoc, one of the pure vessels of a higher race . . ." Julia listened intently, but nothing betrayed the nature of this higher race, or what was to become of the vessels. Her mind had quite run away, imagining poisonous babies, enormous babies that split their mothers open, babies with vicious claws that tore their way out of their mothers' stomachs, when at last the doctor said, her voice now trembling with emotion: ". . . and you can wear the badge that marks you as the bearer of that greatest trust: the chance to carry Big Brother's child."

"What?" said Julia. "Big Brother's . . . what?"

"I know it will seem too good to be true. But you have heard right. You are to have his child."

"But—I mean to say—how, his child?"

The doctor discreetly lowered her voice. "The semenic materials are his. Quite factually, biologically, your child will be Big Brother's."

Julia was visited by an unwelcome image of Big Brother pleasuring himself, positioned over a bucket. She clenched her teeth against a burst of nervous laughter.

The doctor laid a comforting hand on her shoulder. "Many girls get emotional. You needn't feel at all self-conscious. But I'll leave you to compose yourself. We'll be ready for you in five minutes."

The doctor left. Once Julia was alone, the spasm of laughter entirely passed. She was surprised by a rush of emotion and found herself chilled, looking around the room as if to reassure herself it was real. Through the walls, she heard muted footsteps and voices. It was still the world; she was herself. But this— could it truly be Big Brother's seed? Of course Big Brother had a body, which must produce semen; there was nothing absurd in that. In fact, it had a sadness to it, the mortal taint of all things physical. Again she imagined Big Brother touching himself, with his eyes fixed on—was it the future, or was it Julia? This time the vision was accompanied by a queer anguish. It jogged something loose in her mind, and she realized why she was so affected. It was because, as a girl in the SAZ, she'd often fallen asleep to a fantasy of Big Brother.

In it, she had somehow won a private audience in the Crystal Palace. Behind the glass walls were windblown trees and fields and the violet clouds of sunset. Sometimes the room was a hothouse full of every variety of fragrant rose. Sometimes it was a crystalline hall with a gleaming piano and velvet sofas. Big Brother always sat at a massive desk, and Julia stood alone before him. She was here to tell him what was really going on, all the evils and injustices that were hidden from him by the Inner Party—that must be hidden, or they wouldn't go on.

As she spoke, Big Brother intently listened. His fine black eyes were burning. When she was done, he turned to his telephone, a handsome wooden apparatus, and summoned his ministers to an emergency meeting. Everything would be put to rights and the wrongdoers punished. Big Brother *knew*.

So when the purges came to the airfield, and the villagers were made to watch the pilots' hangings, Julia lay in bed and told Big Brother. She told Big Brother when the quotas rose until every ounce of food from the farms was taken, and anyone who kept back food was shot. The day Mrs. Marcy was arrested, Julia told Big Brother, and told him he *must* forgive her; even if Julia couldn't, he must, for he was Mrs. Marcy's Big Brother too.

Then she lay and masturbated to the fantasy of sex with him. Even before she properly knew what fucking was, she imagined fucking Big Brother in that great glass hall, where all might see. He rose from behind his desk to take her in his manly arms. She was the noble daughter of the people, who'd risked her life to deliver the truth. What could be more natural than that he should recognize Julia as his fit bride? He gathered her to him. Their lips met. His strong hands ably removed her clothes, and his lovemaking was like nothing else. He knew her to the bottom of her soul, and could do as he liked without creeping and lying. In all of Oceania, only he was a man. Only he could feel real love.

That was what young Julia had done, as her neighbors starved and were hanged and shot. And it continued until . . . when had it stopped? She knew she'd done it at Women's 21 at least once. It had carried on for years.

Now a sneaking voice in her mind suggested Big Brother really *didn't* know what was going on, that the Inner Party kept him in the dark. Julia might actually meet him now. She was to be Inner Party—O'Brien had promised it. And now she might have a Big Future baby. Perhaps there was a reason she'd had that dream. She could be the one to open Big Brother's eyes. All she'd done could be made right.

At this, she found she was weeping, and told herself savagely, *What drivel! How can you believe such foolishness! To think, you are twenty-six years old!*

The doctor returned, and looked embarrassed but not surprised to find Julia in tears. In one hand, she held a fat plastic syringe, for all the world like a narrow dick, with a red bulb on the end that looked unfortunately like an ill-treated testicle. Julia wanted to find this funny, but all that feeling was quite gone. She mopped her face with the collar of her gown and tried to smile bravely for the doctor, then was guided to lie down and fit her heels in the leather stirrups. She had never been more relieved than she was when the ceiling telescreen was switched on.

Somewhat disappointingly, the fertility telecast was the same one she'd seen twice before. It began with a montage of happy children in a children's home, marching in formation, singing patriotic hymns with radiant smiles, making beds in a cozy dormitory. The camera zoomed in to show the beds' thick blankets and plump white pillows. The music swelled as the children were shown growing older. The boys now marched in soldiers' uniforms, while the girls still sang patriotic hymns, again with radiant smiles. Big Brother spoke in voice-over, thanking the viewer for her sacrifice and promising a worthy life for her children. Then the film went back to the verdant garden of the children's home, where a small boy was catching a ball, and the camera turned to show who had thrown it: Big Brother. He turned to the viewer with a grave smile, expressive of the troubles they'd endured together and their trust in the fruits of that endurance. He said, "Your body is Oceania's future. You will bring forth our victory."

Meanwhile, Julia shut her eyes and the plastic tube slid into her. She waited to feel the sperm go in, half expecting it would feel different—burn her, or give her an ungovernable pleasure—but, as usual, she felt nothing at all. There was only the cold persistence of the hard tube, slightly nudging to the sides as it was manipulated, then the distant, slippery feeling as it was removed.

Per the doctor's instructions, she lay on her back, hugging her knees to her chest, for twenty minutes. She tried to make a solemn face as the film of Big Brother and the happy children played again and again. Meanwhile, her mind ran in circles. She thought that pregnancy might kill her and would surely make her terribly ill. She thought of the absurdity of having a baby that might be Big Brother's or Tom Parsons's; of the years she'd dreamed of fucking Big Brother, and the men she'd actually fucked, and how many were killed by the Party. She imagined a Party of the future, where everyone had Big Brother's face, where Big Brothers hanged and tortured Big Brothers and sent Big Brothers to die in war. By the time she was allowed to rise and get dressed, and to stagger back into the sweltering day, she felt melancholy to the point of madness.

By then, it was seventeen-thirty. She walked to the hostel, taking back streets to avoid the Hate demonstrations. Even here, litter and broken glass lay everywhere. There was a new fashion for smearing blood from wounds acquired in street fighting on the ubiquitous BIG BROTHER IS WATCHING YOU! posters, to show one had bled for Oceania and was eager to bleed more, and the daubs gave Big Brother the macabre aspect of an idol that fed on sacrifice. As Julia came to Socialists of Industry Circle, the weird sound of thousands of people screaming came from quite nearby; then two prole men ran out of a side street with fearful grins and cricket bats in their hands. They brandished the bats at Julia, who immediately shouted, "Death to Eurasia!" and was rewarded with a cheer instead of a beating. A little farther on, a horrid creaking sound approached from an alleyway, jangling Julia's nerves. It turned out to be a wheelbarrow, pushed by two Outer Party women, each supporting one handle. In the barrow sat a third woman, her arms crossed over her chest and a bandaged foot thrust out in front of her. She called out cheerily to Julia, "Stepped in glass!" and the other women laughed as if in self-congratulation.

At Women's 21, Julia went directly to the community room, hoping to get some time alone with a gin and the musical program. She was annoyed, then, to find two girls already parked at her favorite table. She was mortified to realize one was Vicky.

Since that night at Anti-Sex, Julia and Vicky had tactfully avoided each other. At the hostel, at the community center, at Anti-Sex, they drifted to opposite sides of the room. When they were paired for washing-up duty, they exchanged minimal Party chitchat while avoiding each other's eyes. Once, on a Purity march, they were assigned to carry two ends of the same banner. Then the tension against the fabric in Julia's hands felt charged and sensitive. As she chanted slogans, she was conscious of Vicky hearing her raucous, foolish voice. She kept wanting to glance over, and though she didn't give in to the urge, she forgot to look where she was going, and tripped a few times so the banner drooped precariously near the ground. At last she handed it off to someone else. As she turned away, she saw a look of wounded inquiry in Vicky's eyes. She made a comical grimace and touched her stomach as if to say: indigestion. Vicky smiled in relief, and they went back to avoiding each other with renewed vigor.

Now Vicky was sitting across from Oceania, who'd given birth to her artsem baby two months before and still looked puffy and pale with a yellowish cast, a little like an untinted waxwork. Both girls were knitting Socks for Soldiers, but their needles had fallen still and they were leaning forward, so absorbed in talk they didn't notice Julia come in. Julia heard the name Whitehead, then something about Westminster compound and permissions. That was no surprise; Oceania was always pumping Vicky for tales about Central Committee. Vicky supplied them dutifully, though any mention of Whitehead pained her, and indeed her face now had a pinched look that was at odds with her blooming skin.

Julia stood watching for a second, longing terribly to find her own long-abandoned Sock for Soldiers and forget her troubles. The next instant, though, this was overwhelmed by a more powerful longing, and she found herself saying, "Hello! You won't guess where I've been. Don't try—you'll never guess."

At Julia's voice, Vicky started horribly. She said a word that might have been a greeting, then looked down fiercely at her knitting.

Oceania brightened. "Julia! You're early! Hello!"

"Hello. Well? Are you going to guess?"

"You said we weren't to try," Vicky muttered.

Oceania laughed. "I'm sure I can't."

"Very well, I'll tell you what it is," said Julia, coming to sit down. "I've just gone and done an artsem treatment, and—"

Vicky looked up in shock. "Artsem!"

"Oh." Oceania's hand went to her stomach. "That's . . . congratulations. Doubleplus good."

"Yes, I thought I'd try again," Julia said self-consciously. "And it's paid off, you see, as they've got a new program. Have you heard of Big Future?"

"Is it better coupons?" said Oceania. "When I did it, the coupons didn't always work. You might get all the sweets coupons you liked, but the shop wouldn't part with the sweets."

"No," Julia said. "It's nothing like that. It's a new program where, if you qualify, they give you ... well ... instead of its being any old chap's ... that is, the materials ..."

"The artsem babies are to be Big Brother's now," Vicky said, in an odd, prim voice. "At Central Committee, they speak of nothing else."

"Oh!" Oceania said, and the hand on her stomach convulsed. "All the babies are his? Big Brother's?"

"Not all," said Julia. "Not *all* girls get it. But—well, I've just had the treatment now."

"Yes, it's a very great honor," Vicky said. "I didn't mean that it wasn't."

"Wait, I do know!" Oceania said. "There was a presentation at Anti-Sex House. Oh, dear, that's real? That is, of course it's real. They would hardly tell us if it weren't real. Big Brother's child! How marvelous!"

"Yes," Vicky said, frowning down at her sock. "We are fortunate indeed."

"Julia," Oceania said earnestly, "if anyone deserved to get on that program, it's you. You're ever such a good comrade. I can't think of anyone more goodthinkful than you. And if you can get it, perhaps I might? I'd been wondering how I could face artsem again. But if it might be Big Brother's!"

Julia was struck by a wave of weakness that gathered oddly in her throat and head. Just as she was wondering what it could be, to her horror, she began to weep.

"Oh!" Vicky said, dropping her knitting. "What's the matter?"

"I'm so sorry!" Julia said. "I never cry, and that's twice today. I really never cry!"

"It's true," said Oceania. "You never do. Oh, you must be so happy!"

"I'll get you a tea," said Vicky. "You sit. I'll just find Atkins. She's bound to have tea."

Vicky dashed off. Oceania leaned forward and put her hand on Julia's with a sympathetic smile. "Listen, are you feeling very sick? Or is it lowthink?"

"Hardly sick at all," said Julia. "Well, on the bus."

"Lowthink, then. That's to say, wretched mood?"

"I suppose."

"Well, that's chemicals, and nothing to be ashamed of. Dr. Louis explained it to me. It isn't wrongthink at all, it's only a sign the artsem's taken. You should speak to Dr. Louis. He helped me ever so much. Not only with pills, but with advice."

"With pills?"

"Yes, it's the same ones they give for anti-sex. Two birds with one stone, Dr. Louis says. I didn't like them. They made me queasy. Some girls swear by them, though."

Julia made a sympathetic face, while everything else receded into lovely unimportance. "Oh? Have you any left over?"

"I suppose so. He gave me twenty, and I can't think I took more than three."

"I'll tell you what. Perhaps I might try yours?"

"Mine?" Oceania looked uneasy. "I'm not sure. They were given to me, you see."

"Tea coming!" Vicky sang, returning from her mission to Atkins.

Julia said to Oceania, "But it does seem a waste."

"I don't know," said Oceania. "I only meant to say, the crying is from chemicals. It's a natural consequence of pregnancy. Our ancestors cried so the male would take care of the female."

"Yes, I see," Julia said. "I only thought, if you're not using the pills, I could try them. But never mind, if you feel it's wrong."

Vicky looked from one to the other. "What's this?"

"I'm only telling her," Oceania said, "crying is natural, in her condition. It's not wrongthink."

"Wrongthink?" said Vicky. "Who would think that?"

The door flew open again and Atkins bustled in with a tray of tea things, beaming joyously at them all. She said, "What a day, what a day! Our Worthing to have a Big Future baby, and little Vicky Fitzhugh—"

"Oh, don't!" Vicky cried. "Can we not speak of it?"

"What's that?" said Julia.

Oceania clapped her hands together. "Oh, Julia doesn't know!"

"Comrade Worthing doesn't know?" said Atkins with the face of someone invited to a hearty meal. "What, you haven't told Worthing yet?"

"I suppose you must," said Vicky. "But all the same ..."

Atkins set down the tea things and turned to Julia. "Only fancy, our little Vicky Fitzhugh, whom we all thought such a child, and fussed over and scolded and called a little goose— well, that same Vicky Fitzhugh is now to marry an Inner Party man!"

"Yes," said Vicky crossly. "All right."

"And not just any Inner Party man!" Atkins said.

Julia said, "Oh, so it's—"

"She's marrying Deputy Chairman Whitehead," Oceania said. "We're not supposed to know. He only asked her yesterday."

"Keep it under your hat!" said Atkins gaily, touching her own head.

Vicky said to Julia, "I don't mind *you* knowing, not really. If it doesn't come off, I shan't be embarrassed."

"Not come off!" Atkins laughed. "There's bride's nerves for you. A man such as that, to change his mind!"

"The permissions are still to go through," Vicky said. "James doesn't think there ought to be any trouble about it, but—"

"James!" said Oceania with great satisfaction. "How easily you say his name."

"So you're to leave the hostel," Julia said.

"I should think so," said Oceania. "Fancy living in a hostel when you're married to a CentCom member! She'll move to the Westminster compound, of course."

"Our loss is the Party's gain," said Atkins. "Now, who's having tea? I've made enough for all."

It was an hour later, when all the girls were home, gathered noisily in the community room to watch the evening newscast, that a hand found Julia's under the table. Tiger had just made off with a Sock for Soldiers and been chased down to general hilarity, and all were chattering excitedly about the desperate need for hosiery at the front, saying an army marched on its socks, and infected blisters killed as surely as bullets. In the general commotion, the hand fumbled at Julia's, then grew bold and caught her fingers. Julia held still, blandly gazing at the telescreen. She told herself she was annoyed, but her body filled with hot gratification. She had to fight not to smile. What a pest Vicky made of herself! How silly! As if they both hadn't enough to concern them!

But then, with a little shock of confusion, she felt a tiny parcel being nudged into her palm. As the hand was withdrawn, she caught it with her fingers and recognized the waxy paper and the bulk of the pills within. Then Oceania leaned over and whispered, "That's them. Might you be able to get me some of that nice chocolate?"

Julia made the mental adjustment hastily. Still gazing at the telescreen, she muttered, "Nothing is easier. Look under your pillow tonight."

The pills changed everything for the better. Julia used them only at Weeks, and only when the work became truly unbearable. When she took one, it turned the ceremonies there into a harmless game. Even when she didn't, knowing she could made everything feel less black and desperate. It was as if it were a horror story in a book that she could close at will. In the buoyant mood of the drug, Julia also ventured to lead her men to new, more interesting vices, guided by her sense of what Love wanted. It began with Tom Parsons. One day she reminded him of how she'd once said she could climax seven times like a Frenchwoman, and offered to teach him the trick. He balked only briefly when she told him the secret was to say, "Down with Big Brother!" in her ear. This was not an original request—it was something a certain old flame had liked. It did nothing for Julia, except in that it was calculated to placate Love.

At first Parsons muttered it with no expression, as if he didn't know what the syllables meant. It had the salubrious effect of making him last longer, and Julia was soon able to sincerely moan. With this encouragement, he said it louder until he was barking it into her face. When he reached his own climax, he clutched her against him violently, then pulled away and burst into tears. He sat on the edge of the bed, as he did when he talked about his children's feats of denunciation, but now said nothing. His face was stunned and blank. Minutes later, he dressed and left, still crying, not having spoken one word.

But he came back a few days later, and said his "Down with Big Brother!" again, and wept and sat bereft again. It became their routine. Soon Julia thought little of it. She took a pill before he arrived, and then could endure his stunned, beseeching face and his terrified chatter about his children, and still take him to bed as if it were only sex, as if she weren't killing him.

When Ampleforth visited, Julia would have his velvet slippers ready beside the bed. As he slipped into them, he lost his slumping self-effacement and became the Ampleforth of the room, a tall, pleasant-faced man of thirty, who sprawled and recited poems and exulted dotingly, wittily, at their beauty. She made him tea with real sugar, and he always pressed a few dollars on her so she wouldn't be out of pocket. He grew anxious if she came too near, so she usually sat in the armchair smoking while he lay on the bed writing down his poems or reading them aloud. He did flirt in his way, remarking shyly on her prettiness, calling her "my Abyssinian maid," and comparing her to Milton's Eve. Toward the end of every meeting, he allowed her, once, to hold his hand. This seemed to fill him with exaltation. Still, when she let go, he looked profoundly grateful, stretching and glancing down at his arms as if relieved to find himself still whole.

Even if he wasn't the sort of man she liked, she had come to love him dearly. She even started to think it would be a fine thing to cling to him naked as he said his poems, to kiss his throat and make him sigh and weep with different pleasures. What was more, she knew Love would like it. It was just what they would like.

So one day, when it came time to take his hand, she held it with a new sensitivity. Then she carefully, almost furtively, placed her other hand on his knee. She expected him to resist, to put her off with some excuse about how he "hadn't meant that." But he only sat breathless, staring at her face, while she gently pulled down his zip and let her hand wander inside his clothes. When she stood to remove her own overalls, he waited in mute compliance, his eyes darting toward her, then fearfully away. Everything about him was like a small animal that stops struggling in one's hands and falls still when it finds it can't escape. But of course that was how such beasts were tamed, and they were often far happier for it. When she moved his hand to her bare breast, he fondled it with a terrified focus; when she reached for his prick, she found it already hard—a fine big thing that knew its business even if he didn't. Emboldened, she guided him to lie on his back and climbed on top.

Through this final operation, Ampleforth's face was a mask of suffering. He breathed strangely, shallowly, through trembling nostrils. Both his hands were in childish fists. Julia was passionately grateful when he finished, with a stingy little spasm of the buttocks and face that he seemed to resist with all the rest of his body. She had the mad thought: *I have killed him*. A moment later he was fighting free of her, crying, "Oh, I am so sorry! What have we . . . oh, how dreadful! I am so sorry!"

"Stan," she said. "Oh, Stan, what's wrong?"

"It's loathsome! To treat you as . . . oh, shall we marry? Is that what we must do? What can we do? Oh, it's so vile!"

She stared at him, stricken, finding nothing to say. She was visited by a memory of herself in the clearing, sprawled on dewy grass, spreading her legs to show herself to the sun. A man laughed, striding around behind her head, scratching his chest. That had been sex, once.

Meanwhile, Ampleforth stammered that he'd tried this before and supposed it wasn't for him. Not that he didn't think of it. He was kept awake at night by just such thoughts. But if he ever touched a woman, he felt as if everyone he'd ever respected were there in the room, sneering at his dirty antics with repulsion. "I've had that feeling when a woman brushes against me quite by accident. I react, you see, and then I feel so awfully filthy. It's as if I were a child that had soiled itself. I did soil myself once at school, and I suppose—oh, you can't want to hear all this! Oh, dear, I'm such a wretched fool!"

That was the last day of July. The first day of August was one of Winston's days. She'd arrived an hour early and was drowsing on the bed, having taken the fourth-to-last of Oceania's pills, when she heard his step on the stair. He too was early, and his step was hurried; through the pleasure of the drug, she had a thrill of fear. One became very sensitive to things like that, to any change in routine, any urgency. As he opened the door, she was already on her feet.

"My dear!" she cried out. "What is it?"

Winston stopped in the doorway, smiling broadly. When she didn't smile in answer, he laughed and lunged forward to embrace her. She squirmed in his arms unhappily, saying, "Oh, let me go! Well—if you must. But what is it?"

"It's happened at last! It's come! I have spoken to O'Brien. It's all real!"

At this, she went still. Her first impulse was to say he *couldn't* speak to O'Brien. She would speak to O'Brien, if anyone did. O'Brien wasn't his.

Then a chill went through her. "You went to O'Brien? You've done it?"

He let her go and stood grinning before her. "No. That's just the marvelous thing. O'Brien came to me."

The story that emerged was this. Winston had been walking down the long corridor that led from Records to Research. At the very place where Julia had given him her note, he became aware of a large man walking behind him. He slowed instinctively. He'd never liked the feeling of a person creeping up on him. At that moment O'Brien—for it was he—coughed softly as if about to speak. In the shock of seeing who it was, Winston found himself turning to greet O'Brien as if it were quite an ordinary thing. His heart was pounding in his chest.

O'Brien started by speaking of an article Winston had written in the *Times*. It was a squib dashed off to fill a gap, and couldn't have impressed a man like O'Brien. Of that Winston was quite sure. But O'Brien fulsomely praised it, saying its Newspeak was written very elegantly; a friend of Winston's who was certainly an expert had commented on it—his name had temporarily slipped O'Brien's mind.

"And what's remarkable," Winston told Julia, "is that he can only have meant Syme. Do you remember Syme? I can say his name here."

"Oh, pretty well. Yes."

"You'll know, then, that he was vaporized."

"Was he? Are you certain of that?"

"Quite certain. He vanished and his name vanished from all the lists, all the rotas, that same day. It will have been a month or two ago. Well, to speak of an unperson in the Ministry, even indirectly! You see what it means."

"It's thoughtcrime."

"Not only that," said Winston. "He was sharing a thoughtcrime with me, one that I might have reported. By that very act, I am now his accomplice. Even if nothing else happened, we would be bound together by that."

"Perhaps you ought to report it," Julia said.

This he ignored, saying, "Here's the thing, though—he then told me he'd spotted two words in the article which are now obsolete, and he wondered if I'd seen the new edition of the Newspeak dictionary. Of course I haven't—it hasn't been issued yet. Well!"

"He'd got one."

"That's it. He asked if I'd like to have a look at it. 'Perhaps you could pick it up at my flat,' he said. His flat—you see? Then he stood beneath a telescreen to write the address. He was making a show of having nothing to hide, you understand. I've got the note here."

"Oh—I don't need to see it, thanks," said Julia.

"But the handwriting—no, you must see. It is quite a thing of beauty."

He found the slip of paper in a pocket of his overalls, and sat beside her on the bed to show her. Julia was sickened to see the familiar address, the elegant hand with its loops and flourishes. She looked away, saying, "Well, I shan't be going, after all. Perhaps it's better if I—"

"Not going! But of course you will go!" Winston frowned at her, affronted. "Why, don't you see what this means? This is what we have spoken of, all this time!"

"But he hasn't asked me, dear."

"I can't think that will matter, not once he hears you're one of us. No, I shan't hear of you staying behind. We shall join the revolution together."

"He has only offered you the loan of a book. You can't know—"

"I have never been more certain of a thing in my life." Winston stood up again restlessly. "It isn't just the book—if it were only that! It's the subtlety of O'Brien's mind. One can see at a glance he couldn't believe all the rubbish, all the lies. A man like that! Do you know, as I came here, I was imagining him singing the Hate Song: 'Death to the ownlifer, death death death! Death to false botanists, death death death!'" Winston sang in a fair approximation of O'Brien's voice, and did a few steps of the Hate Song dance, a simple march with a kick in each step, while mimicking O'Brien's broad-shouldered stance.

At this, Julia couldn't help laughing, and Winston laughed too, triumphant. "There! You do see! It's quite absurd. It is a miracle he has gone undetected all this time."

Now Julia was struck by the thrilling idea that Winston might be right. If O'Brien was a Brother, after all, he must still do the work of Love just as before. He must recruit people like Julia, and he wouldn't be whispering, "Of course I'm a Goldsteinite, really," to them. No, he would perform his role with perfect fidelity. O'Brien, of all people, was more than capable of this imposture. Looked at a certain way, it all lined up; if he were a clandestine rebel, it made sense that he would use his position at Love to find new recruits. He might have been watching Winston all this time to be sure of his man. He might intend to deploy him against the Party. And Ampleforth, perhaps—although it was harder to believe of poor Tom Parsons.

She said, with less conviction, "But he hasn't invited me."

"Oh, darling! Oh, sweet fool! This is real revolution! There can be no shrinking now!" He laughed at the very idea and went and picked up his paperweight. For a moment, Julia had the wild thought that he meant to menace her with it. But he cradled it to his chest and said, "Only think of it! It's finally to be real! You'll laugh, but I'm not even frightened. I have always known I must die, and now it's as if it has already happened. I am the dead! They cannot frighten the dead!"

15

AGAIN IT WAS THE SOFTLY LIT FLAT, WITH ITS DEEP
carpet and fragrance of spring. Again the enigmatic servant,
Martin, was there as the lift doors opened; again he led the
way with the impartiality of a machine. The cleanness of everything shamed her again, and again she was unnerved by the
way the carpet swallowed the sound of footsteps. She noticed
new details: a leather leash hanging on the wall that must belong to a pet dog, a little tree in a pot, a painting of a country
scene that showed a shining brook and a pony under a spreading oak. Again there was the sense of recognizing the place
where one should have lived, the home of fullness and reality, of
people rightly understood. There was the idea that linked this to
O'Brien, and the leap in one's heart when he was there.

This time Winston was at her side. He looked around at
everything mistrustfully, seeming almost repelled by Martin. But when he saw O'Brien, his face transformed. His eyes
became soft and wondering, his mouth slightly parted. One
saw he would give himself up to whatever this man chose for
him. Here was love, if you liked: love's reality. For the first time
she knew with certainty that he had never loved her, and was
soothed.

Weeks had given her only two instructions. First, she was to
show surprise when the telescreen was turned off. Then, when

O'Brien asked the two of them if they were willing to separate, Julia should say, very vehemently, "No."

"It will be all that you say," Weeks had added. "Mind that."

"One word? Won't Smith find that strange?"

Weeks smiled unpleasantly. "On the contrary. He will be very put out when you say that word."

The memory of it gave her confidence. She was not, as she was last time, the object of the deception, but one of the deceivers. There was the daring feeling of being in cahoots, and a steadying sense of safety. She had done the work entrusted to her, and returned with the sacrifice that was asked. Even guilt toward Winston felt out of place. He had never before been happy, never before in accord with his surroundings; never before had he looked at any other human being with respect. And he knew the result would be torture and prison. In that, she had never deceived him. No, she had given him the wish of his soul.

O'Brien sat at a table heaped with papers, closely studying a note he held in one hand. The shapes of his broad, ugly face were made grotesque by a green-shaded lamp shining close to his eyes. By that light, too, his black overalls seemed made of some opulent capitalist fabric: satin, gossamer, zephyr— whatever stuffs they'd had in the wicked times when magic was still abroad in the world. He didn't look up as they came in. This too created an impression of enchantment, though it could not be said whether O'Brien was the enchanter or the spellbound captive.

Julia thought he would now greet them, but when he moved, it was to pull his speakwrite toward him and dictate into it in a brisk staccato: "Items one comma five comma seven approved fullwise stop suggestion contained item six doubleplus ridiculous verging crimethink cancel stop unproceed constructionwise antegetting plusfull estimates machinery overheads stop end message." Then the note was laid aside, and he rose from his seat with a wintry expression. Julia realized just in time that he was reaching for the telescreen. As he hit the switch and it went black, she made a keen sound of surprise.

Winston said in rapture, "You can turn it off!"

"Yes," said O'Brien. "We can turn it off. We have that privilege."

He was facing Winston now, his ugly face devoid of expression. Winston, by contrast, shone all over. If O'Brien had come and touched him, Julia thought he might have swooned. She too felt the potency of O'Brien's presence, how his big body asserted primacy. She followed him with her eyes, and anxiously waited for him to speak. Though she knew not to expect his attention, when he didn't look at her, she felt forsaken.

Now O'Brien's expression subtly altered. It wasn't a smile but the merest idea of a smile. He said, "Shall I say it or will you?"

"I will say it," said Winston gratefully. "That thing is really switched off?"

"Yes, everything is switched off. We are alone."

"We have come here because—" Winston's voice broke. He glanced at Julia, then went on, "We believe that there is some kind of conspiracy, some kind of secret organization working against the Party, and that you are involved in it. We want to join it and work for it. We are enemies of the Party. We disbelieve in the principles of Ingsoc. We are thought-criminals. We are also adulterers. I tell you this because we want to put ourselves at your mercy. If you want us to incriminate ourselves in any other way, we are ready."

One could hear he had carried these words in his heart for months, that he'd rehearsed them like poetry. At certain words—*thought-criminals*, *adulterers*—his voice was hoarse with defiance. Despite herself, Julia reacted with panic, all the hairs on her body standing up. At the same time, she was startled by a sudden presence rising at her back. It was Martin, the servant, with his rigid face, who had slipped back in noiselessly. He carried a tray with slender glasses and a decanter of maroon liquid.

"Martin is one of us," O'Brien said. "Bring the drinks over here, Martin. Put them on the round table. Have we enough chairs? Then we may as well sit down and talk in comfort. Bring a chair for yourself, Martin. This is business. You can stop being a servant for the next ten minutes."

O'Brien poured for them all as Martin bustled around, arranging chairs. The temper of the gathering was now that of a band of merry conspirators. A feeling of unreality filled Julia. Could O'Brien be a Goldsteinite after all? Could Martin be his accomplice? But the scene was too precisely that of Winston's dreams. When they sat down, he looked wonderfully pleased with himself, like a petted child at his birthday.

Handing out the glasses, O'Brien said, "It is called wine. You will have read about it in books, no doubt. Not much of it gets to the Outer Party, I am afraid." The faint smile on his lips died as he said, "I think it is fitting that we should begin by drinking a health. To our Leader: to Emmanuel Goldstein."

Winston said eagerly, "Then there is such a person as Goldstein?"

"Yes, there is such a person," O'Brien said. "And he is alive. Where, I do not know."

Julia felt a brief shock at this confirmation, before realizing it wasn't a confirmation, only another element of Winston's fantasy. She sipped her wine, then drank it down hastily, faintly revolted at the taste. She'd had it once before, with Gerber, and then thought it terribly refined. Now it tasted only of spoiled juice.

Winston was saying, "And the conspiracy—the organization? It is real? It is not simply an invention of the Thought Police?"

"No, it is real," said O'Brien. "The Brotherhood, we call it. You will never learn much more about the Brotherhood than that it exists and that you belong to it. I will come back to that presently." He paused, seeming touched by a consideration, and glanced at a watch on his wrist. "It is unwise even for members of the Inner Party to turn off the telescreen for more than half an hour. You ought not to have come here together, and you will have to leave separately. You, comrade"—he looked at Julia for the first time—"will leave first. We have about twenty minutes at our disposal. You will understand that I must start by asking you certain questions."

Julia felt a stab of disappointment. Some part of her had cherished the idea that O'Brien would keep her behind for a candid talk. She'd even had a glimmering of a thought that he would take her to bed. Of course none of that was to happen, and, despite herself, she felt insulted. But O'Brien had begun his catechism. She forced herself to attend.

O'Brien asked the questions in a casual voice, as if they'd gone through this many times before, and it had no more significance than filling out a routine form on a speakwrite. It was nominally directed at Julia, too, but Winston answered for them both. Neither O'Brien nor Winston seemed to consider that Julia might respond. O'Brien's eyes dwelled on Winston with confidence. They seemed to say, *I know you are my man. All is already understood between us.* Winston sat very straight and met O'Brien's eye bravely, matching his tone to O'Brien's, answering readily and without evident emotion. Only a tension in his legs betrayed his nervousness.

The catechism went thus:

"In general terms, what are you prepared to do?"

"Anything that we are capable of."

"You are prepared to give your lives?"

"Yes."

"You are prepared to commit murder?"

"Yes."

"To commit acts of sabotage which may cause the death of hundreds of innocent people?"

"Yes."

"To betray your country to foreign powers?"

"Yes."

"You are prepared to cheat, to forge, to blackmail, to corrupt the minds of children, to distribute habit-forming drugs, to encourage prostitution, to disseminate venereal diseases—to do anything which is likely to cause demoralization and weaken the power of the Party?"

"Yes."

"If, for example, it would somehow serve our interests to throw sulfuric acid in a child's face—are you prepared to do that?"

"Yes."

"You are prepared to lose your identity and live out the rest of your life as a waiter or a dockworker?"

"Yes."

"You are prepared to commit suicide, if and when we order you to do so?"

"Yes."

As this continued, always in the same easy tone, Julia's feeling of surprise grew into outrage. She recognized it: it was the list of crimes O'Brien had said the followers of truth would happily commit in its name. He had promised she would someday hear a Brother acquiesce to these crimes from his own mouth; here, then, was the fulfillment of that promise. But how could Winston so glibly agree to these horrors? And how did he think he could agree for her—as if he could choose whether or not she would throw acid in the face of a child! Then there was the absurdity of O'Brien feigning to take Winston's answers seriously, when Winston had no capacity to do the least of these things. Never mind espionage; even to get a job as a dockworker was beyond his powers. He was an office clerk who cowered from rats. He couldn't even buy his own black-market goods! Murder, blackmail, suicide—he hadn't the foggiest conception what these words really meant. It made her conscious, as she'd never been before, that thoughtcrime was nothing to do with crime. It wasn't even a prelude to real crime.

And for this, he was to be condemned? One might as well execute a boy of six for saying he would like to be a pirate. Indeed, the whole scene smacked of childhood—the malignant, Mamie Faye side of childhood. The horrid rhyme Winston loved so much came back to her: *Here comes a candle to light you to bed, here comes a chopper to chop off your head.*

As she thought this, O'Brien's eye slipped unobtrusively to her. That alerted her in time for her to hear him say: "You are prepared—*the two of you*—to separate and never see one another again?"

She jumped to attention and blurted out, "No!"

As Weeks had predicted, Winston reacted to her one word with a grimace of annoyance. But when he saw her face, he balked, and his eyes were touched by sentiment. Only then she understood her role in the comedy. In Winston's dream, his woman would agree to any moral enormity, if it was what he wished. For him, she would die any death and commit any crime, quite without any motive of her own. Would she bring about the death of hundreds of people? Would she burn off the face of a child? For him, readily.

But to give up Winston Smith—oh, no, that was too great a sacrifice! That was the scene she had just played.

Now Winston was faced with a quandary. He was the ruthless terrorist, yes—but was he not also the passionate lover? And if he agreed to give Julia up after she'd defied O'Brien to refuse, mightn't he look a coward? His face filled with exquisite pain.

At last he spat out, "No," and looked back fearfully at O'Brien.

O'Brien nodded soberly. "You did well to tell me. It is necessary for us to know everything." He turned to Julia, saying, "Do you understand that even if he survives, it may be as a different person? We may be obliged to give him a new identity. His face, his movements, the shape of his hands, the color of his hair—even his voice would be different. And you yourself might have become a different person. Our surgeons can alter people beyond recognition. Sometimes it is necessary. Sometimes we even amputate a limb."

She started to ask what purpose amputation served, then remembered she wasn't to speak and bit off the word. O'Brien nodded as if she'd agreed to his terms and said, "Good. Then that is settled."

Now the atmosphere became more relaxed. Martin was sent out. O'Brien distributed cigarettes. Julia smoked and felt fatigue steal over her. Her part was done and she would soon be released. Perhaps Winston would be arrested immediately, and this unseemly farce could end. As she fought sleep, something niggled at her mind, something about the smoothly choreographed scene, the coordination between O'Brien and Martin. There was something important here, but exhaustion wouldn't let her think.

Meanwhile, O'Brien began to pace the room, one hand in the pocket of his sleek overalls, the other gesturing with his cigarette. "You understand," he said, "that you will be fighting in the dark. You will always be in the dark. You will receive orders and you will obey them, without knowing why. Later I shall send you a book from which you will learn the true nature of the society we live in, and the strategy by which we will destroy it. When you have read the book, you will be full members of the Brotherhood. But between the general aims that we are fighting for, and the immediate tasks of the moment, you will never know anything. I tell you that the Brotherhood exists, but I cannot tell you whether it numbers a hundred members, or ten million. From your personal knowledge, you will never be able to say that it numbers even as many as a dozen. You will have three or four contacts, who will be renewed from time to time as they disappear. As this was your first contact, it will be preserved. When you receive orders, they will come from me. If we find it necessary to communicate with you, it will be through Martin. When you are finally caught, you will confess. That is unavoidable. But you will have very little to confess, other than your own actions..."

Julia woke in a panic to find she'd nodded off. O'Brien was in a different part of the room, and Winston was now leaning breathlessly forward. Mercifully, no one appeared to have noticed. The cigarette was still in her hand, and its ash hadn't even grown that much. Perhaps she'd slept only a few seconds.

The great difference was that she'd woken knowing what her doubt had been. This choreographed scene was all too similar to the one played for her when she first came to this room. If it was clear that O'Brien was acting out the fantasies of Winston Smith—the secret society of fearless men, the poetic doom that awaited them—was it not also true that he had played out Julia's fantasies? What had he told her? That being a Hero of the Socialist Family wasn't cowardly, but brave; that she was destined to join the Inner Party because of her special qualities; that her sexual exploits weren't a weakness but a sign of superiority to the herd. He'd even called her a whore—a thing Julia had often called herself, and enjoyed as a badge of thrilling shame.

"When finally you are caught," O'Brien was now saying grandly, "you will get no help. We never help our members. At most, when it is absolutely necessary that someone should be silenced, we are occasionally able to smuggle a razor blade into a prisoner's cell. You will have to get used to living without results and without hope. You will work for a while, you will be caught, you will confess, and then you will die. Those are the only results that you will ever see. There is no possibility that any perceptible change will happen within our own lifetime. We are the dead."

When O'Brien said this, Julia thought even Winston must smell a rat. "We are the dead" was Winston's favorite saying. He must see that O'Brien had been spying on him, that O'Brien was actually parodying him. In a moment he would stare about him, seeing captors where he had seen friends.

But nothing of the kind took place, just as nothing of the kind had taken place when the performance was for Julia. Oh, she'd been terrified, of course. But had she not also been se-duced? She remembered herself saying seriously, "What is hate?" and hanging on O'Brien's answer. In fact, these past weeks, she'd been trying to hate. She had taken that duty seriously, as if Love were monitoring her spiritual development.

Now she saw that it was all a farce. No one cared what she felt, or thought, or was. No one cared even that she had com-mitted sexcrimes, or bought black-market goods. Nothing she did had meaning to these men. She could believe every tenet of Ingsoc and perform all its commandments, she could even do the work of Love, and she would still be killed when it suited their convenience—as Margaret had been killed, and Essie; as

Gerber was condemned not because of anything he'd done, but because Plentymen had been designated a class of scapegoats. Oh, how had she so easily been made to forget her whole life's experience?

Meanwhile, Winston remained bewitched and blissful as O'Brien repeated his own phrases back to him. "Our only true life is in the future. We shall take part in it as handfuls of dust . . . it might be a thousand years . . . in the face of the Thought Police, there is no other way." Julia, too, made a show of rapt attention, while thinking, *It makes no difference. Nobody cares what I am. I make no difference.* Even the cigarette was forgotten in her hand. She was experiencing sanity for the first time in months, and finding it unbearable. She had killed Winston. She was killing him all the time he tried to love her. She too would be killed, at an hour she didn't expect. All this she'd known, but had refused to know. This was her only life.

At last O'Brien again looked at his wristwatch and said to Julia, "It is almost time for you to leave, comrade. Wait. The decanter is still half-full." He poured out more wine and raised his glass. "What shall it be this time?" he said to Winston. "To the confusion of the Thought Police? To the death of Big Brother? To humanity? To the future?"

Winston reflected, then said, his voice hoarse with feeling, "To the past."

O'Brien nodded gravely. "The past is more important."

At this, Julia could bear no more. She drank off her wine, and as she rose to go, O'Brien stopped her and handed her a pill. "It is important not to go out smelling of wine," he said. "The lift attendants are very observant."

She took it mutely and went out, still holding the pill, grateful that he hadn't insisted on watching her swallow it. Once she'd shut the door behind her, she put her hand in her pocket and crushed the pill up in the cloth. Of course it wasn't likely to be poison, but she trusted nothing here.

The lift was waiting for her. Martin stood beside its open doors with his blankly knowledgeable face. How many times had he witnessed this ritual? How many Winstons had beamed in gratitude at O'Brien's lies? How many women had played Julia's part, and where were those women now?

Outside, the sun had set. The thousand lights of the Inner Party district shone in a thousand unharmed windows. Across the street, one window showed a pair of emerald velvet curtains, tied neatly back at their waists with golden cords. Beyond was a spacious room, in which warm light shone over a gleaming piano. Two pale-blue armchairs sat on either side, as if awaiting the piano's song, and the walls were lined with bookshelves full of clothbound books. Even the ceiling was ornamented with plaster flowers, and the piano had its own lovely rug to stand upon. Most strange of all was that no one was in the room. All that beauty sat unattended. The piano alone received the wasteful flood of electric light, light someone somewhere had worked to produce. One saw the hours of a stranger's life pouring uselessly over the silent piano.

16

FOR DAYS AFTER THAT, JULIA SAW NOTHING OF WIN-
ston. Hate Week itself had begun, and every waking hour was
spent marching, shouting, singing, burning, smashing. She
lived in the streets, and the streets were a delirium. What she
felt wasn't hate, but it melded her to the crowd and made her
feel multitudinous, godlike. It was as if the mob revolted and
screamed against the treatment Julia had received, as if the
people raged and broke windows in desperation at the coming
death of Smith.

Then Hate Week had passed, with no greater consequence
than that the name of the enemy had changed.

This happened in the midst of the great Hate Rally that
crowned the week's festivities, at which every person in London
crammed themselves into a few large squares and howled orgi-
astically at a series of speeches. Every year a dozen people were
trampled to death, and this was written about in every newspaper as evidence of the public's fervor. Julia had decided to sit it
all out and was hiding inside the ruins of a float, napping next
to a mechanism she'd repaired earlier in the week. She'd taken
the third-to-last of Oceania's pills, and the screaming outside
felt like a sea on which she was adrift while she dreamed about
falling asleep in various places. Long after dark, she woke and
clambered out drowsily to find squads of people hurriedly past-

ing up posters that said, EASTASIA: THE ETERNAL ENEMY over the previous week's ubiquitous poster of the Eurasian soldier. She staggered to the nearest telescreen and soon gleaned the necessary information. Eurasia, yesterday's eternal enemy, was now our gallant ally—had always been our gallant ally. Eastasia had always been the evil power that sought to destroy our way of life.

This affected Julia not at all, except that it meant she still couldn't see Winston. The Records people were kept working day and night, replacing all mentions of "Eurasia" with "Eastasia" and vice versa. Every book, every newspaper and telecast, even the archived letters of long-dead revolutionary figures were affected. Parsons and Ampleforth were also swept up in the effort. For the first time in months, Julia had free time.

That Sunday, she took advantage of this to go out on a Junior Anti-Sex League hike. She wanted a day of playing at her old life, singing patriotic hymns in ragged harmony and laughing at anodyne jokes; of being what she no longer was. The outing began with the usual speeches in the street, where young firebrands and hardened fanatics took their turn with the bullhorn. The others leaned against the coaches, fighting yawns, as one zealot after another speculated about new surgeries to render people incapable of sex, spoke with disgust of the "unwholesome slimes" that issued from human bodies, and sang the praises of True Vegetarianism—which meant not only eschewing meat but exterminating all animals for their obscene lives. Today the True Vegetarians were celebrating; during Hate Week, a new edict had been issued that forbade the keeping of domestic pets, or, in the language of the decree, "parasitic beasts." Some in the crowd had lost cats or dogs; many others had paid steep bribes to keep them. At Women's 21, there had been a scramble to get Commissar and Tiger registered as pest-control workers and to grease all the necessary palms, and still the cats could no longer be let outside, lest someone kill them and turn their tails in for the reward. The listeners thus showed a tendency to fidget and clench their jaws. Still, every speaker was applauded enthusiastically, with cries of "Hear, hear!" when they paused for praise.

During the speeches, Julia had the time to ascertain that none of her old friends were there, or none but Vicky, who had arrived late, in a gaggle of other Westminster girls—assistants and secretaries at Central Committee and the Chamber of Deputies. These didn't trouble themselves to cheer the speakers, except when one of their own number took the bullhorn, whereupon they instantly began to shriek and clap in ecstasy. Vicky looked wan and restless among them, and Julia kept thinking of going to her, then deciding against it.

At last the drivers began to toot their horns, and all gratefully gathered their picnic things and filed into the coaches. Julia went into one, Vicky and the Westminsters into another. On the drive, Julia was tormented by the nausea that had dogged her these past weeks. She leaned her forehead to the window and pretended to doze, repeatedly swallowing down the saliva that kept gathering in her mouth. She tried to think about being pregnant, but instead was plagued by thoughts of O'Brien and Smith. The scene O'Brien had played kept returning to her, with its skullduggery and masculine glamour. So much effort, just to make a single condemned man as guilty as he could be. Surely O'Brien was not simple enough to believe Winston Smith was a threat to the state, nor could Love believe such rubbish. No, they must know it was a lie, and only played these cruel games for . . . for what?

But she couldn't say she didn't understand it. It was the instinct that had driven her to get Tom Parsons to say "Down with Big Brother!" and to coerce poor Ampleforth into sex. Once the rules of the game were determined, one strove to win as best one could. Indeed, when Smith and Parsons and Ampleforth were taken, what could follow but more nights with more doomed men, who would perform at Julia's suggestion, then be tortured and killed for whatever they did? And she must finally die the same way—for she knew with certainty now that all O'Brien's promises had been lies. She might hope for some months or years of safety, at the price of condemning dozens of others. Then she too would die.

When the coach stopped at last, she was desperately grateful, and stumbled out with a mind for nothing but the clean air and the stable ground. At first, even walking made her queasy, and she lagged behind the group, feigning an interest in the butterflies. Her old leafleting partner Peggy dawdled with her, telling an endless story about a lost coupon book that was returned by a man who turned out to know her cousin. Only very slowly did Julia realize where they were. It was the same path she'd taken the day she found the clearing with Lou; the place Winston called the Golden Country.

The hike leader called a meal halt just then. As often happened, all the speechifying had made them late, and now the hike would be curtailed. Those who hadn't made speeches began to grumble. They wouldn't mind, of course, if the speeches were truly partyful, but . . . and they now found reason to fault each speaker for some error in doctrine. Overhearing, the speakers whispered to their friends that these criticisms were founded in wrongthink. All cast suspicious glances at each other and the atmosphere turned foul. To make things worse, the picnic turned out to be entirely made up of class-three goods. The bread and cheese were only stale, but the SocHealth "apple juice" had never had anything to do with an apple and had a potent aftertaste of bile. The smell alone made Julia queasy, and she was plagued by a feeling of wretchedness. Even this brief holiday was to be spoiled. Peggy had wandered off to join a blanket occupied by more energetic grumblers, and, for the first time ever on a hike, Julia found herself sitting alone.

That was how she ended up leaving her stuff and drifting toward the blanket where Vicky was sitting with the Westminster girls. Of course it wouldn't do to single Vicky out; that risked being pairthink. With this in mind, Julia raised her empty picnic bag and said, in a vaguely inclusive way, "I thought I might go looking for mushrooms. There are often good ones here."

As Julia had hoped, the Westminsters' snobbishness precluded them from thinking of joining her. But Vicky said, "Oh, that's just what I would like," and scrambled to her feet, while the others yawned and regarded Julia through narrowed eyes.

As they set out, Julia's nausea had vanished and she walked with a buoyant pleasure she hadn't felt for months. It now felt clear that, beneath all the misery and preoccupation of these days, she'd been thinking of Vicky, exalting her, possibly cooking up a proper crush. Vicky was Central Committee; she was unspoiled youth; she had been a good comrade in danger. Then there was the history of the baby and Margaret, which had once tainted Vicky in Julia's eyes, but now made her a kindred spirit. Julia too was steeped in crime and walking into doom with both eyes open.

They walked in silence, and the silence was charged with that feeling. It gave a solemnity to the sunlight and the drowsy heat of August. When she heard the stream, Julia ran forward, ducking and pushing through the awkward branches. Vicky followed. This too was strange and intimate, if only because they still didn't speak or laugh. At the bank, Julia turned to face

Vicky, who stopped several paces away, her face flushed. Neither of them smiled.

"It's here I was thinking of," Julia said.

"Yes," said Vicky. "There should be mushrooms here."

Julia had forgotten the mushrooms. She looked at the banks and the trees around, where there were none to be seen. "Oh. I thought the damp ..."

Vicky came closer, peering around like Julia. "Perhaps someone came here before us. It does seem as if there would be some here."

"It is splendid, though, by the water. Wouldn't it be lovely to go in?"

"Well, yes, on a swimming excursion. One couldn't now." Vicky smiled over her shoulder at Julia and went on along the bank, tramping through some muddy leaves and ducking under a low branch. Julia followed, feeling sensitive and a little cross. She hadn't meant they should really bathe. And why was Vicky the leader now, when Julia was the elder and this had been her idea?

At last Vicky crouched down at a place where the stream tumbled noisily over rocks. Julia hunkered down beside her. She looked in the water for fish, but here it was too shallow. Some part of her mind was remembering swimming, how one could open one's eyes underwater and see the pebbles, so still on the bottom, like a thing preserved in glass.

Then Vicky said, "Can I trust you? Can I trust you absolutely?"

Everything stopped. Julia still gazed at the water but felt her face had become entirely strange. If she said no, the day would be spoiled, and whatever was between them might be at an end. Curiosity would torment her, too—though the thing with which she was to be trusted could only be a confession of love.

Worse, she herself had brought on this calamity. It was rash to invite Vicky on this outing, and wholly inexcusable to speak of bathing. How could that be heard but as flirtation? And if she said, *Yes, you can trust me*, it was clear—Julia knew herself—they would soon be kissing and rolling together among the fallen leaves. There was normally no harm in such things, not even any risk of pregnancy. But there was Weeks. There was O'Brien. Nothing Julia did in that way was without harm.

When Julia looked at Vicky then, she found the girl's face pale and altered. One saw the shape of her mature beauty: the strong jaw and small pink mouth; the finely shaped eyes a little too close together, giving her an air of tender concentration. With her very fair coloring, she looked like the girl on the old packet of Valkyrie cigarettes.

"You can trust me," said Julia. "Yes."

Vicky smiled and relaxed, as if a dreadful danger had passed. She said, "You know I'm at Central Committee."

Julia was so wrong-footed, she spent several seconds trying to guess what Central Committee had to do with lovemaking. Then she said cautiously, "Well, of course."

Vicky nervously pulled her hands into the cuffs of her overalls. "Well, I sometimes come to know things there. Just from being in the room, you understand."

"Oh, yes? What sort of things?"

"It's mostly nothing of consequence. Who's in favor and who's out. Something off with the quotas. It's never that I'm spying, not intentionally. But I overhear conversations, or sometimes I have to read the first pages of a file to know where it's to be put away. I haven't any power, so no one thinks anything of it. And, anyhow, I'm Whitehead's fiancée." She said this last very flatly. Inside the cuffs of her overalls, her hands had gone into fists.

Now Julia wished fervently that she had told Vicky not to

trust her. The last thing she wanted on her day out was to learn some Central Committee gossip, or, worse, some secret she wasn't meant to hear. What good did it do to know such things?

Vicky seemed to intuit what Julia was thinking, because she said hastily, "I know it must seem that I'm revealing secrets—dangerous secrets—just to make myself important. But you'll see there's a reason I must tell you. What I want to ask can make no sense unless you know about the maps."

The mention of something to be asked only added to Julia's unease. But she said, "Maps?"

"Yes. There's a room at Central Committee that has maps on every wall. It's where they hold meetings about the war. Of course I don't attend those, but I bring coffee in sometimes, and it's my job to clean up afterward. And, you understand, their maps aren't like the ones we see. These show all the streets in Inner Party districts, all the closed towns in Semi-Autonomous Zones, all the military roads between those towns. If one wanted to know where every airfield is, it's on that map. Well, there's no reason I would want to know, and I never took much notice, as you can imagine. But in that room, on the great map of Airstrip One, there are places that have changed."

Julia frowned. "How, changed?"

"Their color has changed. That's how."

"But isn't the color of a place on a map—well, it's not its real color, is it?"

"No. But it still has meaning. If Oceania is red and Eurasia is blue—well, it matters when the red pushes out the blue. It shows Oceania has conquered territory."

"Is that what it is? Has Oceania conquered more territory?"

"No," said Vicky. "What is that to us? I shouldn't take any notice of that."

This statement flatly contradicted all a Party member was

meant to feel, and, despite herself, Julia was taken aback. Vicky misinterpreted her expression and said, "Don't worry. No one can hear us here. I know this place well. I've been here many times with Whitehead."

"With Whitehead? Here?"

"All around here, yes. There's a clearing where we used to meet, and we swam in this stream. He liked to see me do it, anyhow. He dabbled his feet."

Vicky glared into the water with a mutinous expression. Julia wanted terribly to know if the clearing was her clearing, but didn't like to ask. It could only lead to uncomfortable questions, to which the answer was Winston Smith.

Now Vicky went on: "Now, all the time I've been at Central Committee, Airstrip One was colored red for Oceania. But not long ago, the Shetland Autonomous Zone began to have black stripes. And an edge of the East Scots Economic Zone—that was red with black stripes as well."

"Black stripes. Could it mean they'd had an atom bomb?"

"That's what I thought at first. Or a plague or a flood— something of that nature. But then a few months ago, I saw it had grown. The black stripes had spread into Scotland. A few weeks later, they'd appeared in the south, the Isle of Wight. After that, they only kept advancing. For a time, the cartographers were extending them with pen. They hadn't time to print new maps."

"That could still be atom bombs. Do you remember some weeks ago, there were great explosions?"

"No, it was before that," Vicky said impatiently. "I'm sure it's not that. And listen—those maps are gone now. They've all been replaced by maps without any stripes. And the cartographers who worked on the maps, they're gone."

"Gone?"

"Vaporized," Vicky said cold-bloodedly. "No one speaks of them now. There are new cartographers, and everyone behaves as if they were always there."

"But what can it mean?"

"Why, it's clear. That area has been conquered."

"How, conquered? You're saying we have lost part of Airstrip One itself?"

"I think so. Yes."

"Wait, where are these stripes? How far have they gone? Are they near London?"

"Not when I last saw. They'd come right through the north of England, though. And of course I can't say what might have happened since the cartographers went."

Julia sat digesting this. The peace and luxuriance of the scene around them made it seem impossible. But of course there could be troops and tanks just out of sight behind the trees. Half of London might have already been taken. Anything was possible when one was never told the truth.

"There are other things, too," said Vicky. "There are troops guarding all the main buildings of Westminster now, and fleets of armed microcopters on the roofs. They started to pile sand-bags around some of the buildings, too, but then they stopped. I suppose they saw how it looked. That district's not been bombed since the fifties."

"So you think Eurasia . . . or rather, Eastasia, has invaded Airstrip One?"

"No." Vicky leaned close and said vehemently, "Do you know, I don't believe there is an Eastasia or Eurasia, not as we've been told. If they exist, I don't think they give two pins for us. *That's* not who we're fighting."

"Who, then?"

"Rebels. You know—Goldstein followers."

At this, all Julia's excitement vanished. A sick disappointment washed through her, and she cried out, "Oh, no, don't tell me you have fallen for that, too!"

Vicky's face fell. "How do you mean?"

"Goldstein. The almighty Goldstein! Eurasia doesn't exist, but there's a Goldstein? And he's conquering Airstrip One?"

"But it needn't be Goldstein! I only mean that they're rebels."

"And have they spoken of rebels at Central Committee? Is that what you've overheard?"

"Not as such. When they speak of it at all, they speak of bandits. That's how I know it's not Eastasia."

"Well, there you are! Bandits!" Julia's voice was triumphant, but she felt a vile misery all through her body. "Those areas are plagued with bandits, that's all."

"But that's the same thing," said Vicky stubbornly. "Bandits *are* rebels, aren't they?"

"Oh, to Central Committee, no doubt. Who isn't? You've just said you don't believe in Eastasia. Draw a black stripe here—another rebel area."

"Well, they would be right in that," said Vicky. "I am a rebel, or mean to be."

"How? You aren't thinking of going to these bandits?"

"Of course I'm going. I'd have gone already, but I couldn't go without asking you."

"Asking me?"

"Asking you to come. Don't you see? Oh, Julia, you must come too."

This sent a jolt of panic through Julia. "Don't be a fool. You must put all this from your mind. I'm from a SAZ—no, of course you didn't know. How could you? But there were bandits there when I was a girl, and I can tell you they're not a bit like rebels. They're escaped criminals and boys hiding out from conscription. They do a lot of mischief, but it's not war. It's—oh, robbing people on the roads and violating women— that's their style."

"I know there is that sort of bandit! I'm not a child. But I don't believe that sort of thing would be put on a map. And then there are the sandbags."

"Sandbags? What does that prove?"

Vicky shook her head with a look of despair. "Oh, how can I convince you?"

Julia had the feeling she'd had so often with Vicky of want- ing to shake her by the scruff of the neck. Why was she—why was Winston—why were so many people determined to put an end to themselves?

Julia said, in the most reasonable tone she could muster, "But, Vicky, why would someone like you think of such a des- perate step? Can Whitehead be so terrible? Think: you could have such a lovely flat."

"A flat!" Vicky laughed disbelievingly.

"Babies, then."

"Oh, you don't know! You don't know what they are. Do you know what Whitehead said to me when I told him I'd joined Anti-Sex? He approved and said it would be grand cover. They don't believe any of it! It's all a sham. And when he saw I was serious, when he saw I wouldn't be alone with him anymore—that was when he asked me to marry him. And he did it in front of all the others, so they applauded and spoke of my duty to the Party, and I couldn't say no. I shouldn't won- der if they weren't coached by Whitehead. All to show me I couldn't escape! And you think—they all think—I shall have a fine life. But do you know, I've hardly met a man at Central Committee with a wife of more than thirty? As soon as she starts to lose her looks, the wife becomes a thought-criminal.

They send their own wives to Love—that abattoir! And, as often as not, the children go to a children's home. That's how it is." Vicky reached out and grasped Julia's hand. "You look so strange. Don't you understand? Oh, Julia, don't you see why I *must* leave?"

Julia said weakly, "But they can't all be like that."

"There are some, I suppose. But Whitehead's not one. And what does it matter if so much is rotten? Oh, you can't think how I hate them! Don't you see—to leave is our best chance. I shall be a nurse there. It's all I ever wanted to do. And you—you're a mechanic. They're sure to want mechanics. And if there are rebels, or even a chance of rebels, then we have to help them. What are we, if we don't help?"

Julia sat stunned, chilled to her bones. Vicky's hand still clutched hers, alarmingly soft against Julia's work-rough skin. The girl's blue eyes were blazing, exalted. Julia had a terrible, marvelous sense of lost balance, a wild lurch of hope that altered everything. The sun shimmered. The millions of leaves excitedly trembled in the clear blue air. She looked at the water pouring past like reckless light, and, for one glorious moment, she believed. The rebels were there, or *might* be there. Vicky wanted her. Of course she would go.

But then she remembered Winston saying, "This is real revolution! There can be no shrinking now!" She remembered O'Brien's smile as he said to Winston, "Shall I say it or shall you?" She remembered Winston and O'Brien saying, with grave satisfaction: "We are the dead."

She blurted out, "You mustn't. That's all a sham. There's no Brotherhood at all. There isn't anything—a few boys hiding from conscription. You can't."

Vicky gave a little sob of breath. "But, Julia—"

"No! You can't say this to me, anyway. You mustn't. I shall tell you—I'm Thought Police. I am! So you see why you mustn't say these things."

Vicky stared at Julia. She began to smile tentatively, thinking it a joke. Then her face changed again. It had become dead white.

"Yes, you see," Julia said, freeing her hand from Vicky's. "I would know if there was any rebellion. There's nothing. It's all a damned trick, no doubt. They will lure you into showing yourself and kill you. I've done that sort of thing myself! Oh, I'm a damned, rotten person, and here you are trusting me. Do you see? You don't know what you're about."

"It's not true," said Vicky weakly. "You can't be that. You're only afraid for me, so you're making up a story."

"It is true. It is! That's why you can't ever speak of this to me, or to anyone. You mustn't trust anyone. No one! And you must put all this from your mind."

"But it's true? You're Thought Police? Oh, please don't lie. Do say if it's not true."

"It's true."

"But then . . . is that why you came and sat on my bed that night? When they had the program about our friend the potato? Were you being Thought Police then?"

Julia crossed her arms against herself. "Not then."

"Do you know," Vicky said, "I always think of my baby—*my baby*, I can say those words to you—well, I think of it as our friend the potato. And I think how you came to my bed, how you forgave me when no other would."

"Vicky, don't! Only think. How can you say such things to me? When I am what I am?"

"I don't care! Do you hear me? I love you just the same."

"No, you *can't* love me. You mustn't."

"I shall forgive you as you forgave me. How am I any better?

Even if it's true, I'm no better. I killed my baby! I let that girl Margaret die for what I'd done."

It was what Julia had been thinking for weeks, but now she said, "You mustn't think that. It was they who made you—"

"Oh, rubbish! Who's *they*? I'm at Central Committee. You're Thought Police. We're *they*! That's just why we've got to get out. Oh, *won't* you come?"

"Where? To join some bandits? What would we get from that but rape?"

The next moment, Vicky was sobbing unrestrainedly. Cautiously, Julia put her arm around her, and Vicky let her head fall to Julia's shoulder, crying with soft, desperate sounds. Despite the tears, the girl's warm weight felt wonderfully consoling. Julia breathed Vicky's scent of youth and soap and frightened sweat, and felt as if the crisis had passed. Vicky must have been convinced. They would be safe; the breakthrough had already been achieved. She stroked Vicky's hair, muttering softly, "Yes, please don't. Don't do anything. You won't..." And it seemed nothing great, no significant difference, when Vicky turned and kissed her on the lips.

Then it was easy for Julia to say to herself, *We will kiss and Vicky will stay. I'm saving her.* That vindication was in their tongues touching fearfully, in Vicky's sigh of pleasure. Julia loved Vicky too—that was true. It wasn't false. Her body loosened and lost itself, as if she'd finally slipped into the water naked and let its force carry her free. Vicky's mouth tasted of the vile apple juice, but even this was only a reminder that Vicky lived the same life as she. This was a person she could know. It was someone's real life in her arms. Vicky forgave her, and if this were possible ... She had the old memory of the exiles dancing to the gramophone, heavy rain blowing at the windows, and Julia peering from beneath a nest of coats to spy on the anarchist man as he danced with his wife, too slowly for the music, and she changed under his hands. He changed, and everyone gave them room.

But behind this came the thought of Love.

Suddenly Julia was fumblingly pushing Vicky away. Vicky cried out and tried to catch at her, but Julia broke from her grasp. She stood up, strangely out of breath, as if she'd needed all her strength to escape from Vicky's arms.

She said, "I shan't tell anyone about this. I swear it."

Vicky stared, seeming at first unable to grasp that anything so terrible could happen. Then she stammered, "But you must come. There are the rebels. There is everything."

"We can't. We can't do any of it. Don't you see?"

"No, you might think about it. You might change your mind."

At that, Julia grabbed her picnic bag from the ground and started back the way they'd come. As she went, she felt Vicky horribly not behind her. There was the ache in her throat of needing to cry, that strangling, even after she'd begun to cry. She kept blundering into branches, scratching herself. She had a feeling that she must hurry. If she didn't make haste, there would be no way back.

When she heard Vicky coming after her with a great clashing of branches, she slackened her pace. The awful clenching in her throat eased. She felt light-headed. Vicky caught up and touched Julia's elbow. Julia looked back at her wildly, fearfully, but Vicky only said, "Don't cry. Oh, please don't."

"No, I won't," Julia said. "I'm not."

"If you would think—but I won't bother you."

They walked on, Vicky one step behind. Soon Julia was able to dry her eyes. She didn't try to look at Vicky, she only looked at the trees and sky, as if she wouldn't see them again.

She hugged herself as she walked. Though the day was warm, she felt wretchedly cold.

Only when they came out into the pasture and saw the main group did Julia realize they hadn't got any mushrooms. The Westminster girls were already on their feet, cleaning up their picnic articles. They turned to watch Julia and Vicky approach. Julia had the sudden thought that Vicky might say the wrong thing, revealing they hadn't gone for mushrooms at all. She stepped forward hastily, holding up her empty bag, and called cheerfully, "No luck!" Behind her, Vicky waved her arm and echoed: "No luck! We've had no luck!"

17

IT WAS CONFIRMED AT LAST: SHE WAS PREGNANT. ALL
the artsem nurses gathered in the examination room to sing
"The Birth of a Socialist." The doctor presented Julia with a
MOTHER OF THE BIG FUTURE badge: a large bronze medallion
stamped with a baby's face and embellished with a red satin
ribbon. She was given three booklets of extra sweet coupons
and invited to sit and watch a teletape of Big Brother thanking his honored comrades for being the vessels of a purified
race. As she watched, she imagined she would run away with
Vicky after all. They would go far away, to Eurasia—or Eastasia,
now that they were the enemy. The idea became a chaos of images: she and Vicky in a smugglers' boat; she and Vicky held at
gunpoint by leering bandits; Vicky laughing as she told police
every compromising word Julia had said. At last she saw Vicky's
almost-baby in the toilet, smeared and dead and terrifyingly
minuscule, as if it had died of shrinking. Her heart started beating so unsteadily, so fast, she felt she might be dying.

The teletape ended with an Oceanian flag rippling behind a
line of beautiful women, all pregnant, all smiling and saluting
the viewer. When the screen went to black, Julia asked in a daze,
"So is it truly to be Big Brother's child?"

The nurses all began to applaud. The doctor said, "That's
right. And you will have a certificate."

"A certificate," Julia said. "Plus good."

A very young nurse hugged Julia impulsively, saying, "Oh, yes! I should want that too!"

When Julia got to her feet, she felt surprised there was no perceptible burden. She'd somehow expected to feel the weight of the baby, now that it was a fact. The young nurse led her out. She was a red-haired girl with crooked teeth, all now displayed in a beaming grin. As they came into the waiting room, the nurse's triumphal manner made all the women in the chairs look up.

The nurse said, "Comrades! Please congratulate our newest Mother of the Big Future! Long live the Party! Long live Big Brother!"

At this, all the women hastily leapt to their feet, all applauding and cheering, with fixed smiles. Julia felt horror and joy together, and the joy felt threatening, while the horror felt like a kind of security. Her face slipped, shifted, and involuntarily assumed that same fixed smile. She'd gone astray, had been a criminal, but now was saved, was lost, would live after all, but with a child; no, the child would be taken away—without a child.

There were papers to fill out then, and instructions she must learn and repeat. She was given vitamins and packets of powdered protein, and tutored in their use. All the while, she felt that smile tightening her face. She saw it on the faces all around. It almost seemed to grin from the air. By the time she was released through the street door, an hour had passed and she was weak with smiling.

As the door swung shut behind her, a voice in her head said pragmatically, *But it's all a joke. Every woman there knows artsem babies are mostly bastards. What hypocrites!* At this, the horror eased somewhat. She looked about herself at the quiet street. The smile on her lips was almost hers. She remembered she was to see Ampleforth that evening, for the first time since Hate Week began, and felt better. Whatever his shortcomings, Ampleforth would never have that smile.

She still had two of Oceania's pills and decided to go to the little room early. She took the bus and was surprised when a man stood up to offer her his seat. Then she saw the smiles all around and remembered her new badge. When she sat, all the passengers began to ask if the badge meant what they thought, and if it was true about the Big Future program. All were proles, and very genuine in their enthusiasm. Proles generally despised the Party, but loved Big Brother without reserve, believing he was their only defense against the depredations of the "blues." Now they said how queer it was to think of all those Little Brothers running about, but grinned happily at the idea, and said the little beggars would beat the "Easties" ragged. As they fussed around her, Julia's hand came to rest a little tentatively on her belly. It was there—it really was there. And now she felt a rush of joy, a thrill so wild she was glad to be sitting down. Yes, the child was probably Parsons's or Smith's. Nonetheless, it would be raised as Party royalty. It would live in a pristine, carpeted realm, with a pet dog and a grand piano. And suppose that, by a fluke, the baby was Ampleforth's—might it not be able to read old poetry? Were such books really off limits to the Inner Party? Or suppose it was Smith's—it would have all the power and dignity Smith so clearly craved. Of course Parsons already had children, and both were wretched brats—she had met them at a Truth picnic, where they'd set the skirt of a prole servant on fire, and justified it by claiming the woman pulled a face when "Rule, Oceania!" came on the radio. But mightn't the brats be very different people if they'd grown up in an Inner Party children's home? She'd heard the children there rode ponies and swam every day in a lake. And many were adopted by

Inner Party parents who couldn't have babies of their own. A child of Big Brother would surely be adopted straightaway.

Yet somehow Julia found her smile was gone and she had treacherous tears in her eyes. The keen-eyed woman in the seat beside her patted her arm and said, "Never mind, love. You'll have your own kiddies someday. Here, show me your palm."

Julia readily offered it. Then all pushed in to peer over the woman's shoulder while she read four children in the lines and two of them "keepers," a boy and a girl. "Now, there!" the woman concluded triumphantly, releasing Julia's hand. "It ain't over yet."

"You'll want to get out at this next stop," a man said helpfully. "It's prole streets after that."

"Oh, no," said Julia. "I'm going to a shop in the prole district, two stops on. I know the streets well. It's not a bit dangerous."

"Not dangerous!" said the man, as if this were an extraordinary statement.

"Not dangerous!" echoed others.

All then exclaimed at her carelessness, and vied in telling tales of the crimes that plagued the district now, and the delinquent youth who had lost all fear of the Party and ran amok, who would cut your throat as quick as saying good morning. And this young comrade carrying Big Brother's baby! Not dangerous! Knows the streets! Who knew the streets better, they would like to know!

Julia climbed out hastily at the stop they recommended to save herself from arriving at Weeks with an honor guard of scolding proles. The instant the bus pulled out of sight, she hastily removed the badge and hid it in her tool bag.

On the walk to Weeks, she was uncomfortably aware that the brief bus ride had made her nauseous. She felt peculiarly moved that the baby was already giving trouble, was already a person who edged one out and made a nuisance. She had decided it must be a boy (Big Brother, after all), and it had somewhere acquired the name John. That was the name of two of the more dashing airmen—two Johns who'd once lived together at Mrs. Marcy's, making noise on a guitar neither knew how to play, and teaching the kittens to ride their shoulders. One John might walk around the yard festooned with kittens, singing an old Spanish war song out of tune, while the other played an out-of-tune accompaniment. So beautiful they were: dark-haired, broad-chested, brave as a flag, and young as a tight-closed bud. They'd inhabited Julia's dreams before those dreams were properly filthy, when the airmen were still half love, half father. Yes, John was the name. One John had survived— he'd lost a leg and been demobbed as an invalid—and so the name was lucky too.

A flood of love washed through her that made her stumble as she walked. She was making an Inner Party baby, a baby valuable enough to be safe. At the same time, it struck her that, while it lived inside her, Julia too was safe. More than that: she might be freed from her duties in the little room over Weeks. Surely it wasn't right for Big Future mothers to do that sort of work.

For just a moment, she thought of going directly to O'Brien's flat to tell him the news. She could explain what had happened and ask his opinion, which must be that Big Brother's infant couldn't be exposed to crime and obscenity. As she thought of it, she was filled with a passionate longing to see O'Brien's flat again, the green-shaded lamp, the painting with the brown pony beneath the oak. And to have O'Brien's ear, to speak at last to a person who had power...

When she woke from her reverie, she saw that, from old habit, she'd wandered to the market at the end of Mrs. Melton's street. However, it was so changed as to be almost unrecognizable. If it was poor the last time she was here, now it was hardly a market at all. The government stalls were gone, as were the make-do-and-mend girls with their spools of bright thread. In their place, a handful of people had spread blankets on the ground and were peddling miscellaneous junk—a pair of scissors, old clothes, a battered saucepan, heaps of cardboard. Still worse was a pair of shabby tables with a banner reading SMALL PORK, above which were strung a few dozen narrow carcasses with the unmistakable forms of roasted rats. Less immediately striking but just as chilling was the lack of patrols. Normally there were two or three at the market, guarding the government stalls and extorting bribes from illegal merchants. Now their absence felt like a presence. Julia shivered to think how she'd been walking in a daze through these changed streets.

Despite this, the familiar row of housefronts gave Julia a pang of nostalgia. Since she'd begun her work at Weeks, she hadn't been to see the Meltons at all. No need—she had every sort of Inner Party goods for the asking. Now it struck her that it would be delightful to see old friends. The beautiful Harriet might be married now, or preparing to marry and eager to show off her wedding overalls. Courtesy of Weeks, Julia's bag was full of coffee and sugar; these treats were intended for Winston, but they were just the things to thrill Mrs. Melton's heart. Of course it meant giving up her time lying on the bed in the loving spell of the pills—but there was a thought: Perhaps Mrs. Melton traded in such pills? It was just the sort of thing she might have tucked away in some dark cupboard.

With this pleasant idea in mind, Julia hurried on to Mrs. Melton's door and knocked smartly. In the house, she could hear raised voices, and the footsteps that came to the door were impatient. This was wonderfully familiar, and Julia smiled as she braced herself for Mrs. Melton's rudeness. Indeed, when the door opened, Mrs. Melton was reassuringly unchanged: the same crimson veins decorated her nose; the same stout build filled out the same plain trousers. She even wore the same AIR-STRIP ONE CAN BUILD IT! headscarf she'd worn the last time Julia saw her. On seeing Julia, she frowned and said, "You, is it?" then peered out into the street as if some more interesting person might appear. There was perhaps a longer pause, a more convincing reluctance, before she half closed the door to unhook the chain, saying, "As you're here, you'd best come in."

Mrs. Melton led the way to the familiar sitting room with its well-worn armchairs and heaps of various goods. As they went, she entertained Julia with the usual jeremiad about how times were hard and goods were scarce and people were unwilling to pay their worth. But a new complaint had appeared: the customers too had now grown scarce. "I never thought to see you again, for one. Ain't many of the old Party lot that still come. Here, I hope you weren't reckoning on finding those cigarettes you like. That trade's all gone."

"Oh?" Julia said politely. "What's happened?"

"What's happened? What hasn't happened? Now, what I have got, I've got some lovely Inner Party tea. You can take that off my hands, if you like."

"Tea? Not today, I don't think."

"Tea keeps, and it's good in trade. But suit yourself. I've got little else in that way. If you had any goods yourself, I'd be glad of them."

"Well, I might." Julia let her hand drift to her tool bag. "But what I was hoping you might have, it's a sort of a pill. Perhaps you know them. We call them anti-sex pills."

Mrs. Melton frowned and studied Julia more closely. "That . . . well, I can get it. There's little enough I can't get. But I can't sell them pills to just anyone, when, next thing I hear, they're dead by their own hand. And often enough, the Party was after 'em, and that's why they did it. The Party don't like that. That's the sort of thing makes them take an interest in a trader. They call it 'aiding an escape' and 'conspiracy,' and Big Brother only knows what else. You see it ain't worth the risk. Especially when it's someone such as you, who never had no use for such medicines before. I ask myself where you've been these months, and if you're not in some trouble. You see my position."

Julia nodded, as if these considerations were very well known to her. "That is a shame, as I can pay quite well. And I'm in no trouble. Look here." She fished in her pocket and brought out the Big Future badge. "Do you know what this is?"

Mrs. Melton kept her face blank, but her posture was suddenly keenly upright. Her hands rearranged themselves around each other. "Yes, I should say I know it."

"I've just been given that today," said Julia. "So, you see, I'm in no trouble at all. I am in rather a lot of discomfort, though."

"Yes, you'll want it for your aches and pains. Ain't nothing wrong in that." Then she looked at Julia craftily. "And if you're willing to trade me that badge for it, that might suit me very well."

Julia's hand closed over the badge. "What, this?"

"Now, you see, it ain't much use to you. Just a bauble. You've got the proof you are what it says, so the badge is nothing but idle show. But there's others can make good use of such badges. And a little thing like that—well, you can easily say it was lost."

For just a moment, Julia was tempted. The urge to please Mrs. Melton was strong, and it was true that badges were often lost. But some instinct made her shake her head and slip the badge back in her pocket. "No, best not. I don't like to lose it. But I have some Inner Party coffee and sugar, if those are any use to you."

Mrs. Melton's eyes remained on Julia's pocket. "Well, coffee and sugar is all very well. But if you ever change your mind, I'm—"

At that moment, a great booming shook the house. Mrs. Melton sprang back with a curse as a tremendous crashing rushed in from a distance and blew past, rattling the windows. A tin canister slipped from a shelf and plunged to the floor, rolling resoundingly over the lino. In the quiet that followed, the bare lightbulb that hung unlit from the ceiling was swinging back and forth on its wire. Then pounding footsteps came down the stairs, and Harriet appeared in the doorway, wearing old patched trousers and a shapeless sweater, her red hair mussed as if she'd been roused from sleep.

She cried out angrily, "Bloody bombs! The bastards will kill us! How long are we—" Then she saw Julia and broke off, narrowing her eyes. "You! What do you want here?"

"Harry!" said Mrs. Melton. "That's enough. Now, you get over to Mr. Tyler. Comrade Worthing's here for what he sells."

Harriet's face lit up with a spiteful smile. "Oh, that's it? I might have known it would end in that."

"None of that! Get on!" said Mrs. Melton.

Harriet sniffed and went. She slammed the front door violently on her way out, and the house shook once again.

Mrs. Melton sighed. "Don't mind her. Her fellow Freddie's thrown her over, and she's gone and made a scene. Burst into the community center while they were having their tea and called him filthy names. Of course the pols are all over her now. 'Tain't safe for her to leave the district at all, and she ain't half evil with it."

"She can't leave the district? How is she to get her Party husband?"

"She's not," Mrs. Melton said. "That's done. Anyhow, it ain't them times now, is it?"

"What do you mean?"

"Oh, when she was a girl, when I first seen she were going to be a beauty, of course I thought of a Party husband. There wasn't many prole girls marrying blue, but it did happen. And them girls had fine homes and big fat children. Money coming back to their families, and the families moved to the parts of the district nearest the border, where the bombs don't go.

"But you look at your Party now! It's this one vapped, and that one vapped, and the others in a camp. Her fellow Freddie—half his friends went, inside of a month. Old Party families, and the men all gone. That's what spooked him out of marrying her. He ain't marrying a prole and getting vaporized for his pains.

"And if that weren't enough, now our side's giving more and more trouble. A girl like Harriet . . . Well, we've had to put it about that she dropped Freddie, so she don't get grief from the lads in the area. If you remember Mrs. Bale that lives here— well, she's now thought very moderate in her views.

"If you want to know, you coming here . . . well, I always liked you. Harriet does and all, when she's not being a cow. But you'd be wiser not to come back, and I'd be wiser not to open the door to you. Now, if you ever want to part with that badge, my door's always open for that. But if it's anything else—keep away. Because I look about myself and I see what I see, and I say: it ain't them times."

The door banged again, and Harriet stomped into the room, energetically lovely even in her dowdy clothes. She tossed a paper bag at her mother's feet, then ran up the stairs without a word.

The rudeness seemed invisible to Mrs. Melton. She only bent to fetch the sack and held it up to show Julia the penciled number "25" on it. "Count 'em if you like, but I've never known him to be out. Now, let me just see that coffee..."

The walk back to Weeks took scarcely a minute. It was queer to be reminded how close she'd been to Mrs. Melton's all this time. The shop was closed for the night. In the window, Julia could make out the spot of a lamp moving among the tumbled junk in the rear. A shadow fretted about it, flaring and shrinking. As she watched, it put out one impossibly elongated arm that swept across the ceiling, worrying at something, then was abruptly retracted. Julia used her key and came in feeling weightless with nerves. It had been her last time at the Meltons'; perhaps it would be her last time here.

Weeks was working at a desk in the back. He still wore his gray Charrington wig but had washed the makeup from his face and took no trouble to stoop, so it was obvious the man was six feet tall and strong. He had an aura of Party authority, making the rumpled velvet jacket and bent spectacles incongruous enough to be sinister. One saw them for what they were: sheep's clothing.

Julia called out, "Hullo! You won't guess what's happened!"

"No," Weeks agreed. "I won't. Don't expect it."

"Oh, you needn't be like that. Listen, I've just come from the artsem clinic, and I'm pregnant. I've only just found out."

"Oh, bother." Weeks shook his head and turned back to the work he'd been doing, which, Julia saw with a start, was cleaning a gun. He had the brushes and oil set out on a stained yellow cloth alongside the black, dully gleaming pieces.

"I wonder if you know," said Julia, "about the Big Future program."

"Yes, I was afraid it might be that."

"So you see why I came to tell you. It's Big Brother's child!"

He looked up from his work. "But is it?"

"Well, of course, it's not certain. But it might be."

"Yes. Might be. A rather tasteless situation."

"But it must be all right, or why else did they accept me? They checked my records and took me straightaway, ahead of everyone else. They must have known what I do."

"Oh, they certainly didn't know about this. No, this isn't that easy to learn about."

"They clearly knew *something* about it, though. Why else would I be shown such preference?"

"You are a Hero of the Socialist Family. How soon they forget! A mother means nothing nowadays." He shook his head and began to reassemble the gun.

"But it *may* be Big Brother's child," she said stubbornly. "It is his child officially."

"So you mean to deceive the Party? To leave a cuckoo in the Party's nest? But we can't address this now, as we've come to a point where we need all your attention. I would ask you to put it from your mind."

"Might I speak to O'Brien? He should know of it, after all."

"I shouldn't think that's necessary."

"Perhaps *I* think it necessary. And if—"

"Don't think." Weeks opened a drawer, took out a little brown box of ammunition, and began methodically to fill the gun's cartridge. Julia watched and was reminded of once being allowed to help an airman with this task. It had been a very satisfying business: the resistance of the spring was just great enough that a child could make the bullets go in, but only with effort and a feeling of accomplishment. For Weeks, of course, it was easy.

Weeks said, "We are coming to the close of the operation.

I know it's been great fun, but the summer will soon be over. Autumn approaches—endings, the death of the earth, renewal. So we shall need to say goodbye to some old friends. Comrades Parsons and Ampleforth will be arrested Saturday morning. Smith may take a bit longer—the case goes higher up and they want a big arrest. That plays the devil with the timing."

"Saturday," Julia said, stunned. "That's two days' time."

"Very right. I keep thinking today is Wednesday, but it's already Thursday. It's working odd hours does that." He slotted the last bullet into place, then looked up. "Is that all understood?"

"I needn't take part in these arrests?"

"Perhaps with Smith. I've heard nothing on that. It scarcely matters, as of course you are to be taken by surprise. Please do be taken by surprise, or it will cause a great deal of pointless trouble. He can't know you are with us. You are to be his last illusion."

Julia wanted to ask why Smith couldn't know the truth. What point was there in lying to a man who would so soon be killed? But she only said, "I am to meet Ampleforth this evening. Must I—"

"Oh, bother the man! Take him out for a walk. I have things to do in that room." Weeks fit the magazine into the gun; it clicked into place. He raised it, saying, "Never point a gun at anyone unless you mean to shoot him. Not even if it's not loaded." He pointed the gun at Julia's chest. "There: you will feel that it's not safe."

Her heart began to tediously pound, but he immediately turned the gun away and slipped it into a capacious pocket of his velvet jacket. It bulked out the pocket and pulled the hem askew in a lopsided way that was familiar. The gun must have been there all the time.

She said, "Might I ask—"

"Yes, comrade?"

"Why have we targeted Parsons? He's so loyal. The others I can certainly see. But Parsons wasn't really wrongthinking, not a bit."

"Oh, but you're quite mistaken there. There's been another report. He woke his children in the night, shouting, 'Down with Big Brother.'"

"'Down with Big Brother'?"

"Yes. Still waters, eh?"

With a sick feeling, she studied Weeks's face, trying to determine if he knew the phrase had come from her. But he only frowned as if pondering, then added, "Of course, one wonders whether such a story is true. It does sound rather the sort of thing a child would invent, and they're giving very good rewards in the Spies nowadays. Still, we can hardly let a man go when his own children say he's called for the Leader's death, can we? And if the children are found to have made a false report, well, there are penalties for that too. So it will all come right in the end."

As soon as he said this, Julia saw that this was what was planned. The man would be arrested and shot. Then the children would be determined to have lied and be sent to a juvenile labor camp—if only because it was cheaper than providing for them in any other way. The wife, too, must be arrested, for failing to report these dangerous criminals. Some neighbors and colleagues would be drawn in—it never passed without that. All this from Julia's whim of getting Parsons to say naughty things in her ear.

Ampleforth was glad at the notion of a walk out of doors. His eyes were too tired to be noting down poetry, he said;

like all workers at Records, he'd been replacing "Eurasia" with "Eastasia" all week. They walked south, maintaining a discreet distance from each other and keeping to the prole districts when they could. At times, he had to stop and rest. Then he apologized for his "poor lame legs." Julia said she was glad of the rest herself, and added that it was nonsense to speak of being lame when he was now so strong and straight. This emboldened him, and he insisted on going on as far as the riverside. They found a place far from any streetlamps, and Julia poked around until she felt certain they were out of range of all microphones. The tide was in, so they couldn't go down on the sand. They sat on the wall above.

Then Ampleforth talked about his brother, saying he might stop in to see him on his way home. One couldn't wish for two brothers less alike, however, and it always ended up in a quarrel. "When I see him, he will always chaff me for having been excused from military service. He calls it 'the luck of the invalid,' and says I could have fought if I'd had the right spirit. He works at Peace and was always in the army, you see. He doesn't mean to be unkind."

"But if it is unkind?"

"I daresay it is. But I'm sure I say many unkind things without realizing."

"Some might, dear," Julia said. "Never you."

"Did you know, Alexander Pope was an invalid? He suffered from tuberculosis of the bone."

Julia didn't know who Alexander Pope was, but she shivered and said, "Oh, how unfair."

"He lived in London, too. He might have sat here and looked across to that bank. So many of them lived here. Shakespeare!" Ampleforth dreamily smiled. "Do you know, I often think of being, not Shakespeare himself, but Shakespeare's friend. I imagine him speaking to me about his poetry, though I can never think what he would say. It really is the only thing—poetry. One feels that something has visited the world that isn't of this world."

Julia should have been able to agree with some sincerity. For some time, she'd looked forward to Ampleforth's visits, not only for his amiable ways, but for the verse. Kubla Khan and his pleasure dome were now old friends, and, when she was alone in the room, Julia sometimes read to herself from Ampleforth's notebook. There was one poem she particularly liked, about a soldier fighting in Eurasia:

> If I should die, think only this of me:
> That there's some corner of a foreign field
> That is for ever England. There shall be
> In that rich earth a richer dust concealed;
> A dust whom England bore, shaped, made aware...

At first it had seemed fussily oldthink that the poem said "England" for Airstrip One, but once she grew accustomed to it, she found the word had a glorious sound, like a cymbal clashing. She would look at her own hand and think, *A dust whom England bore, shaped, made aware.*

Now, however, when it crossed her mind, it only reminded her Ampleforth would soon be dust.

She took a deep breath and said, "Poetry. Yes."

"They can't get rid of it, can they? Not altogether. The world would stop existing, in a way. It would be like the eons before anyone lived on earth, when there was no one here to see anything. Great lizards lumbering about, without knowing anything."

"The new Party platform has come out against the lizards. That's bourgeois biology now."

"Oh. I'd missed that. No lizards, then. How lonely." Then he looked cautiously at her. "Do you know, I've had the most peculiar feeling recently? I feel people drawing away from me. At Truth especially, but now in my hostel as well. I walk about in a sort of hush. Do you suppose it's because of Syme? People knew we were friends. But then I've also made a very silly mistake. I left the word 'God' in a poem. It was a rhyme for 'rod,' and, for the life of me, I couldn't think of any other word that fit. But one does make such errors, and then nothing comes of it. Do you think I'm very silly to worry?" He looked at her hopefully.

She wanted to say he had nothing to fear. She kept thinking of ways to say it, but only frowned at the river below. From here, the water was pure black. It had fine wrinkles over its surface and looked like nothing more than the coarse leather of a policeman's uniform.

Ampleforth looked away at last. "I suppose you can't—"

"Would you want an answer—that is, if I knew? Would you honestly want me to say?"

Now he looked properly afraid. He was staring at her as if behind her face lay a terrible mystery.

She went on in a softer voice, "It's only that I feel such things too. I get frightened. And I always think I wouldn't want to know."

"I would. Yes, I most certainly would."

"But why? If there's nothing you can do?"

He looked about himself, in the way of one checking for spies, then leaned closer and said, "Once before I failed to rewrite a poem. I scarcely remember what it was, but it seemed very bad, and I was sure I'd be arrested. So I decided to jump out of a window at Truth. I thought I'd jump, and then I'd be dead, and I wouldn't have to go through the things they do at Love. I'm terribly afraid of all that—pain.

"Now, on the twentieth floor, there are windows that open. I'd learned that somewhere, and thought I would be clever and make use of that knowledge. You'll laugh—you know I can't climb stairs, not easily. I must have been on those stairs an hour, and I had time to think it through then, once and for all. And what I wished for most in that time was certainty. I dreaded to think I might put an end to myself when the danger wasn't real.

"As it happened, when I got up there, I found they'd installed iron bars across those windows. They'd thought of that escape and prevented it. There was a time, too, when one could cut one's throat with a knife. The knives are far too blunt now. Perhaps a cook might have a sharp knife, but you and I—we would never get near one."

"Oh, Stan."

"I do like it when you use my name. You say it so sweetly."

"We might drown ourselves."

He shuddered. "I couldn't. That's my greatest terror, drowning. Oh, I wish you hadn't said that. Now I can't look at the dear old Thames. I know I'm a terrible coward."

"What if . . . well, if it were pills?"

"Yes, that wouldn't be so dreadful. I did think of joining Anti-Sex for that purpose, for the anti-sex pills. But then I met you. I know how that must sound, given past performance."

"Oh, Stan."

He laughed. "Well, as you say my name again and again, it begins to sound quite different."

She reached out impulsively and took his hand. He stiffened, but, after having looked around for spies, relaxed. She was thinking of all the things she might want those pills for in the coming weeks. She thought of Mrs. Melton telling her not to come back. She thought of how perilous it was to ask Dr. Louis for pills, when he was sure to report it. Then Love might come to know, and she knew without asking they wouldn't approve. The pills from Mrs. Melton should be just enough for someone Ampleforth's size, but that left Julia with only the two last pills from Oceania. She had Winston's arrest to get through, and the uncertainty of what came after, when all the men she'd been working with were gone. She imagined Weeks finding out she'd helped Ampleforth die to escape arrest. She remembered the horrid feeling of him pointing the gun at her chest.

At the end of all this agonizing, she had freed her hand from Ampleforth's and taken out the pills she'd bought from Mrs. Melton. When she went to put the packet in his chest pocket, he startled horribly and looked at her with an indecipherable expression.

She said softly, "Hold still. I'm only giving you something."

He sat passively then while she put them in. When she was done, he felt inside the pocket with his fingers, and drew a ragged breath. "Is it . . . ?"

"One must take them with gin. Then it ought to be enough."

For a moment, he was absolutely still, with his hand in his pocket, as if sheltering his heart. Then he said, "So you think . . . it's as I fear?"

"I do think it. I'm so awfully sorry."

Then, for the first time, he reached out and took Julia's hand himself. He crushed it in his, breathing strangely, glaring down toward the murky water. His other hand was pressed violently to his heart, his whole body hunched. By the scant moonlight, one saw only the river's surface as a restless shape. She remembered the Kubla Khan poem, its sunless sea, its caverns measureless to man. For the first time, she thought she understood. It was not a place on earth: it was death.

At last he released her hand and looked at her with the dazed face of a sleepwalker. He said hoarsely, "I suppose I had better see my brother. Yes, I believe he would still want that."

"Yes, dear. I'm sure that's right."

"I did love you in my way. Do you know it?"

"Oh, yes. And I have loved you in mine."

"My dear—it wasn't you, was it? You didn't tell anyone what we did?"

"No," she said at once. "It wasn't me."

"I ought really to hope it was you, so you might be safe. But I haven't got it in me to hope that. Isn't that selfish?"

"It wasn't me. It could never be me."

"I am so grateful for—oh, for everything. But I must go to my brother. I did love you. Oh, my Abyssinian maid!"

She was still searching her mind for a poetic name to give him when he rose and hurried fearfully away. In a moment he was lost in the crowds of proles coming back from the evening executions.

18

SHE TOOK HER SECOND-TO-LAST PILL BEFORE WORK
the next day, but found it had no perceptible effect. The whole
morning she was fretful and haunted. Everything appeared
through a fine veil of black. The figure of Ampleforth, hunched
in terror, kept recurring to her mind, then that of Parsons and
his wife and children—all of them killed by her. She was meant
to see Winston Smith that evening, and he seemed to her now
almost a ghost, a Kubla Khan in a sunless world, intoning pite-
ously, "We are the dead." Vicky she remembered as a gleaming
whiteness, the woods where they'd walked as a tracery of gold,
and all beauty of that kind as lost to her through her own vi-
ciousness. All were to be murdered, and Julia their killer, Julia
never again to be good or beloved. Even Big Brother's baby
made no difference. It would be killed inside her. It would be
erased from memory. She and everyone she cared for would be
vaporized. They would have never been born.

She took the last pill at fourteen hundred, not even being
fully conscious of doing so. As soon as she realized what she'd
done, she instantly craved another. She thought of finding Ampleforth and asking him to give back one or two. He wasn't that
much bigger than Julia, and twenty-three pills might do the
trick. Of course she couldn't do that—and even as she thought
of it, a dread washed over her, a black and bottomless feeling

she'd only had before in nightmares. She knew, with the instinct that had served her all her life, that giving Ampleforth the pills had been a fatal error. He wouldn't use them in time. They would be found. When the men at Love began to hurt him, the first word out of his mouth would be Julia's name.

Her last hours at work she spent in a daze of fear. She kept dropping tools and failing to respond to questions. It took a full hour for her to perform a basic repair on a pneumatic tube. Then, at the bus stop, she found she was afraid to go to the prole district, a thing she'd done every week for years. She was haunted by a memory of the altered market, with its roasted rats and air of sordid menace; by Mrs. Melton's *It ain't them times*. To calm her nerves, she put on her Big Future badge, hoping to earn the friendship of the proles who took the interdistrict bus. But this time no one took any notice, and she was left to stand. She clung to a pole and shut her eyes, reassuring herself that nothing would change today. Ampleforth and Parsons weren't to be arrested until Saturday—tomorrow. The pills could not be found until then. She would not be hurt today.

There was a back door to the little room over Weeks that Winston always used. Julia usually didn't, as it was a sure way of arousing Weeks's suspicions. "We are sneaking," he would say. "We hide from the light. Now, I wonder why that is." Tonight she did use it, however, feeling an obstinate need to hide from the light. If Weeks saw her face, he would see the despair, the panic—all the things she couldn't be seen to feel. Entering the dark corridor, she slowed to enjoy the feeling of being hidden. She thought of going to Vicky and saying, *Yes, I'll leave. Only let us go tonight*. They could flee . . . but when Julia tried to picture it, it seemed outlandish, impossible. The thought of what lay outside London brought back fearful memories of SAZ-5: the skeletal, shambling people; the airmen dangling from the gallows; the reek of graves. They wouldn't be allowed on a train at night, anyhow. After eighteen hundred, one needed special permission, and if they left on foot, there would be checkpoints. No, she needn't decide right now. She had better take the night to think it through.

On the landing of the narrow stairs she paused, looking up at the scarred door to the little room, and tried to compose her feelings. There was a mirror here, hung between two rows of coat hooks, and partly obscured by musty old coats. Julia peered into the glass and was queerly surprised to find her face unchanged. She'd expected some mark of depravity, but she was only pale. She fished her lipstick from her tool bag and dabbed some color onto each cheek, spreading it about with a fingertip. Winston never minded if this was done inexpertly. To him, all makeup was pretty. The narrow stairs had a sharp smell of damp, which she now breathed with appreciation. This might be the last time she mounted these stairs. This was the last safe day in the world.

When she came in, Winston was on his feet, waiting for her. He'd already removed his boots and his long, bony feet seemed vulnerable in their threadbare, much-darned socks. Cradled to his chest was a hardback book with a plain black cover, with no words on it at all.

Seeing him flooded her with relief: there was still someone else in the world. In that moment, she felt all her old irritations with him as a species of fondness. One grew close to someone and let him matter, and so one brooded on his shortcomings, counting them over in private moments as if they were a miser's hoard. It was how she had been with her mother. It was a rage that was a kind of love.

She dropped her tool bag on the floor and fell into Winston's arms. He yanked the book out of the way and embraced her impatiently, clearly waiting for her to be done. Then, when she stood back to look in his face, she found his eyes shining with excitement. He said, "I've got the book!"

Only then she understood. The book was Goldstein's book, the one he'd been promised by O'Brien. Then she felt the reality of annoyance, which was nothing like love, not when one felt it.

"Oh, you've got it?" she said shortly. "Good." She went to the oil stove, turning her back to him to put on the kettle. The oil stove was old and its pressure valve worked unpredictably; it was easy to inadvertently create a flare of sooty flame. The fussy chore settled her nerves, and soon she was able to smile at Winston's carping comments—"It's so dreary to see you in Party clothes. It is like a swan dressed as a pigeon"—and to make her own teasing remarks about the sad state of his socks. She brought the coffee and submitted to his caresses, even though tonight they stirred nothing in her but a terrible wish to cry.

When their lovemaking was finished, he immediately reached for the book. "We must read it," he said in a didactic tone. "You too. All members of the Brotherhood have to read it."

"You read it. Read it aloud. That's the best way. Then you can explain it to me as you go."

She knew this offer would be irresistible to him, and wasn't disappointed. He settled in with a contented air and began: "Chapter One. Ignorance is Strength..."

For a while, she tried to pay attention, if only out of curiosity about how the Truth boys had approached this task, for of course the book was their work, not Goldstein's. But now the exhaustion of the day was making her drowsy. There was some stuff about High and Low classes...and a minute later she woke to Winston nudging her, saying, "Julia, are you awake?"

"Yes, my love," she managed. "I'm listening. Go on. It's marvelous."

He went on, and she fought to stay awake and listen, but

soon was nodding off again. To her ear, it was just like the stultifying works on socialist electronics she'd had to read at polytechnic, rotten with phrases like "Given this background, one could infer..." and high-sounding observations about historical periods no one remembered. She woke up a bit when it got to *doublethink*, but, even here, all the book seemed to say was that believing contradictory things amounted to believing what wasn't true. The dimmest schoolchild could have told you as much, though they might not have said it aloud. The futile tone of it wearied her more than anything. It tasted of the stale breath of men for whom opinions trumped life. But Winston was reading as if it contained revelation after revelation; as if it were a book of spells that would give him superhuman powers.

At last she gave up the struggle and let her eyes close. Some time later she was aware that the droning, contented voice had ceased and Winston's body was nestled to hers. She turned and embraced him sleepily, feeling the natural physical attachment she'd always felt when they were able to sleep together. He was warm and the room was cool. The noises of the prole district outside were a lullaby; they meant that nothing had changed.

She woke to the washerwoman singing. She felt a loose heaviness in all her limbs. It was as if she'd slept for a very long time, though when she looked, the clock said twenty-thirty. Winston was stirring. She stretched luxuriously, saying, "I'm hungry. Let's make some more coffee," then the next instant startled to the realization that she'd left the oil stove lit. She was already on her feet, quite naked, when Winston looked up groggily.

Crouching beside the oil stove, she found the flame was out. "Damn! The stove's gone out and the water's cold." She picked the stove up and shook it. "There's no oil in it."

"We can get some from old Charrington, I expect."

The thought of seeing Weeks woke her more fully, unpleasantly. She now felt the hangover from the pills, a nasty fatigue that weighed in her head. She said irritably, "The funny thing is I made sure it was full. I'm going to put my clothes on. It seems to have got colder."

As she dressed, the specific gray in the window suggested to her that it was morning. She glanced at the clock again suspiciously. Was it possible it was not twenty-thirty, but eight-thirty the following morning? That made a wretched sort of sense; it would explain how the stove had burned through all its oil. Winston had been dressing, too, and now zipped his overalls up and went to stand at the window as if he, too, doubted the light. She went to join him, and he slung an arm companionably around her waist, gazing into the yard.

"She's beautiful," he said.

It took Julia a moment to realize he was speaking of the washerwoman, who had her back to them and was singing lustily while pegging up men's shirts on a line. Her old annoyance returned. Of course he didn't really find the washerwoman beautiful; if he did, he would be in this room with a barrel-shaped woman with a red, raddled face. This was just more of his sentimentality about the noble prole.

She said, "She's a meter across the hips, easily."

"That is her style of beauty." Winston smiled at Julia. "Do you remember the thrush that sang to us, that first day, at the edge of the wood?"

"He wasn't singing to us. He was singing to please himself. Not even that. He was just singing."

"The birds sing, the proles sing, but Party members don't sing. Did you ever think of that?"

Julia was about to disagree—one could scarcely get through

a week in the Party without singing patriotic hymns—but at that moment, the washerwoman turned and looked directly at Julia, still singing, shaking out a damp white shirt. In this light, she seemed changed. Her face was no longer so seamed and red and her figure had a robust grace. Indeed, she had a certain beauty. What was more, the woman's black eyes now showed a mischievous intelligence. They were uncannily like the eyes of Weeks. An icy suspicion flooded Julia. The woman turned away again, singing in her rich and characterful contralto, in what Julia suddenly heard as an expert parody of a prole voice.

Winston said, continuing his thought, "We are the dead."

"We are the dead," Julia parroted without thinking.

"You are the dead," said an iron voice behind them.

Julia and Winston sprang away from each other. She felt all the blood drain from her face. Winston looked wild and weak, almost like a young girl in a moving picture cowering from her Eastasian ravisher. But the girl would be shrieking. He was small and silent.

"You are the dead," the voice in the wall repeated.

"It was behind the picture," Julia said. In that moment, her confusion was sincere. Only after she spoke did she realize it was just what Weeks would have wanted. She was being surprised. She must continue to be surprised.

The mechanical voice agreed: "It was behind the picture. Remain exactly where you are. Make no movement until you are ordered."

The next moment, a click came from the wall and the picture fell crashing to the floor. Behind it was an ordinary telescreen, glowing blankly as they did between programs. The feeling of exposure was extraordinary. She had always known there were cameras, and yet she said stupidly, "Now they can see us."

"Now we can see you," the voice said. "Stand out in the middle of the room. Stand back-to-back. Clasp your hands behind your heads. Do not touch one another."

She moved as instructed, and was amazed to feel that her hands were icy cold on the back of her neck. She was afraid. Why should she be so afraid? This was Winston Smith's arrest, not hers, and she was playing her part more realistically than anyone could have expected. She tried to think she was afraid for Winston, but that was a lie. She had no room in her fear for him. All her body was trembling. Her legs felt flimsy. Oh, why should she be so afraid?

Outside, the washerwoman's singing was cut off abruptly. There were clanging, scraping noises, then a confusion of male shouts that ended in a yell of pain. At the same time, there came a murmur of trampling boots both from inside and outside the house. It made Julia think of infestation.

"The house is surrounded," said Winston.

"The house is surrounded," the mechanical voice agreed.

A new flash of terror went through Julia, and she thought desperately that she must go now. She tried saying, "I suppose we may as well say goodbye."

To her relief, the voice agreed with her: "You may as well say goodbye." But it was instantly interrupted by the thin, insinuating voice of Weeks: "And by the way, while we are on the subject, 'Here comes a candle to light you to bed, here comes a chopper to chop off your head!'"

At this, the head of a ladder shattered the window, breaking through the frame with a deafening noise. The meager sunlight there was blotted out by a black-clad, burly shape. At the same time, boots came pounding up the stairs. In a moment, the room was filled with huge men in black uniforms, wearing iron-toed boots and carrying truncheons.

Two moved past Julia, both sneering into her face, so the

urge to cringe from them was overwhelming. But then both responded to something behind her, perhaps a signal from their leader. Their truncheons reacted in tandem, seeming to stiffen in their hands. She thought distantly that Smith was about to be beaten. She must show fear, she thought, and flinched horribly as something smashed to the floor behind her. A tiny piece of coral rattled across the floor to land beside her foot. *The paperweight*, she thought. *It was only the paperweight.* They hadn't yet hurt Smith.

Then one of the men squared off before her. That was all she knew before she was doubled over, gasping, her legs giving way, her body terribly not working as she fell. He had smashed his fist into her solar plexus. The carpet broke her fall, but she was evilly unable to catch her breath. Her mind jabbered, repeating what had happened. He had punched her—punched her in the stomach, when she was pregnant with Big Brother's child! She felt the knot of pain, and a vile defenselessness all over her skin. She was a prisoner in a body that could be hurt in countless ways. It was as if she had a body for the first time. And if they'd punched her, what could it mean? But no, it must be a mistake. The very fact that he'd punched her stomach showed that. In a moment, Weeks would come and put a stop to it. Weeks must come. He had spoken; why wouldn't he come?

A black wave swooped toward her—more men—and before she could even cower, two had seized her by the wrists and ankles. She writhed, instinctively trying to free herself, to get her feet on the ground. But that panic was followed by a marvelous relief. Of course! They'd only punched her for show. Now they were taking her out of Winston's sight, his damned sight that endangered her. This wasn't capture; it was rescue.

She was carried down the stairs, gasping gratefully even as her head was carelessly knocked into a wall. She even laughed at their clumsiness. At the bottom, they dumped her on the floor. When a boot smashed into her back, she cried out angrily— that was an error! Then, uncomprehendingly, she saw the flash of another boot and tried to scramble clear as it flew blackly into her face. It was a numb blow that immediately felt wet across her nose. Then the pain came, filling her head. In that last moment of disbelief, she groped at one of the men's ankles, wanting him to see her, to recognize who she was. His foot was snatched away effortlessly, then instantly the iron-toed boot stamped down on her hand with all the man's weight. There was a terrible sound of snapping bones. She screamed.

The boot lifted and moved on. She saw her hand, already red and misshapen, and sobbed out, no longer able to stop herself: "Weeks! Help me! They're killing me! Weeks!"

Then, like a miracle, Weeks's dusty, creased shoes appeared beside her eye. She sobbed gratefully. How she loved him! Oh, he was here! But he raised his foot and neatly, deliberately, set it down on her broken hand. Everything stopped in her throat. She saw the room as a thing composed of pain, of bones. It hurt so entirely it had to kill her.

The shoe twisted, grinding down, and she screamed again. It hurt more! It could hurt more! She cried out: "Please, I oughtn't to have done—tell me what I have done! I shall do what you want!" Another boot slammed into her head, and that small pain was newly terrifying. It told her she couldn't make it stop. It wouldn't stop.

Weeks's voice said calmly, "Worthing 6080-F. Class C. Keep for Room 101, ancillary to Class A Smith 6079-M." Far above, his eyes dwelled on her and narrowed with intellectual pleasure. It was the face of the sated spider looking down curiously at the beetle's husk.

19

SHE WAS IN LOVE. THAT WAS ALL SHE UNDERSTOOD.
She didn't know why she had been arrested. She didn't know
if she might still be freed. She didn't know if the cell was
above ground or below; she'd been too disoriented when she
was brought here, her head spinning as she was dragged up
and down eternal flights of stairs. She didn't know how long
she'd been here. Without daylight or clocks it was impossible
to judge the passing of time. Even that it was Love was a thing
she'd intuited, and not a fact she'd heard. She knew it from
the imponderable cold of meters of stone around her; from the
pallor of the guards who appeared from time to time to drag
other prisoners to their fates; from the multitudinous sounds
of misery that seethed in the walls. She knew it because she'd
been waiting to be brought here all her life, and it had lived in
her body and taught her to know it.

The walls in the cell were of white porcelain tile, the floor
of achingly cold concrete. The lights never went off and had a
peculiar straining quality that got in one's nerves like noise. The
air was all stench: urine, feces, rot, and bleach. A bench, just
wide enough to perch on, ran along the walls and was always
overcrowded with prisoners of all kinds: thieves, prostitutes,
black marketeers, bellowing drunks, and the occasional terrified
political in blue overalls, like Julia. There were four telescreens,

one on each wall, which played no programs but only added another harsh note to the jarring light. They also unpredictably erupted in threatening shouts in response to some infraction by the prisoners: "No hands in pockets in the cells! Silence in the cells! No touching!" The politicals meekly obeyed these commands, while the common criminals shouted back defiantly or paid them no mind at all.

Many of the criminals, indeed, seemed quite at home. They called the guards by name, cadged cigarettes from them through the spyhole, made rough gibes about what their wives were doing while they were out of the way. A few even fought back when guards burst in to enforce the rules, though they were invariably beaten down. Despite their troublemaking, they had a rapport with the authorities and were favored in a hundred ways. Cigarettes *were* sometimes passed to them. They could coax the guards into bantering and bargaining. Misbehavior from them was only sporadically punished, while even "disrespectful posture" from a political reliably brought a savage beating. The politicals were also abused by other prisoners: shoved off the bench first when space ran out, kicked in passing by the larger men, routinely robbed of their share of the bread that was sometimes distributed. One beefy robber delighted in describing to the politicals the tortures they would soon endure when they were taken to the special cells. He concluded by saying contentedly, "Me, I'll be off to a nice little camp. Been before, and I don't mind going back. And if I see any of you terrorists there, I'll roast you and eat you with peas."

In one corner of the room was a lavatory pan. The use of it in that crowded room was a wretched humiliation. It was especially hard on Party women; overalls were always tricky when a woman had to piss. At home, Julia often stepped out of them entirely and hung them up to keep them safe from soiling. Here, of course, no woman ventured to do that; instead she shrugged them off while twisting the fabric hastily to cover her breasts. As there was no seat on the lavatory pan, her bare backside remained fully exposed, hovering in the air, for the duration of the procedure. Of course the criminals leered, made mocking comments, and demanded a better view of the woman's crotch. If she took too long, the telescreen too might begin to screech at her for obscenity. This happened to Julia every time; with her broken hand, it took an age to get her overalls off and on. Catcalls and insults rose, to mounting hilarity, only to be cut off by the bellow from the telescreen: "6080 Worthing, no public obscenity in the cells!"

In between these performances were empty hours of waiting. Julia's mind was alternately occupied by longing for the pain in her broken hand to ease so she could control the fear, then for the fear to abate so she could bear the pain. All was infused by the nausea from the pregnancy, which intensified and eased in response to the odors from the lavatory pan. The hand had swollen horribly, and she could scarcely move the first two fingers. It seemed the slender bones leading to those fingers had snapped in at least one place, and the ends were shoved down into the muscle. What happened to a broken bone that wasn't set? She found she didn't know. She once attempted to straighten it herself, but only caused herself such pain that she curled up involuntarily and elicited yet another screeching rebuke from the telescreen. Sometimes she had the tormenting idea that there might still be a pill in her overalls pocket. The memory of taking the last pill felt very distant and uncertain, and the promise of relief from pain so important. And perhaps Mrs. Melton's sack had had a hole in it, through which a pill might have escaped? Again and again, Julia's good hand crept toward her pocket, only for the telescreen to bark: "6080

Worthing! No hands in pockets in the cells!" Then she whimpered and both hands flew of their own volition to her sides.

It was in one of these attempts that she discovered the Big Future badge still pinned to her chest. She must have worn it all through her last visit with Winston, and he had never noticed. It was so typical of him, it flooded her with a weak and wistful love. How could she have betrayed that child, who had never understood the world around him, who had looked to her for every practical thing? That led her to suffer for Ampleforth, too. She found herself wishing on the badge that he might not be here, that he'd been able to use the pills and perish in a sweet narcotic sleep. She also suffered from yearning memories of Vicky, and febrile daydreams in which Vicky led a band of rebels to Love to free her.

When guards came to collect a prisoner, it couldn't help being a blessed distraction, even though it generally only consisted of them saying the name and number of a prisoner, who rose and went without complaint. Sometimes they barked out: "Interrogation!" Then even the boldest prisoners quailed. Some tried to preemptively confess, and went off helpfully reciting their sins and listing those who'd sinned with them. A few times, too, a prisoner was collected personally by a black-overalled interrogator. These prisoners were all politicals and, Julia soon came to understand, "Class A." Some clearly recognized their interrogators and were stunned to meet them in this place. She gleaned that, in these cases, the interrogators had played the role O'Brien had played with Winston. Once there was a little comedy when a Class A prisoner greeted his interrogator by crying out in sorrow, "They got you, too?" only to have the interrogator light a cigarette and smoke casually while guards beat the man bloody.

The most dramatic scenes came on the handful of occasions

when guards collected someone with the words "Room 101." Every prisoner summoned in this way lost their reason. They begged and fought; they crawled underneath the bench; they shoved other prisoners in the path of the guards and shrieked, "It's him you want, not me!" Each one must be beaten into submission and dragged from the cell, struggling all the way and shrieking pointlessly for help. One man tearfully begged the guards to break his neck, and swore they would be rewarded for it, but was carted off whole nonetheless.

During these ceremonies, Julia remembered hearing "Room 101" from Weeks as he stood crushing her hand. Then again, she was Class C: he'd said that too. Surely that meant she was insignificant enough to be spared interrogation, much less whatever "Room 101" was? Perhaps she could even hope to be sent to a "nice little camp." Barracks, thin gruel, barbed wire, guard dogs—those held no particular terrors for her. She could befriend the more powerful prisoners and find a way to be hired out as a day laborer. If only someone would set her hand, she might thrive there as well as anyone.

In her final hours in this cell, her situation markedly improved. This was because one of the other prisoners had recognized her Big Future badge and explained it to the others. Even here, it had a magical effect on proles. She was not only spared the poor treatment meted out to politicals but given extra bread and invited to lie down on the bench to sleep. All were enraged at the state of her hand, which they'd never noticed before, and a prostitute who'd once worked as a nurse's aide tried to fix it, massaging the bones excruciatingly and wrapping it in a rag torn from a burglar's shirt. When they solicitously asked how she'd come here, she saw immediately she mustn't tell the truth. One could hardly tell a lot of criminals one had worked for the Thought Police. Instead, she said she'd been caught violating the "parasitic beasts" policy by hiding her hostel's two cats. Then all the criminals grumbled in disgust about blues who murdered puppies and kittens and didn't shrink from imprisoning a Big Future mother. They asked each other if the bloody Party had forgotten who Big Brother was. When the guards came for her at last—with no word of where they were taking her—all the criminals yelled at them and swore that, if she was hurt, there would be hell to pay. This was nonsense, of course. They could do nothing. Still, it cheered Julia wonderfully. She was able to feel more herself as she bid goodbye to her new friends.

Again she was led down long corridors and up and down dark stairways. Slowly the jabbering of the common cells gave way to solitary moans and cries, seeming to come from all directions, queerly echoing around the concrete and steel. At last a door just like all the others was opened, and Julia was thrust into a small dim cell. Here there was only one other prisoner, a woman political with a messily broken nose and bloodstains down her overalls. She shrank from Julia with a grimace, as if terrified she might be mistaken for a friend.

This new cell stank of bleach and had no lavatory pan, only a drain in the floor, crusted with what looked to be dried blood. A seething of little cockroaches perpetually foraged along this brownish crust. Only one wall had a telescreen, whose light flickered unendurably. If Julia shut her eyes, it flickered even through her eyelids. Once Julia tried to cover her eyes with her hand, but the telescreen promptly shouted, "6080 Worthing! No faces covered in the cells!" Then the other prisoner muttered, "Damn you! It's you and your like! Can't follow simple rules!"

Soon after this, the door opened again and the guards let in a straight-backed, white-haired woman in black overalls, whom Julia first took for an interrogator and shrank from in instinctive dread. The guards treated this woman with careful respect, even with what seemed to be fear, while she bore herself arrogantly, scowling at all about her. Only after she was shoved through the door and it clanged shut behind her did Julia notice her jaundiced, unkempt look and the purple bruise on her temple. She stared at her in amazement then: an Inner Party prisoner!

From the moment this woman arrived, the telescreen was eerily silent. In fact, it was she who scolded the telescreen, ranting at the incompetence of the guards and jeering at the fear they'd had of her. "In my day, they'd be cleaning me off the floor by now. A poor show!" She listed all the errors that had been made in her arrest, naming the people responsible and citing the edicts that had been violated. She laughed and said, "Be sure to tell them the information came from me. And if you think you needn't listen to Diana anymore, remember that people have thought I was finished before. And where are those people now?" She pointed to the drain in the floor with a flourish. "We cleaned them off these floors and washed the bits into the sewer." Through this, the woman with the broken nose huddled down and finally ended with her thumbs pressed into her ears and her eyes squinted shut so hard it distorted her face.

Then suddenly the Inner Party woman—Diana—rounded on Julia, snarling, "What the hell are you gawping at? I suppose you're pleased. Oh, yes, I should say you're terribly pleased to see me here."

Julia started. "I? Why should I be pleased?"

"Doesn't know! What have they got you in for? Stupidity?"

Julia stared at her, not knowing what to say.

"Ha! Doesn't know what she's in for!" Diana turned to the telescreen. "What lambs are you arresting now? Pitiful!" Then she looked back at Julia and said, "Here. Would you like to know what you're in for?"

"Oh," said Julia. "I don't think…"

"Don't be absurd. Of course you want to know. You tell me about yourself, and I'll say what it is. There's little enough to occupy the mind in this place."

Julia glanced at the telescreen warily, but Diana laughed and said, "Oh, if you're afraid of them, you can lie. I'm only after entertainment. I shall have that either way."

After some hesitation, Julia started to tell the story she'd told the other prisoners about parasitic beasts. But Diana kept interrupting to correct her. First it was: "You're from a SAZ, you've left that out. Don't deny it: one hears it in your voice. SAZ-5? A village, not a town. And you'll have only got to London by denouncing a parent. A mother? There you are, a mother. But do go on—I'm not stopping you."

The rest was much like this. Julia mentioned her work at Fiction, only to have Diana interrupt to say that the point was not that, but the sexcrimes, which must have begun when she was quite a child. "An older Party man, it would have been. Since it's the SAZ, I would guess it was a Plenty worker. If I had my files here, I could give you his name." In desperation, Julia confessed to Gerber, and even admitted he'd shot himself. But Diana had moved on and asked if, by any chance, Julia had been shagging a chap from Records. Before she could answer, Diana said, "No, now I see it. You were taken up by Love and set to fucking the Records boys one by one. You have our stink all over you. Yes, I should have known it at first glance. I'm losing my touch. Which one of us got you?"

Julia thought of denying it, but she knew by now how that would end. So she said cautiously, "O'Brien."

Diana burst into a cackle. "Bill O'Brien! That pompous ass! You poor shit. Don't tell me—he said he'd been watching over you for seven years? You're the healthiest mind he has ever encountered?"

"Well, yes."

"He loves that. Has he told you about the boot and the face? Two plus two make five?"

"I don't think…"

"Oh, he will. It's what he's famous for. Mind you, the boot-and-face thing was originally mine, though I hadn't thought to use it in interrogations. A few of us were having a whisky after golf, and it came to me: 'If you'd like an image of the future, think of a boot stamping eternally on a human face.' I might have known Bill O'Brien would steal it. The man never had an original idea in his life. See here, if he says it to you later on, will you tell him from me he's a mediocrity and a thief of others' ideas?"

"All right," Julia said to be polite. "And what is two plus two make five?"

"Oh, now, that is really quite good. He asks the subject what two plus two make. When the man says four, he gets an electric shock. Correct answer's five, you see. You won't believe it, but a certain sort of pedant sticks at that and can't make himself agree—or not at first. When you shock him sufficiently, of course, he can't agree to it enough. But here's where it gets really interesting, for now our friend O'Brien isn't satisfied. He insists the fellow doesn't truly believe it, as indeed he doesn't. So on they go, with the poor sod wailing that two plus two make five, and O'Brien holding up fingers and asking how many the man can see. It's really very humorous, if rather a waste of time. Still, it's that sort of thing that wins popularity. I understand it. You've got to keep your spirits up, working in this place. One doesn't see the sun nine months of the year, and the stench gets into one's hair and clothes, and it's the very devil to wash out. And then, of course, one is an object of public loathing. No, it's not a job for people with no sense of humor."

"Shall I tell you the rest of my story?"

"What's that?"

"You said you might tell me why I'm here, if I—"

"Oh, I can tell you that now," said Diana. "I knew it from the moment you said you were at Fiction. They're all at each other's throats, that's why. It was bad enough when one man denounced the other because he wanted his job. Now whole departments are being wiped out so another department can have their funds. In your case, Fiction is after Records. Wants to take over its functions and its budget. Why keep records, anyhow, if you've only got to change them all the time? Better make them up from whole cloth as they're wanted. That's their line. Then the Fiction Department will have to grow and become a division, and its masters will rise in rank.

"Of course they can't come out and say that's what it's about. They daren't even say the thing about whole cloth to anyone but a chosen few. If Records got wind of it, they would fight back, and they might just win the day. So, instead, Records must be called rotten, and all its workers proven to be criminals. Nothing easier, if you can get a chap like Bill O'Brien on your side. He gets the rumor mill going, hires a few disposable people to lead the Records lot into sin, and there you are. Now you—you ought to have been safe at Fiction. But you went and caught the eye of Bill O'Brien. Just a rotten roll of the dice.

"Oh, don't look like that. Did you imagine you'd committed a crime, and they were punishing you for your very own crime? Oh, we think ourselves very important! No, you're a toothpick, a tissue—a thing that gets used once and thrown in the bin. Even I—do you think I'm here because I've opposed the government? Hardly. I'm not an ingrate, nor am I a fool. I see the need for this government. Anyone who's lived through the fifties sees it. There are no atom bombs falling on you anymore! You're welcome! That's our sterling work.

"No, I love this Party more than any of them. And, God help me, I love Big Brother. I love him as I did in '51, when we drove down from Oxford in Rutherford's Anglia to man the barricades together. I've been in a bloody gun battle with him, with nothing but a single Enfield rifle between us. Love Big Brother? I've had him climb in my bedroom window and fuck me, without saying a goddamned word. How do you like that? Oh, he was a man back then. You never saw such a man! You never will—the race has gone extinct. In my day, there were men who were real men, who hurled atom bombs at each other and breathed the ashes of the millions burned in the conflagration and didn't blink. They had to go extinct or we all would. One in the world—that was all we could have. But when that one's gone, they may as well burn it all up. There will be no human race to mourn.

"Well, they've probably got me this time. But I'm of the generation of titans, and they'll not easily erase me from their damned history. I doubt they will try. No, I shall be another Rutherford. A Goldstein! Children will sing songs gloating over my death for a thousand years. Even you have heard of me, I'm sure. Listen: you're sharing a cell with Diana Winters! Now, say you haven't heard of Diana Winters, and I'll call you a liar."

For a moment, Julia really thought she didn't know the name. She was trying to think how to lie, when her mind cleared and she said in shock, "Oh, I have! My mother knew you."

Diana started. "The mother you killed? You *are* a liar!"

"She said she had met you at Oxford. They called you Icy Winters. Her name was Clara Winthrop then. You were kind to her once. She had bled through her skirt and you gave her your cardigan to tie about her waist."

"No," said Diana dubiously. "That doesn't sound like me. I was at Oxford, though, that's true. So perhaps..."

"Comrade Winters, might I ask a question?"

"As you like."

"What is in Room 101?"

Diana instantly smiled with malicious amusement. "Have they mentioned that at your arrest?"

"Yes. Only once, but—"

"Oh, that's no good. And you'll be an ancillary, not a primary. Yes, you're in for it."

"But what is it? Does it mean torture?"

Diana laughed. "Don't be a fool! All here are tortured as a matter of course. No, Room 101 is rather special."

"Yes, I thought it couldn't just be torture. But I can't see what is worse."

"You won't at first, not even if I tell you. Shall I tell you? It will do you no good."

"I should like to know."

"The stuff of nightmares, that's what's in Room 101. It's your own personal chamber of horrors. That is to say, it's your worst fear."

"Worst fear?"

"Let me guess." Diana narrowed her eyes, an unpleasant smile playing about her lips. "Being burned? No, you haven't that look. Being buried alive?"

"I am rather afraid of caterpillars," said Julia hopefully.

"Don't be a fool. Let me see . . . you like to be liked. Ah, disfigurement! That's what it will be. They won't let you leave here with that face. They'll make you into a freak from nightmares, then put you out to walk the streets for a season and spread the fear of justice. Yes, disfigurement. An old favorite."

Julia's first impulse was to insist she wasn't afraid of that. For what was disfigurement, really? An insult to vanity, perhaps, but no horror. Essie had had that dreadful scar, and it meant less than nothing to Julia. And Essie had been married—what horror was that?

But even as she thought it, weakness flooded her limbs. She was covered in sweat and part of her wanted to pound at the walls, to offer to betray everyone she knew, to beg to have her neck broken by the guards. It was all she could do to prevent her hands from going up to protect her face.

She said, "But if I confess, they won't do it? If I tell them what they want?"

Diana scoffed. "Not a chance. We all confess."

"But if I name other people? What if I—"

"None of that's any use. What do you think you know? You didn't even know why you were here."

"But is there nothing I can do? How can there be nothing?"

Diana studied her. A narrow smile appeared again on her lips. "Well, as it's O'Brien who's to suffer by it . . . would you like a tip? Knowing it's not likely to work?"

Julia nodded, not trusting herself to speak.

"Well, you might try to run out the clock. You see, they call it Room 101, and that's just what it is—a room. A very special sort of room, of course. It can be flooded with water or lit up with flames or pumped full of poison gas. One needs Room 101 for anything of that kind. But there is tradition, too. Even if a man is only to have his prick cut off, it must be in Room 101 or no one feels it was properly done. Well, you can imagine that it's tightly scheduled. Each operation now gets only fifteen minutes. Of course some will get as much time as it takes, but not you. You're a toothpick. They'll set you free just to avoid the extra paperwork. In due course, you'll be taken back and shot, of course, but that's not Room 101.

"Yes, you try to run out the clock. I can't play that trick my-self, but I give it to you as—oh, as a cardigan, if you like. And do remind O'Brien from me that he's stolen the boot stamping on the face. Get your own lines, Bill! You're a hack! You tell him that and we're quits."

As if summoned by this mention, a clamor of boots now came down the corridor. Julia instinctively cringed back against the wall. Diana laughed and turned to the door with a commanding air, as it opened to admit a little crowd of guards. An interrogator emerged from among them, the same man who'd casually smoked the cigarette while he watched his charge being beaten.

Diana said casually, "Neil. What's it to be today?"

"Afraid your luck's run out, old girl." He made an apologetic face. "It's 101."

"Very humorous. Now you can tell me where we're going."

"It's 101."

"Rubbish. I've scarcely been here two weeks. I'm not ready."

The interrogator shrugged and took out a cigarette. As he lit it, Diana took a quick step forward and snatched it from his hand. He smiled and watched her take a drag as if enjoying the playfulness of an old friend. He said, "I am sorry. You know it's not my decision."

"It's not true," she said irritably. "You think I'm a fool."

"See for yourself." He took a slip of paper from his pocket, unfolded it, and held it out to her. She hesitated, then took it and glared at it with the cigarette in her mouth. Whatever she read there struck her horribly. In seconds, all the rage drained from her. One saw suddenly that she was a sick old woman, much abused and very frail. In the cell's harsh light, the skin of her face was green.

The next moment, the interrogator made a gesture, and the guards surged forward and seized her roughly. She was dragged down the corridor, cursing viciously, saying, "Oh, you think I'm afraid? What's it to be? I'm afraid of heights. Shall I be dangled from an eminence? How? You can't frighten me! Don't even try it! You can't do it! You can't!" On the last word, her voice rose to a savage wail that was abruptly cut off when the door was slammed shut.

At that moment, the other woman in the cell, whom Julia had entirely forgotten, came to sudden life. She hissed, "Can't you see that woman was a plant? And you've gone and told her everything!"

"I can't think she was," said Julia coldly. "And anyhow, I've not told her anything they don't know."

"Of all the bloody fools! It's those like you!" And the woman huddled back into her corner.

A minute later, the sound of boots came again. The door ground open on two bored guards. One barked, "Worthing 6080. Interrogation."

20

IN THE WEEKS THAT FOLLOWED, JULIA CAME TO UN-
derstand she was bad at being tortured. The interrogators were
after particular stories. Their art was employed to coerce their
subjects into telling them, and the pain was the guarantor of its
truth. In Julia's case, they wanted to hear about how Records
consisted of a criminal cabal that was out to corrupt the nation
with its lies. She was to admit being privy to this effort, and
explain how the conspiracy worked.

She was not to talk about Weeks, or her work above the
shop, or the pills, or Deputy Chairman Whitehead. She understood this sometimes—she tried to understand it. But the mere
threat of pain confused her, and when they hurt her, everything
flew from her head. She needed to live, to be safe at least for a
moment. Most of all, she needed to be loved and forgiven. It
was this, perhaps, that made her stupid.

Even on the first day, she struggled to tell their story, but lost
her thread and found herself babbling, "But Syme ran away, so I
never could bring him to the room. We suppose he might be in
Eurasia." For this she ended up hanging from hooks in the ceiling, her arms tugging out of their sockets, struggling to breathe.
After that, whenever they approached her, she wept and begged
to be told what to say. That was wrong. It wasn't an answer. It
resulted in hair being torn from her head and the soles of her

feet being beaten with truncheons and her breasts being struck with whips that made welts on top of welts, and at last cut through the skin. Later mistakes brought knives stabbed into her fingertips or into the tender arches of the soles of the feet. All her toenails were torn away, then a fingernail. It felt as if the bone came away with the nail, and she spoke disjointedly, raving about Winston Smith being a prig, about Ampleforth conspiring to meet Shakespeare, about how she didn't believe there were rebels, no matter what those maps said. Wrong, wrong, wrong. Her unbroken hand was secured and cigarettes put out in its palm, and she stared as it was about to happen, then screamed so hard it hurt the wounds in her feet and she forgot what question she'd been asked.

All her life, she had slept very well. Now she was seldom allowed to sleep at all, and hallucinated from weariness. In these fits, she often thought she was having sex with various parties, from Big Brother to Vicky Fitzhugh, to whom she said coyly, "No, I don't like that. I don't like you to touch me. You're a girl," while somewhere men in black uniforms rose and bent, kicking and beating her, their writhing movements making them appear like swimmers. When they gave her truth drugs, she confessed to having registered Tiger and Commissar as pest control workers though they were afraid of rats, to being weak-willed and obliging though she knew it was irritating, to having killed her mother. From somewhere, too, she'd dredged up the false idea that she'd been an illegitimate child, and she confessed this repeatedly although she was punished for it by her frustrated jailers. Some mistakes were worse than others. When she talked about Whitehead, her mouth was stuffed with gauze and closed with tape. Then she was beaten about the face until her nose filled with blood and phlegm, and she passed out for want of air. Her torturers called her stupid, a mad bitch, an imbecile, while also accusing her of thinking she was clever. She saw she was wrong but couldn't see how to change. It had to happen again and again.

Once, she was taken to an infirmary for wounds that had begun to fester. Then the broken hand was set properly and secured in a tight brown bandage. A note was also stapled to the chest of her overalls with the instruction: *Pregnancy. No abdominal.* She wept then and stroked the note. It was keeping her alive. It was keeping her baby alive. She closed her eyes and approved of the note as if her approval would keep it there. But this happiness too seemed to make her simple; she saw a doctor and called to him, "Oh, may I have anti-sex pills, Dr. Louis? I am hurting so terribly, you see." Then the nurses laughed at her. She thought she saw the joke and laughed, as much at the relief of understanding as at the joke itself. Back in interrogation, she tried to amuse her tormenters by telling them how she'd asked for pills against pain. "That would rather defeat the purpose, wouldn't it?" But they didn't laugh; they said the purpose was the defense of the Party against unpersons like her, and they beat her broken hand until she passed out in agony and woke with cold water streaming from her, shivering and screaming. The bandage, of course, was ruined.

Between interrogations, she was housed in a series of concrete cells with nothing in them but drains. Here she was sometimes left for days at a time—or so she surmised from the frequency of meals. Increasingly, too, she was left in corridors, strapped to the cot they sometimes used for torture. These cots had straps that restrained every part of her body. One couldn't even turn one's head from side to side. Once she was left long enough that she had to soil herself. Then the reek of shit and the mushy feeling at her buttocks seemed like the worst thing yet. They were right to hate her. She no longer existed as anything but shit and pain. And of course she must then be stripped, hosed down, beaten. In the midst of it, she thought to beg them to save her Big Future badge. She was kicked for this and called a mad bitch again. But in one of those anomalous gestures that sometimes occurred, when she was in her new overalls, a guard pinned the badge on her collar, then patted it. She replayed that moment in her head for hours. One could still live. People still did things like that.

On the last day, lying on that cot in the corridor, she over-heard two men with cultivated voices, Inner Party voices, speak-ing around a corner. The rich smell of their cigarettes drifted to her. She was happy. She was staring at the lights in the ceiling, fantasizing about how one would go about installing lights like that, when what the voices were saying caught her attention.

One man said, "Subject by the name of Parsons. They'd found a good trigger. He was awfully afraid of burning, so that's what 101 is very good for."

"Yes," the other said. "The asbestos tile."

"Quite so. They wanted him to give up his children, and went so far as to spell it out. Very simple-minded sort of chap, you see. But he wouldn't agree to the switch, so they had to go at him piecemeal. Very tricky to manage with burning, you know, as the damage is so profound. They were fairly begging him to save himself by the end. They even made out that his children had asked for him to do it, and didn't mind being burned in his place. But here's the joke: the children were already dead. They'd been shot in the arrest of the wife."

"Ah. He never suspected that."

"No. It's the stupid ones that cause trouble. I've seen that time and again."

"Yes, no imagination. They can't work up proper fear."

"That's it. Well, this Parsons held out to the end. But when they told him the truth about the children, he died just like that. Like a flame snuffed out."

"Pun not intended, I hope."

"Would you believe, I hadn't thought of it? I *am* sorry."

"And had they done an injury that ought to cause death?"

"I should say they had. The wonder was that he didn't die in the first five minutes. Not much left by then. My friend thinks he had clung to life in the belief that it protected his children. Remarkable what the will can do."

"Remarkable. Even in them."

"Yes, remarkable."

She fell asleep after that and had a dream in which she was confessing and getting everything right, all the stories flowing out of her beautifully—but it made no difference. It even seemed to exasperate her jailers, who now began to carve flesh off her body. They denuded her fingerbones, then chopped off the fingers. They lopped off her breasts. They carved the flesh from her face, excising the nose and tossing it lightly away. She kept trying to die, but they whittled her to nothing but a faceless head and skinless torso, and still she couldn't die. Still they busily hacked at the mass of flesh. The child's foot appeared, kicking outside the bloody belly. Julia's eyes stared lidless and naked from the gory, grinning head.

And she woke into a real interrogation. O'Brien was beside her at last, and she gasped with relief to feel that she had lips, she had cheeks. She could blink her eyes. She badly had to urinate, and let herself, sighing at the warm and pleasant liquid, then felt sorry when it grew cold. O'Brien was speaking, but the words couldn't be understood. She was still strapped to that cot, and she gradually became aware of her dread of a mechanism fixed about her head. Now she remembered: a current came through that mechanism. It was electric shock.

She had been here a long time already, and they had shocked her again and again. It had taken her memory away, but the memory was coming back. The electric shock caused a bizarre, wrenching agony that seemed to pull her joints apart; the bones of her spine ground together and snapped. She'd been told this wouldn't harm her baby, but how could that be true? She wanted to ask about it again, but was lost in inspecting the white tiles of the ceiling where they met the white tiles of the wall. They were a kind of tile she'd worked with before, very easy to clean. O'Brien was speaking of hate. He had a short pug nose. In the nostrils, straight brown hairs could be seen, very orderly as if combed. His hairline was receding unevenly. He was asking her to feel hate, specifically for Winston Smith. She should want Winston Smith to be tortured and killed, and feel pleasure in knowing it was being done. That seemed simple, now that she understood. She said, "That's fine. I should like it very much."

She hadn't been confident she could still speak, and was proud for having managed it. But O'Brien was shaking his head. He said, "No, that is no use. You are lying."

Was she lying? No, wasn't it doublethink? How could it be understood? She remembered Diana Winters, and wondered if this could be the game of two plus two make five. She found she was saying it aloud: "Is this the game of two plus two make five?"

He said, "Four hundred."

She was trying to see this as arithmetic when the electric shock drove through her again. It was a thing that couldn't happen, an agony a body couldn't have. It wrung her into an anger that felt like death. The baby was kicking frantically, causing a pang in her pelvic bone. He was hurt! All they'd told her was lies. Doublethink. How could it be understood?

"I see that you would like to please us," said O'Brien. "But we are not to be pleased. It is no use to dissemble or play a false part. You must *be* what is wanted and nothing more."

It cost her some effort to remember what she was meant to be. Then she said, "Yes, it's only rather difficult to wish pain on someone else when one is in pain. One feels it too plainly. I'm sure that's true."

"That's no good," he said regretfully. "That is just what you must master. You must know the pain you cause, and wish it on other people. You must long for their suffering."

"I shall do that. Thank you. Now that you say it, I see it's possible."

"Another lie, I'm afraid."

"How am I to know if I'm lying? I think you've said. I do wish to understand."

He said, "One thousand."

The number frightened her, but when the shock came, she knew she'd had it many times before. It was familiar; the paralyzing agony, the hideous snapping in her spine, the feeling of something absolutely wrong in the brain. The destruction of the brain. Then she was breathing again. She had survived. His face was blurred, then horribly clear.

She said, "Tell him from me he is a mediocrity and a thief of others' ideas. Diana Winters. She gave my mother a cardigan."

He said, "One thousand."

It came again. She had meant to be careful, but there was always so much pain. Even as the shock faded, she was babbling nonsensically, "Oh, my baby is kicking. He's alive. He is Big Brother's son. He will live in your flat and have a dog."

He said a number but she didn't understand. The shock came. Her mind fled and she found herself floating in the air, looking down on her own body. She noticed its shape with surprise, much more pregnant than before, and the little pool of urine on the floor beneath. She now saw there was a second man in the room, standing just out of sight of the body. He was the one who operated the shock machine. He had greasy black hair and pronounced dark circles under his eyes. He bent over the dials of the machine, biting his lip. O'Brien was still talking and it struck her as strange that he addressed the body on the cot, not Julia where she was on the ceiling. He took a hypodermic needle from the pocket of his overalls, and she curiously watched as he pressed this into the body's shoulder. Then a sharp black snap came, and she was awake again, back in her body, jolting and trembling.

Now she heard O'Brien's inexorable voice again. "Don't imagine that you will save yourself. No one who has once gone astray is ever spared. And even if we chose to let you live out the natural term of your life, still you would never escape from us. What happens to you here is forever. We shall crush you down to the point from which there is no coming back. Things will happen to you from which you could not recover, if you lived a thousand years. Never again will you be capable of ordinary human feeling. Everything will be dead inside you. Never again will you be capable of love, or friendship, or joy of living, or laughter, or curiosity, or courage, or integrity. You will be hollow. We shall squeeze you empty, and then we shall fill you with ourselves."

For a time she lay shivering, uncomprehending, looking at the tiles in the ceiling. Then she said, "I don't believe it. There is the child. Big Brother wouldn't do it to his own child. Not to a baby who can't deserve to have anything . . . something from which he could not recover for a thousand years. You give his baby electric shocks. Why? Why would you hate Big Brother's baby? It can't be for me—I'm not anything. Are you hurting me for having Big Brother's child?"

His face came closer. She was confused by panic. Then she knew she was going to die and said, "I am sorry. I wish I could have helped. But I am grateful for all your work."

He said, "Three thousand."

She woke. She must be long dead, but she woke into a room subtly different from the others. There was a distinct, dank heaviness to it. Its air was utterly inert. She realized she must be in the deepest level of Love, many floors beneath the earth, perhaps even miles underground. She was aware of guards around her. One she could fully see, a red-haired man with a freckled face, leaning in a corner and methodically filling a small pipe with tobacco.

She was on the same cot as before, but its back had been manipulated so she sat almost upright. A different constraint confined her head, a padded frame that pinched her temples painfully but left her whole face free. Her forehead smarted in a way that was new. In her writhing, she must have cut it on something. Her hair was wet and she was terribly cold. She'd been stripped and hosed down—she recognized the feeling— but they'd put her back in the same dirty overalls. The urine had dried at the crotch and was stiff.

The cot faced a telescreen that showed another cell, very like the one she was in, but with a darker tile. At its center a man was strapped to a cot like hers, also cranked up so he sat upright. In front of him stood two tables covered in green baize. It was the brightest color Julia had seen since she came to Love, and at first she stared at the tables in fascination. Only then did she turn her attention to the man strapped to the cot.

He seemed a very old man at first. With his sharp nose, he had the toothless, wizened, gray-pink face of a new-hatched bird. After a moment, though, she saw it wasn't age but advanced starvation. He'd been tortured, too, and like many people here, was covered in bruises and abrasions. Only after she knew all this did she recognize Winston Smith. He had lost most of his hair and half his weight, but it was Winston Smith.

There is the cause of all my trouble, she thought. At that moment, the red-haired guard in her room struck a match and lit his pipe. The smell of the match was a lovely thing, as the sharp green of the baize had been. When the sweet-smelling pipe smoke reached Julia's nostrils, it nauseated her but it was still beautiful. She breathed intently, staring at Winston's face.

Now a sound came from the telescreen, the sucking noise of a heavy door coming open so its opening broke a seal. O'Brien appeared on-screen. He came toward Winston, looking down at him with a paternal air, and Winston gazed back with timid reliance. The tableau bespoke a deep familiarity. One would have said O'Brien had come many times before to save Winston from monstrous fates, and had arrived again on that same errand.

O'Brien said, "You asked me once what was in Room 101. I told you that you knew the answer already. Everyone knows it. The thing that is in Room 101 is the worst thing in the world."

The door opened again, and a guard came in carrying an object made of wire. He set it down on the farther table. Here, Julia supposed, was the worst thing in the world—yet how could it be? It was no bigger than a picnic basket, and in fact rather resembled a picnic basket. It had something affixed to the front: an oval, also of wire, a little like a fencing mask.

O'Brien said, "The worst thing in the world varies from individual to individual. It may be burial alive, or death by fire, or by drowning, or by impalement, or fifty other deaths. There are cases where it is some quite trivial thing, not even fatal."

Winston's face had changed. The reliance was replaced by doubt, and his eyes were fixed not on O'Brien but on the wire basket. For the first time Julia wondered why she was in attendance. They were torturing Winston Smith with some small evil: very well, but why was she here?

Now O'Brien moved aside to let Winston have a better view of the basket. At the same time, she now made out a restless movement in the basket itself. It was a cage. That was what it was. As she thought this, O'Brien said to Winston, "In your case, the worst thing in the world happens to be rats."

"You can't do that!" Winston cried out immediately. "You couldn't, you couldn't! It's impossible."

"Do you remember," O'Brien said, "the moment of panic that used to occur in your dreams? There was a wall of blackness in front of you and a roaring sound in your ears. There was something terrible on the other side of the wall. You knew that you knew what it was, but you dared not drag it into the open. It was the rats that were on the other side of the wall."

"O'Brien!" Winston said, his voice cracking. "You know this is not necessary. What is it that you want me to do?"

O'Brien went on in a didactic tone, "By itself, pain is not always enough. There are occasions when a human being will stand out against pain, even to the point of death. But for everyone there is something unendurable—something that cannot be contemplated. Courage and cowardice are not involved. If you are falling from a height it is not cowardly to clutch at a rope. If you have come up from deep water it is not cowardly to fill your lungs with air. It is merely an instinct that cannot be destroyed. It is the same with the rats. For you, they are unendurable. They are a form of pressure that you cannot withstand, even if you wished to. You will do what is required of you."

"But what is it, what is it?" Winston said. "How can I do it if I don't know what it is?"

O'Brien turned and lifted the cage. As he brought it forward, one saw the considerable weight of the thing. Winston writhed but could scarcely move against the confinement of his cot. Julia's body moved in sympathy. She could see Winston's chest heave with his panicked breath.

"The rat," O'Brien said, "although a rodent, is carnivorous. You are aware of that. You will have heard of the things that happen in the poor quarters of this town. In some streets a woman dare not leave her baby alone in the house, even for five minutes. The rats are certain to attack it. Within quite a small time they will strip it to the bones. They also attack sick or dying people. They show astonishing intelligence in knowing when a human being is helpless."

The cage jerked in his hand, and a burst of furious squealing came from it. Julia stared, fascinated, at its shape. Now that it was closer to the camera, she could see it was really two cages, joined together. She could just make out the shadowy shapes inside; two enormous rats, fighting to get at each other through the intervening wire wall.

Julia tried to tell herself that she was safe. Rats were Winston's fear, not hers. Two rats—even if they were very large rats—that didn't frighten her a bit. She'd eaten rat a dozen times. Let the rats fear Julia; she had no fear of them. But why was she here? Her head was clearer than it had been in some days, and still she could make no sense of it.

O'Brien brought the cage toward Winston and, as he did, he pressed a switch at the side of the cage. There was the click of a release. Again Winston writhed ineffectually, groaning.

O'Brien said, "I have pressed the first lever. You understand the construction of this cage. The mask will fit over your head, leaving no exit. When I press this other lever, the door of the cage will slide up. These starving brutes will shoot out of it like bullets. Have you ever seen a rat leap through the air? They will leap onto your face and bore straight into it. Sometimes they attack the eyes first. Sometimes they burrow through the cheeks and devour the tongue."

Winston had shut his eyes. His whole face squinted, seeming to try to shut itself in a fist. Julia too cringed back sympathetically and felt the constriction of the pads that immobilized her head. Now she remembered Diana speaking of disfigurement. Could that be what was meant? Eating the eyes, burrowing through the cheeks . . . The shrieks of the rats went on as, achingly slowly, O'Brien moved the cage forward. It now covered Winston's face. There was a sound as the mechanism clicked in place; it must be designed to latch onto the pads. The cage was shaking with the frenzied activity of the rats. Winston's moans rose through their noise, low and hoarse, to the rhythm of panting breath.

"It was a common punishment in Imperial China," said O'Brien. He bent over the cage. His hand had found the second lever. His ugly face benignly smiled.

Suddenly Winston burst into a despairing cry, so loud it gave the effect of violent movement. "Do it to Julia! Do it to Julia! Not me! Julia! I don't care what you do to her. Tear her face off, strip her to the bones. Not me! Julia! Not me!"

Once the cage had been removed harmlessly from Winston's face, the door to Julia's room was opened. Then she could see through the doorway to that other room with its darker tile—Room 101. It had been right there all the time. A guard wheeled Winston in beside her. His face expressed only bliss at his escape, and he stared before him with a gap-toothed smile, panting through colorless lips. He never saw Julia. Even when the guard took her chair and wheeled her past him, his eyes didn't turn to see.

Julia thought: *The rats have not fed at all.*

The door closed behind her with its sucking noise. She was rolled to Winston's place. The cage waited on the green baize, now twitching and rocking with the fury of the cheated rats. O'Brien repeated his lines about rats attacking the eyes, devouring the tongue, while Julia tried desperately to think. Winston had escaped by betraying her, but whom could she betray? She'd betrayed everyone already. There was no one. In the back of her mind, she remembered Diana Winters saying they wouldn't let her leave with her face—and about the clock. She had said to run out the clock. She had said it would be fifteen minutes. But how was Julia to do it? She couldn't even move her head. She could do nothing at all.

Now O'Brien had the cage in his hand. He brought it hugely into her field of vision so it blotted out the light. The stink of the rats was overwhelming, an animal smell of dung that shouldn't have been frightening. It wasn't unlike the friendly smell of a cowshed. But there were the sinuous movements, the squeaking, the hungry leaping at the wire. They were huge creatures, as big as cats, with the powerful bodies and grizzled muzzles of veterans of the sewers. She could see the mouths working in anticipation, the dense rows of yellow teeth. She knew the power of the jaws. It was quite true that rats killed babies and infirm people. They ate the flesh from their hands, stripped their faces from their skulls, devoured the nose. Julia's dream returned to her of the skinless head. She wanted to scream like Winston: *You can't, you can't. It is impossible.*

Now the mask closed over her face. The wire knocked glancingly at her cheek, then the structure was locked onto the pads. The rats threw themselves at the wire, only an inch from her face, her eyes. The wire shivered. She felt the jolting in her head. In the confined space, the stink was suffocating. She heard herself rhythmically moan with her panting breath.

"Don't be concerned," O'Brien said. "We will preserve the body intact. The pregnancy will not be affected. You may console yourself with that."

There was no time left, and still Julia had no answer. If it were a matter of outwitting the construction of the cage, she might do it. But her hands were confined at her sides. All she could move was her jaw. She moved her jaw experimentally and thrust out her tongue. Immediately a rat's claw reached through the wire. She whimpered and hastily withdrew the tongue, clenching her jaws shut. Her teeth could guard her tongue; that was safe. O'Brien was wrong about that. But her cheeks, nose, eyes—she could do nothing about it.

They might have used three minutes already. But how much flesh two rats could devour in twelve minutes! Being told to run out the clock was only a taunt. She might have known that was all it was. Diana Winters was probably a plant, as that other woman said. Just another vicious game.

She tried to tell herself again that one could live without a nose. Without lips, without a cheek. Even if she lost both eyes, people did live blind. But nothing in her understood this. She had the feeling of falling and falling into a hole that was disgustingly, unnaturally deep, into the singular horror that could not be.

One of the rats made a series of shrill, eager cries, so close she felt its breath on her face. O'Brien's hand was at the cage. In a moment he would release the doors. Through the wire, behind the furious bodies of the rats, she saw him smile.

Then a slight, awful jolt went through the metal, and both doors sprang open. The rats leapt forward. She felt the confused scrabbling of their claws on her face, her eyes, her chin. There was the horrible intimate dampness of their eagerly sniffing noses. The first sharp nip came at her brow.

But in that pause, in the rats' momentary disorientation, Julia saw it. These were animals. They weren't torturers. They would behave as animals behaved and react as animals reacted. Even now, they hadn't leapt out ravening and bored into her as O'Brien had predicted. One was gnawing at her brow, attracted by the blood from the cut already there. The other rat inspected her lips, flinching back when the lips writhed beneath it, then being drawn back in fascination to the fresh living meat. Yes, they would eat her flesh. They wanted a meal. But that was all they wanted.

She saw her chance. It was horrid, impossible—but it must be tried.

She bit down on the tip of her tongue as hard as she could, until she tasted blood. Then she opened her mouth, careful not to dislodge the rat there, and thrust out her bloodied tongue. The rat at first seemed oblivious, moving aside to sniff at her cheek. Meanwhile its fellow was biting agonizingly into the flesh at the top of Julia's eyelid. She made herself ignore this and opened her jaws wider, thrusting out her tongue and turning its bloody tip enticingly toward the rat's muzzle.

With a pain that jolted her whole body, its teeth seized on the end of her tongue. She almost snapped her jaws shut, but made herself hold still while electric horror ran through her whole body. Her tongue twisted despite her. She gagged. But the rat had the taste of the meat and wasn't deterred. Now, gently, with a patience that hurt in all her tense muscles, Julia drew the tongue in, while straining her jaws as far open as the dimensions of the mask would allow. The rat, intent on its food, allowed itself to be drawn forward, its teeth slicing awful chunks from Julia's tongue. Tears streamed from her eyes and Julia still waited and drew the tongue in more, needing to be sure. At last she felt the nudge of the rat's head inside her cheek. In an instant, she snapped her jaws shut.

The beast fought violently, squeaking. Its claws scratched at her cheeks and mouth, and she felt its strength pull awfully at her teeth. There was the awful texture of fur in her mouth, the dirty taste, the head jerking against her tongue. Then came the crunching of bones, the sickly, hot blood in a rush. The rat jerked again but without strength. It went limp. At last she was able to spit out the head.

The other rat had been temporarily dislodged from its meal by the violent kicking of its fellow. Now it moved experimentally back toward her eye, its sharp, intelligent foot pressing down the lid. She tried to edge the dead one's body away from her mouth, with a thought of enticing the second rat into her jaws, but couldn't make the corpse shift. It was too big. The surviving rat was at her eyelid, its tiny nose snuffling. She felt its breath. She filled her lungs and screamed as loud as she could, but this only slightly discommoded the beast. It winced back only to get a tighter grip on her face. It nipped the eyelid now, a terrible pinching and shearing that Julia horribly felt in the eyeball itself. Then, miraculously, it let go. It turned, gripping Julia's nose with one foot, moving more confidently now. It had been drawn to the corpse of its fellow, a more familiar kind of food.

While the second rat gobbled the first, Julia squirmed and mimicked the sounds of agony. The surviving rat's claws grasped at the bridge of her nose companionably, jerking with the movements of its feeding. Julia was smiling beneath it, loving the rat and its rank smell of life. At the same time, she was aware of O'Brien watching, of the unknown stretch of time that still remained. It might still fail. He must see what was happening. But no: he had gone to the wall and was muttering into a speakwrite. The rat sniffed curiously at her nostril, tickling her, then turned back comfortably to its food. It was a fine, clever beast. A friend. But it must eat more; it mustn't fall still. She squirmed her face to keep it moving.

Now a new sound came; Julia flinched. The rat squeaked in protest and shifted its feet in a way that felt almost reproving. Only when O'Brien said, "What is it?" did she understand that the door to the room had opened.

A voice answered: "Alberts needs the room for prep."

"I'm waiting on medical," said O'Brien.

"I can do medical if it's not a surgical job."

"Could go either way. Rats."

"That's all right. I've got the gauze. They'll do the rest at the infirmary. Alberts needs the room."

"This one isn't to die. It's a pregnancy."

"I said I have gauze. If it's that bad, all right, we'll wait for medical. If not, I've got Alberts behind me with a Class A."

"Very well."

Through the mask, she saw the black bulk of O'Brien looming toward the cage. Once he saw her, he would insist on more time. More rats would be fetched. Or he would simply carve her face away with a knife. It would take seconds. The other man would help.

O'Brien had grasped the cage now. She felt it budge against her face. As he unlatched it, the living rat burst onto the floor and scrabbled off in headlong fright. The mangled body of the dead rat flopped free and fell with a solid thud. Both men recoiled. The decapitated head still adhered to her chin until Julia took a gasp of breath. Then it, too, detached and tumbled lightly away.

O'Brien bent over her, looking very strange. Involuntarily, she shut her eyes against him. She squinted to see and not to see, breathing convulsively. The wound from the rat's teeth stung on her brow. The other man bent over her, probing her face with his fingers, his gaunt face incredulous. Then a bell sounded. The door opened again.

It was the bustling noise of guards that told her it was done. She opened her eyes fully, sucking her bloody tongue. Her face didn't smile—it still wasn't quite a face—but her heart rejoiced in the guards, in O'Brien, in the gaunt-faced man who looked at O'Brien quizzically. Here came the red-haired guard with his smell of pipe tobacco, and behind him a guard she remembered from her first cell whose name was Worth, almost like hers. Since he was small, all the criminals called him "Little Worth." It was thrilling to see the guards' boredom; jolly to see them dance out of the way and curse when the living rat escaped among their boots.

Then she was rolled gaily, bouncingly, back into the room from which she'd come. The pipe smoke was still swirling, and in its luxurious haze she saw Winston Smith. He'd been set before the telescreen just as she'd been, so he must face it from close quarters. The bluish light of the screen made his face look grave. But he wasn't watching. He hadn't been watching. He drooped in his restraints, his narrow jaw lolling open. He was fast asleep.

PART THREE

21

JULIA SAW WINSTON SMITH AGAIN SOME TWO MONTHS after her release.

In that time, she'd spoken to almost no one. At Truth, she'd been taken off the Fiction floor and given the title of Facilities Consultant. The Facilities Consultant had no duties and was sequestered in a tiny room at the end of a little-frequented corridor. The room was furnished with a single folding chair, and all there was to do there was to watch the telescreen. Indeed, it was impossible not to, as the volume was stuck on high. In the first days, Julia was mesmerized by the simple stories and triumphant music without taking much of it in, but as her health recovered, imperceptibly she came to feel real outrage at the child molesters, gangs, and terrorists featured in the crime news and to fret about the fortunes of the ongoing war.

Eurasia was again the enemy—no, it had always been the enemy. One must remember that. She had a curiously hard time believing it, though. All that sort of mental work now gave her trouble. She didn't understand why war was peace, and the very thought of "doublethink" made her feel sleepy and cross. She also embarrassingly cried at the televised executions, though she scarcely knew why. Once her baby was born, she too would be shot or hanged, and she regarded this not as a sorrow but a comfort.

In her diminished state, it had taken her time to understand the new rules of her life. She blushed to think of her behavior on the first night, when she was left outside the hostel by the van with her old boots in her hand. Of course she couldn't wear boots at that time. Her feet were still hideously swollen and she had them wrapped in rags. Still, she was proud of being able to walk, when so many unpersons had to go on all fours. Julia stubbornly refused to crawl even when she got to the hostel steps.

To be free was a riot of conflicting feelings. The wonderful knowledge that she wasn't to be hurt flooded through her again and again. She wasn't to be shocked! She wasn't to be beaten or burned! On the other hand, she felt a dreadful insecurity without any guards to tell her what to do. The cloudy sky felt dangerous, like a suggestion from the enemy; she glanced at it and fearfully ducked her head. Worst of all was the sense of being no longer among her own kind. At Love, one seldom got to speak to other prisoners, but they were always present as a murmur or a smell, fellow sufferers who knew what one's pain was like and could respect one's tiny victories. Even the guards and torturers were of one's society; comrades of a kind.

The people outside understood none of this, nor was one allowed to explain it to them. Indeed, one wasn't to speak, beyond the simplest communications necessary for survival, and even then one must be prepared to be ignored. As she approached the hostel door, Julia's hand kept going to the Big Future badge, still miraculously pinned to her collar. Its ribbon was soiled and crumpled but the medallion with the baby's face was unharmed. Might she be tolerated for her pregnancy? With the baby inside her, after all, she was a hybrid creature. That might ease her way.

In the back of her mind was a dark unease, a memory wanting to come into focus. It was something to do with the hostel—but Julia chased the thought away. She couldn't indulge in painful ideas. There were the girls to face, and she mustn't cry. She was resolved to be a good unperson: to be invisible, to spare everybody anxiety and embarrassment. Perhaps then she would be rewarded with the occasional sympathetic glance. If even Vicky didn't look at her—but there was the memory. She chased it from her mind again as she mounted the final step.

Atkins wasn't at her desk. Of course: at this hour, all would be gathered to watch the evening newscast. The door to the community room was ajar, and Julia was able to peep in discreetly without attracting attention. The girls were just the same, pink and unconcerned, their chairs gathered in a clump. Atkins sat behind them on her portable stool with her usual expression of happy weariness. There was a new girl who was a Nationality, sitting right among the others on terms of equality. Not every hostel would be like that. The girls of 21 were really comradeful. Julia was lucky; she must remember that always. Vicky wasn't there.

Julia went to the dormitory door. Vicky might go to bed early, after all. However, she must be prepared for Vicky to be gone altogether. This would mean she had married Whitehead, nothing more. One didn't have to worry. It was even good, in a way—but now Julia had opened the door to the dormitory and halted in confusion.

Vicky's bed was gone. In its place were two wooden chairs of the type meant to promote muscular development, their seats tilted slightly forward so the sitter must brace herself with both legs. Perched uncomfortably in these were Oceania and a new girl Julia didn't know. They both saw Julia and flinched. Their faces stiffened into masks of loathing.

Julia blurted out, "Why, the bed itself is gone!"

Both girls turned away. Oceania said curtly, "Bed? What nonsense! Leave us alone!"

"Of course, Vicky—her marriage—"Julia said. "But the bed . . ."

"Damn you!" the other girl said. "What do you want by speaking to us?"

"There never was a Vicky," Oceania said. "That's insanity. And we don't want *you*."

It was then that the dreadful thought that had been troubling Julia came into focus. Had Julia mentioned Vicky at Love? Under drugs, she had spoken of Deputy Chairman Whitehead; she clearly remembered that. She'd had her mouth stopped up with gauze for it. But did that mean she'd spoken of Vicky? The interrogators hadn't ever asked about Vicky—they'd only wanted to speak of Records. But had Julia babbled about her anyhow? Dreadful thought—had she spoken about the bandits and Vicky's plan to flee? The memory was almost there, a half-formed thing like the remains of a nightmare. Yes, she had said something. Why couldn't she remember what she'd said?

A sob escaped Julia. "But if the bed's gone . . . was someone taken? Oh, I won't say her name. Only tell me—"

Then Atkins was there, red-faced and furious. "What's this? What's all this?"

"Oh! Comrade Atkins!" Julia said. "Please—"

Atkins slapped her.

It was a clumsy blow, more startling than painful, and in itself, it scarcely bothered Julia. To someone fresh from Love, being slapped seemed quite in the order of things. What stunned her was the look on all three women's faces as they watched her stagger and hold her cheek. There wasn't a trace of humanity in them, only revulsion and panicked hatred. And Julia was weeping now, as she'd sworn to herself she would not do.

"I'm sorry," Julia stammered. "I'm sorry."

Atkins said, "I'll thank you to leave my girls alone. Not another word from you!" She turned to the others and said,

"Damned criminals! Of course they never think of the harm they do!"

After that, Julia took great care to abide by the rules of her ostracism. She came back to the hostel just before curfew, when the others were already in bed, and waited until the voices all fell silent to enter the dormitory. On a good night, the cats would come and curl against her. She sometimes called them wrongthinkers and chaffed them about their criminal ties, being careful to do it in a whisper. In the morning, her telescreen helpfully barked to wake her before the others, and she rushed to the ownlife and washed herself with a flannel while the citizens all did Rhythmic Jerks. These hasty sessions at the sink were all the bathing she could hope for now; though she still had bathing coupons, no bathhouse attendant would accept them. Mealtimes were also a struggle. The servers sometimes neglected to notice her waiting with her tray, and she was turned away hungry. Even if she got food, she could seldom sit. The canteen at Truth was always crowded, and if she tried to join others at a table, they blocked the empty chair with their bags. It was the same if she went to an A1 dining hall, except that the people there were more frightened, and so she felt more guilt. As a result, Julia soon began to take all her meals at the Chestnut Tree Café.

Through the coldest weeks of winter, this restaurant was her haven. It was where unpersons traditionally went, so instead of the dreadful feeling of being a blight, she had a sense of fitness. In fact, there were a few tables in the corner reserved for people such as she. Cheery music trickled from the telescreens. A vast BIG BROTHER IS WATCHING YOU poster, in unusually crisp and vivid colors, looked down paternally from the wall. In this stage of pregnancy, every position quickly became uncomfortable, and the need to urinate was almost constant, so she was especially glad of the cushioned chair and clean lavatory facilities. On her first visit, a waiter discreetly offered her a book to read, one of the salacious Fiction products Julia hadn't bothered to open in years. Now she devoured it in one sitting. When the waiter brought the next book in the series, she gratefully accepted, and soon she'd read the whole *War Nurse* series and had started on *Revolutionary Nurse*. The soup had real meat sometimes, and was served with toasted bread. The waiter silently came and went, refilling her glass with Victory gin without being asked, always adding a few drops from another bottle with a quill through the cork. That was saccharine water flavored with cloves, the specialty of the café. Though Julia found the taste revolting and feared the weakness and confusion of the gin, she drank it as bravely as she could. She loved the waiters for helping her without seeing her, and never would have caused them trouble. Through the inhospitable, sleeting weeks of January, the café was warm and snug. Once she knew she would be given no work at Truth, she sometimes spent whole days there.

Here Julia sometimes felt that the rituals of Love had really been a kind of cure, and this was the final stage of convalescence. She even had an intimation of the final alteration still to come. It took the form of a furious feeling that surged in her sometimes, especially when another unperson entered the café and sat at a table too close to hers. It also emerged when she thought of certain things—of Vicky being gone, or the moment Winston Smith had suddenly screamed, "Do it to Julia, not to me!" The feeling was always just beneath the surface: a threatening-promising rage that contained the germ of an idea. It was important; she was sure of that. It might even be the purpose of everything. Still, she instinctively suppressed it. She was tired. She wasn't ready. Each time it threatened to overwhelm her, she shut her eyes and drank off her glass of gin.

She was also aware of her role as one of the cautionary figures for which the café was famous—and which, she now realized, were also an attraction of the place. Of course she wasn't as gruesome as most. She herself shrank from some of the grotesques that crept and hobbled to her corner of the room. Still, when she once saw herself in a café mirror, she thought: *That's one of them.* The wound on her forehead from the rat was healing jaggedly and gave her a sinister look. Her jaw was swollen where she'd lost two teeth and the gums were now infected. Both hands were marked with scars from cigarettes and the messier scars from frequent beatings. The broken one had healed in an odd, thick shape, and the first two fingers were clawed and paralyzed. All her fingertips had a gory crust where new nails had only begun to grow. The many wounds in her feet were slowly healing, but she still limped and couldn't stand up straight. Then there were the subtler signs: the yellowed skin, the thin and lifeless hair, the slack, stunned expression of the face. It might have been a corpse that turned from the mirror and hastened to its table.

This Chestnut Tree phase came to an inglorious end one day when Ampleforth came through the café door.

At first sight, Julia didn't know him. All she saw was the skeletal look and lurching progress of another unperson. He leaned on every table as he crossed the room, panting audibly and screwing up his face into an ingratiating, gap-toothed smile. He was clearly fresh from Love; the places where his hair had been torn from his head were still bloody. Julia braced herself against the likelihood that he would try to speak to her, as new releases often did. When one had been out a few weeks, one lost one's taste for that sort of company. Their piti-ful mumblings and desperate pleas—so wrongthinkful. It only held one back.

It was with a shock that she knew who it was, and with a greater shock that she saw he was headed to sit with her, though there was no sign of recognition in his eyes. It was rather the instinctive movement of a beast that gravitates to its own kind.

He slumped into the chair with a grunt of pain and smiled his awful smile at no one as a waiter came to pour his gin. Julia thought with relief that he might leave her alone and looked back at *Revolutionary Nurse III: Mirabella*. But once the waiter had gone, Ampleforth leaned forward and said confidentially, "You will have seen what I am. I am so terribly sorry . . . you see, it was a matter of a poem. I could find no rhyme for 'rod,' and I left a terrible word. I don't know what it was anymore. They have been so kind; they took it from my head." Here he touched his crown, where Julia now noticed a deep, peculiar wound. One would have said that a trench had been dug into the skull. He caressed the indentation lovingly.

She knew she oughtn't to encourage him, but she found her-self saying soothingly, "You should try the soup. It is really very good here. It comes with toasted bread."

Ampleforth went on as if he hadn't heard: "A terrible word. It rhymed with 'rod.' But I have also done filthy things, a"—he lowered his voice to a whisper—"sexcrime. I never would have mentioned it, but everybody knows. It is written in my face." His hand now moved down to touch his face experimen-tally. He seemed to find whatever it was he sought. His mouth twisted painfully and his eyes shut.

Julia said rather desperately, "That's all right. Anyhow, it's no good speaking here. Try the soup. It is really quite good."

He nodded gratefully and opened his eyes. Only then did he

seem to properly see her. He shuddered horribly, crying out, "Is it you? Have I ruined you too? Oh, I have killed you!"

At this, she almost fled. Why couldn't unpersons leave one in peace? Loathsome people! One saw why they must be shot.

But something in this idea felt wrong. It tasted of the ersatz gin and the sickly saccharine mixture. That furious feeling that always lurked beneath the surface of her consciousness rose. She took a swallow of gin, and when she looked at Ampleforth's face, with its yellow and purple bruises, she was filled with a chilling compassion. She knew it was wrong to feel this—but it mattered little whether she was right or wrong. Julia too was an unperson. Whatever she did, she could be no worse.

She said, "But you have not ruined me at all. You are very wrong to think it."

"No?" he said humbly. "Who are you, then?"

"But you know me. I am Julia."

"Julia," he repeated dutifully. "Yes? Who's that?"

"We read poetry together. You called me your Abyssinian maid. Do you remember?"

"Did I? Now, what could I have meant?"

"It was from a poem. 'In a vision once I saw: it was an Abyssinian maid, and on her dulcimer she played...'"

At this, he looked terrified and covered his face, shrinking back into his chair. But when she stopped, he leaned forward timidly and said, "Do you remember it? Don't tell it to me—please don't! Only say if you remember."

"Yes. I remember that one, and the one about the soldier. 'Some corner of a foreign field that is for ever...' But I won't say it."

"I've forgotten it all." He touched his crown again. "All gone. I have killed it with my filthiness. It is gone from the world forever."

"But it isn't gone. You see that I remember it."

"No," he said simply. "They told me I had killed it, and it's true. The poetry is all gone from it. Even when I remember the words, they are quite dead."

Once he said this, she saw it was true for her, too. She knew the words, but they no longer moved her. They only reminded her that she was corrupt.

"That's all right," she said, feeling desperate again. "Only listen, there's a song on the telescreen now. That's every bit as good. It's better. These songs are what people really like."

He nodded, looking at her with trusting eyes. But the next moment he was trembling again, saying, "Oh, I know who you are! You are Julia! I have given them your name. I told them . . . Oh, I have killed you!"

"But it's quite all right. You can see I'm all right."

"No, I told them . . . and those pills you gave me. I had to die but I wasn't allowed. They took them from me when I went to see my brother. Oh, my brother! He was drowned. It was Room 101. I betrayed him! Oh, how filthy!"

"No, don't remember it like that," Julia said. "I'm sure it wasn't like that."

"No, it was. 'Do it to Geoffrey, not to me!' That's what I said. They showed it on the telescreen. He fought so terribly."

"But you know that what a telescreen shows is often false. I work at Fiction, so I know. And even if it was true, we have all done the same. But it's very likely false."

"False? I don't think . . . but I get very confused. And who are you? I seem to have forgotten."

"I am Julia."

"Oh, yes. You betrayed me. I remember. They told me about it so many times."

"I did. I should like to have saved you, but I had no choice."

"Yes," he said simply. "That's the horrid thing. One has no choice, and yet one must live through it exactly as if one had."

At that moment, something changed in the music coming from the telescreen. The strings became subtly screeching, the horns played flat. The voice turned coarse and jeering. It had a yellow note—the yellow of contaminated water, of jaundiced eyes and dying skin. It sang:

> Under the spreading chestnut tree
> I sold you and you sold me
> Oh, how cheap we proved to be
> Under the spreading chestnut tree

At this, Ampleforth thrust his face in his hands and sobbed, "But why has anyone done these things! Why did I? Oh, my brother!"

That was the end of the Chestnut Tree Café for Julia. Now, whenever she wanted to go there, that song came into her mind, with the memory of Ampleforth sobbing into his hands, and she turned from the idea with a shudder. It also spoiled her enjoyment of the telescreen. Every voice that came from it had that coarse, yellow note, the taste of saccharine and bad gin. And always beneath it, the furious feeling pushed at her, wanting to be born.

Every morning now she left the hostel and spent hours walking the wintry streets. If it was raining, she sometimes went to the Ministry, intending to shelter in her office, but the telescreen always drove her out. She would walk to a bus shelter, then a Tube station, then a war museum or patriotic fair. When the weather was especially foul, she would take the Tube from station to station and wander up and down the platforms. On fine days, she wandered out of doors for hours, wearing out her boots in an endless circuit of the local public toilets. From time to time she would stop at a store to buy a brown loaf to eat on a bench. Then she stretched in various ways to relieve her aches and felt something akin to happiness.

She was aware that what she was enjoying was *ownlife*, a thing forbidden to her when she was a person. She hadn't missed it then, but now could not imagine anything sweeter. She was grateful for the grimness of February, for the muddy parks that people shunned, the cutting winds that emptied streets. She even found herself devising routes to avoid the outdoor tele-screens; their jabbering grated on her nerves. She would gaze at the sky, which no longer frightened her, but filled her with fond exaltation, and recall episodes from childhood. Snatches of jazz came into her mind, and her feet moved to its peculiar beat. The furious feeling troubled her less. She sometimes thought it might go away completely. The walking soothed her, even when her clothes were soaked by unexpected rain and she stumbled with fatigue. Something in it felt important. Her feet grew rapidly stronger, and she felt proud of how soon she became acclimated to the pain from their old wounds. Almost worse was the backache from the baby's weight, which griped very irritatingly, even though her belly hadn't grown that large. In fact, its modest size troubled her; she couldn't entirely shake the fear that the baby had been harmed at Love. But it kicked very ably, and, anyway, Julia's mother had been the same. Clara had often spoken of it, saying she'd never grown huge as some women did, and that the last months of pregnancy had given her a marvelous feeling of well-being, even though she'd had to piss every fifteen minutes. It was just how Julia felt.

One day she remembered what Vicky had said of sandbags being put around Westminster, and set out to see if they were there. But one couldn't get in on foot anymore. The whole Westminster district was closed off, with new metal gates that rose far overhead. After that, Julia noticed such gates all around, always blocking streets with government buildings. There were also streets barred by military vehicles attended by restive soldiers. In fact, there were soldiers everywhere now, speeding through the streets in open trucks, congregating on corners, guarding doorsteps. On the other hand, there were fewer copters. Sometimes Julia could walk for blocks beneath a sky that was entirely clear. She couldn't see how these things went together, and it gave her a queer, unsettled feeling. Could there be a real rebellion? Were the helicopters off fighting it? She was aware, more than ever, that the telescreens told one nothing, or nothing real.

Another time she was drawn by some perverse longing to return to the Inner Party district where she'd met O'Brien. Here she thought all was unchanged, until she entered the park with the fountain where water flowed from Big Brother's hands. She found the fountain dry and its statue buried in fat burlap sacks; here at last were the sandbags she had sought. A hand-lettered sign said this was the work of the Belgravia Preservation of Heritage Committee. Julia turned away, and only then realized the other thing that was different. It being February, she'd taken the quiet for granted—but surely it was strange that she should be the park's *only* visitor? There was not one black-overalled mother, not one white-jacketed servant or white-aproned maid. The streets, too, were almost empty. Only the occasional servant scuttled past with a harried air. At first, she thought the dogs were gone—perhaps the parasitic beasts edict had reached here—but then she came across a little knot of servants, their heads together in intent conversation. All had dogs on leashes, who sniffed gaily at each other's rears and sought to entangle themselves in the servants' legs. Then a disturbance passed through the group. All the servants looked suddenly at Julia, with what she was surprised to see was fear.

This encounter sat oddly in her mind. Again she thought of Vicky, and was now able to think it possible she had fled the city after all, that there were real rebels she had joined. Julia thought of the smugglers' boat, the black sea, her dream of the oars and the sleepy moonlight. It was futile to think about, yet she found her mind straying to it time and again.

She also visited prole districts, though she didn't dare venture very far inside. The sight of blue overalls nowadays was liable to draw bands of hostile children, and once, she had to run away with stones flying dangerously around her ears. The border streets, though, were still safe. These were populated by proles with Party connections, who didn't look twice at a blue. It was here that Julia found a prole bathhouse that would accept her coupons. It was a ferociously clean place, and when she passed the men's section, there were none of the catcalls and ribald jokes she had feared. On the women's side, her blue overalls earned her hostile mutters at first, but after she undressed and the women saw her scarred body, the grumbles died away. She even won a few glances of sympathy, of exactly the kind she had once longed to get from the hostel girls.

Only when Julia was sitting in the iron tub, half-submerged in lukewarm water and trying to work up a lather with the cake of hard soap, did she realize what this meant. Those women hadn't known what she was until she'd shed her clothes. She'd passed as a blue. Then Julia was flooded with grief at the thought that she must die nonetheless. She couldn't live this life she'd scraped out for herself. The furious feeling surged in her again, and she plunged her head underneath the water and concentrated on soaping her greasy hair until it passed. When she'd rinsed off and wrapped her head in a towel, she looked up and saw a young girl in another tub smiling timidly at her. Julia smiled back, and something changed inside her. She thought: *I am almost here.*

The day the feeling overwhelmed her at last was a bitter day in early March. She had found another street of her route blocked off and turned back to do a second circuit of Martyrs of December Park. Here, coming toward her in the opposite direction, shambling and glaring resentfully around, she spotted Winston Smith.

He looked, if anything, worse than he had when he was strapped to the cot in Room 101. His face was red and bloated, with sagging cheeks, his bald pate coarsely pink. His limbs were still scrawny, but fat had pooled at his waist and bulged on either side of his belt. In the thick winter overalls, he looked like an inexpertly stuffed Hate dummy. As he came up, she noticed with a shock that he was now shorter than she. The eyes were changed most of all, dull and obscene.

As he passed, his eyes narrowed but his step didn't slow, and she thought with relief that she hadn't been recognized. But when she looked back, he had turned and was following after her. She hastened her step and turned aside onto the soggy grass, hoping to discourage him, but the degraded figure still came behind with a resentful gleam in its eyes.

It was the first time she had felt afraid since her release. He knew she had betrayed him—he knew! Now, at last, he would knock her to the ground and break her skull with a stone, as he'd once wished to do. He would steal her last precious months. He would murder her baby. No one would intervene. Indeed, no one would acknowledge their existence. She could hope for no help at all.

But when she dared to look back again, his face showed only a feeble sullenness, and she saw he was no danger. Her fear eased. After all, it was only natural he should want to speak to her. He must have seen that she was pregnant, and would be sure the child was his. She slackened her pace and let him draw up beside her, braced for him to ask about the baby—how many months along it was, how it had survived her time at Love.

But she soon realized this was not to be. Although he openly surveyed her body, it was only with the petty disappointment he'd often showed when she appeared without makeup or hadn't had time to change into a dress. Then she realized with amazement that he hadn't noticed she was pregnant. All he saw was that his lover had lost her figure. He'd been cheated as a man: that was all the bloodshot eyes expressed.

They stopped among a clump of leafless shrubs, though the sparse branches gave no shelter from the weather. On the ground, the first crocuses were out, and the wind harassed their dirty petals. Here Winston put his arm around her waist, and she accepted without resistance, indeed with a certain curiosity. As she expected, she felt nothing. His embrace wasn't even unpleasant. It was like touching a piece of furniture.

He, however, seemed to shrink with disgust from the contact he had himself initiated. He grimaced at the scar on her temple and fingered her waist as if performing a dreaded chore. He was muttering almost inaudibly under his breath, seeming himself unaware he was speaking aloud: "It's not only that the waist is thicker, it is stiff. Like a corpse. The face scarred . . . yes, horrid. Even the feet are broader. All coarsened. If one touched the skin, its texture would be quite different . . . don't even want to touch it . . . no . . ." She smelled gin and cloves on his breath.

There was a pair of iron chairs nearby, their legs sunk unevenly in the wet grass, and Julia moved to sit. Winston gratefully released her and took a seat beside her. He had fallen silent now, but still stared at her with hating, beseeching eyes. Then she had the dreadful thought that Winston might dog her steps from now on. She must break whatever compulsion he had woven around her, if only to drive him away.

She said flatly, "I betrayed you."

He responded glibly, immediately, "I betrayed you."

This she felt like a slap in the face. Julia again saw his new ugliness: the gin-dulled face, possessed by a fixed and mournful imbecility. The eyes were no longer even gray; they were like glass paperweights that enclosed nothing. Her breath hurt in her throat with dislike. And wasn't this what he'd always been, underneath? How had she ever wanted him?

But then a memory came to her of Winston as he was, slight and handsome, smiling as he dreamed about the Brotherhood or lectured her about the Party's lies. No, she hadn't been wrong to want him then. He was a boy who had fallen in love with the truth, and even if he never quite grew into a man, he had a fine and austere spirit that was absolutely real. And he had almost loved her. When the rocket bomb knocked them to the ground, he had wept in the rubble at the thought that she was dead. He had loved birdsong and woods. Of all that Love had done to him, the most cynical perhaps was confining their affair in that dingy, infested room, when he might have made love to her in meadows all summer and swum with her in streams.

Yes, at the end of it all were the rats, and his cry of cowardly betrayal; there were the empty eyes and the reek of gin. But none of this was Winston. It was rather as O'Brien had said: "We shall squeeze you empty, and then we shall fill you with ourselves."

In that moment, she felt something pass from her, some resistance of which she had not been aware. She saw how to free him from her. It was obvious, once one cared.

She said, "Sometimes they threaten you with something—something you can't stand up to, can't even think about. And then you say, 'Don't do it to me, do it to somebody else, do it to so-and-so.' And you may pretend afterward that it was only a trick and that you just said it to make them stop and didn't really mean it. But that isn't true. At the time when it happens, you do mean it. You think there's no other way of saving yourself, and you're quite ready to save yourself that way. You *want* it to happen to the other person. You don't give a damn what they suffer. All you care about is yourself."

"All you care about is yourself," he repeated gratefully.

"And after that, you don't feel the same toward the other person any longer."

"No. You don't feel the same."

The work was done; she could see the relief in his eyes as he looked away from her once and for all. He'd been named to himself, and forgiven. She had cut through the knot of love.

She said, "I had better go catch the Tube. It's going to rain."

He nodded solemnly. "We must meet again."

For a moment she thought she'd failed after all. Then she saw with relief that he'd said it only to be spared from parting speeches. She was of no importance to him now; not even enough for that.

She said, "Yes. We must meet again."

*

Having left him, she didn't go to the Tube, but back in the direction of Truth. There was something left to understand, and it dogged her and drove her on.

At Rightwork Circus, her way was blocked by a crowd gathered before the great telescreen. It was showing a new teletape, and this small novelty was enough to draw a hundred people, even though the rain had begun. She automatically gazed up with the others and saw a clip of a young Big Brother charging out of a trench with a squad of cheering heroes behind. His build was massive, almost godlike; he stood head and shoulders above the others and carried his submachine gun like a twig. This was followed by a series of tamer clips of Big Brother's most beloved speeches. Julia couldn't make out the words over the din of traffic, but the footage was so familiar she could follow the speeches from their rhythm alone. It was the usual stuff about victory and ruthlessness and sacrifice. The great face gazed into the radiant distance and warned of the tricks of the enemy. The voice insisted and the eyes believed.

It was then the change began. It was something in the cadence of that voice, its boom that mixed into the grinding of traffic. It was the same voice that scolded from every wall, from speakers in the parks, from radios carried by passersby, and often from some place unseen, so it seemed to declaim from the sky or murmur from inside one's head. The inevitable face glared down from the screen and, when she turned away, the same face was repeated along every wall in every direction. It waited at every corner, it flickered on screens in every window, it looked from the newspapers in every hand. Big Brother groped into her mind, and when she repulsed him, he grasped at her again and again. At every moment he fumbled for an opening and probed to be let in. He watched and said: *I shall squeeze you empty and fill you with myself.*

A wave of weakness passed over her, and was replaced by that furious feeling she'd fought for so long. It was a feeling, she now saw, that had lurked inside her all her life. She had fled it through sex, through work, through screens, through gin, most lately through her hours of walking. Without ever naming it to herself, she had always feared its power. Now she let it rise and consume her. She felt invincible, reckless, aflame. She had the urge to march, to shout, to break windows, to burn down houses. It was as if she were in a mob, and all were red-faced, screaming with rage, chasing after a man who ran desperately, tripping and scrambling, from their braying might. Now she saw where she had been headed all along. She understood the truth of Love, the lesson that had struggled to be born in her as O'Brien applied his electric shocks. The baby kicked hectically, beating like a heart, and it hurt in a way that was glee, that was death to her enemies. It was a pain that would rule for a thousand generations. The voice from the telescreen boomed indistinctly, and she stood with chin raised, gazing up at the enormous face. Twenty-seven years it had taken her to learn what kind of smile was hidden behind the black moustache. But it was all right, everything was all right. She had won the victory over herself at last. She hated Big Brother.

22

SHE WENT TO TRUTH. AT THE ENTRANCE TO THE STAIRS, instead of going down to Fiction, she went to the bicycle bay. From the racks she chose an old Ruthless Warrior, scabby with rust but fundamentally sound.

She rode south, taking a route that led around the perimeter of the Inner Party district to Big Brother Bridge. As she pedaled, she gloried in hate. She hated Big Brother again and again, with undiminished pleasure. Every poster she passed was a charge of hatred. She imagined him being starved, beaten, humiliated, stabbed, beheaded, drowned, torn apart. She hated his Party and now understood she had hated it all her life. She had always known who had killed her mother and her schoolfriends and the airmen. She hated O'Brien, and hated his immaculate flat with its thieving luxury. She hated Martin for his cadaverous face that could still smirk and gloat. She hated Weeks, the spider, and would have liked to crush him underfoot just as he'd crushed her hand. She hated Gerber—oh, she hated Gerber! What bliss to discover she hated Gerber! She thought of more people who had wronged her and hated them one by one, and she felt cleansed. But always she returned to Big Brother. Without him, she would never have hated, and indeed, no one would have deserved her hatred. He was the source of it all.

Now she saw that Vicky had been right. If there were rebels, of course one must go and join them. One must fight to cleanse the world of this great evil. The rain intensified and pelted Julia's face, and even that was headlong pleasure. She was filled with the blood of rage, the implacable blood she'd inherited from her mother, with hatred that was love.

At the bridge, the traffic thickened. The few cars were stopped, and the bicycles had clogged among them. Around these was a thick churn of pedestrians crowded shoulder to shoulder. Only the police lane was clear. Ahead Julia saw the obstacle: a military checkpoint where there had been none before. The way was blocked by the usual trucks, and several soldiers were checking papers, backed up by a wall of black-uniformed patrols. What was strange was that most of the cyclists and pedestrians were being turned away and sent back via the police lane, though occasionally one was let through with only a cursory inspection of their papers. Sometimes, too, for no visible reason, someone was shoved toward the line of patrols, where they were clubbed to the ground and manhandled into one of a line of waiting vans.

The people still approaching the checkpoint called out questions to those who had been rejected. Some of the latter stopped by the concrete barrier of the police lane to share their observations, but they had little to report. The soldiers and patrols were divulging nothing. All Julia could learn from the general chatter was that other bridges, too, were closed, and even Party members who lived south of the river weren't being allowed to go home. Some people had been trying different checkpoints for hours and were now exhausted and frantic.

Julia thought of turning back and trying to get out of London to the north. Her papers were covered in RELEASED PRIS-ONER: PENDING EXECUTION stamps, and presenting them at a checkpoint was a risk at the best of times. Then again, if she meant to leave London, she had to get through a checkpoint sooner or later. The general chaos here might be in her favor. She only needed to get lucky with a plausible lie. Mechanics were always at a premium in an emergency, and she was a mechanic; that might work. They might well believe the Ministry of Peace was in need of mechanics south of the river.

Despite these resolves, as she approached the barrier, she found herself giving in to fear. It was hard to keep her eyes from dwelling on the policemen's truncheons and the waiting vans. Her broken hand was hurting abominably, as it always did when she was scared, and of course she badly wanted to urinate. She started to take her papers out of her tool bag, then changed her mind; perhaps she could claim they were lost. She mentally repeated various lies, trying to anticipate the ways they could be doubted and rejected. When it was her turn to present herself, she formed her hands around the bike's handlebars in a way that concealed their scars.

All these preparations were wasted. The soldier only had eyes for the badge on Julia's collar, at which he frowned in consternation. "Big Future?" he said. "Where's your escort, comrade? Don't tell me they've sent you here without an escort."

"Escort?" she repeated. "I'm not quite sure ..."

"Not sure? Has he up and left you?"

"That's it."

"Blast! You can't very well go on without an escort."

"I've got this bike," she tried.

This only made him shake his head disgustedly. "Where have you got that bike from? A bike! I can't make it out at all."

At that moment, a superior officer came over, saying, "What's all this? What's the holdup?"

"Sir," said the soldier. "Got a Big Future girl on a bike, no escort."

"Here, comrade," said the officer to Julia. "Where are you being evacuated to? Tell me that, and we'll have a man to take you to your pickup."

"Oh..." Julia said. "My escort knew the name."

"It'll be Lewisham, Dulwich, or SAZ-1," said the officer.

None of these places meant much to Julia, but she said, "Lewisham! That's it."

The officer said, "Your vans will be at the Ministry of Plenty. If you'll stand to the side, I've got a man who can take you—oh, here he is. Jackson!"

The soldier so addressed was a boy of about eighteen, whose black uniform marked him as a London soldier—one whose parents had pulled strings to get him posted to the city barracks instead of being sent to the front. Julia knew this type from community-center dances, and had always found them rather dimwitted but refreshingly free of Party piety. Once again she had been lucky; she couldn't have wished for a safer escort.

Jackson heard his instructions with frightened eyes, but when he turned to Julia, his face changed. With a fluttering feeling, she realized that, to him, she was still pretty. He said gruffly, "Not to worry, comrade. I'll get you there safe and sound."

Her bike was taken away and she was invited to mount behind Jackson on a motorcycle. At first she couldn't make herself hold him about his waist; the habit of being an unperson had made her frightened of touching other people. But when he took her hands and secured them firmly about himself, she began to helplessly smile. He leaned back into her as they set off, and veered immediately around a van, making Julia gasp with pleasure. As they picked up speed, she clung more tightly, until her face was close enough to smell him, even as the wind exhilaratingly blew around her. He smelled of boy, of whatever soap boys used. Her hate had opened out now and become a madcap spirit of adventure. No one had even looked at her papers. She was lucky. She would live.

The Ministry of Plenty was a thirty-story glass tower, with a colossal statue at the front of a naked man brandishing a scythe and holding a sheaf of grain that decorously concealed his groin. Proles called it Bare-Arsed Death, and told their families it walked at night and harvested the heads of ill-behaved children. From the scene at the bridge, Julia had half expected to find the Ministry's glass all shattered and a battle in progress. She was somewhat disappointed that Bare-Arsed Death stood as before, his square-jawed face glaring up at the sun beneath his menacing scythe, and the Ministry's glass was intact and its lights all shining, creating a yellow glare in the mist above.

Two white police vans were parked beside the statue, with a few soldiers leaning against them. Jackson pulled up behind, and steadied the motorbike while Julia dismounted, then got off himself with a broad, relieved smile.

"There!" he said. "Now you see it was nothing. Nothing to fear, just as I told you."

"Yes," said Julia. "It *was* silly of me to be afraid."

This won a broader grin from Jackson, and he put his hand on her shoulder to guide her toward the open back of the second van. When she saw what he meant, she instinctively balked. Somehow it had not occurred to her that the vans that had been mentioned would be police vans. At her alarm, Jackson looked even bolder. "Don't worry. These will take you right to Lewisham. There hasn't been anything there."

"Anything?" Julia said. "What's anything?"

"Well, just anything." He shrugged uncomfortably. "They wouldn't send Big Future mothers there if it wasn't safe."

Julia hesitated for another moment. But out of London was

out of London. She allowed herself to be coaxed toward the police van's open doors.

As was usual in such a van, the rear compartment had no windows and no seats. A tiny overhead light was the only illumination, and the only concession to comfort was a loose piece of carpet laid on the floor. On it were seated seven women in various stages of pregnancy. All wore blue overalls with Anti-Sex sashes, and had Big Future badges pinned on their chests. Among them was a plump and very pregnant Harriet Melton.

Harriet was as lovely as ever, her radiant face and red tresses striking even in the dim interior of the van. The blue overalls she wore had been let out to accommodate her belly, and were brand-new and suspiciously well-made. By contrast, the Anti-Sex sash looked authentic but was shabby with age. The Big Future badge was also well-worn, its ribbon tawdry and fraying. Mrs. Melton must have found someone to sell her these items secondhand. Julia now remembered the baggy clothes Harriet had been wearing when Julia saw her last; Harriet would have already been pregnant then, by that Freddie character, no doubt. No wonder she'd gone and made a stink at his community center.

At the sight of Julia, Harriet's face became wary. Julia smiled reassuringly, saying, "Oh, you've made it too? Good show."

"Yes, I'm ever so glad to see you," Harriet replied, in her best Party accent. "I suppose you never thought to find your old friend Marion Parker here."

Julia almost looked around for this Marion Parker, but realized just in time that this was Harriet's pseudonym. Of course: along with the sash and badge, Mrs. Melton must have obtained false papers.

Julia sat down between Harriet and a gloomy-looking black-haired woman, who made room with a frown of annoyance. Harriet gave Julia a shy look of gratitude. Julia herself had seldom been so glad to see a person. After all these months, it felt miraculous to be greeted by a friend. It was also calming to reflect that if Harriet was here—if Mrs. Melton had gone to such lengths to ensure that she was here—it must be the safest place in London.

A soldier had started to close the back doors, when Jackson appeared alongside him, speaking confidentially and waving his hands. The other shrugged and Jackson jumped in, looking about him at the women with a grin of satisfaction. "Not to worry, comrades," he said. "We'll get you there safe."

Now the van's engine started. The women braced themselves as it pulled away, and for a time, there was only the pleasant sensation of being borne passively along. All the women now looked at each other comfortably. Each looked subtly satisfied, as if the others had been foolishly concerned, and they were now proven right for not worrying. But they'd only been driving a minute when the van suddenly picked up speed in a way that felt suspiciously like panic. A moment later, a roaring sound came from above and grew steadily, trembling in the walls of the van, until all were cowering and covering their ears. The van sped on faster and faster, as if trying to escape. At last the noise ripped directly overhead and passed, diminishing and easing in timbre. Then a woman could be heard sobbing; Julia realized she must have been doing it for some time. Someone else cried out, "What is *that*?"

"That'll be our planes!" said Jackson in an odd, high voice. "Exercises, that's all it is! Only exercises!"

A small moon-faced girl said anxiously, "But, tell me—why are we being evacuated? No one will tell us. Is something happening?"

"Just precautions," said Jackson. "Not to worry!"

"Precautions against . . . is it Eurasia?"

Now an anxious muttering rose all around, and Jackson said unhappily, "There's no need to speak of Eurasia. The Party's taking every—"

He was cut off by a burst of gunfire, shockingly close and deafeningly loud. One girl shrieked. The van sped up again with a jolt, then suddenly swerved. The black-haired woman sprawled on top of Julia, gasping, "I'm sorry!" All the others were hanging on to each other, some with obvious terror and some with seeming impassivity. More gunfire came, now from behind, and Jackson raised his rifle as if to defend against an assault on the doors. Just then the van veered more violently than ever, and his gun swung, pointing crazily left and right. The shriek came again, and the black-haired woman yelled angrily, "Watch where you're aiming! You—" only to be drowned out by the deafening crash of an explosion that kicked and rocked the van. There was a series of pinging noises against the side. One couldn't tell if they were being struck by bullets or only a spray of debris.

The van braked, then gained speed again, jolting and bucking over some obstacle. It smoothed out, and all the noise fell away magically. Again there was no sound but the engine and the occasional jarring of bumps in the road. All the women now raised their heads and looked around with sweaty faces. Jackson bent over and neatly, briefly vomited between his knees. The smell was sharp in the enclosed space, and the black-haired woman said in Julia's ear, "Well, it only wanted that."

After this, they drove on for what seemed an inordinate span of time. No one spoke. All were listening for bullets and explosions that did not come. The only interruption was when one of the girls leaned forward to vomit, too. This made the stench in the van unendurable, and by the time they slowed and came to a halt, Julia felt decidedly ill. Jackson got the doors open and peered cautiously out. The street revealed was completely ordinary: a row of shabby terraced houses with puddles on the pavement from the day's rain. A man walking past with a rake over his shoulder glanced at the tableau in the van with an expression of mild surprise.

Jackson smiled at the women and said triumphantly, "What did I tell you? Here we are, safe!"

All crept out, looking uncertainly about them, and were led inside a large brick building of the late capitalist type. The interior was a hangar-like space with a gallery running around the top. Every inch of the walls was lined with glass display cases, now empty. Above each one was a telescreen. Eerily, these were now dead and blank. As the women came in, they all gazed up at them superstitiously. Julia was no exception. It was no doubt just an electrical fault, and yet that row of inert screens was chilling.

There were only two other things in the room. The first was a folding table set up with a few plates of hard-boiled eggs, a stack of paper cups, and a jug of some yellow liquid that might have been juice. The other was far more remarkable: a stuffed dead creature on a plinth, looking something like a seal but five times the size. Indeed it was nearly as big as the van, and very rotund, with a small, somewhat embarrassed-looking head. It had long tusks that pointed downward and gave it the comical appearance of a man with a drooping white moustache.

Jackson said cheerily, "Some of you will know this place. This is the Museum of Socialist Science, and that's the world-famous beast. The smaller exhibits have been taken to the countryside."

"Precautions, I suppose," said the black-haired woman.

"That's it. Safekeeping."

"So it's not safe enough for exhibits, but it's safe enough for us?"

The moon-faced girl put in, "There aren't even any chairs. Where are we meant to sleep? We can't really be meant to stay here?"

Jackson's face became a bit strained. "Maybe we'll be moved on. We'll see."

"We'll see?" said the moon-faced girl. "But—"

The others gathered around, peppering Jackson with questions, which he fielded with increasingly desperate expressions of optimism. Meanwhile, Harriet had drifted away to inspect the beast. Julia went to join her.

For a time, the two girls stood silently inspecting a plaque that identified the animal as a walrus, complained about its overstuffing at the hands of bourgeois scientists, and extolled the social arrangements of the walrus as an example of natural communism. Then Julia ventured, in a carefully low voice, "Listen, Harriet. Have you any idea what's happening?"

"Yes," said Harriet negligently. "War is happening. Didn't you guess?"

Julia grimaced, and Harriet gave her an unpleasant smile, saying, "Yes, it's not very nice when war affects *you*, is it? One does wish one knew what was going on, doesn't one? *We* always wished to know. But we just got bombed, and never did learn why."

"Harriet, don't be like that. *I* haven't bombed you. And I can see you know."

"Oh, well. It's the Brotherhood, isn't it? The bloody Brotherhood of Free Men. I expect you've figured that out by yourself. Even this lot will have guessed, whether or not they dare to say."

"Goldsteinites?"

"I never noticed that they cared much for Goldstein. My mother used to pay them off, just the same as the patrols. As far as I could tell, all they really cared for was their five percent off the top."

"But you told me you didn't believe in them. You denied they existed. Why, you said it to my face."

"Oh, before you scold me about it—*of course* we lied to you. What good would it have done you to know? And who even thought it mattered? The Free Men have been around forever, and *I* could never see that they made any difference. Just another lot of bullies that took bribes from my mother and called me names for going with blues.

"But now they've thrown in with Eurasia, or Eurasia's thrown in with them, and so the game's all changed. And here *I* am. Girls like me aren't safe in the district now. Too many revenge-minded Free Men about."

"So you think they can really win?"

"Of course they won't win," said Harriet crossly. "It's Oceania they're fighting. You wait and see. The Yanks will put an end to it. That's what I think, anyway."

"But they *might* win," said Julia. "It isn't certain."

"Oh, please don't tell me you of all people are enamored of the Free Men! Listen, you *can't* throw in with them. You work at a Ministry, you great booby. They'd roast you on a skewer. Why, you're a Big Future mother, a real one. The Free Men would kill you for that alone."

For a moment, Julia balked. Harriet picked at a seam in her overalls and frowned angrily at the great beast. But at last the need for knowledge overcame Julia's caution.

She said softly, "But Harriet, don't you see how I am? I'm not . . . Well, look at my hands." Julia held them out to show the scars on her palms, then turned them so Harriet could see where the fingernails still hadn't fully grown in.

Harriet's eyes widened. "Oh! How awful. Oh, Julia. I was so wrapped up in my problems I didn't see at all. I am so sorry. Was it—you were arrested?"

"Yes. And the soldiers here don't know about it. Can't know. So you see, I'm as great a fraud as you. And I haven't any false papers. I've only got the old ones with 'pending execution' stamped all over them."

"How despicable. To you, who wouldn't harm a fly! They *are* bloody."

"So would the Free Men do a thing like that?"

"Oh, don't ask me. All men are rotten, if you want my opinion. The Free Men say they're very wonderful, of course, and wouldn't harm anyone—who didn't deserve it. Well, I deserve it, by their lights, so I can't say I'm very impressed. But they're not Love. Not yet, at any rate."

"And are they all proles?"

Harriet let out a sour laugh. "No, it's the usual joke. Proles at the bottom, and your sort of people at the top. Of course, they *say* they're very different, and terribly concerned to help us proles be free. Not that I care. I just want to live. I suppose that's terribly bourgeois of me. Or, if you're a Free Man, it's socialist of me. Either way, I'm not to be allowed."

"But are you set on staying here? You know they'll take your baby from you."

"They're welcome to it! I haven't a scrap of interest in babies. I hadn't when Freddie gave it to me, and I've far less interest now."

"Well, if not for that, then for yourself. I can't think we're safe here."

Harriet frowned at Julia. "Wait, now. What are you thinking?"

"Thinking of going, that's all."

"Going out of here? You're mad."

"I *can't* stay. If I could find the Brothers—the Free Men— wouldn't they value that I'm a wrongthinker? That I've been in Love?"

"Perhaps," said Harriet dubiously. "Those hands ought to make them sit up and take notice. If they see them before they shoot you."

"If I weren't in these overalls, though?"

"Oh, this is all talk. You can't go, anyway. Those soldiers will stop you straightaway. And causing a fuss like that is the surest way to get them to look at your papers."

A flash of fear went through Julia. Then she said defiantly, "How could they stop me? Why, it's only that one man in here with us. And they think they are defending us, not keeping us captive."

"You'll see how quickly that changes if you try to leave."

"They won't have time to think of it. Look, it's one boy, and he isn't even near the door."

"Go on, then. But don't blame me for what happens."

Thus challenged, Julia turned quite easily and started for the door. After a few steps, she balked and looked back to find Harriet gazing abstractedly at the walrus, as if their conversation had been a thing of no importance. That emboldened her; whatever Harriet thought of Julia's plan, she would raise no alarm. Indeed, a prole never tipped the authorities off to any wrongdoing short of murder.

When Julia reached the door, Jackson, still besieged by the others, called after her anxiously, "Comrade! Please! We're all to stay here!"

Julia answered in a careless voice, "I shall be straight back. Not to worry!"

As she opened the door, she looked one last time at Harriet, who was pressing her fist to her mouth, as if hiding laughter. Julia smiled, then turned and simply walked out into the gray afternoon.

*

She passed the two drivers, who were standing guard outside, with an embarrassed, "Toilets all taken!" They looked away respectfully as she rounded the corner. Then her way was clear. She trotted for a while, turning left and right, until her feet and swollen breasts began to hurt too awfully. By then, anyway, it was clear no one was chasing her. The doubt she'd felt while talking to Harriet had passed, and Julia eased her pace and looked about with a return of her madcap feeling. Nor was there anything to cause her concern. It was the same staid Outer Party district—rows of little houses with vegetable gardens at the front and fences decorated liberally with Oceanian flags and BIG BROTHER IS WATCHING YOU! banners.

In the distance, a crackle of gunfire rose and fell away. Julia listened but couldn't tell its direction. There were the Brothers—but where, exactly? And how was she to safely get past that gunfire? When she'd impetuously taken the bike to leave the city, she'd imagined running into rebels in a wood, or riding south until she hit the coast, where she would luckily happen on a boat and somehow convince its owner to take her to Eurasia. Now she saw this was based on a lack of real hope. Once a plan began to succeed, and all became real, it was a hundred times more difficult.

Still, south was the way out of London, the way that led away from the Party. Southward, she decided, she would go.

Within minutes, this took her into a more than usually battered prole district. Half the houses had been reduced to rubble, and much of the damage seemed fresh: no willow herb grew, no tents were set up in the wreckage. But the eerie thing was that there was no one in the streets, and no sound came from the houses. This was unheard of in a prole district, where people lived out of doors year-round, and were always laughing, fighting, singing, playing radios as loud as they would go. Up ahead, she saw a mass of wreckage, with a wisp of smoke still rising from it—no unusual sight in prole streets, where rocket bombs were always falling—but when she came closer and saw it properly, she stopped dead in her tracks. This was not the rubble from a bombing. It was a helicopter—a full-sized military helicopter crashed in the middle of the street. Two of the blades had been shorn off its rotor, and thin black smoke rose from its smashed tail. The glass of its cabin was busted out, and no one—dead or alive—was inside. The pilots must have either fled or been dragged out.

Now the silence became truly frightening. Julia thought of turning back, but as she looked over her shoulder, her eye was caught by a fluttering shape. It was down a narrow alleyway whose cobbles had been torn out of the ground, so it was now a canal of mud. Above this, someone had strung washing lines from one house to the next. The sheets were startlingly white amid the grubby ruins. Julia thought of Weeks's shop and the washerwoman and felt a queer nostalgia—as if that had been a happy time; as if she wished it back.

Then she had another thought and ventured cautiously to the top of the alleyway. She listened all around. Nothing stirred. Even the wind had died down and the laundry moved only languidly on its short lines. She almost called out to ask if anyone was there, but thought better of it. If an irate householder caught her trespassing, that was the least of her worries. She set her boot into the mud and crept forward.

The washing was wet from rain, of course; indeed, it had begun to drizzle again. She supposed it had been pegged up on a sunny day, then abandoned by a fleeing family. From the line, she chose a long black skirt and a gray shirt that buttoned up the front.

Changing in the alleyway would have meant setting her bare

feet down in the mud, which, by the smell of it, routinely received the contents of the houses' chamber pots. So she came back to the street and stripped there, in full view of all the houses, with the thin smoke from the helicopter wreck weaving over her head. It gave her the thrill she'd always felt from going naked out of doors, made more intense by fear and strangeness. She stood a minute entirely bare, feeling the drizzle on her skin and luxuriously shivering, running her fingers over the gooseflesh on her arms, finding the shallow scars on her breasts and belly. She was still herself. She was alive.

While naked, she took the opportunity to squat down and urinate. As she did, she heard more gunfire. It was far away; still, the stream of urine turned into a poor, frightened trickle. She laughed at herself and, for the first time, spoke to her baby aloud: "Never mind. Mummy won't be such a coward all the time."

The skirt fit her poorly, digging into her belly so she couldn't fasten the top hook. Then the wet shirt was horribly cold, though she knew it would soon warm up from her body. She thought of going to hunt for a coat in the houses, but was doubtful that anyone would leave such a valuable article. At that moment, anyway, the wind changed and brought with it the sound of voices—many voices, all speaking together. She shoved her feet into her boots and laced them up hastily, shivering with cold and nerves.

She decided to keep her tool bag, which a prole woman might well carry. The overalls she bundled up with the sash and badge and left on a garden wall; perhaps another Harriet could make use of them. As she did, she noticed a sheet of paper fluttering in a bush, and realized she was surrounded by many others; they were scattered down the street as far as she could see. She plucked it out curiously and read:

WHY DIE FOR THE PARTY?

In fighting and dying for the Party, you are only being sacrificed on the altar of a corrupted Lie. You and your children and your parents and grandparents have been sacrificed to this Lie for generations. You see your families beaten, tortured, starved in the dungeons of the tyrant, blown to pieces in endless wars without reason. You toil all your lives for another man's wealth, and you are fed on crumbs and clothed in rags so the Party oppressor can live in his degraded luxury, indulging in the vile Sex Crimes of which your honest men stand falsely accused. Every Englishman who lays down his life for the Party is not only a loss to his own country; he is a loss to the common cause of decency…

It went on like this in a dense block of print to the bottom of the page, where in larger print was written: A MESSAGE FROM THE BROTHERHOOD OF FREE MEN. Julia was too nervous to read the whole message, but folded the sheet and put it in her pocket. Then she went on, moving southward as best she could on the meandering streets. She was increasingly aware that the sound of the muttering crowd was ahead of her, growing ever more constant and more distinct. The voices didn't sound distressed, however, and there were none of the harsher sounds of combat. It might be no bad thing to find other people, especially now that she was rid of the incriminating overalls. With this in mind, she followed the sound to a broader street, where a few hundred people, who all looked to be proles, were gathered outside a train station. Its entrance was guarded by men with rifles, which in itself was nothing unusual; any sort of station or depot was often made into an impromptu checkpoint. What was bizarre—even uncanny—was that these men were not in uniform. In fact, they were dressed as proles. Most wore gray shirts very like the one Julia had just stolen. One had a funny sort of coat, very ragged and soiled, with a high, boxy collar.

The sight of proles with guns gave Julia a peculiar feeling. It was almost like seeing a dog using a pen. There was a joy in it, but it was the joy of absurdity, and underneath was dread. At that moment, she heard a gunshot, quite near, and flinched. The crowd, too, was startled and began to look about themselves. The men guarding the station shouted something out. Then all the proles burst into laughter and applause as another gunshot came.

Julia drifted along the outskirts of the crowd, not quite daring to join it. She realized belatedly that she was wearing Party boots; those could still give her away. But no one seemed to take her presence amiss, and a woman who caught her eye smiled. Julia dared to smile back—here it was no shame to be missing teeth—and almost decided to push on to the station. A train away from the city would be a damned useful thing, and surely the armed men here were rebels? This might be the chance she wanted. But another shot came. From the same direction, a shrieking, babbling voice rose up, and was cut short by another shot. Then it came to Julia what she was hearing. It was a sound she hadn't heard since she was a child: a group of people being executed in the street.

That made up her mind. She turned away, being careful to show no haste. As she went, she was struck by the bleak suspicion that Harriet Melton had been right, that Julia could never be safe with the Brotherhood people. Proles did tend to be right about dismal things. Julia briefly considered retracing her steps, finding her overalls, returning to the strange museum with its tutelary walrus.

But she doggedly carried on southward, taking only a minor

detour to stay clear of the crowd. Soon she came to a narrow dirt road between two rows of ruined houses, leading roughly in the direction she wanted. Most wonderfully, at the end was a dense, dark wall of trees. This turned out to be what she hoped: a wood deep enough to show nothing but trees as far as her eye could penetrate. She gratefully ventured in, ducking under the first low branches and laughing when she unwarily jostled a bough and it released a shower of water onto her head.

It soon became evident that this was not a proper forest but one of the suburbs leveled by fire bombs in the all-consuming raids of the fifties. Thirty years on, the ruins were little more than a hilly terrain over which the wood had shaped itself. Here and there among the trees, clusters of windowless, roofless houses still showed, grown over with moss and ivy. Full-grown trees now stood within their walls. In the valleys that had once been roads, crumbs of tarmac appeared among the roots. Most curious of all was to see an iron streetlamp leaning at a rakish angle, its glass very dingy but still intact.

In one roofless ruin, Julia found a rectangular pool of standing water, troubled along its surface by the gentle rain. She knelt down, skimmed away the litter, and drank thirstily. Then she remembered she still had a heel of bread, left over from the loaf she'd bought that morning. She brought this out of her tool bag and ate with a feeling of extraordinary happiness. If she'd been shot then, she would have been content. For perhaps the first time in her life, she was doing what she felt was right.

She thought of making some kind of shelter among the trees. It would soon be dark, and, even if it was damp and uncomfortable here, it would be safe. But then she noticed a thinning of the foliage ahead, an openness where the forest came to an end. Curiosity got the better of her, and Julia ventured on.

She found a field of grass that stretched away to a hilly horizon. To the east, there was the smoke of a fire, very fine and pale like an animated cobweb. It was the only detail against the bare gray sky. She went onward, pleasantly aware of her tired legs and the exalted feeling of ownlife, of her mind coursing free and unimpeded. It felt even better here than it did in London. It was as if the land was happy at her wild presence in it. She was wading in grass to knee height. Little grasshoppers leapt from under her feet like sparks. The sun had begun to set in the mist, and a diffused radiance spread along the westward horizon. Julia considered whether she could walk all night. There was a way to find south in the stars, she remembered, although she couldn't think how it worked, and the overcast sky might not show stars. Was there a way to tell south from the moon? Even her growing hunger didn't worry her. She was a child of the SAZ and knew that, in a pinch, the grasshoppers leaping at her feet were food.

A wind came across the hills and a lovely rustling-flowing sound rose all around. It felt as if the grasses were a sea on which she floated, or as if she and the grass were sailing together over the coursing land. She came to the bottom of a little valley and, as she started up the other side, felt the familiar ache in her back from the baby's weight, and welcomed it. It reminded her of her days of walking, and the pains and exhaustion that were preparation. They had delivered her from prison. They made her what she needed to be.

In this mood of exaltation, she almost didn't notice the new sound. As it rose, it might have been heavier rain coming, or thunder too distant to concern her. She was focused, anyway, on climbing the hill, and what might appear on the other side. When she saw the lights, she was still not frightened. It felt somehow as if she were still hidden. She'd never felt more safe.

It all came into focus in a moment, the moment in which a

man's voice called out. The lights were headlights, the noise a vehicle's engine. A jeep had come to a halt on the hill above. The wind died again, and she heard the doors opening. Two people jumped out—men in those gray shirts, wearing tall black boots over dark trousers. Both carried rifles, and, as they approached, one raised his to his shoulder, aiming at her. But he didn't fire. He called out again, and when she heard his cultivated accent, her heart leapt. She thought of Brothers, of airmen. She raised her hands to show them empty. In a minute, the men would see the scars on her palms. They would know her for their own.

Only then did she notice, in the valley beyond, a line of neatly pruned black trees. Behind them stood the glittering domes and silver tracery of the Crystal Palace.

23

THEY TOOK HER IN THE JEEP. THAT RIDE, WITH THE mad wind in her hair and the jolly bouncing over hills, was as thrilling as such rides had been when she was a child being driven about by airmen. But now she'd defied Oceania, escaped death and torture, and was fleeing with the Free Men to the Crystal Palace. From time to time, she was handed a bottle— not of gin, but of Big Brother's personal wine, looted from his cellars. This was rich and heady, as wine had never been when she'd drunk it with Gerber or at O'Brien's. She was with two young men who blinked at her shyly and made gallant comments, who'd insisted on fetching a blanket from the boot and tucking it around her when they saw her shivering, who had been so moved by the state of her hands that it might have been a scene from a *War Nurse* novel.

Reynolds was a fair-haired man with the rumpled look of having slept out of doors on an errand he found cheerful. He kept up a steady stream of comments, shouting over the noise of the jeep, twisting back in his seat to grin at Julia. Whenever she laughed at one of his jokes, he looked amazed and burst into his own happy laugh, glancing at his comrade to check that he'd noticed.

Butcher was the driver, and used this as an excuse to stay quiet through most of the conversation. He was dark and rather glowering, and seemed to regard himself as Reynolds's keeper. He spoke mostly to check the other man, and seemed uncomfortable addressing Julia directly, although he'd been the one who thought of the blanket.

They'd been out inspecting sentries, and assured her there would be a great stink that she'd managed to evade them. However, she mustn't feel nervous. A stray like herself might slip through, but the main assault was miles away, and the palace grounds were full of Brotherhood soldiers. Indeed, the war was as good as won. Reynolds expanded excitedly on this theme: how London was now surrounded, and the final assault expected within weeks, and no question remained about the outcome. Why, the Crystal Palace had been taken without a shot! "The Party lot have been surrendering in droves. Proper droves. Can't turn on their side fast enough! Oh, I daresay there are still loyal troops around London," he said, with a look of cheerful ferocity, as if he would be rather sorry if there weren't. "But for days all we've seen are a rabble of village boys and proles with rickety legs. The state of some of them! At the sight of us, all toss down their rifles."

"Some didn't," said Butcher.

"True, some ran," said Reynolds. "Couldn't find a white rag to wave, I expect. All they had on was far too dirty. A filthier lot you couldn't imagine, Julia. Even those that guarded the old CP—that's what we call the Crystal Palace. They'd been sleeping in the dirt without tents. They looked made of mud. They weren't ever let inside, you know. No, old Humphrey didn't like to rub shoulders with his own people. Afraid they'd cut his throat, I shouldn't wonder."

"Humphrey—that's Big Brother," Butcher put in.

"Oh, yes! You wouldn't know, Julia, would you? His real name's Humphrey Pease. 'Big Brother'—rather a childish sort of nickname, I always thought. But I guess he wouldn't have got very far if he let people call him Humphrey Pease! The great Pease! Doesn't have quite the ring, does it?

"Well, as I was saying, nobody was let into the old CP except the high muckety-mucks and the servants who ran the place, and they all ran off and abandoned him. There was hardly a soul in the place when we took it. No one at all in the whole great hall but Pease."

"There was the tiger," Butcher put in.

"A tiger isn't a someone," Reynolds said. "But, yes, Julia, can you imagine, he had a pet tiger cub? Hell of a thing. That's the sort of rubbish he spent the wealth of England on—tigers and Grecian statues and racing cars. And golden bathtubs! He's got ten of those. They *are* quite luxurious, I'll admit. Piping-hot water from the tap. You must have a bath while you're here."

"Perhaps not polite to suggest a lady wants a bath," Butcher said.

"Well, I didn't mean that. I didn't mean …" Reynolds craned his head back toward Julia. "I say, you didn't think I meant you were dirty?"

"Well, I *am* quite dirty," Julia said.

"Not at all! Anyhow, any little dirt will be fixed up in grand style. We've all gone mad for baths there. There is even a special tap that dispenses bubble bath."

"Bubble bath?" Julia said. "What's that?"

"A sort of soap … well, I can't describe it exactly. It smells very nice. Lily of the valley. Not that you don't smell nice."

Julia laughed full-throatedly at this. Reynolds looked pleased as punch and laughed too, glancing at Butcher to make sure he'd witnessed this triumph. Then he went on, "Well, Pease is to have a proper trial. It's to be all the glorious old English ways.

Any one of us might be in the jury! There shall be barristers with wigs! A judge!"

"Shouldn't think there's much doubt of the outcome," said Butcher.

"Oh, yes, he shall be hanged," Reynolds said. "No doubt of that! Indeed, none of the guilty shall escape. Not those who took part, nor those who winked at it, nor those that grew fat on it. But all are to get proper trials, in the light of day. They shall be shown on the telescreens, I shouldn't wonder. And if an old Party member doesn't like it—well, he'd best keep it to himself, or he might find himself part of the program! Oh, I'm making it all too simple, I'm sure, and you shall think me quite a fool. Why, I've only been in England three weeks!" He looked back at Julia to see the effect of these words and laughed happily when he saw her confusion. "Yes! My family escaped to Eurasia when I was a child. On a raft! Nearly drowned, too. The Channel's no joke. But it's as well, for I got a proper education among the Free English of Calais. I can do multiplication like nobody's business, and I'm not even clever. These days I've been running around quoting Wordsworth at anybody who will listen. 'Bliss was it in that dawn to be alive, but to be young was very heaven!' Education! Nothing like it! There are a great many of us Free English here at the old CP. Our boys are running the show."

"And were you in Eurasia too?" Julia asked Butcher.

"No," Reynolds answered for him. "Poor Butcher's never been out of England. A proper Newspeaker, he is. Don't ask him about Wordsworth, for he can't answer. No education, you see."

"I got out only six months ago," said Butcher.

"You've got to respect the Newspeak chaps, though," Reynolds said magnanimously. "Even if a Newspeaker doesn't know

Wordsworth, he can tell us how the enemy thinks. In battle, that's a damned sight more useful than *The Prelude*. Trouble is, though, not all can be trusted. Now, Butcher's all right, but a lot of them were in the Party up to their chins. Say, what did you do, Julia?"

"I was a mechanic."

"Now, there you are!" Reynolds said. "A girl mechanic! No harm in that. But a lot of them worked at those Ministries— Peace, Truth, Whatsit. We've even had a fellow who collaborated with the Thought Police! Not that he told us about it. Someone recognized him, or we might have gone along with that snake in our midst."

"How dreadful," said Julia. "Is there any more wine?"

Butcher had the bottle and handed it to her with a look of commiseration, though she doubted he would have been so sympathetic if he'd known. But, she reminded herself, no one here *could* know. Weeks, O'Brien, Martin—all were in London. Winston and Ampleforth, too, and poor Tom Parsons, of course, was dead.

At the awful memory of Parsons, she raised the bottle and was aware as she drank of closing her eyes gratefully like a nursing kitten. She handed it back to Reynolds, who was still chattering happily about the coming victory. Julia sat back, looking for comfort at her ruined right hand. No one could argue with that.

All this time, the jeep had been bounding wildly over hummocks, tossing its passengers from side to side. Now it found a road and smoothed out, and the palace stabilized ahead of them, suddenly serene and immense. Its great central domes were lit up, and the thin rain shimmered vastly in the air around them. The main structure was surrounded by lower rooms, all with gracefully curving glass roofs. Some rooms were brilliantly lit and seethed with tiny motion, while others were dark. Now that the sun had set, the silver tracery of the frame seemed barely sketched in pencil. It had the delicate forms of a botanical drawing. The whole was strikingly alive and real, though the eye kept refusing to believe in it. It was too gigantic, too ideal. The full-grown trees alongside were dwarfed even by the lower rooms.

They now came to a sloppily constructed barbed-wire fence, of a kind that had been everywhere in the SAZ. Somewhere in the dark, a dog was angrily barking. Here, for the first time, Julia had to show her papers. This was reassuring in a way; she was aware of the RELEASED PRISONER—PENDING EXECUTION stamps as a vindication. Still, she wished she had a five-dollar bill to slip into the pages, as she'd once routinely done.

This proved unnecessary, however. The guard glanced at the papers, then looked back at Julia with a startled, worshipful expression. His voice wavered emotionally when he said, "Welcome to Free England, Miss Worthing. You will be safe with us."

After this, they drove straight toward the palace. It loomed above them, growing impossibly, until the feeling was of driving beneath it. At last the jeep turned and mounted a road that ran alongside the building. Their wavering reflection trickled from pane to pane, skipping startlingly where a room was brightly lit. Here the glass offered flashing tableaux of elegant furniture crowded about with dirty equipment and unkempt men in military garb.

Finally they passed the end of the building and entered a cobbled yard where a hotchpotch of other dirty vehicles stood. They pulled up beside another jeep with a red Eurasian flag painted crudely on its door. As he clambered out, Reynolds grinned at Julia, saying, "You will sleep in a palace tonight."

He offered her a hand to help her out. As she took it, she was struck by the old romance of being treated as an attractive girl—or was it only as a pregnant girl? No, it wasn't just that; when she was on her feet, he let go of her hand with obvious reluctance, and his eyes lingered on her face as he escorted her to the entrance. Accompanying them, Butcher kept glancing over with tolerant amusement.

"Now, don't be alarmed," Reynolds said to Julia, "for it is bedlam, rather. The staff have been flown in from Paris and Calais, and they've thrown a bit of a victory party, so you'll see a great many people in civvies. But we're also setting up offices—the old CP is to be the Free Men's HQ. Oh, they shall all embrace you. I don't believe we've had a person before who'd escaped from Love, not on his own feet. *Her* own feet."

The entrance had a green-and-white striped awning. Under this were low marble steps, partly covered by a grubby tarpaulin, for what purpose Julia couldn't see. It almost seemed a simple assertion of the military's conquest of weak pleasure. The soldiers posted here inspected Julia's papers. Like the man at the fence, they reacted with admiration, even referring to her "heroism," but apologetically said she would still need an entrance permit to proceed. Reynolds ran inside to obtain this, and Butcher and Julia waited to one side of the steps.

She was at first so captivated by the palace that she saw nothing else. At this place, heavy curtains hung inside the glass, and light only escaped above, where it made a glamorous haze in the ongoing rain. A din of happy voices came from inside, and a music like the jazz of Julia's childhood, but sweeter and more languid. Through the glass, Julia could see the curtains' folds, so intimately close she imagined being nestled there, hiding to peep out, as she had once hidden in a nest of coats. On the outside, the glass was streaming with rain that reflected the lights of passing vehicles, glittering white and red. All this had an impossible glamour. It was dreamlike and thrillingly real at once. Only slowly, among the tracks of raindrops, did she start to notice the dim reflection of a barbed-wire fence, with a teeming crowd behind.

She turned in fright and saw, to one side of the yard where they'd left the jeep, a crude enclosure. It was so full of people they were pressed together in a solid mass to avoid being shoved into the barbed wire. Though they were stripped of their guns and equipment, their uniforms marked them as Oceanian soldiers. However, they looked nothing like any soldiers Julia had seen in victory parades or newsflashes. Most were boys, and some seemed no more than thirteen. All had the afflicted look of long malnourishment. Their postures were almost comically woebegone: they hung their heads and hugged themselves in misery. One was openly crying, rubbing his nose and making the sniveling faces of a miserable child. Others looked sick with fear, staring about themselves as if expecting a new blow from any quarter. An especially small boy looked up at Julia wistfully. Horribly, his nose had been smashed flat, and the center of his face was dark and bloodied.

"Captured troops," said Butcher, seeing where she was looking. "They're waiting to be shipped off."

"Shipped off," Julia repeated. "Oh, where?"

"They've liberated some camps hereabouts. The prisoners in them have all been released. So there's that."

"Oh, that is good. But these—"

"They are prisoners of war. That's how it is."

"I see . . . Well, of course."

"Yes," Butcher said in a lower voice. "I can't help thinking I'd have been one of them, if I'd waited just a bit longer to run. Or I'd be dead. For all that I hate the Party, I don't think I'd have liked to surrender."

The small boy was still gazing at Julia, and now her mind played her false. It transported her into the palace, through the crowded room she intuited there, and on into a quiet, soaring hall where the jazzlike music was faint and distant. Big Brother sat before her among the familiar furniture of her old fantasy. He was still at his massive desk, broad-shouldered, wise, and sternly handsome. The carpet was the silk carpet of her fantasy, only somewhat soiled by soldiers' boots. Behind the glass walls were windblown trees and fields. She was here to ask why those boys must suffer, when they had never had a choice. Why must they, of all people, be put in camps? Why should there still be children who were punished for things they had no power to change?

All the while, Julia knew this made no sense. Big Brother would be in a cell himself. He hadn't done this, and couldn't undo it. Big Brother had no power now, not even the power those poor boys had, of being able to hope for better days.

Butcher was standing beside her with his hands in his pockets, frowning at the ground. He said quietly, "If anything is worrying you, you may ask me. Perhaps I could clear it up. The Free English—those like Reynolds—they're very good chaps, but they don't always understand."

"Well," Julia said cautiously. "I wondered about . . . well, Humphrey Pease."

He smiled. "Isn't that funny? I bristle every time they say it, though I'm sure I hate him more than they do."

"Oh, I felt that too. But he is real? That is to say . . . he is a person?"

"Quite real. I couldn't credit it, either, at first."

"Yes," Julia said, grateful to be understood. "It didn't seem as if he could be. Not just a man."

"He's a man. Would you want to see him?"

"See him?"

"If they haven't put a stop to it, you can see him. We've all gone."

"Isn't he—well, being interrogated?"

An indefinable disquiet passed over Butcher's features. "No, not him. And I can't tell you more than that, I'm afraid. Those who go must sign a paper agreeing they won't speak of what they see. The brass are very keen to stop rumors. Most of them would rather no one knew he was here. But General Dormer, who's in charge here, feels that all who suffered at Big Brother's hands have the right to confront him. Even I was let in, and I'm in rather bad odor here."

"You? But why? Were you at a Ministry?" Julia said hopefully.

"Nothing like that. I was an airman."

Julia was speechless a moment. She looked away from Butcher, afraid he would notice what she felt. She was hazardously close to weeping, close to speaking of the SAZ and the airmen's hangings. But what could she say? And what was the point in speaking of it, when Butcher would know only too well? He might be from a SAZ himself. He would surely have lost comrades. And to speak, to weep, amounted to demanding that he speak of it. No, one mustn't ever speak. Her eyes found the small soldier boy in the enclosure. He had given up gazing at her, and was exploring his broken nose with his fingertips. Julia flashingly imagined Big Brother with a broken nose, her fist slamming into it. What he deserved...

Butcher said softly, "I'd say you ought to see him. It might do you good. It's something one needs to see, I think."

"Yes," she said. "Yes, I'll do it."

Just then Reynolds returned, more jovial than ever, waving a slip of faintly printed paper with JULIA WORTHING scrawled into a blank in black ink, and two signatures at the bottom. He thrust this at Julia, saying, "They gave me no trouble at all. I knew they wouldn't."

"Listen," Butcher said to Reynolds. "We've been talking, and she'd like to see old Pease. I think it best I take her. You might get her processing papers started while we go."

For a moment, it seemed Reynolds might object. Then he frowned and said, "I do see. We Free English can never truly understand, not truly . . . but I'll do her processing, shall I?"

"Oh, yes. You're far better at that."

"I am," Reynolds said to Julia. "Butcher's solid as a rock, but he hasn't the knack of paperwork. You want to get it right first time, or it causes no end of trouble later. They're proper devils once they take an interest in a fellow."

"Oh, yes," said Julia. "Plus good."

"There, that's just the kind of thing!" said Reynolds. "You aren't to say 'plus good' anymore. That's Newspeak. But you'll learn very quickly."

"Yes," Butcher said patiently. "Now, if you'll start the processing, we'll come and find you. We shan't be long."

"Right you are." Reynolds turned to the door, saying over his shoulder to Julia, "But remember—'Bliss was it in that dawn to be alive! But to be young was very heaven!'"

As he opened the door, a wash of intense, wildly complicated sound burst out, then was dimmed as it closed behind him. Butcher gave Julia a look of wry warning, then opened the door again on its blast of sound and gestured for her to go ahead. She went timidly toward the noise as if venturing into an unruly sea and entered a dark vestibule that was only dimly lit and surprisingly chilly. But beyond was an open doorway, stunning with light.

Here was the great hall under the triple domes—but not hushed and stately as she'd always imagined. Loud music was playing from speakers all over the hall, a music of impossible and alien loveliness, composed of sexual horns and hoarse, longing voices. Hundreds of people rushed in various directions, dodging around each other, and all seemed to be talking at once. Their clothes were bewilderingly strange. Only those in military uniforms, like Butcher's and Reynolds's, made sense to Julia's eye. The other men were dressed in the sort of suits proles wore to go to dance halls: queer "lapel" jackets and trousers with belted waists—but cut differently, outlandishly, and not shabby as prole clothes were, but fresh with an almost supernatural newness. The few women were strangely magnificent. All wore the sort of vibrantly colored dresses Harriet Melton used to have, which could scarcely be shown outside the house. One skirt was even printed with pictures of flowers, and Julia stared after that girl with a startled feeling of breathlessness. Their hair was even more glorious, worn very long, in shining curls. On some, it swept down their backs. Many girls had roses behind their ears—red, yellow, or white, but all full-blown and of marvelous size. These had sometimes come loose and sat at crazy angles, yet the blooms gave everyone a festive look.

Julia had just decided these people must be Eurasians, when a handsome girl passed by in a flame-red satin dress, with matching lipstick and dainty red shoes. She waved at a man and said crossly, in unmistakable Party tones: "What *are* you about, Mr. Fowler! The colonel has been waiting half an hour, you know!"

Julia was trying to keep up with Butcher as they wove through the crowd, and now couldn't help looking at him in wonder.

He said, "It's just there up ahead. Never fear."

"Oh, fine. But isn't this splendid?"

He slowed, smiling at her. "Yes. They do clean up rather well."

"Those roses the girls are wearing—how lovely!"

"From Big Brother's hothouses," Butcher said. "I'm sure Reynolds will fetch you one, if you ask."

"Not you?" she said, daringly meeting his eye.

"Oh, no. I'm far too serious."

She laughed up at him, and almost collided with a girl who was running across the room amazingly clad in nothing but a towel—a thick, snowy-white towel of impossible dimensions that covered her from her armpits to her knees. The girl was giggling breathlessly, pursued by a grinning soldier in a soaking-wet uniform, who chased her with leaping-dodging strides. As they passed, they left behind a positively dizzying dose of floral scent.

The two had come from a dainty, exquisite structure, free-standing in the middle of the floor. It was like a delicate cabin, all of lacquered wood, with little painted panels showing peacocks and—most amazing yet—lovely naked girls. The door had been left open, and Julia saw the glint of a golden something. With a shock, she realized that here, in the midst of the swarming room, was one of the vaunted golden bathtubs.

Now they came to the far wall and a silver-framed door, guarded by two soldiers. Butcher said something to them Julia didn't hear. As he opened the door for her, Julia cast one final glance back at the great hall, elated and chastened, and seeking vainly for the tiger cub. Then she smiled and passed through.

She had expected another grand room, but instead they came into a low-ceilinged glass walkway that led away through the wooded grounds. Trees and shrubs were thickly planted all around, and their boughs shook in the rain, so the way seemed to tunnel through a seething blackness. A thousand lamps were softly shining, embedded somehow in the ceiling's frame. It was dark and brilliant at the same time, the lamps reflected and reflected again, so swarms of lights moved with every step. Julia and Butcher, too, were reflected on both sides, and the reflections of their reflections receded blurrily, so they were paced by a multitude of ghostly selves.

Here Julia first became properly aware that she was going to see Big Brother. Not just Humphrey Pease, the comical figure over whom Reynolds gloated, but Big Brother. With Butcher at her side, what she remembered was the hangings of the airmen—how the condemned men were made to cut down the bodies of their friends, so they could take their place on the gallows. The hatred was back, feeling dreamier, but more sure. She remembered her fantasies of seeing Big Brother beaten, stabbed, torn to pieces. She had the right to confront him— what did that mean? Suppose she was allowed to strike him; if Butcher was watching, would she be ashamed to do it? No, Butcher understood. She could show him her hands again. He would give her a cigarette to burn Big Brother as she had been burned. No one could fault her.

The walkway took a turn. Here a guard was posted who must look at Julia's papers. Some five hundred meters beyond him, a pair of soldiers waited at the very end of the walkway, standing on either side of a desk. One was a woman, in a uniform with a neat wool skirt. Behind them was a peculiar and lovely thing, a flight of stairs, made of ironwork wrought in a floral pattern, going up in a corkscrew shape. Above, indistinctly through the glass ceiling, one saw the looming shape of a tower.

The woman soldier came forward to meet them. She searched Julia painstakingly, apologizing as she explored her buttocks and crotch. Then Julia was invited to sit and sign a paper agreeing to the statement: *I will not write anything, make any recording, speak to any person, or communicate any information by any means, about my meeting with Humphrey Pease, the man once known as "Big Brother," on pain of imprisonment or death.*

Julia frowned at the sentence for a minute to give an appearance of gravity. In fact, it meant little to her. All her life she'd kept secrets on pain of death. If she'd had to sign a paper every time she held her tongue on pain of death, she'd have gone through a ream of paper every week. When the woman soldier came concernedly to look over her shoulder, Julia nodded as if coming to a decision and put the pen to paper, only to find the physical act of writing gave her trouble. The index and middle fingers of her writing hand were still stiff and useless. The shape she made for a signature was passable, but she struggled to print her name beneath, until the woman soldier kindly offered to do it for her.

At last these ceremonies were complete, and she was invited to mount the stairs. Butcher said, "I'll be here when you're done," and she felt a chill of panic when she saw she must go alone. There was a heaviness in his manner. He knew what she was soon to learn—about the torture, it must be torture. Images chased each other through her mind: a godlike, young Big Brother charging from a trench; Big Brother on the telescreen above her pillow, speaking quietly when she woke from a nightmare; Big Brother in her fantasy leading her to a white bed and pressing her down on it ardently. She remembered the little she'd been told by people who had known him: Diana Winters saying he had crawled into her bedroom window and fucked her; Julia's mother speaking of seeing him at marches and offering him a bottle of pear juice. The stairway was in moody shadow, thick with an oppression that seemed to hang upon the darkness. As she started up, this took on a physical character, then in sudden awfulness became a smell. It was a faint stink of rot, feces, urine, in which was intermingled a harsher reek of bleach: the smell of the Ministry of Love.

She paused, feeling sick and weak. The hatred was still there, but mixed horribly with pity. At any moment she might give in and be swept under, lost, undone. In the play *The Sin of Big Brother*, an old revolutionary teaches Big Brother: "Never pity the enemy. He doesn't pity you." The play ends with Big Brother conceiving of his third great maxim: "When you spare the enemy, you kill three others: your comrade, your family, and the man you might have been." Julia had acted in that play and gone home and killed her mother, but in fact Big Brother had killed her mother. He had killed her comrades, her family, the woman she might have been. Being nothing but Humphrey Pease, the drinker of pear juice, he had murdered all the people she loved. She would not pity him. He had not pitied her.

When she came up into the room, she first noticed two guards standing by the railing in relaxed postures, turned toward each other. They'd been having a private conversation, it seemed, which her arrival had interrupted. The room was a sumptuous bedroom, its glass walls curtained all about with crimson velvet draperies, as if to close in that smell. The bed, too, was thickly hung about with draperies, tied back with heavy gold ropes. A chandelier hung above, and there was a dainty wooden structure like that of the bathroom cabin Julia had seen below. This one's paintings showed Eastasian women and butterflies beside a little stream.

At the center of the room was a leather chair, in which an emaciated old man sat. At first glance, he looked to Julia like Winston Smith—not the Winston she'd once loved, but the one she'd seen in Room 101, with his caved-in face and ru-

ined frame. The man's skin was blotchily yellow, except the eyelids, which were bright pink and swollen. Withered skin hung
under his chin, and the nose and ears seemed magnified on his
shrunken face. His moustache was mostly white and its sparse,
coarse hairs looked unwholesomely wet. His toothless mouth
worked unhappily, and a white crust showed at the corners. The
man was almost bald, and his age-spotted pate was scabbed
and bruised. His limbs were so fleshless that, at first glance,
the sleeves of the heavy silk dressing gown he wore seemed
empty. Despite the man's obvious weakness and the guards in
the room, he'd been strapped into his chair with thick leather
bonds, against which he hung lopsidedly, as if unable to support
his own weight.

Even after Julia's mind had registered the features and
thought, "Yes, it is he," she continued to look around the room
for Big Brother. As she sought him, she knew with evil lu-
cidity what she really wanted here. She didn't want to punish
Big Brother. She didn't want to see him brought low. No, she
needed to find him handsome, wise, and powerful, as he'd always been—and for him to explain that the Party wasn't as
it seemed. She needed him to make sense of everything that
had happened, to explain why the murders were justified, why
none of the sacrifices had been wasted. She needed to tell her
story, and to sob in his arms, his strong and capable arms, and
for him to prove it was all for the best. He would learn he was
the father of her child, and honor and love her. It would be as
in her dreams at last.

The wretched figure had noticed her now, and reacted with
a grave frown. She'd seen that frown before in a thousand tele-
casts and on countless posters on every wall of the city, every
day of her life.

Then, for one last moment, she hoped. He was old, but it was he—Big Brother! In that instant she saw in his face the cha-risma, the transfixing intensity, of the man from the telescreen. Perhaps it could still be made right. He was ill and mistreated, but he was himself.

Then he turned to the guards and said, in a querulous trav-esty of the old voice: "What does the fellow want of me? You must send him away. I don't want him!"

Julia caught her breath. A chill went through her. She tried, "Big Brother—comrade. Do you see—"

"Bring Rutherford!" Big Brother howled at the guards. "He'll see to this. Damned fools, bringing strange fellows here . . . no, I see. We are going to catch a plane now, are we? This fellow will see to my bags."

Julia turned to the guards and cried in distress, "Why, what have you done to him? Is it the beating? Has it harmed his brain?"

"No, miss," said a guard, unperturbed. "He was like this when we come. That's himself, you might say. Just old."

"Old!" said Julia. "Just old!"

"All must go," Big Brother said peevishly. "It is time for my banana." Having reached this conclusion, he slumped back in his chair and closed his eyes.

Again she saw the slack face, the reddened eyelids, the scabs and bruises on the old head. But now she also noticed signs of care. The last strands of hair had been combed neatly, and his face was shaven around the familiar moustache. Among the animal smells, she now recognized the dusty scent of talcum powder.

Julia tried to remember her hatred. If she couldn't be con-soled, she could at least feel avenged. She didn't even need to strike him. Big Brother was helpless, as she had been helpless; bound, as she had been bound; shamed, confused, incontinent, as she had been at Love. No doubt he was in discomfort and pain. She might be glad of that.

She could not feel it. She couldn't want the blighting of his eyes, his confusion and illness. No: she passionately wished him better. If he couldn't be healed, she only wished Big Brother to be helped with gentleness. She felt a shuddering repulsion at the thought that she had dreamed of beating him, of putting cigarettes out on his skin. No, she couldn't want a suffering person to suffer more. She could not find it in herself.

Then she was distracted by a new horror—the baby! But of course it wasn't his; no baby could have come from those poor loins. Indeed, not even the Party could have wanted it. That must have all been lies. Quite possibly the "semenic materials" had never been anything but lukewarm water. Everyone knew most artsem girls were already pregnant, so there wasn't any risk of the program failing. Babies would be born, and everyone would agree they were the image of Big Brother. No one would dare to question it, not even in the silence of their own minds.

All was false. It was known to be false, but everyone lied about the lies, until no one knew where the lies began and ended. That whole life had been a game of make-believe, everyone pretending together like little children. Even at Love, they had played at torture and murder, knowing it was all pretense. No one cared that Julia was not a real Goldsteinite; in their make-believe game, she was.

But what had made them willing to kill for a lie? Julia should know; she'd betrayed men and seen them tortured. She'd played that bloody game. But that was different; she had done it from fear. Oh—terrible thought—was it all fear? Had no Party member ever killed anyone from anything but fear?

Then this too passed. There was nothing. She put both hands to her face and felt an unbearable, hollow want. She needed Big

Brother. He had no right! Her breath stopped in her throat, and her legs went weak underneath her. For a moment, she thought she would die and felt gratitude. But it was only tears. A sob broke out and she was crying.

She cried for the loss of the hostel and its noisy camaraderie, for the bunk where she'd slept with her friends around her in the dark. She wept for her years of work in Fiction, the pride of a useful job well done. She cried for the meetings and marches where she'd played her part and met with comrades and believed. Oh, yes, she had sometimes believed, and it had felt like joy and faithfulness. All chanted as one, and marched together to a future of strength and goodness. They sang, and the singing was beautiful. The people had been so brave and kind—yes, they were brave even as they cowered and let each other be dragged to prison. They had dared so much for each other. Think how she'd gone out to meet Winston, how they'd made love in the forest, risking their lives, and thrilled to the bird's wild song. All that world! Julia's life—not just gone, but trampled, scorned, turned at a stroke to worthless rubbish.

She had sunk to the ground, sobbing terribly, gasping. All her face was wet, and her throat still hurt. She couldn't breathe for the weight of tears. A guard touched her shoulder, and she tried to turn from him. Only slowly she realized he was offering her a handkerchief. He said, "I am sorry, miss. We dries 'em out best we can, but there's so many takes it like this. Why I myself—"

"Oh!" she said in surprise. "You are a prole!"

Both guards laughed kindly at this. The one with the handkerchief said, "Well, don't mince words, miss. But yes, I am. Nor I ain't taken no offense. I am a prole, and no worse for it."

The other said, "We all has to feel what we feel. Ain't no easy way. It takes each of us different."

Now Julia looked up through her tears and saw the two guards properly for the first time. The one with the handkerchief was young and black-haired, with a three-day beard like a scattering of pepper. The other was a doughy fellow in early middle age, with the rosy cheeks of a drinker. She smiled and took the handkerchief. As the guard had warned her, it was damp, but she used it without fastidiousness, and found the unpleasant sensation calmed her tears. When she dared to look back at Big Brother, he'd opened his eyes again and was watching her curiously.

The younger guard said, "As it happens, we proles are the only ones can do this job. The Free English are too busy bossing everyone, and you can't let a blue in here alone. Half of 'em would do violence to the old man, and they need him in one piece to stand trial. And the other half would lose their heads the other way and try to set him free. Us, well, we're a bit sensible. Or that's how the Free fellows see it, and I can't say they're wrong."

"Salt of the earth, we are," said the other man.

Julia and the young guard laughed, and Big Brother laughed along with them, muttering, "Funny, funny. Now for my banana."

"Miss," said the young guard, "not to hurry you, but the nurse is due in a minute. Mr. Pease is quite right: he's to have his banana. And he's got to be cleaned up and changed before he eats. You don't want to be here for that." He turned to Big Brother and said, "We've had an accident, haven't we? Not very nice."

"Not nice," Big Brother said, then added gravely, "It's the Goldsteinites. They have their hands in everything."

The older guard laughed. "There, he thinks the Goldsteinites have soiled his underpants for him. It's a shame to live that long. Who'd want it? Sores from head to toe, and he don't know what's happening. Couldn't happen to a nicer person, mind."

"Yes, that's how it is, miss," said the young guard. "So you'd best go along. And don't mind that you cried. A great many do. You has to cry or you'd laugh, as they say. Or is it the other way around?"

When she came down, Butcher was waiting at the bottom of the stairs with a look of worried inquiry. His face changed at what he saw. Together they went by the two soldiers, who nodded them past with expressions of reserved sympathy. As they started back down the glass walkway, Butcher said, "It's always hard to know if someone should go. I hope I didn't guess wrong."

"No, you weren't wrong," she said. "Anyhow, I *would* have gone, just as soon as I knew I might. It wouldn't have mattered what anyone said."

"Yes. That's how I was, too."

Butcher paused and Julia stopped beside him. The glass hall was at once dazzling and murky. It felt achingly familiar to her now, as if she'd lived here many years.

He said softly, "You know, as a boy, I always imagined I'd get to see him somehow, and I would tell him all that really went on. I believed he didn't know, that he couldn't know, or else he'd put a stop to it. I thought, once he knew, it would all be fixed."

"Yes," Julia said. "It would all be fixed."

"I would lie in bed and work on the speech I would make. I thought they might not give me much time, so I'd better have it off pat."

"I thought he would love me. Now I see every girl must have dreamed of that."

"When I saw what he was, I wanted to kill him or myself. I couldn't grasp it."

"Yes," Julia said. "How can one trust oneself, or anyone? After that..."

Butcher said more quietly, "You know, Reynolds—all the Free English—they can't understand. They think we were all great fools—that is, when we weren't being tragic heroes. But you mustn't think ill of them for it. No one could understand who hadn't grown up in it." He glanced down the walkway then with the unmistakable manner of someone checking that he wouldn't be overheard, then went on: "One can't be entirely frank with them. I was hoping to have a chance to say. I did try frankness, and nearly got myself shot. I shouldn't like you to go through that."

"Yes," said Julia gratefully. "I did wonder, when Reynolds spoke of the Ministries." She hesitated, then added in a near whisper, "I worked at Truth, you see. That's where I worked as a mechanic."

"Yes, I shouldn't mention that to anyone. But no one will push you to tell, you know. That was my mistake. I said straight-away I'd been in the People's Air Force. I thought I might be useful, but it only made me suspected. They won't let me any-where near an airplane now, that's certain. Mind, it's not only the Free English who have that prejudice. Many of the London crowd are no better. They want to erase the past so badly, they forget they were part of it themselves. But they won't go hunt-ing for dirt on someone like you, not without cause. We all have things we don't speak of, and they're glad to leave the past well alone, as long as one doesn't rock the boat. When you do your processing with Reynolds, though, you must take care not to say too much. Do as Reynolds tells you, and nobody will look at you twice."

"Yes, I shall. Keeping secrets is no trouble."

"It *is* better here. It is simply…" He grimaced and seemed at a loss.

"I do see. Yes."

"Well, let's go and find Reynolds. It is good to get processing over with. And Reynolds will make sure you're all right. He's taken rather a shine to you."

As he said this, his eye darted away, distracted. Julia followed his gaze and saw a white-clad girl approaching down the long walkway. She was carrying a tray, and, as she came to the soldier on guard, he held out his hands, offering to take it from her. She smilingly shook her head and came on with a light step. Something about her troubled Julia, even as she saw it was only the nurse.

Butcher said with better cheer, "Now, here is a person you should know. Another Londoner. She'll show you all the ropes. She's been with the Brotherhood a few months, and she's already quite the native."

As he said this, his face had softened. Julia looked jealously back at the nurse. At first she was distracted by the sight of the banana, riding brightly on its tray. It was a fruit she had seen only once before, and whose taste she couldn't imagine. When she did look at the nurse, she was not surprised to find the girl lovely, her great youth made touching by her practical manner and crisp nurse's cap. She was amazed, however, that it was Vicky.

In that first moment, Julia thought she'd made a fatal error. Here was a person who could expose her. Vicky might turn to the soldier now and cry out: "That is Julia Worthing! She is a member of the Thought Police! She has told me so herself."

Then Vicky had recognized her, and Julia saw that this could never happen. Vicky stumbled and her mouth came open. A strange joy appeared in her eyes. Julia felt something—perhaps what Vicky felt—as if her face grew soft with light. The idea that Vicky would betray her now seemed shameful, meaningless. Oh, it was not about that! It could never be about that! Julia was giddily, childishly happy, as she'd thought she never would be again.

"Victory!" Butcher said. "There's someone here I'd like you to meet."

Vicky came with a faltering step, her hands tightening on the tray. She looked at Butcher but her body was conscious only of Julia.

"This is Miss Worthing," said Butcher. "She's just come today. Walked out of London, just as you did. When you have some time, you might show her around. She needs a bed and might like to bathe and, I don't know..."

Vicky now dared to look at Julia. Her mouth smiled, and seemed to fight against a greater smile. "But I believe we know each other already."

"Yes," Julia said to Butcher. "We were in the same hostel in London. Women's 21."

"Old Women's 21!" Vicky said. "Monitor Atkins! Tiger and Commissar!"

"Those were our cats." Then Julia turned back to Vicky, almost not daring to look her in the eyes. "I'm ever so glad you're here. How simply lovely."

"Yes," Vicky said. "It's—I'm so glad."

Butcher now was beaming, looking from one to the other. "Well, that's splendid. You will have a friend here. You will both have a friend."

Vicky said, "I shall be free in twenty minutes. I get my break then. I could meet you ... where are you going?"

"Processing," Butcher said. "Reynolds is taking her."

"Oh, he's a dear!" said Vicky. "That's all right, then. Yes, I shall come and find you. And I know you may think it silly that I call myself Victory now. But I *am* silly now. I am happy all the time. And shall be happier now."

"Oh, yes!" Julia said. "I am so happy, too."

"I could hug you, if I hadn't got this beastly tray." Vicky laughed and glanced at Butcher, then said to Julia in a more measured tone, "Well, I shall find you. I'll come very soon."

She went off with a hasty, self-conscious step. Julia looked after her, then didn't. She had the old awareness of having a feeling that wasn't for public inspection. Butcher clearly had no such compunction, and burst out as soon as Vicky had mounted the stairs, "Now, isn't she a lamb? Do you know, the other nurses treat the old man roughly, and I can't say I blame them. But Victory's famed for her gentleness, even with him. And she's been through—well, not what you have, but enough. When I see a pure heart like that, and see how it's respected here, I just know we'll be all right. We can't not be."

"Oh, yes," said Julia. "I know we'll be all right now."

"Yes, we boys are all in her thrall. She came out of London on foot like you. Worked at Central Committee, and gave it all up. And do you know, no one holds Central Committee against her? Oh, she had some trouble at processing, just as I did. But that was soon forgotten. One sees at a glance what sort of girl she is..."

He went on chattering about Vicky's wondrousness as they made their way back down the walkway. They were all things Julia felt herself, but they sounded fantastical, even callow, on his lips. He was a darling, but didn't he see? Vicky and Julia were the ones. What was between them was the reason things were all right. But oh, it was marvelous of him not to see! For he was right that there were truths one didn't speak of. She was grateful to be with people who understood her, in a place where secrets could still be good.

Thinking this, and smiling at Butcher's chatter, she followed him back into the majestic, deafening crystal hall. He was forced to give up enthusing here and beat a path through the thickening crowd. In this chaotic progress, Julia spotted the tiger cub, being teased with an Anti-Sex sash by a girl who was wearing soldier's clothes but was barefoot. Julia was entranced to see the girl's toenails had been painted red to match her lipstick. Julia would paint Vicky's toenails that color, and kiss her toes. The tiger cub would sleep at the foot of Vicky's bed. What sort of bed might it be? When beds were in short supply, two girls were often asked to share. Would it matter very much that Julia was pregnant? No, Vicky must have seen, and it made no difference. Nothing of that kind could make any difference . . . The cub raised a desultory paw at the sash, then unceremoniously collapsed on its back and stretched to show its belly, its striped tail coiling. The girl very gingerly stroked the pale belly. The cub instantly twisted to attack, and she snatched her hand away, laughing musically. Just like Tiger or Commissar. How Vicky had said their names! What a dear!

The room Butcher brought her to was one of those they'd glimpsed while driving up, where sumptuous furniture shared space with heaps of dirty backpacks, helmets, and mud-encrusted boots. On the side adjoining the great hall, it was inadequately curtained off with a piece of canvas. The word PROCESSING had been written on the glass door in what looked like lipstick. Julia smiled, thinking of toenail paint and lily of the valley, thinking, *Bliss was it in that dawn*. She was grateful to see a bottle of wine waiting on the desk among the papers, and even glad to see Reynolds grinning at her with admiration.

Butcher left them, saying they would all meet again at dinner that night. Reynolds poured two glasses of wine. Something in the gesture of pouring troubled Julia's memory, but he gave her no time to consider this, launching into a cheerful explanation of how easy processing was, and how impossible it was to go wrong, as long as one did it with a trusted person. "It's only two parts, you see. Then, once you're done, you'll get new Brotherhood papers. We must take your old papers, of course. They go in a file somewhere, and I suppose when the war's all over, someone will put it in some kind of order.

"Of course, if there's cause to suspect a fellow, they take a much closer look at those papers. There are people here who are proper scientists at decoding what all the markings mean, the identity numbers and whatnot, and if someone seems unsavory, they go all through it until the chap's sorry he's alive. Take Butcher, who was rather naughty in his Party days. He wasn't just an airman—bad enough—but he went and got himself the command of a squadron. Well, our boys gave him the proper third degree, and had a dozen people poring over his papers and needling him to catch him out." Reynolds clearly found this very funny, but at the look on Julia's face, he recollected himself, saying, "Yours won't be like that, though. No, I shouldn't think it will take ten minutes."

He became doubly solicitous after she confided that she couldn't write the answers herself—her hand wasn't up to it. He was only too glad to read the questions out to her, and take down her responses. Indeed, he said it was just as well, as then he could be sure she didn't go wrong.

This proved immediately useful on Part One, which consisted entirely of the question, *What was your role in the Party of Ingsoc?* The answer must be at least three pages, Reynolds said, but one was better off with six. "Short of six, they fancy you're holding back. That's all rot, of course, but you've got to know how they think. The bureaucratic mind!"

Julia saw, without being told, that the key to this question was to admit nothing. In the account she gave Reynolds, accordingly, there was no Ministry of Truth or Junior Anti-Sex League, never mind any Big Future program or Hero of the Socialist Family badge. She did not hint, either, that she might have played a part in anyone else's downfall. No matter how strange it was to imagine a Party member who had never helped the police with their inquiries, never joined a mob in setting an enemy's house alight, never signed a petition calling for the execution of colleagues for falling afoul of some new rule, this was who she must claim to be. Of course, Julia had told such implausible lies all her life, so this was second nature. By the age of ten, she was writing letters at school to ask Big Brother to send all the SAZ's food to London, saying she didn't feel hunger because she was too passionate for the cause.

However, Reynolds had to steer her into referring to other Party members as "bloodsuckers" and "murderous wretches," and it was he who knew that her parents' deaths should be given two full pages. He insisted, too, that two pages be devoted to her time in Love. Some of this he wrote without help, holding up one hand for silence as he scribbled away with a ferocious scowl. Another page must be filled with expressions of hatred for Humphrey Pease. This too he wrote himself, assuring her that Newspeakers all needed help with this. Julia let herself drift off, sipping wine and watching the door for Vicky. Her mind drifted back to the tiger cub and the toenail paint. The golden bathtub . . . lily of the valley . . . She and Vicky would enter the cabinet alone.

Reynolds rudely broke this reverie by saying, "I am sorry to ask, but they will like to know . . . forgive me if I'm wrong, but you are expecting a child?"

"Yes," said Julia guiltily. "That's right."

"Well, if your jailers forced . . . at the prison . . . I do hate to have to ask this question."

"Oh, no, it was nothing like that," said Julia, feeling a tightness in her throat. "The father and I were arrested together. He betrayed me there, in Love." It was on the tip of her tongue to say, *I betrayed him, too,* but of course she mustn't say that. Instead she added, "Of course they had tortured him awfully, or he never would have."

Reynolds's face had stiffened into rage again. "He still played the part of a coward, I should say."

"I don't know. But you may put it down that way, if it's what they want."

He looked down at the page, then at her. "No, I don't think we ought to mention that—the betrayal. I'll say he was killed there, shall I? We don't want anything to hang over the child."

"Of course," she said gratefully. "If you think that's right. Perhaps they killed him because he stood up to torture to protect me?"

"Yes!" Reynolds's face brightened. "The very thing!"

He scribbled feverishly for another minute, then stapled together the pages he'd filled and set them aside with a sigh of satisfaction. "Now," he said, "Part Two can't really be got wrong. It's more of a formality, really. But you mustn't mind if some of the questions are rather fearsome. It's just an old tradition, you see."

"All right," said Julia dubiously.

"Oh, now, you needn't worry. I'll tell you what to say."

He settled the paper a bit nervously and read, "'Are you prepared to dedicate your life to the cause of overthrowing the red dictatorship?'" He looked up and added, "That's the Party, you see."

"Yes."

"Is that a yes to the question, or—"

"Yes to the question. This *is* easy."

They smiled at each other. He said, "Now I think of it, all of the answers are yes. But I suppose I ought to ask them nonetheless." He looked down at the paper and made an unhappy face. "Well, here we have the first tricky one. 'Are you prepared to commit murder if it is necessary to the Brotherhood of Free Men?'"

"Murder?" Julia said. "That is …"

"Oh, this is all just a funny old tradition. I mean, fancy anyone asking *you* to murder!"

Now something stirred uncomfortably in Julia's memory. It was somehow connected to the taste of wine …

Reynolds said, "I shall put that as a yes."

"Oh—yes. If you think I should."

"Yes. After all, it's a war. You can't very well say you won't kill people in a war."

"That's right. In a war—that's true."

"Now, we're coming to the worst of them. Brace yourself. 'Are you willing to commit acts of sabotage which may cause the death of hundreds of innocent people?'"

With a little shock, she realized what the questions were. It was the list of crimes O'Brien had said truth-followers would happily commit—the list he'd had Winston Smith agree to, when pretending to recruit him to the Brotherhood.

"Wait, these are the real questions?" said Julia. "The things one accepts, when one joins the Brotherhood?"

Reynolds made a little grimace. "It's all rather cloak-and-dagger, I know. I certainly don't blame you for thinking twice.

But of course you would never really be asked to do these things. Can you imagine?" He laughed uncomfortably.

"And is there really a Goldstein?"

"Goldstein?" Reynolds frowned a little quizzically. "Well, there was. But he was never ours. Indeed, he was never much better than the rest of them. He only made the error of winning too much popularity, you see, and looking like he might oust Pease. Old Pease was too quick for him, though, and had him done away with."

"Is that it? I see."

"Now, naturally you're upset by that last question, and I don't think less of you for it. This tradition does look gruesome to outsiders, only the older chaps won't hear of it being changed. But it's just an exaggerated way of speaking. It's as if one said, 'I like you so much I would fetch the moon from the sky for you.' One doesn't literally mean..." Now he blushed and turned back to the paper, saying, "Oh, I can't let you take this so seriously. I'm writing *yes*." He scrawled in the word and looked up with an air of defiance.

Despite herself, Julia felt some relief at having the problem taken out of her hands. She sat back in the chair, resting the glass of wine against her belly. "Well, if you think..."

"Very good. Now, you won't like this one, either. I can't say I'm very happy about it, but try to remember—just a tradition. So: 'If it would somehow serve the Brotherhood's interests to throw sulfuric acid in a child's face—are you prepared to do that?'"

"No," Julia said with a flash of rage. "I will not."

He put the pen down with a troubled expression. Only then did Julia see what she'd done and feel a thrill of fear. What if Reynolds should start to doubt her? No, Julia *couldn't* arouse suspicion. If the people here once properly inspected her papers—

people who knew what they were seeing—no scars or pleasing manners could save her. She would be sent to a camp or shot.

"I am sorry," she said. "I was only teasing. You may write . . . well, as you think."

Reynolds snatched up the pen and wrote in the word hastily, then looked back at her with an uncertain smile. "Well! I do see that I deserved some ribbing. We all do, putting a girl through that. But that's the worst of it past. Shall we go on?"

"Yes. I do see now. It's fine."

From here, Julia felt herself detach. It was almost the feeling she'd had at Love, when she'd fled from her body and floated to the ceiling. After all, she couldn't stop what the Brotherhood would do, or make her do. Julia was a criminal. Worse, she was pregnant. She didn't have the freedom to think of what was right. She must do what was safe. It was as Ampleforth had said: one had no choice, one must only live through it as if one had.

Reynolds went on, and Julia made herself answer brightly. She poured more wine for them both and drank hers off. She watched the door where Vicky would arrive, and let her mind drift to the thought of Vicky's soft hair, her smell of soap and clean sweat. One had no choice. One was carried forward, and tried to be kind whenever one could. One survived, and then was sorry. And she would go in the cabinet with Vicky and they would laugh about the golden bathtub. She would put a rose in her hair like the Brotherhood girls. The jazzlike music would play in the walls, the exalting music of another universe. She would shed her clothes and stand naked. She would kiss Vicky's face.

"'You are prepared to lose your identity and live out the rest of your life as another person?'"

"Yes."

"'You are prepared to separate from everyone you know and never see them again?'"

"Yes."

"'You are prepared to cheat, to forge, to blackmail, to corrupt the minds of children, to distribute habit-forming drugs, to encourage prostitution, to disseminate venereal diseases—to do anything which is likely to cause demoralization and weaken the power of the Party?'"

"Yes," said Julia. "Yes, I will. Yes."

Acknowledgments

Extraordinary thanks as always go to the superb Victoria Hobbs, who has been my agent from the very beginning. She always goes above and beyond, but really outdid herself this time by being the one who suggested I write this book. Many thanks also to Bill Hamilton for entrusting me with *Nineteen Eighty-Four*, and for his help along the way. Thanks also go to Jessica Lee; and to Prema Raj, Tabatha Leggett, Alexandra McNicoll, and Jack Sargeant for their extraordinary work selling *Julia* around the world.

I also want to thank everyone at Granta for their brilliant work: Jason Arthur, Pru Rowlandson, Bella Lacey, Lamorna Elmer, Sigrid Rausing, Noel Murphy, Christine Lo, Sarah Wasley, Daniela Silva, George Stamp; and the team at Mariner: Nicole Angeloro, Peter Hubbard, Tess Day, Liz Psaltis, Eliza Rosenberry, and Tavia Kowalchuk.

Thanks to my early readers, John Muckle and Clare McHugh, for their encouragement and advice, and to others who helped and supported me in various ways while I wrote this book: Jeff Newman, Sally Greenawalt, Anita Vanca, Timothy Paulson, Clive Merredew, Bethany Raymond, Arlene Heyman, Peggy Reynolds, Jim Gottier, Paul Bravmann, Mandy Keifetz, Wendy Jones, Gail Vachon, Ellen Tarlow. A special thanks also to my friends in Small Twitter. And finally, as always, thanks to my husband Howard Mittelmark, the smartest editor, best friend, most long-suffering roommate, and the reason I mystifyingly and very unfairly still do not have a dog.